# The Regency

## LORDS & LADIES
### COLLECTION

*Two Glittering Regency
Love Affairs*

My Lady's Prisoner
*by Ann Elizabeth Cree*
&
Miss Harcourt's Dilemma
*by Anne Ashley*

# The *Regency*

## LORDS & LADIES

### COLLECTION

# The Regency

## LORDS & LADIES
### COLLECTION

*Ann Elizabeth Cree &
Anne Ashley*

MILLS & BOON®

*First published in Great Britain 2005 by
Harlequin Mills & Boon Limited,
Eton House, 18-24 Paradise Road, Richmond, Surrey TW9 1SR*

THE REGENCY LORDS & LADIES COLLECTION
© Harlequin Books S.A. 2005

The publisher acknowledges the copyright holders of the
individual works as follows:

My Lady's Prisoner © Annemarie Hasnain 2001
Miss Harcourt's Dilemma © Anne Ashley 1998

ISBN 0 263 84571 0

*138-0805*

*Printed and bound in Spain
by Litografía Rosés S.A., Barcelona*

# My Lady's Prisoner

*by*
*Ann Elizabeth Cree*

**Ann Elizabeth** wrote her first books when she was five years old. She took a break from her budding writing career to attend grade school and high school, and then University. Her favourite form of daydreaming during that time was weaving exciting and romantic stories in her head. With the encouragement of a friend, she finally started putting those stories to paper nearly 30 years after she wrote her first books!

Ann Elizabeth lives in Boise, Idaho, with her husband and two lively school-age sons. Their family also includes two eccentric cats and a house rabbit. In addition to writing, she loves to garden and plays the piano and oboe. And, of course, reads as much as she can.

# *Prologue*

*London, 1817*

She had never expected to see the ring again. And certainly not on the hand of Nicholas Chandler, Viscount Thayne, a man who, as far as she knew, had never crossed paths with Thomas.

So, at first, when Thérèse Blanchot had told her that she had spotted the ring, she was certain Thérèse must be mistaken. But she had gone to Thérèse's exclusive and very discreet gaming house to see for herself. And when she stood by the hazard table and watched Thayne throw the dice, her heart had taken a sickening dive. For on the fourth finger of his left hand was a ruby signet ring. A ring with an intricately carved gold band, the stone surrounded by two small diamonds. The ring was unmistakable. Her eyes had gone to his face: a lean masculine face, just bordering on handsome with a pair of cool dark eyes. His hard gaze went briefly to her masked face and she froze. But he returned to the dice, clearly uninterested.

She must obtain the ring. And discover what he knew. No matter what it took.

# Chapter One

Julia, Lady Carrington, paused in the door of Thérèse Blanchot's richly appointed saloon, her legs suddenly shaky. There was no reason to be so apprehensive, she had merely to find Lord Thayne and, at the appropriate time, abduct him.

She glanced around the elegant room, its colours muted reds and golds. Already the saloon was crowded with patrons. Both men and women frequented Thérèse's saloon, where the suppers were superb, the guests carefully chosen and the stakes high. Admittance was by invitation only. Many of the women chose to come masked, although Julia had no trouble recognising the Duchess of Langston at the EO table—but perhaps that was because she took no trouble to hide her flaming red hair or disguise her husky laugh. Julia's own hair was a muted brown and completely unremarkable. Not that she was likely to be recognised at any rate; since her return to England she rarely graced London society.

She moved into the room and looked more closely around, hoping to spot Thayne. But there was no sign of his tall, broad-shouldered figure. Or of a man with tawny brown hair that glimmered with gold. Thérèse had sent word he would be here tonight. Perhaps he was in one of the private parlours. It would be too awful to contemplate if he was to change his mind. She hadn't come up with an alternative plan and she wasn't quite sure if she could work up the courage to do this again.

Thérèse materialised at her side. 'My dear, you have arrived. I was not certain you would come.' In her early thirties, she was still a beauty with high cheekbones and violet eyes under a crown of thick black hair.

'Yes.' Julia took a deep breath. 'Is Lord Thayne here?'

'He is. In the gold saloon. However, he is not in the most jovial of moods.' Her brow creased with worry. 'My dear, I do not know what you have planned, but he is not a man you can cross. If you only would tell me, I could help.'

Julia shook her head. 'No. I do not want you implicated in any of it.' Thayne's hard gaze sprang to mind. She did not want his wrath to fall on Thérèse.

'That does not matter to me.' Thérèse hesitated. 'My dear, I wish I could convince you that it is most unlikely he knows anything about Thomas's death.'

'Perhaps not, but he has Thomas's ring. If anything, I want to at least know how it came to be in his possession.' She put a reassuring hand on Thérèse's arm. 'I will be careful.'

'I only want you to be safe.'

'I will be. Eduardo is waiting for me outside so I will be well protected.'

'Yes.' Thérèse still appeared unconvinced.

'Will you take me to him, then? I wish to play a game with him. Perhaps piquet.'

'And what then?'

'I will, I hope, have my ring,' Julia said lightly. She had no intention of telling Thérèse that she planned to abduct one of her most wealthy and powerful patrons. 'And one more thing—I think it would be best if you would pretend you do not know me.'

'If that is what you wish. What should I call you?'

Julia frowned. 'Jane, I think.'

Thérèse's brow shot up. 'Jane? Such an ordinary name.'

'I am less likely to forget it.' She had thought of taking something closer to her own name, Juliana, for instance, but she feared she would blurt out Julia instead. And certainly she did not want him to connect her with anything related to her real identity.

'Then come with me.' Thérèse led her through the saloon.

Several patrons greeted Thérèse as they passed but, to Julia's relief, no one gave her more than a cursory glance as they crossed the rich-hued oriental carpet, winding their way among the baize-covered tables. And then she caught sight of someone she knew all too well, her neighbour, Lord George Kingsley. He was hovering near the EO table. The Even-Odd wheel had just been set into motion as Julia and Thérèse passed by. Preoccupied with the spinning wheel, he did not even glance up. Thank goodness for that. If anyone were likely to recognise her under the mask it would be him. She quickly averted her gaze and prayed she could avoid him.

Thérèse stopped in front of the door of one of the private parlours. She looked over at Julia. 'Are you certain this is what you wish, my dear?'

Julia took a deep breath to steady herself. 'Yes. I do not think I have a choice.'

Her knees started to shake. She was about to confront the man who perhaps held the only clue to her husband's murderer.

\* \* \*

Nicholas polished off the remainder of his brandy in one smooth move and leaned back in his chair. 'Another game?' he asked his companion.

Henry Benton gave the pile of vouchers in front of Nicholas a meaningful stare. 'No, thank you. Not if I hope to keep my shirt. Believe I'll try my luck at Faro. Dammit, Thayne, I think your wits only sharpen the more you drink.'

Nicholas laughed, but his laugh was hardly amused. 'Then after another bottle or two I should break the bank.'

Benton frowned. 'Don't know why you're drinking like a fish. You'll have the devil of a head tomorrow. If you don't pass out before then.'

'Which is precisely what I plan to do.' Perhaps in drunken oblivion he'd be able to get through the rest of this anniversary without the images that had haunted him for the past two years.

Benton rose, the frown still on his face. 'Perhaps you'd do best to continue at home.'

'No,' Nicholas said curtly.

Benton opened his mouth as if to say more, but merely bowed and walked off.

Nicholas slouched back in his chair and reached for the bottle. His hand stayed when he realised someone had entered the small, dim room. He saw Thérèse and then his gaze flickered to the woman with her.

She was of average height and slender. The low-cut silk gown she wore revealed a glimpse of soft curved breasts. She was masked, not an unusual occurrence among ladies of the *ton* who did not wish to be recognised in such a risqué place. She looked vaguely familiar. He frowned and had a sudden recollection of her watching him last evening. Her still, watchful manner had

seemed out of place in one of London's most exclusive
and high-stake private hells. The thought had crossed his
mind that it must be her first time in such an establishment. Apparently he had been mistaken. She looked quite
confident as she followed Thérèse towards his table, her
eyes behind the mask fixed on his face.

Thérèse stopped, the young woman a little behind her.
She clasped her gloved hands in front of her in a way
that suddenly reminded Nicholas of a schoolgirl. Thérèse's expression gave nothing away as she addressed
him. 'Nicholas, may I present Jane? She wishes to play
a game of cards with you.'

'Does she? I fear I am not in the mood.' He would
prefer to polish off his bottle in solitude.

'She assures me she is a very skilled player. And she
came here specifically to play with you. Surely you do
not wish to disappoint her?'

His eyes flickered over the woman. He could think of
no reason why she would wish to challenge him. She met
his gaze boldly but he saw her fingers tighten around her
reticule. So she was nervous. In spite of his desire to
remain detached, he felt the faintest stirring of curiosity.
'How skilled is she?' he asked.

Thérèse shrugged and glanced quickly at her companion. 'I cannot say.'

He looked back at Thérèse. 'I don't waste my time on
amateurs. Tell her I must decline.'

The young woman turned her masked gaze on him. 'I
can hear and speak, my lord.' Her voice held more than
a touch of annoyance. 'And I am hardly an amateur. I
never lose.' Her voice was low and well bred.

His eyes narrowed. He wondered what the devil she
wanted, but there was nothing he could think of. Her

voice was completely unfamiliar. 'Don't you? Then sit down,' he said curtly.

She took the chair across from him. As she sat, he caught a whiff of soft rose. The scent evoked memories he'd prefer to forget. He should undoubtedly send her away after all.

A servant entered the room and spoke to Thérèse. She turned to Nicholas. 'I fear I cannot stay. A small crisis with the supper. But I shall be interested in the outcome. My dear,' she said to Jane, 'I wish you all luck.'

Jane nodded and then looked back at Nicholas. He saw her swallow, although the rest of her demeanour was calm.

'What is your game?' he asked.

'Piquet.'

'Very well. What odds?'

She looked straight at him. 'Anything you wish, my lord.'

'Anything?' he asked, his voice suggestive. He allowed his gaze to rest on her lips and then drift down to where her creamy breasts plunged into her bodice. Despite the amount of drink he'd consumed and his indifference, he felt the faint stir of desire.

Her gaze faltered a little. 'Anything.'

He smiled coldly. This was a new tack—usually women expressed their interest in a more direct fashion and never by challenging him to a card game. 'And if I lose?'

She hesitated and then spoke, her eyes on his face. 'Then, my lord, you will give me what I wish.'

His loins tightened unexpectedly, the thought of what she might want damnably erotic. His eyes went to her lips, soft and slightly parted, and the idea of crushing them beneath his was becoming more enticing by the moment.

What the devil was wrong with him? Apparently he had not consumed enough drink after all. The last thing he should want was a woman, particularly tonight. Except for an occasional one-night liaison, he'd been nearly celibate for the past two years. On the other hand, perhaps a night in a stranger's arms was exactly what he needed to make it through this anniversary. He leaned back in his chair and regarded her through half-closed eyes. 'Fair enough. If I lose then I will be at your mercy. However, I would prefer to call you something besides Jane.'

'What is wrong? You do not like Jane?' She sounded affronted.

'No. I'd expected something more exotic from such a woman of, er…mystery. I don't suppose that is your real name?'

'No, but I shouldn't mind if it were.' She lifted her chin.

He nearly laughed. 'I suppose your given name is something quite extraordinary that makes you long for a name such as Jane.' He hadn't expected to feel amused.

'No, it is also quite ordinary.'

'Mary? Elizabeth? Harriet?'

'No. Perhaps we should start the game, my lord.' Now she sounded cross as if she hadn't much time to dally with him. Certainly her voice held no trace of flirtatiousness. In spite of himself he was beginning to feel rather intrigued.

He picked up the cards. Her gaze was suddenly riveted on his hands. 'I assure you I've no intention of cheating,' he said. 'And if I did, watching my hands with such concentration would not reveal a thing. But if that worries you, you may deal the cards.'

She looked up and smiled, although her smile appeared forced. 'I am not worried about that at all, my lord. I was merely curious about your ring. It is quite unusual.'

'Yes,' he said curtly.

'Where did you get it?'

His brow snapped together. 'It was given to me.'

'Indeed. By someone close to you?'

'It is, my dear, none of your concern. I believe you expressed a desire to play a game with me.' He pushed the cards towards her.

'Yes.' She picked up the cards and he noticed her hand trembled a little. However, her movements as she first shuffled and then dealt the cards were quick and practised.

He made the first move and waited for her countermove. She merely stared at the cards in her hand as if mesmerised. He was beginning to wonder if she was a trifle mad.

'Your play. Although I suggest you do it some time within the next hour. I've no desire to stay here until dawn. Unless you would rather forgo the game and leave now.'

Her head jerked up. 'Leave?'

'Yes, leave. Together,' he added carelessly.

'I…' She caught her lower lip between her teeth.

'Well?' he asked. She still hesitated. What the devil was she playing at? For a woman who wanted to seduce him, she was remarkably reticent. He suspected he was dealing with a complete novice. 'Then I will decide. I forfeit the game. Under our terms I am now at your command.' He threw down his hand.

She stared at the cards and then looked back up at him. 'Oh. Well, yes.'

'You seem surprised. Perhaps I misunderstood, but I

thought we agreed that if you won I would do what you wish. I assume you had something in mind.'

'Yes.' She rose, stumbling against the chair a little. 'I would like you to come with me.' She sounded rather prim.

He stood. 'Would you? Very well, I am at your service, my dear Jane. Although I am curious as to where we are going.'

Her lips parted in a nervous little smile. 'It will be a…a surprise.'

His brow rose. 'Indeed.'

'Yes. So, if you will please come.'

He moved to her side and looked down at her. Her demeanour was hardly that of a seductress—if anything her stiff manner reminded him of a governess. He stepped closer to her.

She nearly jumped away. 'Shall we go, then?'

'Perhaps we should before you change your mind,' he said drily. 'I must own at this point I am quite curious as to what you want.'

'Oh.' She hurried from the room as if it was all she could do to keep from running.

He followed her into the passageway and took her arm. Her bones felt delicate under his hand. He pulled her around to face him. 'There's no need for such haste, my dear. Unless you are that eager to have your way with me.'

'No…that is, yes.'

'Are you? Most women who have expressed such a desire show more, er…enthusiasm for the task.' He released her arm.

'I fear I haven't much practice,' she said crossly.

He folded his arms and leaned against the wall. 'So,

why exactly did you decide upon me to improve your skills?'

'I...' She stopped, her eyes fixed on the door of the parlour next to the one they had just vacated. She stiffened and then yanked her gaze away. 'I would rather discuss this outside.'

He glanced in the direction she had been looking. Lord George Kingsley and Carleton Wentworth had stepped out of the room. He looked back at her. 'I see. You wish to converse with me in private. Then let us depart. I am agog with curiosity.'

She threw one last glance at the two men and dashed across the hallway to the staircase. He caught up to her just before she started to descend. 'There is no need for such haste. I am yours until dawn.'

She gave him a startled look. 'Oh. Yes, of course.'

He nearly laughed then. He took her arm again and started down the stairs. He led her to the small front parlour where they waited for the footmen to fetch her cloak. She stood near the door, her posture stiff as if she were about to flee. He came to stand in front of her and then lifted her chin with gentle fingers. 'You need a few lessons in the art of seduction.'

'I...' Her lips parted and even in the lamplight he could see colour suffuse her face. A shaft of desire, hot and fierce, pierced him at this maidenly response. He found himself wanting to push her up against the wall and begin the lesson now. He dropped his hand and backed away. He was beginning to think that she was perhaps a most accomplished seductress after all.

They stepped into the foggy London night, the brisk air cooling his cheeks. It also had the effect of clearing his mind. He glanced down at his companion. She now wore a long, rather unfashionable cloak which hid her figure, but he could see the material was of good quality. What was she exactly? A demi-mondaine? But her speech and carriage were those of a well-bred lady and even in her nervousness she had not slipped into other, less refined accents. 'Well?' he asked. 'Where to?'

'We will go to my carriage,' she said firmly.

They walked in silence along the fog-shrouded street. But when they turned the corner of the square on to a dark, nearly deserted side street his hackles rose. Although he heard nothing he had the prickling sensation of being watched.

His companion apparently noted nothing amiss. She halted next to a carriage. 'We are here, my lord.' Her voice was quite calm. Too calm.

His fingers closed around her arm in a tight grip. 'So, what exactly do you want, my dear?'

She stared up at him, the dark and the mask completely hiding her expression. 'You.'

'I think, then, we had best be certain.' He yanked her to him, his mouth crashing down on hers in a merciless kiss. She froze and then began to struggle. He released her abruptly.

She stepped back, stumbling a little. Her hand dipped into her reticule. 'Please get in the carriage.'

He stared at her, then his eyes dropped to the pistol pointed a few inches away from him. 'What the devil?'

'I am abducting you, my lord.'

'Are you?' He gave a short, surprised laugh. 'Are you that desperate? My dear, after that kiss such measures are hardly necessary. I would be more than happy to oblige you without the use of force.' His eyes roved over her figure.

'Get in, please, or I will be forced to shoot you.' Her

voice was still polite, as if she had just requested he take her in to supper at a ball.

'Can you really use that thing?' he asked carelessly.

'Yes.' She motioned with the pistol. 'Will you just get in?'

'No please this time?' His mouth quirked. 'I will if you kiss me again.'

'I did not kiss you the first time!' she snapped. 'Get in.'

He raised a brow. 'I don't think so, my dear.'

He made a lunge for the pistol and she jumped back. He felt a blow to the back of his head, and the next thing he knew he was pitching forward.


Julia stared at the man sprawled at her feet, then looked up to see Eduardo.

Eduardo gave her an apologetic look. 'Thought I'd best step in before you decided to shoot the lad. Didn't want a scene. You'd best get the ring. What do you want me to do with him?'

'Put him in the carriage, if you please.'

He stared at her for a moment and then nodded. 'And then…what?'

'I…I want to take him back to Foxwood. I need to find out where he got the ring.'

'Very well.'

He glanced over at the coachman who had been watching with a disinterested look. 'Come on, lad, we'll put him in the coach for the Countess and bind him up good and tight. A pity, however, he isn't a less robust man.'

'Yes, 'tis a shame,' Julia said weakly. Her legs were beginning to shake. She watched while they managed to bundle Thayne in the carriage, worried Eduardo might have hit him too hard. But then he groaned and let out a string of curses and she almost wished Eduardo had hit him harder.

She stood by the carriage, her nerves on edge, praying no one had seen the assault. There was only one other coach on the other side of the street, but it was doubtful the coachman could have noticed anything. When they finished, she finally climbed in the carriage and took the seat opposite him. Guilt assailed her when she saw they had not only bound her prisoner, but had gagged him with his cravat as well. She leaned back against the uncomfortable cushions and closed her eyes. Whatever had she done now? She just prayed they would make it to Foxwood without incident.

Brunton watched the carriage turn a corner. They had been following it since it left the French woman's gaming hell. From all appearances, the carriage was about to leave town. He cursed, causing his horse to startle.

Smithers urged his horse next to Brunton's. 'Now what? They're leaving town.'

'Yes.' Brunton scowled. He'd not figured this into his plans. He'd anticipated either waylaying Thayne in a dark street and nabbing the ring or, if he had to, ambushing him while the Viscount rode his big grey through Hyde Park in the early-morning hours. When Thayne had entered Madame Blanchot's he'd been certain his opportunity was at hand. Until Thayne had left with the masked woman. He'd followed them down the street and around the corner. They had stopped in front of a carriage but, instead of climbing in, had seemed to be arguing. Brunton had been forced to dodge across the street when a large, burly man had suddenly appeared out of nowhere and had stopped to watch the two as well. Brunton hadn't actually seen Thayne enter the carriage, but when it had finally rumbled away Thayne and the woman were gone. The burly man now sat on the box next to the coachman. A glimpse of the masked woman in the window of the carriage confirmed she was inside. And, unless Thayne had vanished into the air, he was in the coach as well.

'Don't think the guv'nor will be pleased if he gets away,' Smithers said.

'No.' Never idle, Brunton's brain latched on to an alternative plan. A slow smile crossed his face. 'But he won't. We'll hold them up.'

Smithers grinned, showing several blackened teeth. 'Always wanted to be a highwayman.'

'Keep your wits about you. If we snuff out Thayne the guv'nor will have our heads.'

'Thayne won't argue with this.' Smithers patted the pistol at his side. 'Dare say he'll be occupied with the wench.'

Brunton grinned. 'We'll hope she keeps 'im busy enough so he'll not notice us.'

# Chapter Two

The carriage hit a bump and Julia winced. She glanced over at her prisoner. He had not made a sound since they had left London but she had no doubt he must be horribly uncomfortable. The fifteen miles from London to Foxwood had never felt so long. She leaned forward. 'I am sorry, but I assure you I mean you no harm. You will be more comfortable as soon as we reach Fox—I mean, our…our destination.'

The low sound issuing from beneath the gag was not encouraging. Even with his hands and feet bound, the set of his shoulders indicated he was furious. And his eyes. If they were weapons she would be dead. She suspected he would have no qualms in strangling her if he could. At least the bindings looked sturdy and Eduardo was skilled in tying knots. She hoped they were not cutting too deeply into his flesh.

She sat back against the cushions, wishing she could ride on the coach box as Eduardo was. Despite his incapacitated condition, Thayne's presence seemed to fill the confines of the carriage. It was like sitting with a caged tiger and the sensation was not comfortable. He was quiet, leaning against the cushions, long legs straight in front of him, but she could almost feel his contained power.

She tried to keep her eyes off of him as the coach rumbled through the foggy London streets. She wrapped her cloak more tightly around herself. At least she still wore her mask but it provided little barrier from his hard gaze. Or from the memory of his ruthless kiss. Even now her cheeks heated and her legs felt shaky just thinking about it.

Whatever had she done? She remembered Thérèse's words that he was not a man to cross. She knew little else about him except he had some sort of scandal attached to his name and that his grandfather, the Earl of Monteville, was one of the most powerful men in England. He was unlikely to take the abduction of his grandson and heir lightly. She would undoubtedly end up in Newgate or worse.

But what other choice did she have? She had considered offering to buy the ring or, if necessary, robbing him, but that would still not tell her where he obtained it or tell her if he had had anything to do with her husband's death. Asking him point-blank seemed ridiculous. He would hardly admit it if he had; so, the idea of abducting him and forcing him to give her an answer had seemed the only recourse.

Except she had not counted on his being so, well, unmanageable. She stole a glance at him and saw his eyes were now closed. Not that it made him appear any less unyielding. They hit a bump and he winced. She averted her eyes. Inflicting pain on her fellow man was not something she took pleasure in doing. She peeked out the window. They were finally leaving London. The carriage hit another bump. This time Thayne made a sound like a muffled groan.

'Are…are you all right?' she asked. A stupid question.

He shook his head and made another groaning noise. Concerned, she shifted on the seat and peered more closely at him. The light was dim but she thought he did look rather pale. A dreadful thought occurred to her. 'You are not going to be sick, are you?'

This time he nodded. She nearly groaned herself. Why hadn't she thought of such a thing? She could not possibly allow him to cast up his accounts wearing a gag. She must untie it.

The sway of the carriage told her they were now outside of London. 'Very well, I will untie your gag.' She moved to his seat and nearly fell on him as the carriage lurched. She was beginning to think the coachman was not a particularly skilful driver. He had been in her employment just a fortnight. She only hoped he was not tipsy.

She righted herself and forced her hands to reach up to the back of Thayne's head. His hair was thick and surprisingly soft under her hand. She managed to locate the knot, her fingers trembling. Her face was hot beneath her mask.

Unfortunately, the knot was tight and working it loose proved difficult. She finally pulled her gloves off, but the swaying carriage hardly helped. As much as she tried to avoid it, her body was forced into contact with his hard length. She finally managed to loosen the knot and she tugged. He made a noise like a muffled yelp and her hands fell away. Was he about to become ill? 'Please, try to hold on. I am almost done,' she said. She tugged more violently at the cloth and this time the sound was nearly a growl. Then she realised what was wrong. A strand of his hair had become entangled in the knot.

'Oh, drat!' she muttered. 'I will try not to pull too hard.'

She somehow managed to free the knot without further mishap. The gag fell away and the carriage slammed to a halt. She found herself smashed against Thayne's side. A shot rang out followed by shouting.

She managed to sit upright on the seat, her heart thudding uncomfortably. Her face had hit his shoulder and her mask was completely awry.

'What the devil is going on?' Thayne said.

Julia peered out the window and then her heart sank when she saw two masked men. Eduardo had already climbed down from the coach box and stood by the carriage, his hands up. She sank back on the seat. 'I think we have been set upon by highwaymen.'

Thayne stared at her. 'Good God! I don't suppose you could loosen these damnable bindings?'

'I will try.' She knelt in front of him and started to work on the knot at his feet. Thank goodness, Eduardo had not tied it too terribly tight as her fingers did not seem to want to co-operate. She had just started to slip the thin rope over his boots when her mask slipped completely off. She looked up for a moment and his eyes widened in surprise. She realised this was the first time he had seen her face. And then he glared at her, not at all grateful for her assistance.

The door was yanked open and a nasty-looking pistol was thrust in the opening of the coach. 'If you will be so good as to step out, madam.' The voice was exceedingly polite for a ruffian.

'I would rather not,' Julia said. 'Perhaps another evening.' She sat back down and managed a smile. Where ever was her pistol? It was unlikely she could shoot the man, but if there was the slightest chance she intended to use it. Her hand finally contacted the cold metal and she thrust her hand with the pistol into the folds of her cloak.

The highwayman gestured with his pistol. 'Alas, I fear another evening is not convenient for me. And I should hate to find myself obliged to assist you in a more forcible manner.'

She dared not look at Thayne. She stepped down into the cold foggy night and was relieved to see Eduardo appeared unhurt. He held the horses while the coachman leaned against the carriage with his eyes closed.

'The gentleman as well.' The highwayman waved his pistol at her.

He had spotted Thayne. Her heart sank even further. Surely they would not harm a man in such a helpless condition. 'I fear he is rather unwell at the moment.'

'Not at all,' Thayne said coolly from inside. 'However, I will need some assistance. I am rather incapacitated.'

The highwayman peered into the coach and then reeled back. 'Egad! The man is trussed up like a chicken.'

'I am the lady's prisoner,' Thayne said. 'Perhaps you would be so good as to untie me.'

'Don't think I will. You look a trifle too brawny. So, he's your prisoner, milady?' He turned his masked gaze back on Julia. 'Why would a lovely lady such as yourself be needing such drastic measures to capture a man? Most men would come willing enough.' Beneath his mask, his mouth curved in a smile revealing a blackened tooth.

'I presume you have stopped my coach for some reason other than mere conversation,' Julia said pointedly. She had no idea whether she was afraid or annoyed. Why must they be robbed tonight of all nights? And why didn't the man just get on with it? She glanced over at Eduardo who still had a pistol trained on him. The coachman's eyes were now wide open and he looked as if he was about to swoon.

'Get your prisoner out.'

'I beg your pardon?' Julia said.

The highwayman jerked his head in the direction of the coach. 'Get him out.'

She blinked. 'How?'

'I'll come out on my own,' Thayne said. He suddenly appeared in the door of the coach, his feet no longer bound. Julia gaped at him, too shocked to speak as he awkwardly climbed out of the coach. His hands were still tied behind him. He met her eyes with a grim mocking look.

He glanced at their captor. 'Perhaps you would proceed with your robbery. We'd like to continue our journey.' His voice was bored.

The highwayman chuckled. 'Not so well trussed after all. Hand over your valuables, milady.'

'I do not have any. Unless you want a paste necklace.'

'Give it to me.' The amusement had left his face and he looked like the thief he was.

'Good God,' Thayne muttered.

'Best do as he asks, lass,' Eduardo called.

She fumbled with the clasp and reluctantly gave it to the ruffian.

The man turned to Thayne. 'Your ring, my lord.'

Julia's heart nearly stopped. 'No.'

The highwayman ignored her. 'Your ring.'

Thayne leaned against the coach. 'I am hardly capable of removing it myself.'

'Then you remove it, milady.' The highwayman gestured with his pistol.

Julia stepped closer to Thayne, her hand, still hidden

in the folds of her cloak, gripped her pistol tightly. The highwayman's eyes fell to her side.

'What is in your hand?' he demanded.

'Nothing.'

'Show me your hand.'

She backed up against the coach. 'No.'

'You'd best do as I want, milady.' His tone had lost all affability. He pointed the pistol at her.

'Hell,' Thayne muttered. 'Give the damn thing to me.'

'But you don't have any hands,' Julia said in a low voice.

'Put it in my hand. Behind my back,' he said between gritted teeth.

The highwayman levelled the pistol. Beneath his mask, his mouth had tightened into a nasty line. 'I should hate to shoot you or your, er…gentleman. Show your hand, milady.'

Reluctantly, Julia brought her hand forward. In a sort of dream she heard the shot and at the same time Thayne slammed into her. She hit the hard road and gasped, the breath knocked from her. A heavy weight pinned her to the ground. After an eternity, she heard more shouting and the pounding of horses' hooves and finally silence.

'Are you all right?' Thayne's voice was near her ear.

'Yes,' she managed to say.

The weight rolled away from her and she heard a groan and then he cursed. She managed to rise to her hands and knees, dizziness overtaking her for a moment. When she sat back, her hand encountered something thick and sticky on her cloak. Puzzled, she realised it was blood, except she could feel no pain.

And then she saw Thayne. He was sitting up, less than a foot away from her, a dark stain spreading on his coat. She crawled over to him and was horrified to see the hole in his coat sleeve on the upper part of his arm. She briefly registered his hands were no longer bound. 'You've been shot,' she said stupidly. With a sick feeling she realised he had taken the ball meant for her.

He looked at her and his eyes held a sardonic gleam. 'It appears so.' Then promptly shut his eyes.

Before she could say more, Eduardo appeared. He knelt down at Thayne's other side. He glanced at the wound and looked over at Julia. 'We need a pad for his arm. You'll need to hold it to the wound while I bind it.'

Thayne's eyes snapped open. 'Keep her away from me.' His voice was nearly a snarl.

She supposed she couldn't blame him for being so bad-tempered, but he needn't sound as if she was about to poison him. 'I am only going to help you.'

'How? By knifing me?'

'No!' she snapped. Her face heated when she saw Eduardo's amused look.

She rose, her mind starting to shift into focus. 'I have my handkerchief, and there is his cravat in the carriage.' And the new ribbon she had purchased at Grafton House earlier today. It seemed centuries ago.

Between them, she and Eduardo managed to stop the bleeding and then bind his wound. To her relief the shot had only grazed his arm, but she knew even then there could be complications.

Thayne had said little, his face growing paler; by the time they helped him into the coach, she feared he was about to swoon.

The coachman was revived with a shot of whisky. 'Never thought I'd live to say I was held up by a highwayman. I'll have a tale to tell!'

At least someone was delighted with the night's events. She climbed into the coach and reluctantly de-

cided she'd best sit next to Thayne. If he fainted or
started to fall off his seat, she'd at least try to prevent it.
His eyes were closed, but he opened them as she sat
down. He looked at her vaguely and then grimaced.
'Good God. Not you. Hell.'

He closed his eyes again and she strongly suspected
hell was exactly where he wished her. And she could
hardly fault him.

# Chapter Three

His head felt like it had been kicked by a horse and his arm was on fire, reminders that last night had been more than restless dreams brought on by too much brandy and a conscience filled with remorse. No, he'd been shot by a highwayman. That was after he had been abducted by a woman with the face of an angel who was undoubtedly mad. He opened his eyes and looked up at a ceiling with a brown water stain directly over head. No, it was most certainly not a bad dream. He recalled the stain from last night when his captors had poured whisky into his wound. He struggled to sit up and then groaned as pain shot through his head. He closed his eyes. Fate had seen fit to finally punish him after all.

'My lord?'

He vaguely recognised the soft male voice from last night. He forced his eyes open and saw the stocky grey-haired man who had bound him up hovering over him. 'How are you feeling, laddie?'

'I've felt better.' He barely managed to form the words around his dry mouth.

'You need some water.' The man moved across the small room to a pitcher on a chest.

At least they weren't planning to kill him yet. He'd had some half-formed notion that was exactly what they intended as they forced some vile concoction down his throat last night. He'd drifted into unconsciousness with the brown-haired angel bent over him, something surprisingly like concern in her face. And that was the last he knew until now.

He watched the man pour the water and then bring the cup to the bed. Although his captor was undoubtedly on the shady side of fifty, his tall body was well muscled and he moved with the grace of a much younger man. He placed the cup on the table next to the bed. 'I'll help you sit.'

He supported Nicholas with one arm while holding the cup with the other. Nicholas took a few sips, the water soothing to his parched throat and then fell back against the pillows. He fixed his companion with a cool stare.

'Who the hell are you?' he managed to ask.

'Eduardo Mackenzie.'

'Eduardo's a damnable name for a Scotsman.'

'My mother was Italian.' He looked down at Nicholas, a slight grin tugging at his lips. 'Must be feeling better. You had a bit of a fever last night but in a few days you'll be on your feet.'

'I am delighted.' He stared hard at Mackenzie. 'However, I'd rather know precisely what I am doing here. Or more to the point, why the hell did you abduct me?'

'You will need to ask the Countess.'

Nicholas raised a brow in his most sardonic fashion. 'I presume the Countess is the madwoman I met last night? Perhaps you would be so kind as to fetch her.'

Mackenzie looked apologetic. 'She is out.'

'Doing what? Searching for another victim? Does she

make a practice of luring men into her clutches and then finding novel means of torturing them?'

Mackenzie's lips twitched. 'Nay, you're the first.'

'Splendid,' Nicholas said bitterly. 'How was I fortunate enough to be chosen for the honour?'

'She'll tell you soon enough. Since you were still abed she went out to care for the animals.'

'Animals?' Had he heard correctly?

'This is a small farm.' Mackenzie took in Nicholas's expression. 'Some of the animals she prefers to tend to herself. And one of the mares is about to foal.'

'I see.' Nicholas closed his eyes briefly as tiredness overtook him. From the lingering taste in his mouth he suspected the potion last night contained laudanum.

'You'd best rest and then you'll be ready for a bite,' Mackenzie said. 'I'll be outside the door if you need anything.'

More likely to guard the door. Not that he was in any shape to attempt an escape. And even if he was, he certainly had no intention of leaving before he found out exactly what he was doing here. Nicholas watched Mackenzie cross the room and then he spoke, one more question coming to mind. 'Who is the Countess?'

Mackenzie paused at the door. 'I will let her tell you.'

He quit the room on quiet feet. Nicholas fell back against his pillows and swore, not only from the lack of answers but at his own helplessness. The Countess, or whatever she chose to call herself, had better have a good explanation for why he was lying under her roof with a gunshot wound in his arm—or she would rue the day she had ever laid eyes on him.

Julia closed the door to Betty's pen. The goat gave her a reproachful look, but Julia had no doubt Betty would find a way to escape again. It was nearly impossible to keep the goat contained anywhere. She preferred to follow Julia about like a dog and make everything her business.

Julia pulled the long wool cloak more tightly around her. The spring air was crisp and cool, but there were hints of warmer days to come. She paused by the barn and looked towards the old farmhouse. She had spent most of the day outside, dreading the moment Thayne would wake and ask for her. He'd slept the entire morning while she had attended to business in the study and then she had escaped after the noon meal to the barn. She had already spent more time than usual with the horses and then had played with the new kittens in the barn. From the position of the pale sun, it appeared to be late afternoon. She could not delay facing Lord Thayne any longer, not after he had saved her life.

This had completely confused her. Only an imbecile would fail to realise how angry he had been with her. She would hardly have blamed him if he had stood aside while the highwayman had shot her and then tried to make his escape. Instead, he had taken the bullet himself.

Perhaps Thérèse was right after all and he knew nothing about Thomas's death. For instance, it did not make sense that he would wear such an unusual ring that would be certain to attract notice. The cool intelligence she had seen in his eyes last night told her he was unlikely to do something that foolish.

He deserved to at least know why he had been hit over the head, bound and gagged and stuffed into a coach, and then shot by a highwayman. Every time she thought of last night she wanted to run. Thomas had always warned her that she was far too impulsive. 'You jump first and then think. You must make your plan, think of the possible outcomes, and then act, my sweet Julia.'

Not that he had always followed his own advice. And in the end, all the planning in the world had not saved him.

She reluctantly walked towards the house, the yellow cat, Wellington, trailing behind her. When she entered the house, Mrs Mobley, her housekeeper, appeared in the small hallway, dusting the flour off her hands on her white apron. She was tall with a magnificent figure and a mass of flaming red hair that was never quite concealed under her mobcap. 'Good thing you're back. His lordship is getting a trifle peevish, asking for you. Has the devil's own temper, I can see. Just brought him a tray and I thought he was likely to throw it at me. Said the gruel was only fit for babes, unless we now planned to starve him. Finally sent him some of the roast beef.'

'Splendid.' Julia's stomach was starting to knot up. So he was awake. She should be grateful he was finally conscious, but the thought of facing the man and his temper was hardly pleasing. 'How is his wound?'

'Wouldn't let me look at it. Or Eduardo. Said he wanted to wait for you.' She grinned. 'He's handsome enough, although he'll not tame easily. You'll have your hands full.'

'I have no intention of taming him. He will be leaving as soon as he is well enough.'

Mrs Mobley looked sceptical. Julia forced herself upstairs. Eduardo sat in a wooden chair outside of the door of the small bedchamber Thayne occupied. He rose when he saw her. 'Ah, 'tis you at last. The lad has been waiting impatiently for you.'

'He is not asleep?' Julia asked, praying that he was.

A smile touched his mouth. 'Not at all. He has just

finished his meal. I think, however, you'd best tell him why you've brought him here. He's becoming a trifle impatient.' He opened the door and Julia entered the room.

She paused, her heart thudding. Thayne was in bed, propped against the pillows. His cool gaze found her and the dangerous light that leapt to his eyes nearly made her back out the door. 'So you decided not to run after all,' he said softly.

'I had some business to attend to.' Unfortunately, her voice was not as strong as she might have wished. 'I hope you are better.'

He ignored her inquiry. 'Come here,' he commanded.

'I….' She glanced behind her, relieved to see Eduardo had not completely closed the door. She moved across the room and looked at him with no little degree of apprehension and tried to remind herself that, after all, he was her prisoner. And wounded. Despite that, he hardly looked vulnerable. In fact, with the dark shadow of beard around his mouth and powerful shoulders visible beneath the thin linen of his borrowed night shirt, he appeared even more male and deadly than he had last night. Her heart thudding, she halted by the bed. She saw his face was still very pale. 'How is your arm?'

He stared at her. 'It hurts like the devil.'

'I really am very sorry,' she said, feeling wretched. 'I never thought we would be held up or that you would be hurt. And you saved my life as well.'

'In retrospect I've no idea why.' His hard gaze focused on her face. 'So, my dear Jane or is it my dear Countess? Or is that merely another one of your pretences?'

She tried not to flinch at his cold, sardonic tone. 'No. My husband was an Earl.'

His brow rose. 'Was?'

'He is dead,' she said quietly. 'I suppose you wish to know why you are here.'

'The thought had crossed my mind. We've no dealings together that I can recollect and I already told you I would have been willing to provide my services without such a rash measure on your part. I am still willing.' His eyes raked over her body in blatant insult. 'Of course, I would prefer to know your name first.'

Her sensible, high-necked gown suddenly seemed as transparent as glass. Heat crept up her cheek. 'That is not what I wanted at all! Certainly you are the last man on earth I would...' She stopped and collected herself. Losing her temper would hardly help. 'I am Lady Carrington.' She kept her eyes on his face, watching for his reaction.

'Lady Carrington?' His gaze sharpened for a moment. 'Have we met before?'

'No. But perhaps you once met my husband.'

'Not to my knowledge.' If he had met Thomas before there was nothing in his face that gave it away. He regarded her from under lowered brows. 'What does this have to do with your abducting me?'

'I abducted you because of the ring.'

'The ring?' He looked blank.

'The ring you are wearing.'

He glanced down and then quickly back at her face. 'Ah, yes. My ring. The one you expressed an interest in last night.' His eyes narrowed. 'So, you wish me to believe you abducted me merely for my ring?'

'Yes, but there is more.'

'Is there?' He stared hard at her and gave a short laugh. 'I pray you will enlighten me. For you see, you are not the only person that has expressed an interest in this particular item in the past week.'

A chill ran down her spine. 'There has been someone else? Who?'

'I've no idea. The interested party sent an agent, but wished to remain anonymous.' He studied her face for a moment and then his brow drew together. 'What is this about?'

She took a deep breath. 'The ring belonged to my husband. When he was killed, nearly three years ago, it was removed from his finger.' She looked away. 'Most likely by his…his murderer.'

'How do you know it is the same ring?' he asked sharply.

'I purchased the ring in Spain. It is very old and I think it unlikely there would be another. Most certainly not in England. Our initials were carved on the inside of the band.'

'If they were there, they are no longer. How did you come to know I had the ring?' Then he smiled, but it did not reach his eyes. 'Ah, I remember. You were watching me play Hazard one evening. An amazing coincidence you happened to be there that very night. Or do you often visit Madame Blanchot's premises?'

The knowledge that he had recognised her was more than disconcerting. 'Thérèse told me you had the ring. I came that night to be certain.'

'And then a night later you decided to abduct me. Why?'

'Because I needed to know if you had anything to do with my husband's death. I did not think you would tell me if I merely asked you so I decided I would need to abduct you instead. And I wanted the ring.'

'I see.' Amusement briefly touched his mouth. 'Before we proceed further, I think you'd best look at the ring and be certain it is the same one. It would be a pity to discover you had gone to all this trouble for naught.' He pulled the ring from his finger, wincing slightly at the effort, and then held it out to her.

She took it, her hand trembling as she held the ring for the first time in nearly three years. The band still held the warmth of his hand. She ran her finger over the intricate carving on the band, remembering the surprise and pleasure on Thomas's face when she had presented it to him. And afterwards he had pulled her to him...

She forced the memory away and willed herself to look inside the band. Thayne was right, any initials there might have been were gone. When she touched the spot where they should have been, she felt a slight roughness. She moved to the window and looked more closely. The gold was scratched.

'Well?' Thayne said.

'I think they have been removed,' she said. She crossed to the bed. 'See, if you put your finger here.' She bent over him and held out the ring. He glanced at her and then touched the spot.

'Possibly.' He fell back against the pillows. A lock of hair had fallen over his forehead and he suddenly appeared rather vulnerable. She had the most discomforting urge to smooth it away. She jerked up, flustered by the notion.

He looked tired again. 'Shall I leave you?' she asked. 'Perhaps you should rest. We can continue the conversation later.'

'No.' He fixed his hazel gaze on her and frowned. 'Precisely why do you think I had something to do with your husband's death?'

'You have his ring.'

'Then I must be either a fool or remarkably arrogant to flaunt it in public where anyone might recognise it.'

'I had thought of that,' she admitted. She forced herself to look directly at him. 'Did you have anything to do with his death?'

He met her eyes squarely. 'No.'

Was he telling the truth? Some instinct told her he was. Despite his arrogance, she sensed he would not kill a man unless he had no other choice. Not for a piece of jewellery, no matter how valuable. And if had to kill, he would not lie about it. She looked away, shaken at the certainty of her thoughts. Why should she trust a man she had just met and under such bizarre circumstances?

His sardonic voice broke into her thoughts. 'And so, where do we proceed from here? Have we established my innocence or not? Or am I to enjoy your hospitality until you make up your mind?'

She frowned at him. She may have decided to believe him but it did not mean she planned to tell him that. Not until he answered the rest of her questions. 'I still would like to know how you came to be in possession of my husband's ring.'

He eyed her. 'I would like my ring back first.'

The slight emphasis on the 'my' set her back up. 'It is not your ring.'

'No? Then why is it in my possession?'

'That is what I'm trying to discover!' She fought back her exasperation. 'Can you not tell me?'

He gave her a cool smile. 'Not until you return the ring.'

'I have no intention of returning it!' She clenched her hands together in pure frustration.

'Then you will need to come up with another plan. Perhaps you could coerce the information from me at gunpoint. Or threaten to starve me. I presume you have a cellar. Does it have rats? You could lock me up there until I—'

She glared at him and resisted the urge to throw something at him. 'I think you are quite mad! Do you think I would do such a thing when you are so unwell?'

'So you will wait until my arm is better and then lock me in the cellar?' he asked maddeningly.

'Possibly. I would hope you will change your mind by then.'

'It is unlikely. Not until I get my ring back.' His expression was grim. 'For you see, my dear Lady Carrington, that ring is much more to me than a mere piece of jewellery. I have no intention of letting it go.'

'Then I've no choice but to keep you here.' She fought to keep her voice calm, but inside she wanted to scream at him.

His smile was wicked. 'I look forward to it. And to furthering our acquaintance.' His eyes locked with hers.

To her chagrin, her legs suddenly felt weak and her face heated. 'Good day, Lord Thayne. I trust you will change your mind soon.' She turned and forced herself to walk calmly across the room. She could not let him see how much he managed to fluster her. It would only give him all the advantage.


Nicholas fell back against the pillows, loath to admit even to himself that he was exhausted. Certainly he had no intention of letting his lovely gaoler suspect it had taken all his strength to finish their conversation, although it could hardly be called that. More of a verbal fencing. His mouth briefly lifted as he remembered the way her dark eyes flashed before she left.

Then he frowned. What the hell was going on? He knew of her husband, of course. One of Britain's most celebrated agents, Lord Carrington's name had been on every tongue after he had returned to England with his lovely wife, but even more so after his brutal murder. No one, to Nicholas's knowledge, had ever been arrested for the crime. He knew little of Lady Carrington, although that was hardly surprising. Since Mary's death, he had rarely ventured into society and so it was unlikely they would have crossed paths.

Had the ring indeed belonged to her husband? Certainly Lady Carrington had no doubt, not if she was desperate enough to abduct him for it. And how did the rest of it fit in? The man who had approached him had made him an offer that was staggering. He had found it peculiar but, because he had no intention of relinquishing the ring, had put it out of his mind.

And there was last night. The highwayman had requested Lady Carrington's necklace but had appeared oddly uninterested in any other valuables except for the ring. The fact the men had panicked and run off after shooting him had suggested they were amateurs.

So had that been the doing of the same person who had made him an offer for the ring? Or was the robbery a mere coincidence? If not, the implications, combined with Lady Carrington's revelation about her husband's murder, were not pleasant.

His frown deepened. He had no idea what to make of her, which had been his downfall. He had not been able to make up his mind whether she was an accomplished seductress or an innocent playing a game way over her head. So, due to a lethal combination of alcohol, lust and blasted curiosity, he had gone with her.

She had proved to be neither. She was a woman who would go to any lengths to solve her husband's murder. Except she needed to be more ruthless if she hoped to succeed. Instead of showing concern for his wounded state, for instance, she should have threatened to march him into the cellar straight away if he did not comply. A grin tugged at his mouth. At the very least she needed to curb her tendency to blush every time he teased her. He should perhaps drop a hint or two in her ear.

His grin faded. The last thing he wanted was to become embroiled in her affairs. He intended to retrieve his ring as soon as possible and escape. Even if it meant he held her at gunpoint.

The ring was all he had of Mary.

# Chapter Four

Nicholas put his fork down on the plate. He grimaced as he surveyed the remainder of the meal sitting on the tray across his lap. The chicken was stringy and nearly tasteless, and the vegetables so overcooked they fell apart before they reached his mouth. If all the meals were this inedible, he would starve.

With his good arm he managed to shove the tray over onto the small table near the bed. After that he forced himself to sit on the edge of the bed. His head spun for a moment before his vision cleared. But when he stood and took a few steps, he broke into a sweat as a wave of nausea rolled over him. He was forced to sit back down.

He swore, cursing his weakness. Even if he did manage to escape his room he was hardly in any condition to make his way down to the stables and steal a horse to ride back to London. Not until he rid himself of this blasted lightheadedness.

The weakness passed and he forced himself to stand again. This time he waited before attempting a step. Nicholas had just made it to the table near the mantel-piece when he heard the key turn in the lock. Half-expecting Lady Carrington's Amazonian housekeeper, he was startled to see Lady Carrington instead. She carried a basin and a cloth was draped over her arm.

She stepped inside the doorway and then saw him. Her eyes widened as they fell on his half-bare legs and quickly focused on his face. 'Whatever are you doing out of bed?'

'Attempting an escape.'

She frowned. 'You are ridiculous. Please get back into bed.' She set the basin and cloth down on the table and fixed a disapproving look on him.

'I would rather not.' Despite the fact his stomach was beginning to feel heavy again.

'I think it would be in your best interest to do so.'

He raised a brow. 'Why? Do you plan to shoot me if I do not?'

'No, of course not!' she snapped. He was gratified to see that she looked as if she wanted to hit him. 'You are far from well and you must be rather…rather cold in only a nightshirt.' She kept her eyes fastened on his face, slight colour rising to her cheeks.

So that was the problem. 'On the contrary, I feel rather warm. I had considered removing it since I normally do not wear such things to bed.'

Her reaction was all he had hoped for. She blanched as if she expected him to pull the garment off now. 'I… I…' She swallowed. 'Perhaps you are a bit feverish.'

'Perhaps.' Although he was loath to admit it, his head was starting to spin. He reached out for the table to support himself.

Lady Carrington was at his side in an instant. 'I am going to help you to bed.' She took his good arm in a gentle grasp. 'Come.'

Blast. He hardly wanted her leading him to bed as if he were an elderly invalid. 'No.'

'I fear you will swoon if you do not lie down.' She gave his arm a little tug. 'And if you do not do as I ask I may have no choice but to shoot you after all.'

'Very unsporting of you,' he managed to say and then was forced to close his eyes for a moment as sudden dizziness overtook him. When he opened them, he found her looking up at him, her face full of concern.

'You are most definitely going to bed,' she said.

Except for his sister, no woman in the past two years had ever looked at him in such a way, or touched him with such gentle hands. The sensation was more than disconcerting.

He pulled his arm out of her grasp. 'I will put myself to bed,' he said coolly. He turned away from her and managed to make it back to the bed without stumbling. He sat down on the edge. To his chagrin, his head swam and he was forced to lay back on the pillows. Lady Carrington had followed him and now stood next to the bed. He looked up and scowled. 'Now what do you want?'

She levelled a frown at him. 'I need to look at your wound.'

'Why? To pour salt into it, perhaps?'

'Do not be so absurd! I wish to make certain it is not infected. Eduardo will be in with a new dressing in a moment. If you will sit up a little more, I can remove your bandage.'

'I've no intention of having you faint all over me at the sight of blood. I'll wait for your bodyguard.'

'I have seen worse injuries. Much worse.' She was beginning to look exasperated. 'I am going to remove your bandage. And it will hurt much more if you do not cooperate,' she added severely.

'Are you threatening me?'

'No. Merely telling you that if you attempt to pull away you may hurt your arm.'

The last thing he wanted was to have her touch him again with her soft, gentle hands. Or see his bare arm. 'What is your given name?' he asked, hoping to distract her.

'Julia.' She sat down on the bed next to him.

'Julia,' he murmured. 'Much more suitable than Jane.'

From the slight colour that stained her cheeks, he knew he had flustered her again. Good. He intended to fluster her enough so she would leave him alone.

'I need to see to your arm, please.' She did not look at his face. A few strands of fine brown hair had come loose from the knot at the back of her head and he resisted the sudden urge to tuck the hair behind her ear. He forced his gaze to her lips, which proved to be a mistake for a surge of desire shot through him.

He nearly groaned. Lust was the last thing he wanted to feel for her. He had undoubtedly been without a woman for too long. Perhaps it was time he gave up his celibacy and accept Marguerite Anslow's not too subtle offer after all.

'Is something wrong?' she asked. Her brow was creased in a tiny frown. Apparently she had no idea of the effect she had on him.

If she did she would probably run like the devil, which might work to his advantage. He stared down at her pale oval face with its thin, delicate nose and rosebud lips and resisted the urge to pull her into his arms. Instead his gaze lingered on her mouth. 'I might consider telling you what you want to know if you will kiss me,' he said softly.

She stared at him as if he had gone mad. 'I…I beg your pardon?'

He smiled wickedly. 'I am making you a bargain. If you kiss me, I will consider telling you where I got the ring. With a little more enticement I might decide to let you keep it.'

She leapt up and backed away from the bed. 'I think you are delirious!'

'Not at all.' He turned his head a little on the pillows and then allowed his gaze to run insolently down her softly curved body. Even in the candlelight he could see the colour on her pale ivory cheeks. 'I believe you offered me that and more last night.'

'I...I did not!'

'No?'

She jumped when the door opened and gave a little gasp. Mackenzie entered. He glanced at Julia's dismayed face and then looked at Nicholas. A hint of a smile touched his mouth but he only said, 'I was a bit delayed. How does his wound look?'

'I...I have not yet had a chance to look at it.' Her voice was a trifle breathless. 'In fact, I believe it would be best if you saw to Lord Thayne yourself.'

'I see.' Eduardo gave her a curious glance before moving to the side of the bed where, as Lady Carrington had before, he sat down next to Nicholas. Before Nicholas could protest he had started to unwrap the bandage.

'I thought she was planning to leave,' Nicholas said. He gritted his teeth against the sudden pain that shot through him when Mackenzie's hand brushed his tender flesh.

'How is his arm?' Lady Carrington asked, ignoring Nicholas. She had come to stand next to the bed again.

Mackenzie straightened and stood up. 'A bit red. We'll clean it with a spot of brandy and then wrap it again.' He glanced at Nicholas. 'Afraid you'll need to accept our hospitality a bit longer. Can't have you leaving with that arm.'

Nicholas scowled at him. 'I had no idea leaving was a possibility. Lady Carrington does not seem inclined to release me.'

'So you haven't reached an agreement yet?' Mackenzie asked.

'No.' Nicholas looked past Mackenzie to Lady Carrington. 'We are still negotiating. I have laid out my terms. I am certain when she has the time to consider them she will see they are quite reasonable.'

Her mouth fell open and then she glared at him. 'Reasonable? You may count yourself fortunate if I let you go before the next century! Good evening, my lord.' To his immense satisfaction, she backed out of the room and slammed the door.

Mackenzie regarded him with an interested expression. 'You might try a less heavy-handed approach, laddie. Unless you're wanting to stay on for a while.' He moved to the table and picked up the basin.

'No.' Nicholas watched Mackenzie approach him and braced himself for another assault on his arm. He fully intended to be back in London before another night had passed. Unless he had completely misread Lady Carrington, a few more improper offers should have her eager to return his ring and rid herself of him in no time.

Julia entered her bedchamber and then sank down on her bed. She got up again almost right away and stalked to her window, her fists clenched. She forced herself to take a deep breath before she did something childish such as heave a vase across the room.

Whatever was wrong with her? He wasn't the first man who had offered her a *carte blanche*. Thomas had posed as a charming gamester. He rubbed shoulders with some of the most practised rogues in Europe and more than one of this circle had assumed Julia would be amenable to an illicit affair. She had learned to shrug off most advances with a polite smile and had become expert at dodging the more persistent admirers.

So why could she not shrug off Thayne as well? He was proving to be exactly the sort of man she despised; a man who was not beneath attempting to force a woman into his bed. She should treat him with icy contempt instead of losing her temper and slamming doors. Certainly she should not be blushing like a schoolgirl every time he looked at her with an insolent gaze.

Except she had the most stupid feeling he really did not want her in his bed at all and was merely trying to aggravate her. In fact, she suspected he did not even like her very much. Worse, there had been a moment or two when she had looked at him and actually felt the same mixture of exasperation and sympathy she had felt for Thomas when he had been ill. More disconcerting, she had felt the same desire to take care of him.

She wanted to groan. However had she got herself into this fix? She had Thomas's ring—perhaps she should just release Thayne and try to discover whatever information she could on her own. If someone had approached him about the ring, then there was a chance the person might approach her.

Unfortunately, she suspected it would not be all that easy. However else Thayne might confuse her, of one thing she was certain: he was not going to give up the ring without a fight.

The next morning Julia decided she would let Eduardo and Barbara Mobley nurse Thayne. She tried to justify her cowardly behaviour by reminding herself that she did have to attend to other matters and could not spend all of her time worrying about her ungracious patient. Not that she was allowed to forget his presence. Barbara seemed to think she needed frequent reports on his arm, which was less red, his manners, which were surly, and his demands, which included a shirt and breeches instead of the nightshirt.

She finally escaped to the stables; when she returned to the house, she went directly to the tiny room that served as her study. She sat down at the old desk. The first thing that met her eye was the most recent letter from Francis Abbot of Abbot and Sons, Solicitors. Mr Abbot had written to advise her, not for the first time, that she would be wise to sell Foxwood. On sunny days with blue skies showing outside the study window, and roses and larkspur in bloom, it was possible to be optimistic about keeping Foxwood. But on cold rainy days such as today, with leaks in the roof and the dilapidated garden, she was tempted to give in and sell the farm after all.

Foxwood had been Thomas's dream; a peaceful country farm to raise his horses. But he had been killed before the first foal was born.

She had not wanted to give up his dream. She had leased out the land to her neighbour, Lord George Kingsley, and sold several of the horses. There was little of the money Thomas had left her and none of the amount his uncle had left with the farm. She refused to give Thomas's remaining relations the satisfaction of admitting defeat and selling the farm. Or her own relations. Where would she go? To live as a companion to Cousin Harriet? She could hardly take Eduardo and Barbara with her.

'Daydreaming again?'

Julia's head jerked up. She stared at the man who stood in the doorway. And then wanted to groan. A visitor was the last thing she wanted and this particular one was even less welcome. She stood. 'Oh, George. I…I hardly expected you. I thought you had left for Maldon.'

He sauntered into the room and raised a brow. He was of medium height with dark brown hair and a thin, arrogant face. As usual, he was exquisitely dressed, with an elaborately tied cravat and shirt points to his chin. 'Disappointed, my love? No, I had meant to leave London and travel to Maldon today, but, alas, my dear father had other plans. There seems to be a matter or two at Amberton that cannot go without my attention. I would have thought Seton could capably attend to the problem but, alas, my parent decided otherwise with the gentle hint that if I declined, I would find myself without funds. I fear some of my creditors are becoming a bit, er… persistent.'

Which meant he had probably racked up another mound of gambling debts. But why, of all times, must he pay one of his infrequent visits to Amberton? He much preferred Maldon where he kept a small cottage and docked his yacht. 'I see.'

'He also commissioned me to inquire after your well-being.'

'I am well, of course. Would you care for refreshment?' She prayed he would say no.

'Perhaps a glass of claret. However, I will forgo anything of an edible nature. I do not wish to risk breaking a tooth.'

Mrs Mobley suddenly appeared as if on cue. She regarded George with a suspicious eye and stalked out after Julia made her request. George watched Mrs Mobley leave. 'I expect to find myself cursed,' he remarked as he settled himself in one of the wing chairs. 'I have no idea why you surround yourself with such grim servants. Actually, I have no idea why you persist in living in such a grim place.'

'I do not find it particularly grim.' She cast a nervous glance towards the door. She hoped Mrs. Mobley had remembered to lock Thayne in his bedchamber. The thought of him appearing while George was here was enough to give her palpitations.

'Well, perhaps one becomes used to it although that is a rather troubling thought. So, I take it you are not planning to take up my offer and sell?'

'No.' She nearly jumped at the sound of footsteps, but it was only Barbara returning with the claret and a plate of cakes. She watched George take the glass and hoped he would quickly finish it.

He did not. He took a leisurely sip and sat back. 'So, my dear, what have you been about since I last saw you?'

'Nothing very interesting.' Was he looking at her oddly? She gave him a quick smile. 'How is London?'

'Tedious in the extreme. The usual *on-dits*, although the latest gossip is most interesting.'

'Indeed,' she said flatly, hoping to discourage him from elaborating.

'Yes. Indeed.' He took another sip. 'Viscount Thayne has disappeared without a trace.'

'V…Viscount Thayne?'

'The Earl of Monteville's grandson. He was to meet with Monteville yesterday morning and never showed up. He also failed to appear for a dinner at Norwood House last night without a word. The rumours have already begun. Everything from foul play to an elopement. He was last seen at Thérèse Blanchot's establishment the night before.'

'R…really.' Oh, Lord. Was there any chance she had been recognised? But she could tell nothing from George's bland gaze. 'Perhaps he merely decided to go away.'

'Perhaps. But his carriage was found in a nearby street and the coachman reported he never returned to it. And there is the mysterious female with whom he was said to have left Thérèse's.'

Julia managed a laugh. 'A mysterious female as well? How odd. It is beginning to sound rather like a Minerva Press novel. Perhaps he decided to elope and hired a hack.'

George raised a brow. 'My dear, one does not miss appointments with Monteville in order to elope in a hack. Unless one has run mad.'

'I suppose not. At least from what I have heard about Lord Monteville.' The reputation of the cool powerful Earl was well known. The thought of what he would do if he discovered she had abducted his grandson made her feel rather ill.

'No. Which is why that scenario is most unlikely. I am surprised you have not met the formidable Lord Monteville. He is a friend of my father's.'

Monteville and Phillip were friends? The situation was becoming worse by the moment. 'I did not know that.'

'He is not a man one would want to cross. If Thayne's disappearance was not voluntary, one could almost feel sorry for the perpetrators.'

'Oh,' Julia said faintly.

George suddenly polished off his drink and set the glass on the table. 'As much as I am loath to do so, I suppose I must deal with the local peasantry.' He rose in a leisurely movement and looked down at her. 'My lovely Julia, you look most unwell.'

'Do I?' She stood. 'I am rather tired, that is all.'

He took her hand and bowed elaborately over it. 'I am not surprised. You must come and dine with me soon. As dull as Amberton can be, at least I have a decent cook. And by the way, my dear Aunt Sophia has asked me to tell you that you are always welcome to stay with her in London.' He released her hand and picked up his hat and gloves and strode to the door. He opened it. Betty stood outside. She fixed him with her dark unblinking stare. George paused and turned to look back at Julia, a look of disgust on his countenance. 'My dear, I really advise you to sell the place. If it ever gets about you have live-stock running about the house, you will be considered a complete quiz.'

He left the room. Betty wandered into the study and spotted the cakes whereupon she reached up and neatly helped herself. Julia sat back down in her chair, her thoughts in turmoil. Had George recognised her as the unknown female? But surely he would have said something or asked more probing questions if he had. More disconcerting was the knowledge that Lord Monteville and Phillip were friends. What if Phillip decided to make one of his visits to Amberton? George always stopped at Foxwood and she would be forced to ask him to dine, an invitation he never turned down despite Barbara's cooking. And if something went wrong and Thayne managed to escape from his room…she shuddered at the thought. How could she ever explain how he came to be here? Perhaps she could drug Thayne and lock him in his room, but that seemed utterly barbaric.

Aside from that, it was hardly fair to Thayne's family to let them think he was dead or hurt. She had best re-lease him as quickly as possible. But would he leave without the ring? Even if she told him he was free to go?

She fingered the chain around her neck. She had finally decided this was the safest place for it. It was unlikely he would look for it there. At least she hoped not; the thought was enough to make her blanch. Particularly after last night.

Now, instead of persuading him to stay, she must persuade him to go.

Without the ring.

Nicholas swung his legs over the side of the bed and rose. He was still a little shaky and his head tended to spin for a few seconds after he changed positions, but his arm was better. Not that he had any intention of letting Lady Carrington know that. Better if she thought he was still incapacitated. His mouth curled. She had not been by to see him today, but instead, had sent either Eduardo or Mrs Mobley to tend to him. However, he planned to deal with his captor himself. Tomorrow, if possible. He forced himself to move to the window. His room faced the back of the house and looked down on the stable yard. In the fading light he could see the outline of the stable.

Earlier today he had positioned himself in the chair in front of the window. He had been interested to see that Lady Carrington had spent considerable time in the stables. Mrs Mobley had been willing enough to tell him Lady Carrington generally made a daily visit to the stables to attend to the horses. So, he merely needed to make his way to the stables at the same time she was there. Slipping past her two guardians might pose a problem, but he had noted that today his door was frequently left unguarded. The lock was so old he doubted it would take much effort to break it. Once in the stables, he had no doubt he could persuade her, although she may not like his methods, to give him the ring and a horse. And a pair of boots as he'd not managed to locate his own. Then he was leaving.

There was a sound behind him. He turned, expecting to see Eduardo who'd been the last person outside his door. Instead, Julia stood there. His body tensed in anticipation almost as if he had been looking forward to her visit. He forced the feeling down.

'So, you've deigned to visit me after all,' he drawled.

'Yes. I had something I wanted to discuss with you.' She looked at him, biting her lip a little as if she were nervous and did not know quite what to say. 'How are you feeling?' she finally asked.

'Better.'

She frowned. 'Why are you up? Shouldn't you be in bed?'

'No. What do you wish to discuss? Have you come to accept my offer after all?' He had no idea what to do if she said yes.

'No! I most certainly have not.' A touch of colour washed over her cheeks but she held his gaze. 'In fact, I have put it quite out of my mind.'

'Indeed.' He gave her a disbelieving smile. 'What is it you want?'

'Must you be so rude?'

'Am I? I was not aware there was a protocol for when addressing one's abductor.' He had no idea why he was sparring with her except he wanted to keep her at a distance.

She looked completely discomfited. 'Won't you at least sit?'

'After you.' He gestured towards the wooden chair near his bed.

She hesitantly advanced into the room and perched on

the edge of the chair like a schoolgirl. He climbed back into the bed, grateful to be sitting and determined not to let her know. He stared at her. 'What is it?'

'I have decided to release you.'

That was the last thing he had expected. 'Why?'

'Well, I…I cannot keep you here forever.'

'But I thought that was the plan if I did not tell you what you wanted to know. I was quite resigned to spending my life locked up in a small bedchamber with a leaking roof, subsisting on poorly cooked meat and overcooked vegetables with my only visitors two surly servants. And your delightful self, of course.'

'That was hardly my intention!' she snapped, and then seemed to collect herself. 'You may leave tomorrow.'

'So, why the sudden change of heart? I don't suppose George Kingsley's visit had anything to do with it?'

Her eyes widened in surprise. 'What do you know of that?'

'Your delightful Mrs Mobley told me. I am rumoured to be the victim of foul play, I believe.'

She coloured, looking extremely mortified. 'She had no business telling you that!'

'Why not? It is my life after all.'

'Yes, but she should not have been listening!'

'Apparently she fears for your virtue at Kingsley's hands.' At least that was the excuse the housekeeper had given for eavesdropping on Julia's visitor.

'That is ridiculous! George…that is…Lord George would never…' She shut her lips tightly. 'This is an inane conversation! And yes, if you must know, I did change my mind after his visit! I cannot have your family worrying about you and thinking you are dead! So you may go.'

'So you have decided to return the ring to me.'

'No, I haven't decided that at all!' Her hand went to a chain she wore around her neck.

'Then I am not leaving.' He settled back against the pillows and looked at her.

'But you cannot stay here!'

'Why not? What do you plan to do about it? Throw me into the rain and leave me to my own devices? I am hardly well enough to walk back to London. Then you would have my death on your conscience, although, of course, that may not matter to you. I suppose you could abduct me again and take me to my townhouse. But in that case, I might decide to press charges against you.'

'But then you would have to admit you were abducted by a woman. I cannot imagine you would like that getting about!'

He smiled sardonically. 'It matters little to me what tale gets about.' He allowed his gaze to wander over her face in a way that brought colour to her cheeks. 'Some men might actually be envious.'

'I cannot imagine why!' she snapped.

'Can you not? You are a lovely woman.'

Her colour increased and she glared at him. 'That has nothing to do with a thing! Why must men always make some idiotic remark about a woman's appearance that has no relevance to a conversation at all!'

'Referring to you as a lovely woman is hardly an idiotic remark.'

'That is not—' She stopped and shut her mouth tightly as if attempting to hang on to her temper. 'Perhaps we could stick to the point of the conversation.'

'We could, although we seemed to have reached an impasse. You wish me to leave your house and I do not plan to go without the ring. Although you could have Eduardo toss me into the rain.'

'You are ridiculous! I would hardly do such a thing!'
She looked extremely flustered. 'I should think you
would want to leave!'

He gave her a lazy smile, which had the desired effect
of making her look even more disconcerted. 'Why? I've
nothing more pressing to do. I will own, being abducted
by you has been the most entertaining thing that has happened to me in a long while.' Which was, he realised
with some surprise, the truth. His days mostly seemed to
stretch out in a predictable pattern of appointments and
activities designed to fill the time.

She stared at him, a peculiar look crossing her face. 'I
cannot imagine why anyone would find being forced into
a carriage at gunpoint entertaining.'

'You've left out being bound and gagged, jostled over
rough roads, and finally being shot by a highwayman.
Then there is the nearly inedible food and the—'

'I think you are quite mad! Why can you not go? I
will be more than happy to have Eduardo drive you to
London.'

'But then you won't know where I got the ring. I
thought you wanted that information.'

'Yes, but…' She bit her lip. 'Why must you make this
so difficult?'

To his consternation, she looked as if she were about
to cry. After living with a younger sister, he recognised
the signs all too well.

'Don't,' he said roughly.

'Do…don't what?' She avoided his eyes and sniffed.
She looked vulnerable and tired and he had the damnable
impulse to pull her into his arms and comfort her.

'Cry.'

'I am not crying. I never engage in such…such missish
behaviour!' She abruptly rose to her feet, stumbling

against the chair a little. 'I will leave you for now. I…I hope you will consider my…my offer.' She turned and dashed from the room, leaving Nicholas to stare after her.

He fell back against the pillows. 'Hell!' he muttered. Now he'd managed to make the indomitable Lady Carrington cry. Hardly the effect he had wanted. Not that he was sure what he had wanted from her.

If he had an ounce of sense he'd take his leave from this house as quickly as possible. He had no desire to involve himself with the lovely Lady Carrington. No more than she wanted anything from him—her evident desire to rid herself of him as quickly as possible told him that. She was willing to let him go without the information she sought.

But, of course, she still had the ring. And he could not leave without it.

# Chapter Five

At least he hadn't propositioned her again. That was the first thought Julia had on awakening the next morning. The next was that it was raining and the roof was undoubtedly leaking.

And then she heard a curse followed by an indignant bleat. Her eyes shot open and she sprang out of bed, hardly noticing the hard cold floor. Oh, heavens! Whatever was Betty doing inside? And why must she choose to enter Thayne's room?

Betty stood at the foot of his bed, staring at him. He had sat up, the cover falling from his chest. His eyes went to Julia's face. 'There is a goat in my room,' he said.

'Yes.' Embarrassed, she stepped inside. 'It is Betty.'

'Indeed.' He continued to stare at her with an unreadable expression.

'She…she sometimes comes in the house.' Actually, it was on a nearly daily basis, but Thayne didn't need to know that.

'Perhaps you could tell her I'd prefer that she'd find another room. Waking up nose to nose with a goat isn't particularly appealing.'

'No.' Her face crimson, Julia crossed over to Betty

who had a cloth in her mouth. She saw it was one of the clean bandages. 'Just give me that,' she hissed, grabbing the other end.

Betty stared at her with unblinking dark eyes. Julia tugged and the cloth tore. 'Drat!'

'Perhaps you should use what's left of it as a rope,' Thayne suggested. His voice held a slight hint of amusement.

Julia quickly tied the cloth around Betty's neck, not daring to look at him. She tugged on the makeshift lead and Betty reluctantly followed her, her hooves clicking on the wood floor. Julia returned to her bedchamber and shoved her bare feet into a pair of slippers before leading Betty down the narrow steps and to the kitchen. Because of the rain, the door had swollen and would not shut properly which was how Betty had made her way in. Julia supposed it was her fault for raising the orphaned goat in the house in the first place.

She pushed the reluctant Betty out of the door. The goat gave her a reproachful look as if she considered Julia the epitome of cruelty for shoving her into the rain. Julia looked at her sternly. 'You can go into your shed! And please, if you must come in, stay away from Lord Thayne.' He probably thought her mad enough already without a goat roaming about the house.

She watched Betty amble into the garden and then attempted to shut the door. It closed, but barely, and she had to use all her strength to push it tight enough so she could fasten the latch. By the time she was done, she was breathless. And then she noticed the leak in the roof. She stifled a groan and went to fetch a large pot. It seemed as soon as they repaired one leak, another heavy rain would come and bring another.

'Do you frequently have livestock running about the house?'

She whirled around, her hand going to her throat. 'Wh…what are you doing here?'

Thayne was leaning against the doorway. 'I came to see if you needed help evicting Betty. And I was hungry.'

'Hungry?' She stared at him, her heart pounding. He was dressed in a shirt and breeches that had belonged to Thomas. They were a trifle loose on him, but failed to hide his lean, muscular build. His injured arm was in a sling. The faint outline of his beard made him look a little rough and not at all like an elegant lord. She was suddenly aware she was clad only in her nightrail, her feet bare except for her slippers, her hair in a thick braid past her shoulders. No matter that it was a voluminous gown with a high neck and she wore a shawl. She pulled the ends of the shawl tighter and crossed her arms.

'Last night's stew was not exactly edible,' he said. 'What meat was that anyway? For a moment I feared I was eating pieces of boot.'

'Mrs Mobley does her best. And please do not say anything to her! You'll hurt her feelings.'

'I wouldn't dream of it.' He fixed his penetrating stare on her. 'Where is she, by the way, as well as your other faithful retainer?'

'Still sleeping, I imagine.' At his look, she added defensively, 'It is not yet dawn.'

'Leaving the mistress of the house to contend with escaped goats and leaking roofs. And prisoners.'

'They both work very hard.' She gave him a cold look. 'If you want something to eat, I suggest you sit down and keep your unwelcome observations to yourself.'

His brow shot up, but none the less he sauntered into the room and sat down in one of the wooden chairs at the heavy old table. He swayed a little and she frowned. 'What are you doing out of bed? You still look far from well.'

'I am well enough,' he said curtly.

'I doubt that.' Arguing was undoubtedly fruitless. 'What do you want to eat? There is bread and cheese and ham.'

'Bread and cheese will do. I am not certain I trust the ham.'

She moved to the pantry, aware his eyes were on her as she pulled out the bread and found a carving knife. She prepared the food, put it on a plate and set it in front of him. 'Would you like something to drink?'

His cool gaze settled on her face and then drifted down to the high neckline of her gown. 'You have surprising talents.'

Colour rose to her cheeks. 'Hardly. And unless you wish your meal taken away from you, I suggest you make no further remarks in that vein. And I pray you will not say a thing about the fact I am not suitably dressed!'

Amusement leapt to his eyes. 'And risk having my food snatched away? I assure you I would not be so ungentlemanly.'

She backed away, unnerved by the unexpected laughter in his face. 'Anything else, my lord?'

'No. Come and sit with me.'

'I...'

'I have something to say to you.'

Her heart began to pound again. She swallowed and forced herself to look at him. There was no reason to think he was going to make her another improper offer. 'What is it?'

'I apologise for making you cry last night,' he said abruptly.

Her mouth fell open and then she flushed. 'You really did not.'

'Then why did you dash from the room like that?'

'I…I was merely rather tired.'

'And had a sudden urge for your bed, I take it?'

'Well, no.' She felt rather foolish under his penetrating gaze. Of all the men to abduct, why did it have to be someone who seemed to see through her? 'Would you like something to drink? I can make coffee or there is ale.' She jumped up.

Nicholas caught her hand and a tremor ran through her at his touch. 'There is no need to run away. I am not planning to eat you. So, do you accept my apology for upsetting you?'

He was too close. She looked into his eyes which no longer seemed so cool and impersonal and, for a moment, no one seemed to exist except him. His own gaze darkened and he dropped her hand. She stepped back. 'Yes, of course.' Except she hardly knew what he was talking about.

She brought him the ale and forced herself to sit down. She had no idea what to say. Sitting with him in the dark kitchen with the rain pattering on the roof created an intimacy she found unnerving. She stole a glance at him. A lock of hair hung over his forehead, making him look rather boyish. He seemed to have lost some of his defensiveness and for a moment she suddenly caught a glimpse of a younger, more vulnerable man. A man she could quite like.

Disconcerted by her thought, she quickly turned away. She could not possibly allow herself to like him. She might be tempted to forget they were at daggers' drawn.

'What do you do here?'

She started. 'I beg your pardon?'

He was looking at her. 'On this farm. Do you actually farm?'

'No. I have leased out most of the acres to Geor...Lord George. I keep some in pasture for the horses and some is still rather wild although Geo...that is, someone has suggested that I should farm that as well, as it is very good land.' After last night she did not want to bring George's name too prominently into the conversation.

'But you obviously do not wish to.'

'No, I like it the way it is. Part of an old ruined cottage sits there which looks rather romantic, and there are berries and a family of foxes. And a lovely view of the countryside.' If she leased it, she would never feel quite as comfortable about going there when she wanted to think.

'Why are you here? I would imagine such an isolated farm would be rather lonely for you.'

She looked away. 'Foxwood was where my husband wished to live. He much preferred it over his family estate in Hampshire. He used to come here when he was a boy to visit his uncle; when his uncle died, he left the farm to Thomas. And when Thomas died, he left the farm to me.'

'I see. What about your family?'

She looked back at him, surprised. 'My father died when I was six and my mother when I was thirteen. I have no brothers or sisters. Eduardo and Barbara—that is, Mrs Mobley—are my family.'

He frowned. 'There are your husband's relations and your stepfather and your cousin. Do they not care about your welfare?'

She was even more shocked he should know that much about her. 'Thomas and I eloped. My stepfather had wanted me to marry someone else; when I married

*My Lady's Prisoner*

Thomas, he disowned me. And Thomas's family disowned him when he married me. So, no, to answer your question, they do not care about my welfare.'

'There is no one you can apply to?'

'For what?' She gave a little laugh.

'After a night or two in this place it becomes quite apparent it is in dire need of repair. I've no idea what you are leasing your land for, but it is obviously not enough to keep the roof over your head. Did your husband not leave you enough to at least keep the farm up?'

She stared at him, more than a little angry. 'I cannot see that it is your business, my lord. It is hardly polite for a guest to make such rude comments anyway.'

His brow rose a fraction. 'I have now been elevated from the status of hostage to that of guest?'

She ignored that. 'You are free to leave, you know.'

He leaned back in his chair. 'As soon as I get the ring.'

'It is not yours! Can you not understand that?'

'Not at all. I had it in my possession for the last two years. I consider it mine. And so far you have given me no solid evidence it belongs to you.'

She stared at him, frustrated. 'It belonged to Thomas! I gave it to him!'

'How do I know it is the same ring? Perhaps there are two such rings. You admitted yourself you could not read the inscription.'

'It should be quite obvious the inscription was scratched away! Why must you be so stubborn?'

'You are equally stubborn, my dear. And for all I know the inscription had someone else's name.'

'Could you at least tell me where you got the ring?'

'I could, but not until you return the ring. Or until you kiss me. Of course, I still might not leave until I have my ring.' The slow smile that crossed his face nearly made her legs turn to water.

Something she had no desire to let him see. She gave him a cool smile in return. 'I can see you still plan to be unreasonable. Very well, my lord, you may stay and enjoy my hospitality in your leaky bedchamber with inedible meals as long as you wish!' She rose with as much dignity as possible in a nightrail and shawl.

He leaned back even further and regarded her with infuriating calm. 'Thank you. I fully intend to do so.'

'Good. Well, I have too much to do today to entertain you. You may do as you wish. If you need anything, Mrs Mobley will be delighted to assist you.'

'I somehow doubt that.'

She gave him one more scathing look and then stalked to the door. Without looking back at him, she left the room, quite aware that his eyes were fixed on her back.

After dressing, she went downstairs to her study. Barbara had left a tray on her desk with toast, butter and coffee. The rain had stopped and, to her surprise, the clouds actually showed signs of dispersing. She sat down at her desk and stared out at the back garden, which seemed to be nothing but a mess of tangled weeds and forlorn-looking plants. Betty was nibbling on a tall weed. At least one member of the household had time to garden.

She poured herself a cup of coffee and sighed. The condition of the garden was the least of her worries. Whatever was she to do about Thayne? Instead of gratefully accepting her offer and leaving, he seemed determined to stay unless she gave him the ring.

But how could she do that? She touched it gently. She had found it in a shop in Madrid. The ring had been curious and old, and she had been instantly drawn to it.

The proprietor's unlikely tale of love and magic had only added to its mystery, and after a bit of haggling she had purchased it. Thomas had been as intrigued as she had, and until the day he died had worn it.

So how could she possibly give it to Thayne? And however was she to persuade him to tell her from where he got the ring? She could hardly hold him at gunpoint again. Besides, it was doubtful if even that would convince him. He'd probably just look at her in his sardonic way and tell her to shoot him, which, of course, she wouldn't do…as he undoubtedly knew quite well.

Or she could kiss him.

She quickly dismissed that thought. After this morning she was convinced more than ever he merely intended to tease her. It would quite serve him right if she did tell him she wanted to accept his offer. But if he called her bluff…her face heated at the mere thought.

She rose and stood in front of the window. And what of his family? She could hardly justify letting them think he was gravely injured or even dead. Why had she not considered that when she abducted him? But then, she was not thinking about anything but her own desperate need to find Thomas's killer. Thayne had been nothing to her but a means to an end. Certainly not a man with a family that might worry about him.

But there was a way she could solve at least one of her problems of conscience.

A half-hour later she found Eduardo in the barn. He listened to her request with an impassive face. 'So the lad still refuses to leave?' He set the pitchfork against the wall and looked at her.

'He will not leave without the ring.'

'And I take it you will not return it to him.'

She scowled. 'No. Not unless he tells me what he knows. And even then I am not certain I will do so.'

His lips twitched. 'Then you may have him on your hands for a very long time.' He sobered. 'Very well, but are you certain he's wanting his family to know his whereabouts? I do not suppose you told him your intentions?'

'No.' That he would be displeased would be a vast understatement. 'But I cannot think of any reason why they should not know. I remember how worried and desperate I would feel the few times Thomas disappeared for days without word. I cannot inflict that sort of worry on someone else.'

'I doubt you can,' he said quietly. He hesitated. 'Are you certain you'll be all right with Thayne for a few hours?'

'Of course I shall be. Barbara will be here. At any rate, I do not think he is well enough to do much harm.'

'I wouldn't be too sure of that,' Eduardo said. 'I'll take Isabella and return as quickly as possible. At least the rain has let up so the road should be passable.'

She watched him go and prayed she had done the right thing.

A few hours later she finally sat back on her haunches and surveyed the small garden plot near the kitchen door with more than a little satisfaction. Most of the weeds had been pulled and it now appeared quite ready for the vegetables she planted each year. Usually, she set young Joe Partridge from the village to clearing the plot, but her anger and frustration with Thayne had made a physical task most attractive. No matter she had managed to tear a glove and her old gown was hopelessly dirty from the muddy soil. At least she had accomplished something.

She rose and dashed a stray lock of hair from her forehead with a muddy hand, undoubtedly leaving a streak in its place. The cat, Wellington, who had been sleeping on an old wooden bench, rose and stretched, then jumped down. Betty ambled over to the pile of weeds and then paused, looking at something behind Julia's shoulder. Her tail twitched and she bleated.

Julia glanced around but saw nothing near the garden fence. Then she heard a sound as if someone was walking rapidly away. Puzzled, she walked across to the gate and peered over but saw no one. Had someone been there? Surely Barbara would have said something. Or could it have been Thayne? But why would he watch her in such a manner and then steal off?

A drop of rain hit her on the nose and she shivered. She had best go in anyway. The clouds were beginning to look rather ominous. She quickly made her way to the kitchen door, Wellington and Betty trailing after her. She managed to keep Betty out, but Wellington slipped past her.

Barbara was at the long wooden table rolling out a pastry. She glanced up and her brow creased in a disapproving frown. 'Out in the dirt again, I see. You had best change before you sit on any of the furniture. Or before Lord Thayne sees you. He'll think we're unrespectable if he sees the mistress of the house does her own gardening.'

Julia strongly doubted there was much else she could do to lower herself in his eyes. 'Were you outside a moment ago?'

'Now why would I want to be outside in a rainstorm?' Barbara patted the pastry into a dish. 'I don't like the rain any more than the cat.'

'Where is Lord Thayne? Did he go out?'

'He's in the drawing room. I don't suppose he went out either. Not unless he likes to ramble around in his stockings. Eduardo hid his boots.'

'Did he?' She would have to find them straight away in the unlikely event Thayne decided to leave. She wouldn't want him to be deterred by a lack of boots.

Barbara was regarding her with a little frown. 'Was there someone outside?'

'I thought perhaps there was, but I must have been mistaken.' She glanced down at her gown and made a face. 'You are right, I must change.'

But first she would see if Thayne was in the drawing room. Had he decided to leave, boots or no boots, without saying a thing? But that hardly made sense. She left the kitchen, Wellington at her heels, and walked quickly to the drawing room.

Nicholas had just dozed off when something heavy and wet landed on his chest. His eyes flew open and he struggled to sit up. The weight fell off him with an indignant meow and pain shot through his injured arm when he hit it against the cushion. He managed to sit back and, after the usual wave of dizziness passed, he saw with no little astonishment a yellow cat sitting on the floor in front of him. He looked up and was even more astounded to find Lady Carrington regarding him with a dismayed expression from the doorway. 'Do you always send animals in to wake up your houseguests?' He asked. He looked at her more closely. She wore a faded pink gown that was streaked with dirt. Her fine brown hair hung about her shoulders and there was a dab of mud on her cheek. She looked nothing like the impeccably dressed women he knew in London.

He found her absolutely charming.

The thought displeased him enough that he scowled. 'What the devil have you been doing? Ploughing the fields yourself?'

She sniffed and stared at him with an indignant look. 'I have been gardening. Some people do not have the luxury of lying around on other people's sofas!'

The corners of his mouth lifted. 'I beg your pardon.' He started to rise, but the sudden movement made his head spin. He sat back down.

She dashed forward. 'What is wrong? Are you feeling ill again?'

'It's nothing,' he grated out. 'I am still a trifle dizzy whenever I first sit up or stand.'

'And your arm. Does it still hurt?' She sat down next to him, her leg under the faded cotton gown brushing his. He flinched. 'Perhaps I should look at it.'

'There's nothing wrong.'

'You are very pale. Why ever were you down here anyway? You should have been resting.'

His mouth curved in a faintly sardonic smile. 'And you were planning to send me off today.'

'I will own I was wrong. You are certainly not well enough to go anywhere. And I think now you'd best go directly to bed and allow me to check your arm,' she said sternly.

Nicholas looked into her lovely brown eyes with their flecks of green and gold. Why the devil must she look at him with such concern? Of course, she was probably worried she would have his death on her hands if he died. His gaze fell to her cheek. 'You have mud on your face,' he said.

'Oh.' Slight colour rose to her face. 'I had best fetch Barbara and we can help you to bed.'

'Later.'

She sighed. 'Then I will look at your arm here.'

'There is no need to look at my arm.'

'I fear an infection may have set in.'

'And how would you know if you saw one?'

'I do have some familiarity with wounds, including those made by a gun.'

'Indeed.'

She looked both exasperated and concerned. 'I promise I won't hurt you if that is what worries you,' she said more gently.

'And if you don't, my lord, we'll be forced to take matters into our own hands,' Mrs Mobley said from the doorway.

'Good God.' The last thing he wanted was to have two females pouncing on him. Under other circumstances the idea might have its appeal, but Mrs Mobley had the look of a governess about to box his ears. For that matter, Julia hardly looked much more amenable.

He settled back on the sofa and the cat jumped up beside him. 'Very well, look at my arm.'

Clearly affronted, Julia sniffed. 'There is no need to be so rude.'

'You should have thought of that before you abducted me.'

'I can hardly help it now!' she snapped. 'I am going to remove your shirt.'

'*No!*'

'How can we look at your arm, then?' Julia sounded completely exasperated. 'You must take it off.'

'No need for maidenly modesty,' Mrs Mobley said. 'I dare say we've all seen a bare manly chest or two in our time.' Which was not a particularly noteworthy sight, if her disparaging tone was any indication.

If he refused to cooperate, he feared they'd forcibly

rip the shirt off his back. He fixed Julia with his most
cold gaze. 'Very well. Remove it. I would be grateful,
however, if the rest of the audience, including the cat,
would depart. Where the devil is Mackenzie, by the
way?'

He was surprised to see Julia flush. 'I sent him to London on an errand.' She turned to Mrs Mobley. 'Perhaps
you could fetch some clean bandages and water.'

'Behave yourself, my lord,' Mrs Mobley said.

'Good God,' Nicholas muttered. He was hardly in any
condition to think of seduction.

But he wasn't so sure after Julia sat down on the sofa
next to him and untied the sling from around his neck.
Then her gentle fingers fumbled with the buttons of his
loose linen shirt. She studiously avoided looking at him
and kept her eyes on her task, presenting him with a
delicious view of the back of her neck. She slowly eased
the shirt from his shoulder and down his arm. The movement was so sensuous he almost forgot the pain. Except
now his groin was beginning to tighten most uncomfortably. He shut his eyes for a moment, trying to regain
control.

'What happened?' Julia's concerned voice forced his
eyes open. She was looking at a long thin scar on his
chest.

'I was wounded. In a duel.'

Her face registered shock. 'I am sorry.'

'Don't be. I deserved it.'

'No one deserves such a wound,' she said quietly.

'I must disagree. Perhaps you will get on with the
task.'

'If I hurry too much I might hurt you.' She began to
unwrap the bandage from his arm. He closed his eyes,
willing himself to ignore her soft sweet scent and the fact

the gentle touch of her hands was arousing him to a painful degree. Otherwise, he'd be tempted to pull her down on the sofa with him.

'It looks rather inflamed.'

He opened his eyes. 'What does?'

'Your wound.'

'My wound?' he asked stupidly.

'The wound in your arm. You are not feverish, are you?' She looked worried and placed a cool hand on his forehead. 'Your head is a bit warm.'

'Is it?' His eyes strayed to her mouth. Perhaps he was feverish. 'You are very lovely.'

She jerked back as if she'd been slapped. 'I beg your pardon?'

'You are a lovely woman.'

She frowned. 'I hope you are not about to tease me again with another ridiculous offer. I really do not have time for such things.'

'Don't you?'

'As soon as Barbara returns we will clean your wound and bandage your arm.' Her voice was cool and composed and she shifted away from him on the sofa.

So she planned to ignore him, did she? He suddenly had the most devilish urge to tease her. He allowed his gaze to wander over her face. 'I suspect you are very kissable as well,' he said softly. 'I do not suppose you would consider kissing me? I've no doubt it would help my arm considerably.'

'Really!' Her eyes flashed with a mixture of annoyance and anger and he had no doubt she could cheerfully box his ears. And then a peculiar expression crossed her face. 'Very well.'

'Very well what?'

'Very well, I will kiss you.' She sat back, a little smile on her face as if she knew he would turn her down.

'Why?' He fully intended to call her bluff, but he wanted to see how far she was willing to go.

She opened her eyes wider in feigned innocence. 'To help your arm, and for the information you promised me, of course.'

He smiled, a little wickedly. 'Then come closer, my lovely lady. You cannot kiss me properly from that distance.'

A trace of panic fled across her face and he fully expected her to leap up and run. Instead, she scooted next to him. And then she leaned over and brushed her lips over his. Desire, hot and swift, shot through him at her sweet cool taste, but before he could react she had pulled away.

His only consolation was that she was breathing as hard as he was. 'I believe you have something to tell me, my lord.' Her eyes did not meet his.

He scowled, angry with her for taking up his challenge, but even more angry with himself for wanting her. 'That was hardly the sort of kiss I had in mind.'

This time she did look at him. Her eyes were icy. 'Are you trying to back out of your bargain, my lord? I believe you have told me on at least two separate occasions that if I complied with your terms you would tell me how you came to have my husband's ring. You did not specify how I was to kiss you.'

He stared at her and then laughed shortly. She had managed to best him at every turn. 'You are right, I did not. So, my dear Lady Carrington, I will tell you what you wish to know, which I fear is not very much.'

'Well, well. This is most certainly an interesting scene,' a voice said from the doorway.

Julia gasped. 'Oh, no,' she said faintly. She rose, her face turning pale.

He looked over and nearly groaned. Lord George Kingsley stood in the doorway, surveying the room with a sardonic air. His gaze wandered over to Nicholas. 'It appears you've not been murdered after all, Thayne,' he remarked.

'Obviously not,' Nicholas drawled.

'So, that leaves us with the second theory, although who would have guessed the reclusive Lady Carrington would capture the interest of the elusive Lord Thayne?'

Nicholas forced himself to stand. 'I fear your second theory is in error as well.'

'Indeed.' He ran his eye down Nicholas's bare chest in a suggestive fashion.

'George,' Julia said. 'You are mistaken. Lord Thayne was wounded. By…by a highwayman. He made his way here and we took him in. I was just looking at his wound. I fear it is slightly inflamed.'

'I see.' He swung his sardonic gaze to Julia. 'How fortunate he was wounded so near to Foxwood. And that you were here to bind his wounds in such a tender manner.' He managed to sound as if he didn't believe a word she had said.

Nicholas quelled the desire to mow him down. 'I trust you have a purpose in coming here other than insulting Lady Carrington.'

'Was I insulting her? I had merely intended to make a statement of fact.'

'Then keep your facts to yourself.'

Kingsley turned to Julia, who stood rooted to the spot. 'My dear, it appears you have a new protector.'

She unfroze and glared at him. 'He is not my protector!'

'I did not mean it in the usual sense, more of the chivalrous knightly sense in which he will stand up for your honour. Much as the good Mrs Mobley does, whom I see has just entered the room.'

Mrs Mobley eyed Kingsley coldly. 'Good day, Lord George. Here to cause a bit of mischief, I see.' She carried a basin of water and some clean linens.

'Not at all. I was on my way to Maldon and wished to bid Julia adieu. I will own, I was a trifle surprised to find Lord Thayne secluded at Foxwood. I am certain his family will be delighted to know he is not dead. When you deign to tell them, that is.'

'I trust you do not plan to take that task upon yourself,' Nicholas said coolly.

'I wouldn't think of it. My lips are sealed. I am certain you have reasons for your secrecy.' His gaze wandered back to Julia who still looked as if she wanted to vanish. 'I have the sense I am somewhat *de trop*. I will take my leave, but you know, my dear, if you need anything you have only to send for me.'

Julia's smile was strained. 'Thank you, George.'

He moved towards the door and then paused and looked back at Nicholas. 'I would not wait too long, however, before announcing your whereabouts. Your grandfather has asked my father for help in locating you. I do not know if you are aware, Thayne, but the former Lord Carrington was my father's godson. So, Julia, you see, is practically one of our family.'

Nicholas waited until Kingsley had left before swinging around to stare at Julia. 'Why did you not tell me Lord Stanton was your godfather?' he demanded.

'I had no idea it mattered. Besides, he was Thomas's godfather, not mine.'

'Indeed.' He stared at her. 'Were you aware that my grandfather and Stanton were old friends?'

A light flush stained her cheeks. 'George did mention something when he called yesterday. I do not see why it is a concern.'

'It is.' He bit back a curse. 'There's not a chance in hell we'll be able to keep the fact I've been under your roof for three days from my grandfather. Not that there was much hope of keeping this from leaking out now that Kingsley has been here.'

'You should have thought of that before you decided to come downstairs.'

'How the devil was I to know that Kingsley runs tame here?'

Her colour mounted. 'He does not run tame here!'

'No?'

'No.' She looked at him, clearly dismayed. 'Was it really so important to keep the fact you are here from your grandfather?'

'Yes. He has the most uncanny ability to ferret out the truth whether one wants him to or not. I only hope he doesn't discover precisely how I came to be here.'

She paled so much that for a moment he thought she might faint. He bit back another curse, this time at himself. He had no business taking out his frustration on her. 'I beg your pardon,' he said stiffly. 'I did not mean to ride roughshod over you.'

'You undoubtedly have every right to do so,' she said in a small voice. 'If you will pardon me, my lord, I believe I will allow Barbara to tend to your arm.' She walked quickly from the room without looking at him.

This time he did swear. When he turned, he found both Mrs Mobley and the cat staring at him. He raised his brow. 'Well?'

'You'd best sit down, my lord,' Mrs Mobley said mildly.

He did. Mrs Mobley sat down next to him and began to gently clean his arm. He winced and then frowned. 'I assure you my intention was not to overset her.'

Mrs Mobley looked up. 'Perhaps, my lord, you should decide exactly what your intentions are.'

Julia rose from her chair by the fire. As much as she longed to stay in the cosy quietness of her drawing room, she could not put off her mission any longer. The clock showed the hour to be nearly a quarter past eight; if she waited much longer Thayne might be asleep.

She had decided she must give him the ring. And then he would have no reason to stay at Foxwood any longer.

Her hand went to the chain at her neck. The ring felt familiar and strange at once. She had worn it against her skin for the past day, but it had not made Thomas's presence more real. Perhaps because it had been on another man's hand. Somehow the ring had become entwined in her mind with Thayne.

She could not keep him here any longer. Not after this afternoon. Every time she thought of the kiss, she wanted to sink. How could she have done such a thing? It was just that he had been so arrogantly certain she would back down and the thought of actually disconcerting him had been too tempting. And by the time she realised he intended to call her bluff, a mad impulse had propelled her to neatly block him into a corner. She had not, however, counted on finding the brief taste of his lips beneath hers so intriguing. Or having the most insane desire to prolong the kiss a few moments longer.

Thank goodness, she had not. If George had seen them in an embrace… Her face flamed at the mere thought. It was bad enough that he had discovered Thayne on her sofa with his shirt off and her sitting next to him. She could imagine how the scene must have appeared to George, who delighted in viewing any situation in the worse possible light. From the cynical look in his eye, she doubted very much that he believed her halting explanation about the highwayman.

At least Barbara had appeared with the water and clean bandages which surely must lend some credence to her tale. Despite his assurances his lips were sealed, she very much feared he would let something slip for George was a notorious gossip.

But even without the complications George's visit had brought about, she could not keep Thayne under her roof any longer. He was far too attractive and far too dangerous and she did not need a man like that in her life.

She knocked lightly on his door. For a moment she hoped he might be asleep, but his cool voice bade her to enter. She opened the door and stepped inside. He was in bed, his head propped up against several pillows. 'I was not certain whether you would pay your usual evening call tonight,' he said when he saw her.

She prayed he would not bring up this afternoon's débâcle. 'I need to speak with you.' Her stomach was beginning to clench again. She forced herself to walk across the room.

He stilled. 'What is it?'

'I...' She took a deep breath. 'I...I have decided to return the ring to you.'

He studied her face for a long moment. 'Why?'

'I can see you will not go until you have it. And I cannot keep you here. Not after this afternoon.'

'So, Kingsley's appearance distressed you enough that

you are willing to give me the ring? Or,' he said softly, 'was it the other?'

'It doesn't really matter.' She looked away. 'It was very wrong of me to abduct you but I was desperate, you see. I was certain you would do what I wished, but you would not. And to make matters worse you were wounded. I fear I have done you a great wrong, I cannot blame you for being very angry.'

Her hand tightened around the ring she held in her hand. 'And it is only a ring. I had thought that having it again would bring something of Thomas back, but it has not. It has been away from him for so long that it no longer carries his...his impression. Perhaps it carries yours now.' She looked at him, having no idea if he understood or not. He was watching her very quietly, but she saw no censure in his face. 'But I want more than I want anything, even more than I want the ring, to find out who killed him.'

'If you recall, I still have my part of the bargain to fulfil. I fear, however, it is not much to go on.' He looked away towards the window. The curtains had not yet been drawn and raindrops drizzled down the panes. He watched for a moment before half-turning towards her. 'It was given to me by a lady shortly before she died.'

She stood very still, her eyes on his face. 'I...I did not know. I am so sorry.'

'Are you? I doubt if you would be if you knew the whole of it.' His mouth twisted in a bitter smile. 'She was married, but not to me.'

His words shocked her, but the stark pain in his eyes put a stop to any fleeting judgment.

He glanced back towards the window. 'She found the ring in a jeweller's shop in Sheffield. That is all I know.'

The disappointment she felt warred with compassion

for him. The words he did not say spoke more than if he had told her all. He had loved this lady deeply and she had died. No wonder he was reluctant to give up the ring. It was, perhaps, all he had of her.

And they had not married. 'I am sorry,' she said again. At least she and Thomas had lived together and, although briefly, they had been united in every way. She lifted the chain over her head. She undid the clasp and removed the ring. 'Here, my lord.' She held it out in her palm.

He stared at it and then at her. 'I've not given you much to go on. And you do not need to give me the ring.'

She shrugged. 'But it is more than I had. I will proceed to Sheffield and see if there is anything I can discover. I have a sketch of the ring. Perhaps someone in the jeweller's will recognise it.' She tried to sound more optimistic than she felt. Despite the ring's uniqueness, the likeliness of anyone remembering the ring seemed impossible after such a lapse of time.

He still looked at her face, making no move to touch the ring. She took his hand and laid it in his palm and then closed his fingers over it. 'It belongs to you, I believe.' She removed her hand.

As if waking from a trance, he jerked back. For the first time since she had met him, his expression held uncertainty as if he did not know what to say.

'I had thought Eduardo would be back today. But he seems to be delayed. He should be back tomorrow, however, and he could take you to London, if you wish. I dare say your family will be pleased to see you.' She was babbling, but the peculiar look on his face was making her nervous. For once he was neither attempting to intimidate or tease her.

'Just like that?' he asked.

'I beg your pardon?'

'You are returning me without further ado?'

She was puzzled. 'What do you mean? I would expect you would be anxious to leave. And you have what you wanted.'

'Do I?' His gaze flickered over her face. 'And do you have what you wanted?'

'Yes.' She hesitated. 'No. I want to find out who killed my husband.'

'I wish you all luck, then,' he said softly.

'I will need it.' She hesitated another moment. 'I will leave you then, my lord. And you can look forward to soon spending your nights in your own bed with no danger of the roof leaking.'

'Yes.' A bleak look crossed his features and then he closed his eyes. She watched his face for a moment, then left the room, quietly shutting the door behind her.

A few hours later, Julia started awake, her heart pounding. Had she heard footsteps or was it merely a product of an overactive imagination? Or had Eduardo finally returned? She sat up, hands around her knees. The rain still beat against the window so perhaps it was only the storm.

The floorboards creaked again. She had no doubt this time they were footsteps. She threw back the quilt and climbed out of bed. She made her way to the door and opened it. The hall was dark. 'Eduardo?' she called softly. This time she heard a familiar clop-clop. She nearly sank with relief. It was only Betty, who appeared to have made her way to one of the bedchambers at the end of the hall.

No doubt she should put Betty out but the rain was pounding hard on the roof and she was cold and tired and wanted her bed. She could only hope Betty would stay out of Thayne's room. She started to turn when she heard a sound behind her. Julia had no time to react before the dark shape was upon her. A strong, rough hand was clasped over her mouth and an arm yanked her against a hard, smelly body. She struggled and managed to kick her assailant's leg until he subdued her. 'Don't scream or I will hurt you. I want the ring.' His voice was low and menacing and then he took his hand from her mouth.

'I…I don't have it.'

'Get it.'

'I…' She could hardly tell him Thayne had the ring.

There was the clatter of hooves and a loud indignant bleat. 'What the…?' Her assailant's hands fell away and then he shoved her so hard she fell. Julia's head hit the wall and pain shot through her skull as she tumbled to the ground.

The last thing she heard before darkness descended was another angry bleat.

# *Chapter Six*

Something cold and wet shoved her in the face. She moved her head a little, but the pain that shot through her caused her to moan. She heard a familiar bleat. 'Betty?' she whispered.

'Move.' The rough male voice was certainly not Betty. 'Julia, can you hear me?'

Why was Thayne hovering over her? Surely he had not bleated. And why was she lying on the floor? She forced her eyes open. His face swam into focus and she vaguely realised he was kneeling beside her. His face was joined by a hairy one. 'So, Betty is here,' she murmured.

'Yes.' He scowled and shoved the goat away. 'Damn it. Are you all right?'

'There is no need to swear at me.'

'I was not swearing at you. Can you sit up at all?' His face was grim.

'Yes, I…I think so.' She struggled to sit despite the pain in her head. His arm came around her shoulders and she was forced to lean into his chest for a moment. She could hear his heart, strong and steady, beneath the fine linen of his shirt.

'Good girl,' he said softly. He held her for a moment,

his warmth enveloping her. 'I am going to carry you to your bed.' Before she could protest, he had scooped her up in his arms.

'You cannot do this. Your arm.'

'My arm will be fine.' He carried her the few steps to her bed and laid her gently down. She winced as her head contacted the pillow.

He drew the cover up over her and sat down next to her on the bed.

'Julia,' he said gently.

She opened her eyes. He was close enough so she could see the shadow of his beard around his firm mouth. His eyes were dark with concern. And he was calling her by her Christian name. Perhaps she was having some sort of odd dream.

'Damn it, Julia, do you know what I am saying?'

She most certainly was not dreaming. 'You are swearing again, my lord.'

He made an exasperated sound. 'Yes, and I am likely to swear more if you do not give me an answer. Why the devil were you out in the hallway? I hear your goat making enough noise to wake the dead and when I go out to investigate, I find you nearly unconscious. You have a bump on your head. Did you fall?'

'No.' She forced her mind to focus. 'I heard footsteps—I thought that perhaps Eduardo had returned and I left my room. Then I heard Betty.' She faltered, suddenly remembering what had happened next.

'What else?'

'Someone…someone attacked me,' she whispered.

He stared at her. 'Are you certain?'

'Yes. He…he grabbed me from behind. He wanted the ring. And then Betty came. Perhaps she scared him for he shoved me away and I fell. I must have hit my head then.' She had no idea how to read the expression on his face. 'I know it sounds most improbable.'

'It does not,' he said grimly. 'Do you have any idea who did this?'

'No.' She shuddered. 'There was nothing familiar about him.'

He rose. 'Where is Mrs Mobley's room? I will send her to you.'

She sat up, not liking the harshness in his voice. 'Her room is at the very end of the hall. But where are you going?'

'Outside.'

'No! Please, I cannot have you hurt again!'

He glanced down at her, his expression odd. 'I won't be, my dear.'

He strode to the door. 'But you are not even dressed properly!' she exclaimed. He couldn't possibly go out in just a thin shirt and breeches! Her gaze went to his feet. 'And you've no shoes!'

He paused at the door and the corners of his mouth lifted in a brief smile. 'Don't worry. I found my boots.'

Nicholas straightened up from his slouched position against the wall when the door to Julia's bedchamber opened. Doctor Bothwell, carrying his bag, stepped out followed by Mrs Mobley. 'How is Lady Carrington?' Nicholas asked.

Doctor Bothwell regarded him with a slight frown. He was a tall, serious man and although his manner had been all that was polite, Nicholas sensed he did not approve of his presence at Foxwood and found the tale of his being shot by highwaymen and making his way to Fox-wood somewhat suspicious. But if so, he had kept his thoughts to himself. 'She has a bad bump on her head, but since there are no other symptoms it does not appear to be a serious injury. However, she must remain quiet and in bed for a day or two. Nor must she be unduly upset.' He fixed Nicholas with a stern eye.

'She will not be,' Nicholas said coolly.

'I trust not. It could only be detrimental to her health.' Bothwell paused for a moment. 'She asked me to look at your arm before I left.'

'My arm?'

'She was concerned since you carried her to her bed-chamber last night. So, if you will allow me to look at your arm, my lord.'

'My arm is fine.'

Doctor Bothwell allowed a slight smile to touch his lips. 'It will upset her if you do not.'

'The devil. Very well, do it, if you must.'

He submitted to the exam with ill grace. Despite last night, the slight inflammation from yesterday had gone and Dr Bothwell pronounced him able to travel when he wished. The dizziness he still felt upon rising was not uncommon after an injury and as long as he was not losing consciousness should eventually pass. Mrs Mobley entered his bedchamber just as the physician finished the exam. She waited until Dr Bothwell had left before speaking. 'So you will be leaving us soon, I expect.'

Nicholas awkwardly fastened the last button of his shirt before turning. 'No.'

A smile actually touched her lips. 'I thought not, my lord. You may see her now. She is awake.'

Julia was sitting in bed, eyes shut, her head propped against several pillows. Wellington lay at her feet. For a moment he thought she was sleeping, but when he stepped into the room she opened her eyes. He walked to the bed and stood, looking down at her. 'How are you feeling?' he asked. Her face was pale and her hair fell around her shoulders in a light brown cloud. She looked fragile and very young, and he wanted to run the man through who had hurt her last night.

'Doctor Bothwell assures me I will live. And you? How is your arm?'

'My arm is fine. And, like you, I will live as well.'

'I am glad.' She fixed him with her clear gaze. 'Thank you for coming to my rescue and for going out into the rain.'

He shrugged. 'You do not need to thank me. I fear, however, I was too late to catch your assailant.'

'It was brave of you to try.'

'Hardly,' he said curtly, embarrassed by her gratitude.

'But it was.' She smiled a little and then she glanced away for a moment. 'Eduardo should return today. I expect you will wish to return to London as quickly as possible.'

'No.'

Surprise crossed her face. 'No?'

'No. I am not leaving this place until I am certain you are safe, and there are no repeats of last night.'

She looked stunned. 'Surely the man will not return. And as soon as Eduardo is here, I will be fine.'

'Have you thought this through? Someone knows I am here and suspects you retrieved the ring from me. This person was desperate enough to enter your house in the middle of the night and attack you. And have you forgotten the highwaymen?'

Her eyes searched his face. 'Do you think that is connected?'

'I believe so, yes.'

'Oh, dear.' If possible, she had grown paler. 'I had

rather thought he was very interested in the ring but I had hoped it was nothing to signify.'

Hell. He was doing exactly what Bothwell had warned him against, oversetting her. He frowned. 'Do not trouble yourself. I won't let anything happen to you,' he said roughly.

She looked down at the bedcover. 'You are very kind, but you are not responsible for me. This is none of your concern.'

'You are wrong. From the moment you forced me into your carriage it has very much become my concern.'

She looked up. Anger flashed in her eyes. 'Well, I am releasing you from any obligation. At any rate, you now have the ring, so I doubt if I will be bothered again.'

'You don't know that, my dear.'

She glared at him. 'I am not "your dear".'

'No?' Why the devil was he goading her? And in her condition. She looked as if she wanted to throw something at him. He'd best leave before she did and he had the combined wrath of Bothwell and Mrs Mobley falling on his head.

He started when Mrs Mobley stepped into the room. Fully expecting her to take him to task over upsetting Julia, he was surprised to see she looked almost flustered. 'You'd best go downstairs, my lord. Eduardo has returned with company.' She paused. 'Your grandfather.'

'Oh, no,' Julia said softly.

He felt as if someone had punched him in the gut. 'My grandfather is here?'

Mrs Mobley nodded. 'That is what he tells me. So, if he's Lord Monteville, then he is.'

Nicholas paused on the threshold of the drawing room. The faint hope he'd entertained that the housekeeper was mistaken was dashed by the tall, lean and very familiar figure who stood near the window looking out over the drive. Betty was visible, nibbling on some tall grass.

Monteville turned when Nicholas entered. In his seventh decade, he was still a formidable figure with a cool commanding presence. Not quite knowing what to expect, Nicholas paused. 'Sir, I hardly thought to see you here.'

The earl's brow rose a fraction. 'No? You did not think I would come as soon as I discovered you had been wounded? I hope you do not think I am completely unfeeling when it comes to your welfare.' He did not give Nicholas a chance to reply. 'How is Lady Carrington? Mrs Mobley said she was hurt last night.'

'She is better,' Nicholas said.

'What happened?'

'She was attacked by an intruder.'

The brow rose higher. 'I think perhaps you had best tell me what is going on.' Monteville moved away from the window towards Nicholas. His expression gentled for a moment. 'Sit down, you do not look completely recovered.'

Nicholas took the sofa where he had so boorishly fallen asleep yesterday. As if on cue, the yellow cat appeared from behind the sofa and leapt up next to him. He tried to shove it away, but the animal merely looked at him and settled down, paws tucked under its chest and began to purr. Since he had no intention of fighting with the cat, Nicholas gave up. 'I am well enough. It is Lady Carrington who concerns me.'

'Of course. So, do you know why she was assaulted?'

'The man wanted a ring.'

'A ring?' Monteville looked at him, his expression curiously alert. 'What sort of ring?'

'A very old ring. With a ruby in the centre.'

'Perhaps the same ring you are wearing.'

Nicholas looked at him with more than a little surprise. 'Yes.'

'You do not seem to be particularly forthcoming on the matter. So I will guess that the ring you wear is the same ring that once belonged to her husband.'

This time Nicholas nearly reeled. 'How the devil did you know that? Sir,' he added belatedly.

'Phillip was with me yesterday when Mr Mackenzie arrived with Lady Carrington's note.'

'She sent a note? What the devil possessed her to do such a thing?' He'd have thought revealing his whereabouts would be the last thing she would want to do. She apparently knew nothing of his grandfather, because if she had, she would have known a note would bring him here straight away.

'I would imagine from the kindly impulse to relieve your family's mind. She wished to inform your family that you were not dead, but recuperating at Foxwood from a wound inflicted by a highwayman. I will own I am decidedly curious as to why you quit London, leaving your carriage and servants without word. You are usually not so forgetful.'

'I am not at liberty to satisfy your curiosity, sir.' He was hardly about to tell his grandfather he'd been abducted.

'I see.' Monteville leaned back, regarding him with the piercing stare that had compelled more than one man to confess. Nicholas, although not exactly immune, had lived with it long enough to hold out against it, at least for a while. 'Curiously enough, Mr Mackenzie and Phillip knew each other quite well.'

'How?' The Marquis of Stanton was highly placed in

the Home Office. He seemed an unlikely person for Mackenzie to know. He was also one of his grandfather's oldest and most respected friends.

'Lord Carrington and Mackenzie had both worked for Stanton. They were English agents.'

Nicholas started. 'Mackenzie was a spy, too?'

'Yes. When Lord and Lady Carrington returned to England, Mackenzie came with them. As well as Mrs Mobley.'

'Don't tell me she was a spy as well.'

A slight smile touched Monteville's lips. 'On occasion. Thérèse Blanchot was involved also. Carrington posed as a gambler. Information was often passed in the gaming saloon Madame Blanchot kept in Brussels.'

Which would explain why Thérèse had informed Julia of the ring. She had apparently known Carrington well. How the devil had he managed to land in such a hotbed of intrigue? 'Good God,' he muttered. 'But how did you know about the ring?'

'Carrington was killed in what appeared to be a robbery. Among the items stolen from his person was a ring.'

The tale was very familiar. 'Go on.'

'The ring, perhaps, the thief wanted. And the one you wear on your finger.'

'Yes.'

'Perhaps the ring explains how you and Lady Carrington came to cross paths?'

He had no doubt his grandfather would have the story from him one way or the other. Or manage to find out. 'She abducted me from Thérèse Blanchot's establishment at gunpoint,' he said coolly. 'She wanted the ring back.'

At least he had the rare satisfaction of watching his grandfather appear truly startled. 'Precisely why did she find it necessary to abduct you rather than merely rob you of the ring?'

'She wanted me to tell her where I obtained the ring.'

'I take it, then, you were a trifle reluctant to provide this information.'

'Yes, and a trifle foxed,' Nicholas said baldly.

'So where did the highwayman come in? Or did Lady Carrington shoot you?'

'Hardly. Although I think she might have liked to. We were robbed on the journey here.'

Monteville frowned. 'What did they take?'

'Not much. Although they were more than a little interested in the ring. I believe they were amateurs. They fled without much persuasion.'

'But not without shooting you.'

'No.' He had no intention of elaborating exactly how that came about.

Monteville regarded him for a moment. 'And in the end did you tell Lady Carrington where you obtained the ring?'

'Yesterday. After she returned the ring to me. She had taken it from me and would not give it back unless I told her what she wanted to know.'

His grandfather merely looked at him. Nicholas scowled. 'I had no idea if it was even the same ring. The inscription had been scratched off.' Which made him sound the worst scoundrel who routinely doubted the word of ladies and failed to provide grieving widows with whatever help he could render. He could not tell his grandfather the ring had been given to him by Mary.

'So I assume you were planning to return to London once you had the ring.'

'I was. Lady Carrington has made it quite clear she can hardly wait to be rid of me.'

'And now?'

Nicholas frowned. 'That was before last night. I've no intention of leaving her here even under Mackenzie's protection.'

'You will not need to. Phillip will arrive tomorrow. Once we realised you had been under her roof we decided it would be best if she returns to London with Phillip. She will stay with Lady Simons.'

She would be safe at the house of Phillip's sister. Which meant he could be absolved of his responsibility towards Julia and could get back to his life. He thrust aside the disquieting feeling that the thought was not as appealing as it should be.

# Chapter Seven

Julia looked up as Barbara entered her bedchamber. The housekeeper crossed the room and observed the barely touched supper tray across Julia's lap. 'You need to eat more than that.'

'I was really not hungry.' Although the chicken was actually tender tonight, her stomach had knotted up the moment she picked up her fork. 'Although it was very good,' she added.

'You'd best do better than this if you wish to keep up your strength.' Barbara picked up the tray. 'I suppose the cat will be grateful at any rate. By the way, Lord Monteville wishes to see you, if you are well enough.'

'Oh, dear.' Her stomach began to knot again.

'I doubt he plans to eat you. He has been most civil.'

'Then he probably has no idea I abducted his grandson.'

'I wouldn't be so sure of that.' She regarded Julia with a small smile. 'And he plans to stay for the night.'

'Oh, no,' she said faintly. 'Why would he wish to do that?' She doubted if Foxwood had two decent spare bedchambers whose ceilings did not leak. Why had he not taken Thayne back to London? Surely he couldn't want to spend the night in such a dilapidated house?

'Well, at least we won't be worrying about someone creeping about in the middle of the night.' Barbara headed towards the door with the tray. She paused and glanced back at Julia. 'Should I send them up?'

'Now?'

'Yes, now.'

'I…'

But Barbara had already quit the room. Julia straightened up against the pillows, her heart thudding. When she heard footsteps and the unmistakable timbre of masculine voices, it took all her willpower to keep from diving under the bedclothes.

The door opened and Thayne came into the room, followed by a tall, distinguished man with silver-flecked hair.

Thayne came to stand by her bed. She blinked. Not only had he shaved, he was wearing brown breeches and a pair of well-polished boots and over his shirt and cravat was a perfectly fitted blue coat.

'You are dressed,' she blurted out and then could have sunk through the floor at her idiotic and most improper remark.

His brow rose slightly. 'My grandfather brought a change of clothing for me.'

'Of course.' Her face heated. She felt uncomfortable under his scrutiny and his clean, civilised appearance made her feel even more at a disadvantage.

'How are you feeling?' he asked softly.

'Better.' She looked away, finding his intense expression unnerving.

Lord Monteville moved to stand beside his grandson. No one could doubt they were related. They had the same lean countenance, the same hawk-like nose, and the same cool intelligence in their eye. She felt more than a little intimidated.

'Perhaps you will introduce us?' Monteville said.

Thayne started and yanked his eyes away from Julia. 'Of course. Lady Carrington, may I present my grandfather, Lord Monteville. Lady Carrington.'

She found herself looking up into a pair of eyes that reminded her forcibly of Thayne's. 'I am pleased to meet you, Lord Monteville,' she said, feeling more than a little awkward. 'I must apologise for receiving you here instead of in the drawing room. I fear I am not allowed to go downstairs.'

'I would not have expected you to under the circumstances.' He smiled gently. 'I have looked forward to making your acquaintance. And to thanking you for looking after my grandson after he was wounded.'

She saw nothing in his expression to tell her he knew the true state of affairs. Feeling the worst hypocrite, she managed to say, 'You are very kind, but there is nothing to thank me for.'

'I must disagree with you on that point,' Monteville said firmly. 'I was sorry to hear of your assault. I fear neither you nor my grandson has fared very well in the past few days.'

'No. But my injury was a mere trifle compared to Lord Thayne's,' she said, trying to be fair. 'He was wounded when he—' She stopped, mortified at what she was about to say.

Monteville raised a brow. 'When he…?'

'Tried to…to…' She cast a helpless glance at Thayne.

A smile touched his mouth. 'There is no need to worry. He knows everything.'

Her eyes flew to Monteville's face. 'Everything?'

'Under the circumstances, I cannot blame you for abducting my grandson,' Monteville said. 'He told me the whole of it.'

'Oh, dear.' She briefly closed her eyes and then looked back at him. 'I am sorry.'

'My dear, there is no need to be.' For some odd reason, he looked almost amused. 'So pray continue, my grandson was wounded when? He has not yet told me exactly how it came about.'

'There is no need to say more,' Thayne said coolly.

She did not dare look at him.. 'The highwayman was about to shoot me. Lord Thayne shoved me aside and took the ball instead. I had a pistol, that I would not give to Lord Thayne, which was why the highwayman wished to shoot me. So, you see the fact he was wounded was entirely my fault.'

'Hardly,' Thayne snapped.

'So he was shot in order to save your life.' Monteville looked at his grandson. 'I must commend you,' he said softly.

To her surprise, a hint of colour appeared on Thayne's cheekbones. 'Any man would have done the same,' he said stiffly. The familiar scowl had returned to his face. 'Perhaps we could move on to the next matter of business.' He moved away from the bed and went to stand near the window. 'Lord Stanton will be arriving tomorrow.'

'Oh, heavens.' Her stomach jolted. 'Does Phillip know about this?'

'Not the entire story,' Monteville said. 'Only that Nicholas is here with you. Phillip was with me when Mr Mackenzie delivered your message. He, of course, was concerned about your welfare. And my grandson's.'

'Oh, dear.' What an unfortunate coincidence. But why

ever had she thought she could keep this from Phillip? She had no doubt George would say something sooner or later. 'Must Phillip know everything?'

'Most of it, I think,' Monteville said. 'In light of the assault on you, I do not think the matter can be dismissed. Phillip needs to be told.' He looked down at her. 'You must rest now. Try not to worry too much. We will see you are safe.'

She nodded, but it was hardly her safety that concerned her. It was all she could do, after they had quit the room, to not indulge in helpless tears. She lay back against the pillows and stared with unseeing eyes at the wall. She felt nearly as helpless as she had when Thomas had been killed. She had been told to rest and had gone to stay with Sophia while Phillip and George and the others had looked into his death. There had been nothing—no leads, no sign that his death had been anything other than a robbery.

But if it had been only a robbery, why would someone care whether the ring had shown up again or not? Was someone so worried the ring could be traced back to them? Or was it something more?

She was beginning to feel tired so she closed her eyes, her mind in a muddle. One thing she did know, however—she was not going to trust it all to someone else this time.

Stanton arrived mid-morning on the following day. Monteville had wasted no time in relating the events of the past few days. Stanton had listened impassively, although the revelation of Nicholas's abduction had startled him. He had asked to see the ring and Nicholas had removed it from his finger and handed it to him.

Stanton ran his finger over the ring. 'It appears to be

the same ring.' He looked up at Nicholas. 'Julia—that is, Lady Carrington examined it herself?'

'Yes,' Nicholas said. 'In fact, she had it in her possession for a good day before she returned it to me.'

'I am surprised she did so,' Stanton remarked.

Nicholas had the grace to colour slightly. 'I forced her to.'

'I see.' Slight amusement crossed Stanton's face. 'And where did you get the ring?'

'It was given to me.' The words were not so difficult to say this time. 'But I know little else except it was purchased from a jeweller in Sheffield nearly two years ago.'

Stanton looked at him curiously. 'It is a very unique ring. Have I seen it on your hand before?'

'Perhaps. I have not worn it very often until recently.' Several weeks ago to be precise. On the second anniversary of Mary's death.

'A few days ago he was approached by a man who wished purchase the ring,' Monteville said.

Stanton looked sharply at Nicholas. 'Who?'

'A Mr Grayson, I believe.'

'Would you recognise him again if you saw him?'

'Most likely, yes.'

Stanton regarded him for a moment. 'It may have some bearing on the matter.' He moved to the mantelpiece. 'Thomas's murder was, as far as we could determine, a robbery. Ironically enough, he was killed after leaving Thérèse Blanchot's. He was involved in a matter of some importance with the Home Office, but no connection was ever established between that matter and the murder. However, there were several things that were puzzling if it were only a robbery. He carried several items of value but only the ring was taken.'

'So he was robbed for the ring?' Monteville asked.

'It appeared he was. It is very old and very valuable. I will own, I had not expected to see it again. I would have thought it would have been sold privately, if at all.'

'None the less, someone very much wants it,' Nicholas said. 'Enough to assault Lady Carrington in her own home and possibly enough to hold up a coach.' He frowned. 'Although it makes no sense for Carrington's killer to decide he wants the ring back now. Why would he have disposed of it in the first place if he did not want it to turn up again?'

Monteville spoke. 'It is possible he sold the ring and that person in turn sold it to the shop in Sheffield. Or the killer never expected the ring to be recognised, particularly by Lady Carrington herself. It is possible that there is something about the ring that might identify the murderer.'

'Possibly.' Stanton looked grave. 'Julia may very well be correct as well. Tracing the ring to Sheffield might provide a lead to his killer.' He glanced at Nicholas. 'I would have preferred she came directly to me, however, rather than taking the drastic and foolish step of abducting you.'

A brief smile touched Nicholas's mouth. 'It has been a most interesting experience. What is it you want from me? The ring, I assume. I own I would like it back.' As would Lady Carrington, he added silently. He didn't want to touch that yet.

Stanton read his mind. 'I've no doubt Julia does as well. No, if you would agree I would like you to keep the ring. There is a chance that whoever approached you might approach you again.'

'I see. A bait of sorts.'

'Yes, but there is a certain element of danger involved

if this does indeed have anything to do with Thomas's murder. Once a man has killed he will have no qualms about killing again.'

Nicholas shrugged. 'I can take care of myself well enough.' He thought of Julia lying unconscious on the floor and then about her husband, dead by another's hand. If someone had killed Mary he would have gone to any lengths to discover her murderer. Including abduction. He made up his mind. 'Very well, I will do it.'

'Thank you.' Stanton looked at him, some strong emotion in his face. 'Thomas was my godson, you know.' He looked away for a moment before returning his attention to Nicholas. 'I would like Julia to stay out of this as much as possible. Which is the other reason I am grateful you are willing to help us. I fear she may try to take matters into her own hands. If she knows you are involved as well, she will be more inclined to let us handle the affair.'

Nicholas nearly choked. 'Indeed.' She would most likely kick up a dust when she found out. Or abduct him again.

Julia looked up as Phillip entered the tiny sitting room off her bedchamber. She had managed to convince Barbara she was well enough to be out of bed and spent the morning in a chair near the window. She rose and smiled, despite the quaking in her legs. 'Phillip, it is good to see you.'

'And you.' He moved across the room. In his early fifties, he was still a handsome man with receding dark hair and a pair of calm grey eyes. He took her hand. 'Although I wish you had come to me straight away instead of taking matters into your own hands.'

Relief flooded her. At least he was not planning to ring

a peal over her. She sat back down. 'I had no idea everything would become so complicated. But do you not see what it means, Phillip? Thomas's death had to be more than a mere robbery. Otherwise why would someone want the ring so much?'

'Which is why I am taking you back to London with me.'

She stared at him, dismayed. 'Taking me to London? But why?'

'For several reasons. The foremost is to protect you from danger.'

'But surely I am in no danger. The intruder wanted the ring and I no longer have it.'

'We do not know if that is all he wanted. We do not want to take the risk that you might be harmed. You will stay with Sophia.'

'I should love to see Sophia, but I do not wish to go to London. At least not now.'

'You have no choice, I fear. I would never forgive myself if something should happen to you. Neither would Sophia. You are forgetting one more thing as well. Nicholas has been under your roof for several days. We will hope nothing of it leaks out but if it should, I would prefer to deal with the matter with you in London.'

'But I had Barbara here with me. And Eduardo,' she said, appalled.

'My dear, in the eyes of society they are servants. That is not the same thing as having a relative or a companion.'

'But there is nothing to gossip about. And no one knew he was here.' No, that was not true. 'Except for Dr Bothwell, who is very discreet, and…and George.' Who was not.

Phillip started. 'George knew Nicholas was here?' His

brow snapped together. 'Then you most certainly have no choice. We will only hope he'll have the sense to hold his tongue.' He looked at her face and frowned. 'You still do not look well. I fear this whole affair has been too much for you. You must let Sophia look after you and try to think about something else. Perhaps balls and routs, for a change, instead of Foxwood.'

'I don't wish to be distracted. I want to find out who killed Thomas.'

'As I do. And like you, I hope to God that when we discover who is behind these attacks, we will find his killer. But killers are ruthless men, my dear. And dangerous, which is why I do not want you involved.'

'But, Phillip, surely there is something I can do.'

'Just take care of yourself.' He touched her cheek. 'And do not worry too much.' He started to move away and then paused. 'By the way, Nicholas has consented to help us.'

She started. 'Nicholas?'

'Yes.' He smiled a little at her expression. 'He was approached by a man who wished to buy the ring. He will put it about he is now interested in selling it. With any luck, he will be approached again.'

'He cannot do that! I do not want him involved in this at all!'

Phillip looked at her steadily. 'Once you made the decision to abduct him, you embroiled him in this affair. You have no choice in the matter. Nor does he.'

Which was precisely what made his involvement so intolerable. He had no choice. Once again, she had not only managed to muddle her own affairs but his as well.

Nicholas hesitated for a moment before tapping lightly on the door of Julia's sitting room. He waited for her soft reply before stepping into the room.

She sat in a wing chair near the window. The yellow cat sat on the quilt covering her lap. She wore another one of her high-necked gowns and a shawl was draped around her shoulders. Her eyes widened when she saw him. 'Lord Thayne? Oh! I...I did not expect you.'

A smile touched his lips. 'Disappointed?'

'Oh, no. It was just I expected Barbara as she said she would—' She broke off and then frowned. 'I am glad you are here. There is something I must discuss with you.' From her governess-like tone, he gathered she planned to argue with him. Phillip had certainly wasted no time.

She removed the cat from her lap and set him on the floor. He gave her a reproachful stare and then sat down and began to wash. Julia stood.

'There is no need for you to get up,' Nicholas said.

'I would prefer to.'

He moved across the room and came to stand in front of her. Her face was still rather pale. 'Sit down. I've no doubt you can upbraid me just as well from the chair.' His lips twitched. 'Otherwise I will be forced to help you.'

She gasped and fixed him with an indignant stare. 'Well, really!'

His brow shot up. 'Only fitting after all the times you threatened me.'

'I was merely trying to help you.'

'And I am merely trying to help you. Your face is nearly white.' He took a step towards her.

She plopped back down. 'There is another chair, my lord,' she informed him pointedly.

'Indeed.' Instead of taking it, he leaned against the

window pane. 'What do you wish to say to me? Or should I guess? Phillip has informed you that I am to help him with his investigation and you want to tell me that you would rather I declined. Shall I tell you my response to that? I have every intention of helping Phillip.'

She looked at him, clearly agitated. 'I have no idea why. I would think you would be glad to wash your hands of the entire affair. I suppose Phillip told you that once I abducted you, you had no choice but to be involved. You did not ask to be so shabbily treated and so it is hardly fair that you should be asked to do this.' Her clear gaze met his. 'I cannot have you possibly put yourself in any more danger because of me.'

Taken aback, he stared at her. He had been prepared to meet any number of arguments but not this one. 'I doubt I will be in any danger.'

'But you might be,' she insisted. 'Someone broke into this house because of the ring. What if this person attacks you as well?'

'I will be careful.'

'But that is the point! I do not want you to worry about being careful! You should return to your life as if this never happened!'

A wry smile lifted his mouth. 'I doubt I can do that. There is still my sore arm. And the ring.' He sobered. 'Phillip's argument was wrong, however. I was involved in this affair from the moment I decided to wear the ring in public although I did not realise it at the time. As long as I have the ring, I have no choice in the matter.'

'Then I wish I had not returned it to you!' she burst out. 'I should have kept it and waited to see if anyone approached me.'

'Someone did,' he said grimly. 'The results were not

pleasant. Next time you might not have Betty around to fend off any assailants.' Her face was still worried and unhappy and he wanted to pull her into his arms and comfort her. A move that would border on insanity. The last thing he needed was to feel her soft curves against him. His body heated even thinking about it.

He ran a hand through his hair and frowned. 'I came to tell you that my grandfather and I plan to leave within the hour.'

'You are leaving?' She sounded stunned as if she had not expected it to actually happen.

'Yes. Is that not what you had hoped for?'

'No, that is, yes…' She stopped. 'I did not think you would leave so soon. But, of course, you must want to. I have no doubt you look forward to seeing London again.'

Hardly. If anything, the prospect seemed more flat than usual. In some damnably odd way, he would miss this place. With almost a sense of shock, he realised that, for the first time in two years, Mary's ghost had not been his constant companion. The sensation was foreign and he did not know if he welcomed it or not.

'I only wish I could persuade you to give up this idea that you have some sort of obligation to concern yourself with my affairs.' She had risen again and come to stand in front of him.

'It is my affair as well, now.' He looked down at her. Her face was raised to his and her brow was puckered with worry. Why the devil must she look at him like that? As if she truly cared about him. The idea made him feel vulnerable. He shoved the idea away and told himself that was quite impossible. 'I'll be fine,' he said roughly.

'I hope so.' She took a deep breath and gave him a shaky smile. 'Goodbye, then.' She held out her hand.

He took it. Her hand was soft and warm and delicate. He looked into her hazel eyes and suddenly felt lost. 'Goodbye,' he said. He released her hand. 'Perhaps we will meet in London.'

'Perhaps,' she said. 'I wish you a safe journey.'

'Yes. With no highwaymen.'

She gave him a tremulous smile. Without thinking, he bent and kissed her hard on the lips. He straightened. 'Goodbye, Julia.' He turned before he was tempted to do more, almost stepping on the yellow cat who was suddenly in front of him, and left.

# Chapter Eight

Julia smoothed down the fine muslin of her pale green ball gown, her stomach churning. Why ever was she so nervous? She was just attending a ball, not an execution. It was only that she had not been to such an affair since Thomas's death. The last ball she had attended had been with him on the night he was killed.

She turned to the dressing table in the bedchamber Sophia had given her and picked up her fan. Best to not think of such things now—it would only make this even more difficult. She wished she had not let Sophia talk her into attending but Sophia had insisted.

'My dear, now that I finally have you in London, I am not about to let you hide away. And since your poor head is much better there is no reason why you cannot attend Lucy Bathurst's ball.'

Arguing with Sophia was impossible. She had taken such delight in having her mantua-maker fit Julia with a new gown that Julia feared further protests would only disappoint her. Sophia had always been kind and had taken Julia under her wing shortly after her marriage to Thomas. Julia had come to love her as the sister she had always longed for.

'Julia?' Sophia appeared in the doorway of the pleasant bedchamber. 'Are you ready?' She moved into the room with her light, graceful tread. She paused and looked at Julia. 'Oh, Julia, you look lovely. I knew the green would suit you.'

'And you look beautiful,' Julia said warmly. With her soft blonde hair, grey-blue eyes, and slender figure, no one would ever guess Sophia was nearly one and thirty. And that she had been a widow since the age of eighteen after a brief marriage to a man twenty years her senior.

'Thank you.' She smiled at Julia. 'Are you still nervous? There's no need to be. I promise to stay by your side at all times. Except when you are dancing, of course.'

Julia laughed. 'No, really, Sophia, I shall be fine. I suppose it is because I haven't attended a ball for so long that I feel a little apprehensive. I doubt that I remember how to chit-chat properly.'

'You can just smile.'

'Which can look rather empty-headed if overdone.'

'But harmless.' Sophia shot her a quick glance and said carefully, 'Nicholas will be there.'

Julia nearly dropped her fan. 'Will he?' She had not seen him in the six days she had been in London. Not that there was any reason he would want to call on her. Why would anyone wish to pay a social visit to the person who had abducted one? But the few affairs she had attended had seemed rather flat, for some reason; the one time she had caught a glimpse of a tall male figure with light brown hair her heart had beat a trifle too fast until she saw the man's face and realised she did not know him at all.

'His arm must be better, then,' she said, hoping to sound nonchalant. She had avoided bringing up his name although it would be perfectly reasonable for her to inquire whether he had been approached about the ring. Or to ask after his arm.

It was just she did not want Sophia thinking that she had any interest in him, which of course, she did not. Just as he had no interest in her, despite the brief, intimate kiss he had planted on her lips before he left…or his words that he might see her in London. He probably wanted to put her out of his mind, which was quite understandable, just as she wanted to put him and his scowls out of hers. Except, at the most unexpected moments, she would suddenly think of the slight smile that would tug at his mouth when he was amused and the vulnerability she had more than once glimpsed in his face, which was why she needed to avoid him. She could not afford to be thinking of anything but Thomas.

She realised Sophia was speaking. 'I beg your pardon. I was thinking about something else.'

Sophia arched a delicate brow. 'I can see that. I was merely saying that Nicholas's arm is nearly healed.' She hesitated for a moment. 'I hope you will not worry about meeting him. I could see that it might feel rather awkward but once you have this first meeting, the rest will be easier. I have no doubt he will behave in a gentlemanly manner.'

Julia gave her a wry smile. 'And I promise to behave in a ladylike manner. I will not do anything such as force him from the ballroom at gunpoint.'

Sophia laughed, obviously relieved Julia was determined there would be no awkwardness. 'I hardly thought you planned that, although it would create a most interesting diversion.' She picked up Julia's silk mantle from the bed. 'Shall we go, then? George should be here soon.' She made a small face. 'I do hope he will not be too

difficult. I know he is my nephew but I sometimes find
him so terribly trying. I had thought that when Arthur
was sent to Italy George might step into his shoes, but if
anything he is worse. Sometimes I feel such sympathy
for it cannot be easy having such a paragon for an older
brother. And other times I want to strangle him!'

Julia laughed and took the shawl from Sophia. 'I understand very well. I have had the exact same feeling.
Then I remind myself that George can be kind. And
Thomas said much the same thing as you. Living in Arthur's shadow would be difficult.' Actually he had said
it would be enough to drive any man to vice, but it hardly
seemed the thing one should say to Arthur's doting aunt.

'Well, we shall hope he behaves himself,' Sophia said.
'And do not worry about a thing. It is only a ball and,
for the most part, they are dreadfully predictable.'

Two hours later, Julia stood at one side of the crowded
ballroom. She wriggled her toes in her satin slippers and
sighed. Her feet were beginning to ache, reminding her
that although she was capable of walking for miles in the
country in half boots, she was not at all used to executing
dance steps in thin slippers.

Sophia seemed to know everyone and so Julia had not
lacked a partner until now. Nor had Sophia. She was at
this moment performing a country dance with a slightly
balding gentleman who, from the look on his face, was
quite taken with his lovely partner. A twinge of longing
mixed with sadness shot through Julia. Thomas had
looked at her in much that way the first time they had
danced together. She had just returned to her stepfather's
house from school and he had been a guest at the neigh-
bouring estate. They had met at a local assembly. He had
asked her for a dance and from the moment she laid eyes

on the tall, dashing young man with laughter lurking in his eyes, she had been lost. And to her great amazement, her feelings had been reciprocated.

'Enjoying yourself, my dear neighbour?'

She started and turned to find George at her side. Tonight he was dressed in a bright blue coat over an embroidered waistcoat of an amazing yellow. His stiff collar was so high she wondered how he managed to turn his head.

'Very much,' she said politely. 'And you?' She had seen very little of him. He had asked her for one dance and then disappeared into the card room.

'The affair is a trifle dull.' His attention had drifted away from her and then his gaze sharpened. He leisurely brought his quizzing glass to his eye. 'However, I believe it has just become more interesting. Your most recent houseguest has arrived.'

'I beg your pardon?'

'The enigmatic Lord Thayne. He is over against the wall.'

Her heart jumped. She avoided the direction George indicated. 'Indeed.' She had been on pins and needles for the first hour or so, half-expecting to see Thayne, but when there was no sign of him, she began to relax. Although, for some odd reason, she had almost felt disappointed.

'Yes, indeed. Shall I present him to you as a possible partner?'

She turned her most furious expression on him. 'I pray you will not! In fact, if you should even try to do so I will never speak to you again!'

George toyed with his quizzing glass. 'I take it that he was not the most agreeable of guests. Although I never would have guessed that from the day I found you bent tenderly over his wounded arm.'

'If you do not be quiet,' she said through gritted teeth, 'I vow I will endeavour, at the next opportune moment, to do damage to some item of your clothing.'

He held up his hands in mock defence and shuddered. 'I had no idea you felt so strongly. My lips are sealed. I will say no more.'

'Thank you.' Not that she trusted the speculative gleam in his eye one bit.

'My dear, I believe I will adjourn to the card room. Before I inadvertently say something to put you further in a temper.' He made her a bow and sauntered off.

She watched him go. Instead of heading towards the card room, he was heading in the opposite direction. Towards the side of the room where he said Thayne stood. She forced herself to look in that direction. Thayne was indeed there, standing near the wall, a familiar, half-bored expression on his face as he surveyed the room. Her heart began to thud and her hands felt clammy.

George stopped next to Thayne and said something. Her stomach lurched. George could not possibly be suggesting to Thayne that he dance with her! But when Thayne glanced in her direction she feared that was exactly what he was doing. Mortified, she jerked her gaze away and prayed he had not noticed her. She forced herself to look again and saw Thayne had moved away from the wall. He was not heading in her direction, however, but had stopped to talk to a woman she recognized as Lady Bathurst.

She nearly sank with relief. Thank goodness, she had been mistaken. She would rather die than stand up with Thayne. Particularly if George was in some way involved.

The musicians were tuning their instruments. Another dance was about to start. Perhaps she should find Sophia before she jumped to any more silly conclusions and made a cake of herself. She turned to walk towards the card room, but found her way blocked by a group of chattering young ladies. She started to step to one side when she heard someone say her name.

She turned around. Lady Bathurst stood behind her, a curious, almost excited expression on her pleasant, plump face.

With her was Lord Thayne.

Julia froze, her mind a complete blank. Lady Bathurst was speaking. 'My dear Lady Carrington, I have a gentleman here who is very desirous of making your acquaintance. And soliciting your hand for the next dance!' She beamed at Julia.

'In…indeed,' Julia said faintly. She finally stole a glance at him and tried not to notice how devastatingly attractive he was in his elegant evening clothes. His eyes met hers with a slightly mocking expression. A stab of annoyance shot through her. If he did not wish to see her, then why did he ask for an introduction?

'Yes, indeed,' Lady Bathurst said. She looked excessively pleased. 'Lady Carrington, may I present Lord Thayne?'

'How do you do, Lord Thayne?' she said as coolly as she could. She held out her hand.

He took it. His fingers, warm and strong, seemed to burn through her glove. He bowed over her hand. But instead of releasing it, he gazed into her face. A smile touched his mouth. 'I have looked forward to making your acquaintance, Lady Carrington. And to standing up with you, of course.'

She pulled her hand out of his. 'Indeed.'

His brow rose in that irritatingly familiar way. 'I can see you are nearly speechless at the offer,' he murmured.

She was about to say 'indeed' again and then shut her mouth. Lady Bathurst glanced from Julia to Thayne with a puzzled expression, her smile fading. The musicians played the opening notes of the next dance. Her expression changed to relief. 'The waltz is starting. I do hope you enjoy yourselves.' She gave them a brief smile and bustled off.

Thayne glanced down at Julia. 'I believe we are obligated for this dance, my dear.' He held out his arm.

She ignored his arm. 'I really do not wish to dance. And I am not "your dear".'

'No?' He dropped his arm. His lips twitched in a most maddening way which made her wonder why she had ever entertained the slightest desire to see him again. 'I was informed you most particularly wished to dance with me. It is quite ungenerous of you to refuse me now that I have gone to the trouble of procuring a proper introduction.'

She gave a little gasp and stared at him in outrage. 'Who ever told you that?'

'Kingsley.' His voice was bland.

She closed her eyes for a brief moment and then opened them. 'I will strangle him.'

'Later.' He reached down and took her hand. 'For now, we are going to dance. Otherwise, Lady Bathurst will think we have already quarrelled, which will not do.'

He led her to the edge of the floor. Before she could protest, he had placed one hand lightly at her waist and taken her other hand in his. The Spanish ring gleamed on his fourth finger. He began to move in time to the music and she promptly tripped on his foot.

Her face heated and she stared at the lace of his snowy

white shirt. 'I beg your pardon. I have not waltzed for over three years.'

'I fear you have surpassed my record then. It has been two and one-half years since I last waltzed.'

She glanced swiftly up at him and stumbled a little. His hand tightened on her waist as he steadied her. 'It has been nearly two years since I have danced with anyone other than a relation,' he said conversationally.

She nearly stumbled again at that. 'Then you should have asked someone with more recent experience.' Her gaze had returned to his shirt front. 'I really did not ask George to say anything to you.'

'I know.'

'Then why are you dancing with me?'

'Must you address my chest? It is disconcerting to be conversing with the top of your head.'

'I will probably step on you again if I look up.'

He laughed. 'After other things I have survived at your hand, I've no doubt I could survive that.'

The genuine amusement in his voice startled her. She did look up and saw his eyes were alight with laughter. It transformed his face, erasing the hardness from his countenance, and suddenly she realised how powerfully charming he could be. She swallowed, trying to regain her equilibrium. 'I...I suppose so. How is your arm?'

'It is much better.' The corner of his mouth lifted. 'We are making progress. You have not yet tripped again.'

She stared at him. Was it possible he was flirting with her? The thought was so unexpected and so unnerving she nearly froze. She cast about for something to say. Nothing at all came to mind.

'I asked you to dance because I wanted to inquire about Foxwood. I assume Mrs Mobley is well, as are Betty and the cat,' he said.

'The cat?' He was unnerving her more by the second. 'Oh, Wellington. He is fine. So are Barbara and Betty. I think Wellington misses you, however. He sits in front of your…that is, the bedchamber you occupied and me-ows.'

This time he actually grinned. 'Probably hoping for another victim to pounce upon.'

She found herself returning his smile. 'Perhaps.'

His expression changed, the smile fading from his face. He stared at her, his eyes darkening with an awareness of her that made her catch her breath. Her hand trembled in his and for a moment she had no idea where she was. There was only him and he suddenly seemed completely familiar as if she had just come home.

The music stopped. He dropped his hand from her waist and then she was back in the ballroom in the midst of a crowd of strangers. She blinked, feeling as if she had just awakened from a dream. She glanced at Thayne and saw his expression was almost as dazed as hers. He cleared his throat and then frowned. 'I should return you to Sophia.' His voice was abrupt.

'Yes.' She took the arm he proffered, trying to make the least contact with him as possible. She felt shaky and odd as if something had just changed her forever.

Sophia stood near the edge of the ballroom with a man and a young woman she did not recognise. She felt Thayne stiffen. Puzzled, she glanced up at him. He met her eyes, a wry look on his face. 'My cousin and his wife. I've no doubt they wish to meet you, particularly now. By the way, I should warn you they know I stayed at Foxwood. After I had managed to escaped, wounded, from a robber.'

Before she could reply, they had joined the group. Sophia looked at Julia with a peculiar little smile but merely greeted Nicholas before introducing Julia to the others.

Adam Henslowe was a pleasant-looking man of perhaps five and twenty. His wife, Lady Jessica, looked to be several years his junior. She was extremely pretty with thick dark hair curled about her face and a pair of expressive eyes.

Mr Henslowe took Julia's hand, his eyes going over her with frank interest. 'We are delighted to meet the lady who rescued my cousin.'

She felt heat rise to her cheeks. 'I really did nothing.'

'No?' Mr Henslowe glanced at Nicholas with a raised brow and turned back to Julia with a grin. He dropped her hand. 'That was not my understanding. His arm has nicely healed due to your care.'

'I doubt he was the most agreeable of patients. Men are nearly impossible when they are laid up,' Lady Jessica added. 'Although perhaps he was not so bad if you actually agreed to waltz with him tonight.' She cast a laughing look at Julia.

'He wasn't really very horrible at all, considering the circumstances.' She had no idea why she felt obligated to stand up for him. Except it had been her fault he had been wounded. And he had come to her rescue. Twice, in fact.

'Wasn't he?' Lady Jessica looked at her and then at Nicholas. She suddenly smiled. 'I see I will have several interesting things to write Sarah tomorrow.'

Nicholas looked less than pleased. 'I doubt she will find any of them all that interesting,' he said drily.

'Oh, but she will. Do you not think, Adam?' Lady Jessica's eyes sparkled.

'In the interest of keeping the peace, I believe I will keep my speculations to myself.' Adam grinned and then gently took his wife's arm. 'Come, my love. I think a dance is in order. Before we manage to embarrass Lady Carrington or antagonise my cousin.'

Lady Jessica smiled at Julia. 'I am certain we will meet again soon. Perhaps I might call on you and Sophia?'

'That would be delightful.' Sophia glanced over at Julia. 'Would it not?'

'I would like that very much,' Julia said. She felt rather awkward particularly when Nicholas turned to look at her. She couldn't imagine that he would welcome any sort of acquaintance between herself and his family.

She avoided looking at him as Mr Henslowe and Lady Jessica said their goodbyes. Sophia turned to him. 'And I hope you will call as well, Nicholas. You are always welcome, you know. I am certain Julia would agree.' She gave Julia a meaningful look.

'That would be very nice.' She forced herself to meet his eyes.

He stared at her for a moment and then a slow smile touched his mouth. A smile that made her hot and cold at once. 'I look forward to it.' He bowed. 'Good evening, Sophia, Lady Carrington.' He sauntered off.

Sophia turned to Julia. 'Well! I can see I need not have worried about any awkwardness. Not only did he ask for an introduction, he actually waltzed with you. He rarely stands up with anyone and I cannot recall the last time he waltzed!'

'It was two and a half years ago,' Julia said automatically. 'The only reason he did so was because George told him I wished to dance with him. I dare say he only wanted to aggravate me.'

'George? I've no doubt of it, but for once his mischief worked out remarkably well, wouldn't you say?'

'I meant Lord Thayne.' Julia suddenly felt too tired to explain.

Sophia merely laughed. 'I doubt that is the whole of it. Well, you certainly have created a stir.'

Which was the last thing she wanted to do. If she had an ounce of sense, she would avoid him at all costs. The horrible truth was she found him dangerously attractive. She had hoped it might be due to their forced intimacy at Foxwood, but she was wrong. He was just as lethal in a London ballroom. Perhaps even more so, if tonight was any indication.

And she had not even thought of asking him about the ring.

Much later that evening, George strolled into White's. He was hailed by Carleton Wentworth, a foppish young man with an indolent air. 'My dear fellow, you have just come from the Bathurst affair, have you not? Bunty, here, has as well and has proposed a bet on which I've no doubt you'll want to lay odds.'

George ambled over to their table. 'Will I? And what has that to do with the Bathurst ball, Bunty?'

Bunty, who was more properly known as the Honourable William Buntford, raised a languid hand. 'Saw Thayne waltzing with your neighbour. Never waltzes with anyone.'

George started. 'Indeed. You are correct, Thayne never waltzes with anyone. Nor does Lady Carrington for that matter. So?'

'Actually smiled at her. Thayne never smiles,' Bunty explained.

'I will own that is a rare event.'

'Precisely, and so, my dear fellow, what are the odds

he plans to make her his mistress? And that she will accept?' Wentworth asked.

'I begin to see.' George thought for a moment and then a slow smile curved his mouth. 'I will go further. What are the odds they will wed?'

'Marriage? Thayne?' Wentworth raised an incredulous brow. 'Do you perhaps desire to see the inside of debtor's prison? I doubt your sire will increase your allowance enough to cover such a wager.'

George smiled gently. 'My sire will go to any length to protect the family name from scandal. One of his offspring in prison would not further the cause. There would be the unfortunate effect of tainting my sainted brother as well. But that is a moot point. I doubt I will lose.'

# Chapter Nine

Phillip called the next day, driving all thoughts of Nicholas from her mind. He was shown into the drawing room where Julia and Sophia were studying the most recent *La Belle Assemblée*.

He refused Sophia's offer of tea and took the wing chair near the sofa. He did not waste time on the preliminaries. He turned to Julia. 'I returned from Sheffield last night. I am sorry to tell you that I could discover nothing useful there.'

Sick disappointment washed over her. 'Nothing at all? The jeweller did not remember it?'

'No. His son has taken over the business in the last year and the father's memory is impaired. There was no record of any such transaction nor could either one recall such a ring.' His face held a disappointment that reflected her own. 'I am sorry, my dear. I know you had hoped there might be some clue to the identity of the person who took the ring. I do not wish to be harsh, but we may have to accept the fact that we may never know who killed Thomas.'

'I cannot.' She looked away, refusing to allow the tears to fall. She swallowed and glanced back at Phillip. 'There is still Lord Thayne. Perhaps someone will approach him about the ring.'

'Possibly. But that does not mean the person wants anything more than to purchase a valuable and unusual piece of jewellery. I am afraid that Thomas's death may be exactly what it seemed—a common robbery.'

A common robbery that resulted in her husband's murder. 'But why would it be so important for a mere thief to break into my house and demand I hand over the ring? I cannot believe that has nothing to do with his death!'

'You were perhaps mistaken. You did sustain a blow to the head.' Phillip's expression was not unkind.

'No. I know what I heard.' Distressed, she rose. 'I know I have asked you before, but please could you not tell me what Thomas was involved in before he died? I know it worried him very much.'

Phillip stood as well. 'You, of all people, should know I am not at liberty to tell you that information. And I will repeat what I have told you before: his work for the government and his death are not related.'

She looked at him, the frustration and hopelessness she had felt three years ago bubbling to the surface. 'Perhaps I should go to Sheffield. I could make inquiries. There must be something.'

'That is not necessary,' Phillip said coolly. 'And possibly dangerous. Furthermore, I cannot see what you could discover that I could not.'

'But there might be something!' She willed him to understand. 'Last time I waited and waited. You cannot know how frustrating it was! At least you were doing something! But I could only wait!'

'I know.' His mouth tightened. She had undoubtedly insulted him. 'I will still make inquiries, but I cannot allow you to put yourself in danger, if there is any. I promised Thomas we would watch out for you if he could not. And I plan to.'

His face had that uncompromising look that she had come to know well over the years. He had no intention of allowing her to do a thing. And now that she was in Sophia's home, it would be next to impossible to oppose him.

Sophia rose and put her hand on Julia's arm. 'I am sorry as well,' she said softly. 'But, oh, Julia! If anything happened to you we could not forgive ourselves. And I know Phillip is doing everything he can.'

'Of course.' Julia managed a smile, but she could not quite quell the twinge of resentment. Which was mean-spirited of her, because they were two people in the world who would never hurt her.

But her mind refused to let the matter go. That night after the dinner party she attended with Sophia and Phillip, and after the abigail had helped her dress for bed, she sat down at the small desk facing the window. The muslin curtains were parted and the pale light of the full moon bathed the room. She leaned her hand on her chin and thought.

Thomas had escorted her home after the ball and then gone to Thérèse's, which was not his usual habit for he almost never left her after such affairs. She had sensed he was meeting someone there although he did not say in so many words. And he was troubled again—she could tell by the way his ready smile did not quite reach his eyes. She had tried several times over that past week to discover what was behind the shadow in his eyes but he always managed to distract her.

Now she wished she had not been so easily bought off by his kisses and teasing. But hindsight was never useful.

She rose and went to stand by the window. Thérèse had been questioned by Phillip and his men. But Julia had never asked her about Thomas's last night. Somehow, with the horror of his death and the mourning and condolences and then the horrible sensation of moving in a fog, she had never really questioned Thérèse herself—how Thomas had spent his time there had not seemed relevant in the aftermath of his death and had been too painful to discuss.

But time had healed some of the pain and made it manageable. So perhaps it was time she called on Thérèse and found out exactly whom Thomas had been going to meet.

She called on Thérèse the next day. Despite knowing Thérèse was the proprietor of a gaming saloon, Sophia had been pleased to have Julia visit an old friend and had offered the use of her carriage.

Thérèse greeted her in her office, a small room on the third floor. She rose from behind her desk. 'My dear Julia! I could not believe my ears when André said you were here.' She moved towards Julia and embraced her. She stepped back. 'You look well. I had heard you were in London.'

'Yes.' Julia smiled at Thérèse. She wore a sensible dark blue dress and her hair was pulled severely back from her face and caught at the nape of her neck. Her prim appearance only emphasised her exotic beauty.

'And Lord Thayne has returned also.'

Julia's pulse jumped at the mention of his name. 'I believe so.'

'I would hope you know so, particularly as you waltzed with him the night before last.'

Julia started. 'You know that?'

Thérèse arched a delicate brow. 'I am certain all of London know. Come, sit down and I will ring for refreshment. And you will tell me about Nicholas. I have been agog with curiosity since you left with him that night. Or should I say forced him to leave with you?' Her eyes twinkled at the expression on Julia's face. 'Do not worry, I doubt if anyone else noticed a thing. But what exactly did you do with him for five days?'

Her tale failed to shock Thérèse. If anything, except for the highway robbery and the intruder, she was highly amused. 'My dear, you would be the envy of half the women in London. Except they would have taken full advantage of having the elusive Lord Thayne helpless under their roof.'

'He was hardly helpless.'

'No?' Thérèse laughed. 'Perhaps difficult, then?'

'Yes,' Julia said shortly. 'It is not Lord Thayne I am here to discuss. It is Thomas.' She took a deep breath. 'That last night, the night he died. I think he was here to meet someone. Can you remember anything at all about that night?'

Thérèse frowned. 'I told Phillip what I knew, as did my servants. Have you asked him?'

'He will not tell me much about his inquiries. But I know Thomas was worried. Perhaps about something he was investigating. And Phillip will not tell what that was.'

'No. He would not.' Thérèse stood and moved to her desk. She took a ring of keys from a hook above the desk, removed one and then used it to open a drawer in her desk. She pulled out a small stack of papers. 'After Phillip left, I wrote down my observations as well as those of my household. I thought perhaps Phillip would come again or send someone else with more questions and so I thought to write down everything we saw that night. But he did not and then I heard it was decided Thomas's death was a robbery and nothing more. But I kept the papers.' She came to Julia's side. 'You may take them if you would like.'

'Yes, if you please. I will return them to you when I am finished.' She took the papers and for some odd reason found her hand was shaking. She glanced at them and then swiftly up at Thérèse. 'Do you agree with Phillip?'

'I do not know,' Thérèse said cautiously. 'I have wondered. And now with what you have told me about the ring…' She shrugged lightly.

'So you are not convinced it was.' Julia looked down at the precise, elegant writing. As in everything, Thérèse had been meticulous. The first page listed the patrons who had attended that night. The others were narrative accounts by each of her servants. She glanced down at the list of names and frowned. 'George was here that night? But I thought he had left for Maldon.'

'He was here for a very short while. He left early, I believe.'

She looked up, puzzled. 'He never said anything. Did he speak to Thomas?'

'That I do not know.'

Julia returned her attention back to the papers and then felt a surge of excitement. 'And Robert Haslett? He was one of Thomas's good friends. He worked under Phillip as well.' Her hope died down. 'But he has left England.'

'He returned six months ago. He is, in fact, a frequent patron.'

'I would like to speak to him. He was still working for Phillip then. Perhaps he knows something.'

A frown creased Thérèse's brow. 'My dear, are you

certain this is wise? I will help you in any way, but I worry that you will only be disappointed. And hurt once again.'

Julia stood and clasped the papers to her chest. 'I cannot be hurt any more than I was. I need to find out why Thomas was so worried. Perhaps it means nothing and then I will accept that. But I cannot stand back this time.'

Thérèse's face still held worry. 'But you must be careful. You have already been injured once because of the ring. There is someone, perhaps, who does not want the past disturbed. I do not think Thomas would have wanted you in danger, even for his sake.'

'I am doing this for my sake,' Julia said quietly. Thérèse was right, as was Phillip, Thomas would prefer she remain innocent and out of harm even if it meant his killer was never brought to justice.

'I see.' Thérèse looked at her for a moment. 'So you want to speak to Robert Haslett. He will be here tonight. Can you come?'

'Yes.' A twinge of guilt shot through her. She and Sophia were to attend another coming-out ball. She loathed lying to Sophia, but knew that it was one thing for her to visit Thérèse during the day and another at night. Sophia would wonder why and there was always the possibility Phillip would find out. And this time, she wanted to do things her own way.

Julia arrived at Thérèse's house shortly after nine that evening. She finally decided on a lie that held a grain of truth—an elderly friend of hers and Thomas's had asked her to dine. Haslett was at least an old friend. If Sophia found it odd the invitation had been made so late, she said nothing, merely that, of course, Julia must go. And that it might be less tiring for Julia than a ball. Her kindness nearly made Julia confess everything, particularly when she offered to send Julia in her carriage.

Julia had assured her Mrs Sanders would send a carriage. Instead, Thérèse's plain, elegant carriage had arrived at half past eight to fetch her.

Despite the fact she had no intention of abducting anyone tonight, Julia's stomach still knotted as she was admitted to the house by André, Thérèse's butler. He took her card and glanced at it. 'Madame Blanchot awaits you in the saloon, my lady,' he said.

She nodded. 'Thank you.' She made her way across the small entrance hall and up the staircase. The main saloon was on the first floor. She paused in the doorway, her hand going to her mask to assure herself it was still in place. Then she stepped inside.

The room was already crowded. Most of the patrons tonight were men; if she hoped to find Robert Haslett on her own, it would take an age. She looked around and finally spotted Thérèse near the Faro table.

She moved across the room, aware she was the object of more than one curious glance. Thérèse looked up just as she reached the table. She left it and came to Julia's side. 'He is here,' she said quietly. 'I have told him that you very much desire to speak with him and he has agreed to meet you. He is in one of the small parlours. Shall I have Hayes take you to him now?'

'If you please.'

Thérèse nodded to a burly man in livery who stood near the Faro table. He came to her side and she spoke to him in a low voice and then turned to Julia. 'I wish you luck, *ma chérie*.'

'Yes.' She followed Hayes across the saloon and the small hallway. He paused in front of one of the rooms and Julia realised it was the same room where she had met Nicholas. The coincidence was not very reassuring.

'He is seated at the table in the corner,' Hayes said.

'Thank you.' Julia stepped inside, her heart pounding. Two men sat at the table near the fireplace. She saw a solitary man seated at the table in the corner.

She started across the room. And then gasped when someone caught her arm.

'Planning another abduction, Lady Carrington?'

She whirled around and stared up into Nicholas's sardonic face. 'Wh…what are you doing here?'

His brow shot up. 'More to the point, what are you doing here? Or did you decide you desire more entertainment than your dinner with an elderly lady provided?' Any of the warmth she had seen at the ball two nights ago had vanished.

Her mouth fell open. She gave him an angry stare, and then remembered it was probably wasted on him in her masked state. 'That is none of your concern. Will you please let go of me? I have an appointment with someone.'

He dropped her arm. 'With Haslett?'

'Yes. And if you will move out of my way, I will endeavour to keep it.'

'An assignation? My dear, I had no idea you had it in you, although I might have guessed,' he drawled. His face had darkened and he suddenly looked as dangerous as he had the night she abducted him.

A shiver of fear coursed through her. What if he had no intention of letting her move past him? She could not allow Haslett to leave. 'Please, you must let me go. It is not an assignation. He was a friend of my husband's and it is very important I talk to him.'

He stared at her for a moment, his eyes searching her

face, and she had the sense he could see beneath her
mask. 'Very well,' he said abruptly.

'Julia.'

They both turned. Robert Haslett had risen and come
to stand next to them. 'I trust there is not a problem, Lord
Thayne.' His voice was polite but cool.

'I merely wished to determine that Lady Carrington
was safe,' Nicholas said, equally coolly.

'I assure you she will be.'

'She had better be.' The slight menace in Nicholas's
voice was not reassuring.

'I have known Robert for a very long time,' Julia said,
attempting to break the tension.

The only result was to have Nicholas's brows snapped
together. 'Indeed,' he said, ice in his voice. 'If you need
anything, I am at your service.' He stalked off.

Robert looked at her, a quizzical expression in his blue
eyes. But he merely said, 'Come and sit down.'

She followed him to the table and took one of the
chairs. He seated himself across from her. 'It is good to
see you, Julia. Or at least most of you.'

She smiled at him. 'And it is good to see you as well.'
Except for his thinning hair, he had not changed much
since she last saw him, a few months after Thomas's
funeral. He had left for Austria shortly after that. He was
not quite handsome but his thin intelligent face was very
attractive. 'I hope you are well?' she asked.

A shadow crossed his face. 'For the most part.' He
paused, and then said, 'I lost my wife a year ago.'

She touched his hand. 'I am so sorry.' She had not
known he was married, but then she had lost contact with
so many people after Thomas's death.

'So am I.' He looked away for a moment and then
back at her. 'I did not mean to bring that up the very first

thing.' His smile was wry. 'The anniversary of our marriage was today.'

'Then today must be very difficult for you.' She hesitated. 'Perhaps this is not a good time for me to talk to you.'

'No. It is actually better than being alone with my thoughts,' he said. 'What can I do for you? I assume that the matter must be rather grave if you chose to meet me here.'

'It is.' She leaned forward. 'It is about Thomas. I know you were here that last night—the night he was killed. Do you know if he came to meet someone here?'

He frowned a little. 'If he did, I did not notice. We played a few hands together. He spoke with a number of people, but I cannot recall that anyone in particular caught my attention.'

That was disappointing. 'There is something else, then. He seemed troubled, but he would not tell me why. I knew he was involved in some matter for the government and I wondered if that was what worried him. Do you have any idea what he was doing?'

His frown increased. 'Why the questions now, Julia?'

'Because some things have happened and I have begun to wonder if there was more to his death than a mere robbery.'

'Have you?' he said slowly. 'I will own I had wondered myself, but the investigation came to naught.'

'Do you know what he was involved with?'

'I suppose there is no reason I cannot tell you,' he said slowly. 'He suspected that someone in the Home Office was selling secrets to the French. No one was ever charged and, once Thomas died, the investigation was dropped.'

*   *   *

'Lady Carrington is ready to leave, my lord,' Haynes said in a low voice.

'Thank you.' Nicholas turned from the EO Table.

'But you've yet to place your wager,' the young Lord Lawton exclaimed.

'Later,' Nicholas said over his shoulder. He made his way through the saloon and went down the staircase to the front entry. André finished admitting a trio of young bucks and then saw him. He came to Nicholas's side. 'She is in the waiting room, my lord.'

Nicholas nodded and went to the small room off the hall.

Still masked, she sat on a wing chair, her hands clasped around her reticule. She looked up at his footsteps. Her body stiffened. She slowly stood. 'Why are you here?'

'I am escorting you back to Sophia's house.'

'Thérèse has provided a carriage for me.'

'I am taking you instead.' He levelled a frown at her. 'Don't argue. I'll go to the devil before I allow you to leave this place without me. I intend to see you get home without incident.'

'I have no idea what sort of incident you refer to,' she said icily.

He stepped towards her. 'No? Then you are either more naïve or more foolish than I thought.'

'I am neither, my lord.'

'Indeed? Then what sort of a game do you play? I doubt if either Sophia or Phillip know you are here.'

'I am not playing a game.'

It was all he could do to rein in the anger that had boiled in him since he saw her with Haslett. He refused to acknowledge he could possibly be jealous. 'Is this how you abuse Sophia's hospitality? By leading her to believe you are safely dining in the home of an old friend while you are all the while amusing yourself in a gaming hell?'

'I am not amusing myself! Nor is this a gaming hell!' she snapped. And suddenly seemed to fold. 'I would not dream of deceiving Sophia if I did not have to.' Her mouth trembled beneath her mask. 'Please, I do not wish to argue with you. I will go with you, if you insist.'

His anger vanished along with her capitulation. 'What sort of trouble are you in?'

'I am not in trouble.'

'Then what is wrong?'

'Nothing. Everything. I just want to leave this place.'

He picked up her mantle from the chair. She did not protest when he draped it about her shoulders. 'Come. My carriage should be waiting by now.'

They did not speak as they entered the carriage and took their places across from each other. He waited until the footman had closed the door and the carriage had started through the dark London streets before he spoke. 'You can remove your mask.'

Her hands went to the strings at the back of her head. She fumbled with them for a moment and then the mask fell away. He could barely see her face in the shadows of the carriage.

'What happened tonight?' he asked quietly.

'Robert Haslett told me that my husband suspected someone in the Home Office was passing information to the French,' she said dully. 'Before he was killed, he was attempting to discover this person or persons' identity.'

'And did he?'

'No. The investigation stopped with his death. His superiors concluded there was no evidence for his suspicions. Or at least no evidence was found.' She drew in a breath. 'I think he was killed because he did find something.'

'You did not know of this until tonight?'

'I knew he was still working for Phillip and that something was worrying him. But Phillip would not tell me what it was. He assured me it had no bearing on his death.'

Just as Stanton had assured him and his grandfather. 'Will you tell Phillip what you have discovered tonight?'

'I do not know. He returned yesterday from Sheffield. He found nothing. He still thinks, or wants me to think, Thomas's death was a robbery.' Her voice was tired.

'Perhaps to protect you.'

'I do not want to be protected. Not if it means hiding the truth.'

He frowned, not liking her implication. 'Do you really think he would do that?'

'I do not know what to think.'

The carriage had turned into Berkeley Square. The whole affair made him uneasy, but he did not like the turn things were taking. He especially didn't like the fact she was making her own enquiries. He leaned towards her. 'Don't do anything more.'

The carriage stopped. 'I cannot let this rest.' Under the street lamp he could see the stubborn look on her face.

'It may be dangerous. Let me help you.'

'I cannot have you involved any further.'

He laughed. 'My dear, whether you wish it or not, and for that matter, whether I wish it or not, I am involved beyond return in this matter. I am not about to back out now and allow you to risk your lovely neck.'

'Then I wish I had not told you what I was doing tonight!'

'Then I would have threatened to tell Sophia where you were.'

She gasped. 'That is blackmail.'

He gave her one of his most sardonic looks. 'Precisely so. And believe me, I won't hesitate to use it again if I deem it necessary.' The footman opened the doors. Nicholas stepped out and then held out his hand. With some hesitation, she took it and allowed him to help her out. He walked up the steps with her.

He looked down at her face. 'We will talk tomorrow. You can drive with me in Hyde Park.'

'I do not wish to drive in Hyde Park.'

'Yes, you do.' He smiled gently. 'Otherwise I might mention to Sophia how delighted I was to escort you home from Thérèse's.'

She looked as if she wanted to hit him. At least it was an improvement over the dispirited woman in his carriage. Without saying a word, she turned and stalked into the house.

Brunton watched Thayne's carriage rumble away from Lady Simons's house. He had been sent to follow Thayne and, as last time, Thayne left with Lady Carrington. Except this time they left in Thayne's carriage and without the added interest of ropes. A pity. Although his preference would have been to have the lady bound.

He moved his horse forward out of the shadows. No matter. The guv'nor should pay him well for this information.

'Will you need anything else, my lord?' Samuels asked.

'No. Not tonight.' Nicholas waited until his valet departed and then walked over to the wing chair near his bed. He threw himself into it, stretching his legs before him. He doubted sleep would come any time soon. A frown creased his brow as he mulled over the night's events. Did Phillip indeed have something to hide? But Carrington had been his godson and Nicholas had sensed Phillip was sincerely grieved over Carrington's death.

But perhaps Phillip merely wanted to protect Julia, keep her from doing exactly what she had done: come to the conclusion that Carrington's death was connected to his investigation for the Home Office when it was nothing but a coincidence.

His frown deepened. He meant what he had told Julia. He would not allow her to pursue this on her own. She'd been desperate enough for information to kidnap him. He hated to think what else she might do if she thought it was necessary. He'd keep her from doing something else rash if he had to abduct her in return.

How the devil had he managed to get this involved in her affairs in the first place? It was the last thing he wanted. When he first returned to London, he vowed he would stay away from her. But when he saw her at the Bathurst ball, looking rather lost and trying to pretend she did not see him, his resolution went to hell. Kingsley's sly machinations had little to do with his decision, except to make certain he obtained a proper introduction before asking her to stand up with him. He had thought only to tease her, perhaps flirt with her a little and then he would put her out of his mind.

But as he had looked down into her upturned face with her expressive hazel eyes and inviting mouth, his hand resting lightly on the slender curve of her back, he realised he still desired her. He wanted to possess her in a way he had felt with no other woman but Mary.

He was not in love with her. Nor would he ever be.

In her own way, she was as unobtainable as Mary had been. Only an idiot would fail to see Julia still loved her husband.

And he still loved Mary.

So, what to do? As much as he might like, he could not avoid Julia. The ring he wore was a reminder of that. He had avoided wearing it for two years because it had reminded him of his failure to protect Mary.

He would not let the ring symbolise his failure to protect Julia as well.

# Chapter Ten

Julia stood in Sophia's drawing room, looking down into the square. Nicholas was due to arrive any minute. Disgusted that she was peering through the curtains as if she was actually anxious for his arrival, she turned away, only to find Sophia watching her with a little smile.

'Do not worry, I know he will be here soon enough,' Sophia said.

'I am hardly worried about that. If anything, I rather wish he would change his mind.'

Sophia laughed. 'Men do not cry off. And why, if you are so reluctant to go with him, did you agree?'

'He coerced me.' That at least was the truth. Arriving home last night before Sophia had not done much to relieve her guilt. Sophia's kindly questions about her dinner and her elderly friend had not helped either.

'Did he? Splendid! Otherwise, you would have neatly fobbed him off.'

'I doubt anyone could do that,' Julia said crossly.

Sophia laughed again. 'Poor Julia. At least think of it as a chance to show off your new bonnet and spencer. You look lovely.'

The stylish bonnet trimmed with purple ribbon to

match the braid-trimmed spencer had arrived today. Sophia had insisted that she wear them. Julia had to admit having new clothes was pleasurable—she rarely bothered because there seemed little point in purchasing fashionable clothing when she had few occasions to wear them. Particularly when she must worry about the cost as well.

She turned when she heard footsteps in the hall and then Nicholas was shown into the room. Sophia rose to greet him. 'How nice to see you, Nicholas.'

'And you.' He bowed over her hand and then looked up. His gaze fell on Julia. 'Lady Carrington.'

'Good day, Lord Thayne,' she said coolly, trying to ignore the fact his dashing appearance in a perfectly fitting drab coat and light-coloured breeches made her pulse leap a notch.

His expression was quizzical, but he said nothing. After he exchanged a few more pleasantries with Sophia, he turned to Julia. 'Are you ready?'

'I have been ready for the last three-quarters of an hour,' Julia said stiffly. She had no intention of letting him think she was coming with him willingly.

'I am flattered,' he drawled, giving her a sharp look.

'I hope you will enjoy yourselves,' Sophia said. She glanced from Julia to Nicholas with a rather worried face.

Which made Julia feel ashamed. None of this was Sophia's doing, or for that matter, his, and she knew Sophia was fond of Nicholas. She managed a smile. 'I am sure I will.'

She went with him down the stairs and out of the house. His curricle, pulled by a handsome pair of matching bays, waited in the street. He helped her in and then gracefully took his place next to her. After he dismissed the groom, he set the horses to.

He said nothing until they were out of the square. He glanced down at her. 'Are you comfortable?'

'Yes. It is very nice.' She had not ridden in anything so dashing for an age. The sensation was pleasing. She gave him a tentative smile.

He looked taken aback. 'Good.' He manoeuvred around a cart and then turned back to her. 'I take it Sophia did not discover last night's activities.'

For a moment she had nearly forgotten why she was here. 'No. She did not suspect anything.'

'You do not sound particularly pleased.'

'I dislike deceiving her. But she would be even more distressed if she knew what I was doing.'

He frowned. 'What made you decide to meet with Haslett last night?'

'Thomas was killed after he left Thérèse's. Thérèse gave me a list of all the patrons who had been there that night as well as written narratives of her observations and those of her employees. Robert's name was on the list. He had been a good friend of Thomas's and I thought he might know something. He did.'

They were approaching the entrance to Hyde Park. The increasing number of carriages and riders forced him to slow down the horses. 'What did you hope to do next?' he asked without taking his eyes off the horses.

'I have the list. I recognise some of the names and I thought I could contact some of the others.'

His mouth tightened. 'No.'

'No, my lord?'

'No. It is too dangerous. Give me the list. I will make any of the necessary contacts.'

'I do not think—'

He cut her off. 'It makes sense. For one thing, I may know some of the men on the list. And, my dear, I have one other factor in my favour.' He slanted her a glance. 'I am a man. I have access to places you do not and with much less trouble. Unless, of course, you look forward to spending the rest of your time in London deceiving Sophia.'

'Of course I do not. I should hate it!' And he was right, of course. No one would question why he visited a gaming saloon. He undoubtedly belonged to White's or Brook's and could easily meet with any of the members, whereas she had wondered how in the world she would manage to approach most of the men on the list. But she hated to be beholden to him any more than she already was. More troubling, she had no idea why he seemed determined to help her.

'So is it settled? You will give me the list?' he asked.

'I am not certain,' she began, only to be interrupted by a voice.

'How very interesting. First a waltz and now a tête-à-tête drive in the park. Does this mean there is to be an interesting announcement?'

Startled, she saw George had ridden up beside them on a handsome chestnut. Engrossed in their conversation, she had nearly forgotten where they were.

'Good day, Kingsley,' Nicholas said, ignoring his comment.

'And good day to you, Thayne. And, of course, my dear Julia.' He lifted his quizzing glass to his eye and surveyed her. 'Can I believe my eyes? A new bonnet? Most flattering, my dear. Very *au courant*. You look ravishingly lovely, do you not think, Thayne?'

'George!' Julia said, wanting to disappear. 'Do be quiet!'

'I was merely soliciting Lord Thayne's opinion on your appearance. I assume he has one.'

'He is not obligated to state it, if he does.'

'But why not? I thought the purpose for wearing new clothing was to elicit a response from one's companions, particularly eligible gentlemen.'

She didn't want to disappear, she wanted to commit murder. 'You are mistaken in my case,' she said between clenched teeth. 'I really do not care if Lord Thayne has an opinion or not.'

Nicholas turned to look at her. The corners of his lips twitched. 'Actually, Kingsley is right, I do have an opinion. The bonnet is very becoming on you. And you do look lovely.'

'You were not obliged to say that,' she said stiffly.

'Are you accusing me of insincerity?'

'Of course I am not.' Now she was flustered. 'Please, can we discuss something else? I cannot see that it matters what I wear.'

'Actually it does, my dear,' George said. 'However, I will not belabour the point. Ah, I see the charming Lady Jessica has sighted you and undoubtedly wishes for a chit-chat. So I will be off.' He made a slight bow and, with a flourish, turned his mount around.

They were approaching a trio of young ladies on horses. One of the young ladies broke away from the group and trotted towards them at their approach. 'Nicholas!' Lady Jessica exclaimed.

Nicholas stopped the curricle and she reined in her mount, a dainty grey. She beamed at them. 'Good day, Lady Carrington. How nice to see you again!'

Julia returned her smile, finding the girl's sincere warmth hard to resist. 'I am glad to see you again as well. What a lovely horse you ride.'

'She was my first gift from Adam after we were married. Her name is Sultana.' Jessica patted the mare's neck. 'Is she not the sweetest thing?' She turned her gaze to Nicholas and gave him a teasing smile. 'I see I now have something else to write Sarah. I believe this is the first time I have caught you driving in the park during the fashionable hour. She will be quite astonished when I tell her.'

'I had no idea driving through the park was such an accomplishment,' Nicholas said drily.

'Oh, but it is. At least for some people,' she added. She smiled back at Julia. 'I had hoped I might see you soon. I know it is rather late notice, but I wish very much to invite you and Lady Simons to a small picnic we are giving in a few days. It will be at our house in Richmond so it is not a great way from here. I will, of course, send you and Lady Simons an invitation, but I had wanted to extend the invitation in person as well.'

'A picnic sounds lovely,' Julia said, rather taken aback by Lady Jessica's warmth towards her, a person she had briefly met just once before.

'I hope you can come. Nicholas will be there as well.'

His brow shot up. 'Will I?' he asked. 'I am beginning to feel slighted at the lack of an invitation extended in person.'

She grinned at him. 'You have one now.'

She turned her mount to catch up with her two companions. Nicholas urged the horses forward again. By now the park was crowded with fashionable carriages of every sort, as well as riders and a number of persons on foot. Their carriage was travelling at a mere snail's pace.

'Your cousin's wife is very kind,' Julia said.

He glanced down at her. 'Yes, she has been very kind. More than kind under the circumstances.' There was a harshness in his voice she did not understand.

'Sarah is your sister?' she asked, hoping that would be a neutral topic.

His face relaxed a notch. 'Yes. She lives in Kent. Her husband is Jessica's brother.'

'I see.' That would explain several things, although not why he had looked so grim. 'Lady Jessica seems very fond of your sister.'

'She is.' He was forced to stop the carriage while they waited for the occupants of a barouche and another curricle to finish their conversation. 'They consider themselves sisters.'

'How lovely,' Julia said a bit wistfully. She had always longed for a sibling, but Thomas had been an only child as well and so there had been no siblings by marriage either. 'I always wanted a sister or a brother. They are very fortunate. So are you.'

The barouche finally moved on and Nicholas urged the horses forward. He looked down at her. 'I am. Did you not have any cousins or such growing up?'

'No. My cousins were all much older than me. My stepfather did not encourage friendships outside of the family. It was not until I went away to school that I finally had a good friend. And then after I married Thomas, there was Sophia.' She smiled. 'She has always been as a sister to me. And Thomas as well. He was my best friend.'

'You were fortunate,' he said softly.

'Yes, I was.'

He looked at her for a moment, his expression unreadable. 'I'd best take you back to Berkeley Square,' he said curtly.

He said nothing more until they reached Sophia's townhouse. The groom dashed forward to hold the team. Nicholas jumped down and then held out his hand to

Julia. She stepped down and he released her hand. 'Can you send me the papers today?'

'Yes.' She looked up at his face. 'Why are you doing this? After what I did to you, I would think you would run as far away as possible.'

'Because I would never forgive myself if anything happened to you,' he said shortly.

Under different circumstances and with a different man she might be tempted to take his words as a declaration of love. But she had the sense he was not talking about her at all, but some other woman entirely.

The note was waiting for her in her bedchamber. After Nicholas had left, she had gone directly upstairs to change for dinner. She and Sophia were to dine early with Phillip and then would proceed to a ball at Lord and Lady Middleton's home.

She pulled off her kid gloves and went to place them on her dressing table when she saw the note. She picked it up. The handwriting was unfamiliar. Puzzled, she opened the sheet.

The message was short, the handwriting crude. *You were at Thérèse's. Do not interfere.*

She stared at it for a moment, and then dread slowly washed over her.

Someone had recognised her, despite her mask. Someone knew she had gone there for a purpose other than gambling.

But who? Thérèse, Robert and Nicholas, of course. And André and Hayes. But Hayes had been there only a year and had never met Thomas. André had been with Thérèse for as long as she could remember and had always been nothing but discreet.

She could not imagine that Thérèse or Robert would

mention her visit. Or Nicholas, despite his threats to reveal her whereabouts to Sophia.

Or that any one of them knew something about Thomas's death they did not want her to learn.

She sank down on her bed, her legs trembling. The note was clearly an effort to frighten her or warn her, or both. Someone did not want her asking questions.

And it was unlikely the sender of the note would be any more pleased if Nicholas started asking questions. She had already been assaulted, and there had been the highwaymen. What if the note writer decided to progress beyond threats on paper?

Which meant she must explain to Nicholas as soon as possible why she could not accept his help.

Without removing her bonnet or spencer, she sat down at the small writing desk and pulled out a sheet of paper.

The ball was in full swing by the time Nicholas stalked into the Middletons' ballroom. He'd had no intention of attending this particular ball held in honour of the second Middleton daughter, but Julia's polite little note had quickly changed his mind.

He paused just inside the door. A quick perusal revealed no sign of Julia. The dancers were engaged in a lively country dance and the sides of the ballroom were crowded with chaperons and their charges who were not fortunate enough to be engaged with a partner.

A frown crossed his brow and then he spotted Sophia. So, at least she was here, which presumably meant Julia was as well unless she had decided to elude Sophia for another meeting. His frown changed to a scowl. He'd have her head if that was the case.

He started across the room towards Sophia when he suddenly saw Julia standing near the French doors on the other side of the room. She stood with Kingsley, her back to Nicholas. As if sensing Nicholas's interest, Kingsley looked over and saw him. He turned back to Julia and said something to her and then, taking her arm, led her through the French doors to the outside terrace.

Nicholas muttered a curse. What the devil was Kingsley up to now? The music stopped and the dancers began to drift towards the sides of the ballroom. He was forced to step aside as he waited for the crowd to disperse.

'Lord Thayne,' Lady Middleton said. She bustled up to him, beaming. He nearly groaned. Not only was she a notorious gossip, she routinely pounced on eligible bachelors as partners for her daughters. 'How honoured we are to have you! But your poor arm! I do trust it is better! How shocked we were to learn what had happened!'

He stared at her. 'I beg your pardon.'

'The highwayman. How fortunate that you were able to make it to shelter where you were cared for.' She wagged a finger at him. 'Now, if only we can learn the identity of the mysterious lady who bound your wounds!'

He nearly reeled. Where the devil had she heard this? Not from his grandfather or Phillip. Or Julia. Which left Kingsley. He looked forward to killing him.

He realised Lady Middleton was regarding him with an odd expression. 'There is no mysterious lady, I fear,' he said.

'No?' She arched a brow and then smiled in a disbelieving manner. 'Of course not. I quite understand. But come, let me find you a partner. My Lydia would be honoured to stand up with you.'

He glanced towards the doors, only half-attending. Julia still had not appeared, nor had Kingsley. 'I fear I am obligated for this dance.'

'The next one, then?'

'Yes, the next one,' he said automatically.

'Splendid!' She beamed again.

He finally managed to extricate himself and to escape through the French doors onto the terrace. Lamps at intervals provided light. A few couples stood on the terrace and, at one end, a group of men were engaged in a heated discussion.

Julia and Kingsley had to be in the garden. He quickly ran down the steps. A couple stood in one corner, but the lady was too stout to be Julia. He frowned. And then from his right, he heard Kingsley's unmistakable drawl. 'My dear Julia, did I tell you how lovely I find you? A veritable rose in the moonlight.'

'I think you have finally gone mad!' Julia's voice was filled with exasperation.

Nicholas rounded the corner of the terrace. They sat on a bench behind a large potted tree. Julia was attempting to rise but Kingsley's grip on her hand prevented her.

'Well?' Nicholas said between gritted teeth.

Julia froze. She sank back down on the bench, her expression a mixture of mortification and apprehension. Kingsley merely smirked. He released Julia's hand. 'Ah, your protector has arrived. And just in time to save you from my ungentlemanly advances.'

Nicholas fixed him with a hard stare. 'Is that what you were attempting?'

'Yes. I fear the moonlight, coupled with the presence of—'

'He was doing no such thing!' Julia declared. She jumped up, her eyes flashing with fury. 'He has spent the entire time telling me the most idiotic gossip and would not let me go in, and suddenly at the last moment decided to possess himself of my hand and pay me an idiotic compliment.'

'I see.' It was all too apparent Kingsley was amusing himself, but Nicholas had no idea why. Just as he had no idea why Kingsley had decided to spread the tale about his encounter with the highwayman. He was beginning to suspect they were related.

He kept his eyes on Kingsley. 'I believe, Kingsley, it is time you and I meet,' he said dispassionately.

'No!' Julia said. 'Please do not!' She looked almost sick. 'George looks very frivolous but he…he is deadly with swords and your arm cannot be completely well!'

Nicholas swung around to stare at her. 'What the devil are you talking about?' Then it dawned on him. 'Don't concern yourself, I am not planning to call him out. Yet.'

George rose in a leisurely movement. 'This little comedy has been extremely amusing. Despite the ungracious remark about my frivolous appearance.' He turned his gaze on Nicholas. 'Just let me know when you wish to meet me, my dear fellow. I will be completely at your service.' He sauntered off.

'I…I should go in as well,' she said, not quite meeting Nicholas' eyes.

He stepped in front of her. 'Not yet. We are going to talk first.'

She frowned at him. 'Are we? I do not think we have anything to talk about.'

'You are quite wrong. We have a number of things to talk about. Such as your note dismissing me from further involvement in your affairs.'

'I decided I did not need your help after all.'

'Indeed. And what caused you to change your mind?'

'After some reflection I…I decided that Phillip was right and there is nothing more to discover about Thomas's death.'

He merely looked at her until she began to fidget. 'Now tell me the real reason,' he said.

'I just told you.'

'What happened in the scant hour since I left you and before your note arrived at my house?' He smiled coolly. 'I can still tell Sophia about your little adventure the other night.'

'No.' She took a deep breath. 'Very well, I will tell you. I received a note as well. I found it on my dressing table after I left you. The note was unsigned. It said not to…to interfere.'

'What else?'

'And that the sender knew I was at Thérèse's.'

He drew in a breath. 'Do you have the note?'

'Yes.'

'Then give it to me. Along with the other papers.'

'No! I cannot! I do not want you involved.' She glanced away and then looked back at him. 'I cannot allow you to be hurt.'

He stared at her. 'You are worried about me?'

'Of course. You have already been injured because of me. I do not want anything more to happen to you on my account.'

'And you were worried Kingsley was going to run me through?'

'Well, yes. That would have been due to me as well.' Her eyes, fixed on him, were large in the pale moonlight. 'I do not think I am a safe person for you to associate with.'

'Probably not.' He stepped towards her, causing her to step back. 'But, as I told you before, I am too tangled in your affairs to extricate myself.'

'You needn't be.' Her voice was breathless. 'You could walk away right now.'

'I do not think I can.' His gaze strayed to her lips, soft and inviting. 'Because then you might be hurt if I do.'

Her eyes widened. 'I…'

He bent his head towards her. He was undoubtedly mad, but he was going to kiss her. 'Julia.'

'Lord Thayne!'

Lady Middleton's shocked tones jerked him back to reality. He spun around to find her behind him. She stared at him and then her gaze narrowed speculatively as it fell on Julia. 'Good evening, Lady Carrington.'

'Good evening, Lady Middleton. We…we were just about to return to the ballroom,' Julia said in a hollow voice.

Lady Middleton continued to watch her. 'Lord George said I might find Lord Thayne out here. Lord Thayne is obligated for the next dance.' Her tone implied Julia had deliberately kept Nicholas out in the garden in order to thwart her plans.

Nicholas started and then vaguely recalled agreeing to such a thing. Good God. The last thing he wanted to do was stand up with the flirtatious Lady Lydia.

Julia glanced at him. 'Yes. He…he was just saying that, which is why we were about to return to the ball-room.'

'Very good.' Lady Middleton sounded mollified. 'Then you will not object if I whisk him away from you.'

'No, of course not,' Julia said. 'I will go in as well.'

Nicholas had no choice but to leave. He cast one more look at Julia who wore a fixed smile, then he turned and mounted the terrace steps with Lady Middleton. He should be relieved he had been saved from an act of pure folly. Instead, he wanted to roundly curse Lady Middleton for her damnable timing.

## Chapter Eleven

Any hopes Julia entertained that Nicholas would forget about the papers were dashed when he came to call the next morning. Julia and Sophia were having breakfast in the small library which overlooked the back garden.

He was shown in, impeccably dressed in a dark blue morning coat and buff pantaloons, his Hessians polished to perfection. Her heart thudded at the sight of his elegant maleness and she had no idea whether it was from nervousness or something else entirely. Sophia smiled. 'Good morning, Nicholas. Will you not join us?'

He returned her smile and shook his head. 'Thank you, but I am not here on a social call. Lady Carrington has an item she is to give me.'

Sophia glanced over at Julia, her expression bemused. 'Indeed. Did you wish it fetched for you?'

'Oh, no. I can do it.' Julia glanced quickly at Nicholas, who merely raised his brow. Why must he ask her in front of Sophia? She rose from the table and frowned at him. 'Could I speak to you for a moment, Lord Thayne?'

'Of course.' He did not move.

'In the hallway, if you please.'

He smiled coolly. 'After you bring me the item.'

He apparently had no intention of budging. Aware of Sophia's curious look, Julia turned and left the room. Really, why ever had she thought he would listen to her? He was as stubborn as Thomas had ever been. Perhaps worse.

The papers were in the bottom of a wardrobe where she had left them. She pulled them out. She had already gone over the list and marked the patrons she knew had had some connection to Thomas. She took this list and returned the other papers to their place.

She clasped the list to her chest and stood, hesitant to go downstairs and turn it over to Nicholas. What choice did she have? If she did not turn it over, he would undoubtedly hound her for it. She could say it was lost, but he was not likely to believe that.

She reluctantly returned to the library. He was alone and stood in front of the tall window looking out at the garden. He turned when he heard her. 'Well?'

'I do not want you involved.'

'You made that clear last night.' He moved towards her and she was suddenly reminded of last night in the garden. Her gaze flew to his mouth and her heart began to thud. Had he really been about to kiss her? Why was she thinking of that now? She forced her mind on to the topic at hand. He stopped in front of her. 'Let me have the paper.'

She stared at his hand. The ring glinted up from his fourth finger. It fitted his strong, lean finger well, as if it had always belonged there. She swallowed, a peculiar lump rising to her throat. Without looking at him, she placed the paper in his hand.

He took it and frowned. 'Is this it?'

She forced herself to speak. 'I have the narratives Thérèse wrote. I did not think there was anything very remarkable. But this is the list of patrons that night. I marked those who knew Thomas.'

'I see.' He looked at her closely for a moment and then turned to the list.

She covertly watched his face, the strong planes of his cheekbones, the long lashes of his eyes. His golden-brown hair, thick and silky, curled just slightly at his neck and she suddenly remembered how soft and silky it had felt under her hands the night she had abducted him.

He glanced up. 'I will start with those you have identified.'

'Yes,' she said distractedly.

'Is something wrong?'

'I beg your pardon?'

'You are staring at me.'

'Oh!' Her cheeks heated. She hurriedly came up with an excuse. 'I…I was wondering how your arm is. Has it healed properly?'

'My arm? I was talking about the paper.'

'Yes, but I was wondering about your arm.'

His gaze travelled over her face and a slight smile touched his mouth. 'What is it? Are you still worried about my welfare? My dear, if you continue in this vein I may start to believe you care about me.' His voice was lightly mocking.

A stab of hurt shot through her. 'There is no need to be horrid about it!' And then could have bitten her tongue. Why could she have not said something light and mocking in return?

An odd expression flitted across his face. 'I did not mean to be,' he said softly. His hand holding the paper dropped to his side. 'So, are you saying you care about me?'

Mortified, she backed away. 'Of…of course I am concerned about you. I shouldn't want anything more to happen to you because of me.'

'I see. You do not want my death on your conscience?'

'Well, no. That is, I would not want your death anyway. Or anyone else's for that matter.' She had no idea what she was saying.

His expression shuttered. 'It is gratifying to know I at least occupy the same level of esteem as most of humanity in your eyes,' he said shortly. 'I assume that means you don't abhor me.'

'Why would you think I abhor you?' she asked astonished. 'If anything, I would expect the reverse, that you abhor me!'

His brow snapped down. 'Why the devil would I abhor you?'

'Because I abducted you.'

Now, he appeared astonished. 'What the devil does that have to do with anything?' He fixed her with a scowl. 'I don't dislike you at all.'

'Well, I do not dislike you either!'

He stared at her and then suddenly laughed. 'Are we now clear enough on that point? I am glad to discover you do not dislike me.'

'I never have.' She smiled back at him, feeling unexpectedly shy.

'Good,' he said softly. He looked down into her face and his expression slowly changed, the laughter fading from his eyes. She caught her breath, her heart pounding as she met his gaze. Her lips parted, almost as if anticipating his kiss.

He slowly pulled his eyes away. 'I should leave you,' he said abruptly. His voice was husky.

'Yes.' She looked away as well, her cheeks flaming.

She prayed he had not noticed her wanton reaction to him.

After he departed, she sank down on a chair, her hands at her still-heated cheeks. She must be going mad. What else could explain her growing preoccupation with him? No, it was not just a preoccupation—it was an attraction. Almost as if she were developing a *tendre* for him.

Which would be completely horrible. She could not allow such a thing. Undoubtedly it was some sort of aberration due to their forced togetherness under such unusual circumstances.

Which undoubtedly accounted for any attraction he might feel for her as well.

The best thing would be to avoid his company as much as possible except as absolutely necessary. She would be civil, of course, but only as befitting the merest acquaintance. And certainly she would endeavour to never find herself alone with him. She feared she might be tempted to do something exceedingly rash.

A night later, Nicholas sat in Thérèse's and watched the Honourable Edward Palmerston, seated across the table from him, polish off his fourth glass of brandy. Nicholas doubted he'd gain much more information from the man now. Not that he'd been particularly helpful—his recollection of the night Carrington had been killed was hazy—undoubtedly he'd been in the same inebriated state he was in now.

Which presented a problem. Not only was he interviewing witnesses about an event that took place three years ago, most of the witnesses who had last seen Carrington had probably been foxed as well. His inquiries so far had yielded nothing of importance.

Nicholas rose. Palmerston set his glass down. 'Leaving so soon, Thayne?' His words were slurred.

'I've another appointment at White's.' He was to meet Adam there shortly.

A gleam of awareness actually crossed Palmerston's face. 'Look at the betting book. Might interest you.' He slumped back down in his chair.

Nicholas shrugged. In his more youthful, albeit wilder days, White's betting book held some curiosity for him. He rarely glanced at it now.

He left Palmerston starting on his fifth glass and quit the private room. Thérèse left the table where she had been presiding, and stopped him on his way out. 'How is Julia?' she asked in a low voice.

'She is well.'

'Good.' Thérèse put a hand on his arm. 'I am glad you are helping her. I do not want her pursuing this matter on her own.'

He stared at her. 'You know what I am doing?'

'But of course.' She arched a delicate brow at his expression and dropped her hand from his arm. 'It is not a secret you have been asking questions about Thomas's death. The question, of course, is why. The general conclusion is that you wish to fix your interest with Julia.'

'Hell.' He scowled.

She looked amused. 'I see you have been too busy to listen to gossip. Which is rather remarkable since much of it concerns you.'

He stifled a groan. 'What else?'

'There is the tale of your heroic wound by a highwayman and the mysterious woman who nursed you.'

'I've heard that. Kingsley, no doubt.'

'Probably.' She sobered. 'There is the betting book at

White's. I have not heard the precise nature of the wager. I fear, however, most of it concerns Julia as well.'

'Blast.' He felt like uttering something much stronger. The gossips would soon suspect Julia was the mysterious woman—if they did not already. 'She will hardly be pleased.' Which was an understatement.

'I fear she will not.' She caught his arm again and looked directly at him. 'I do not want her hurt, Nicholas. She has a kind heart.'

'I've no intention of hurting her,' he said. 'Or of allowing anyone or anything else to do so either.'


The entry in the book at White's hardly improved his temper. *Wager: Lord G. Kingsley wagers the Hon. W. Buntford a certain sum Lord Thayne will wed Lady C. within two months.*

Adam peered over his shoulder. 'Good God! What the devil possessed Kingsley to make such a bet?'

'A death wish. He knows I will have his blood.'

Adam put a restraining hand on his arm. 'I wouldn't if I were you. Unless you want a scandal. And a rift between your family and his.'

The words he'd left out hung unspoken over Nicholas's head. *Unless you want another scandal. And to cause another rift between two families.*

'Of course, you are right,' he said bitterly. 'I can do nothing.'

Adam dropped his hand. 'Except keep your temper. As much as Kingsley probably deserves your wrath, Lady Carrington does not need the additional gossip.'

'No.' It would distress her no end. Particularly if knowledge of this blasted wager got about. She would undoubtedly find some way to blame herself.

He realized Adam was regarding him curiously. 'Well?' Nicholas demanded.

'I was merely wondering what led Kingsley to think you would not be adverse to, er…accompanying Lady Carrington to the altar?'

'I've not the least idea!' Nicholas snapped and then scowled. 'Just the knowledge I was under her roof for five days, I suppose.' He wasn't about to tell Adam about the scene on the sofa. Which meant nothing.

'Is that all? You are rather frequently in her company.'

'That hardly signifies.'

'No? Apparently to Kingsley it does.' Adam regarded him thoughtfully. 'So, what is your next course of action? You had best hope Kingsley does nothing to advance his cause.'

Nicholas smiled rather grimly. 'He will not have the opportunity. I intend to avoid Lady Carrington's company as much as possible.'

'Indeed,' Adam said. 'Does that mean, then, you are not coming to Richmond tomorrow? Lady Simons and Lady Carrington have both accepted Jessica's invitation. I warn you, however, Jessica will be most put out if you do not decide to come. She will undoubtedly write to Sarah as well,' he added with a grin.

Nicholas stifled a groan. How the devil had everything become so damnably tangled? He'd forgotten about the picnic, but he could hardly cry off now. It would distress Jessica and she had been far too kind to him to disappoint her.

Except as politeness dictated, he would stay as far away from Julia as possible.

Julia and Sophia arrived in Richmond shortly before noon. Adam Henslow's Richmond estate was small but beautifully situated in a large green park. The house, of red brick, had been built a half century ago and stood at the end of a long curving drive.

Since Phillip had gone to his estate near St Albans for a day, George had escorted the ladies. The weather was perfect for a picnic, warm with the sky a nearly cloudless blue. The footman showed them to the large lawn at the back of the house where a number of guests, mostly female, were already present. Long tables had been set up and a number of servants were bringing out trays of food.

Lady Jessica broke away from a small group of ladies when she saw them. She came forward, lovely in a white-sprigged muslin gown tied with a dark green sash and a bonnet trimmed with matching green ribbon. She greeted them, a smile of pleasure on her face.

'I am so glad you could come. How pretty you both look!'

'And so do you,' Sophia said with an answering smile.

Lady Jessica turned to Julia. 'Nicholas has already arrived. I fear, however, the men have already abandoned us to look at the trout stream.' She made a little face.

'Men have a habit of doing such things,' Julia said lightly, trying to ignore the reference to Nicholas. She planned to stay as far away from him as possible.

'Julia?'

She turned and found Robert Haslett standing at her elbow. 'Robert, how nice to see you,' she said, surprised.

He smiled, his eyes crinkling at the corners. 'And how nice to see you as well.'

Jessica looked from one to the other. 'I did not know you knew each other.'

'We are old friends,' he said. His gaze fell on Sophia. 'I do not believe we have met,' he said slowly.

Sophia smiled at him in her friendly way. 'No, we have not.'

Julia quickly performed the introductions. Sophia held out her hand and Robert bowed over it. 'I did not realise Stanton had such a lovely sister,' he said, releasing her hand.

Colour rose to her cheeks. 'I did not realise you knew my brother.'

Several new guests arrived and Jessica excused herself to greet them. 'Shall we find a place to sit?' Robert asked. 'There are some chairs under the trees or we can sit on a spread if you would prefer.'

'Oh, I would like to sit on the spread,' Sophia said. 'I think when one is on a picnic one should be on the grass. Or at least as close to it as possible.'

Robert smiled down at her. 'I agree.'

They found a spot under a spreading oak and seated themselves. Sophia and Robert were soon chattering away with an easy familiarity as if they had known each other a very long time. Watching his rather sober face light up with a smile at something Sophia said, Julia thought he was decidedly smitten.

She could hardly blame him. The light blue of Sophia's gown brought out the lovely blue of her eyes and her porcelain cheeks glowed with soft colour. A pang of envy shot through her.

Not because she wanted Robert for herself. She had always liked him very much, but her feelings were those of a sister. And she could think of no two people who were more deserving of happiness than Sophia and Robert.

So, why did she have such a feeling of longing? She certainly had no desire to fall in love again, to lose herself in another person so completely as she had Thomas. When he died, she felt as if she had died with him.

'Julia? Are you well? You have been so quiet.' Sophia was watching her with concern.

'I was merely thinking. I am fine.' She smiled and attempted to shake off the melancholy that had gripped her for a moment.

Sophia's face relaxed and she smiled back at Julia, a hint of mischief in her eyes. 'Nicholas has returned, I see.'

'Has he?' Julia said with as much disinterest as she could muster. Why did everyone think she was interested in his whereabouts? First Jessica, and now Sophia.

'He is over near the tables.'

'How nice.' She kept her gaze fixed on the stream.

Sophia gave her a peculiar look. Just then Adam appeared near the tables and announced it was time to eat. Robert promptly rose and offered to fetch a plate for each of the ladies.

Sophia looked after him for a moment and then turned to Julia. 'Have you quarrelled with Nicholas?'

Having expected Sophia to comment on Robert, Julia was startled. 'Of course not. Why would you think that?'

'Because he has been casting the most dark glances this way.'

'I have no idea why. We hardly know each other well enough to quarrel.'

Sophia stood. 'Then you won't object if I invite him to sit with us.'

'Sophia!' But Sophia had already walked off towards the tables.

She could get up and leave herself. But that would be too obvious. Besides, whom else would she sit with? Except for Lady Jessica and her husband, and George, she hardly knew anyone else. She was not about to sit near George.

Perhaps Nicholas would refuse. There were undoubtedly a dozen other guests he knew. She stole a glance towards the tables and then nearly blanched. Nicholas was heading in her direction, two full plates of food in his hands. She scooted over onto the other side of the tree. And then felt ridiculous. He might not even be coming in her direction.

Her hopes were dashed when two well-muscled legs clad in buckskin breeches appeared in front of her. She stared at his boots and froze.

'Good day, Lady Carrington.'

Her eyes flew to his face. 'Lord Thayne.' He had a stiff cool look on his face that did not bode well.

'Sophia asked me to bring you a plate of food.'

'How kind,' she said faintly.

'She also invited me to join you.'

'Please sit down.' What else could she say?

He did in a remarkably graceful fashion for a man with two full plates in his hand. She probably would have spilled both of them. He held out one to her. 'This is for you.'

'Thank you,' she said, taking it and then staring down at it. The plate was piled high with lobster patties, and chicken and salad. Even if she had an appetite, she could hardly eat that much food.

'You do not care for lobster patties?' he asked.

She looked up. 'I do. It is only—how much food do you think I can eat in one sitting?'

He made a wry face. 'I beg your pardon. I fear I am out of the habit of procuring plates of food for ladies. I did not want you to go hungry.'

'That seems unlikely.'

He settled back against the tree trunk and balanced the plate of food across his legs. 'So, Haslett is here as well. I imagine you were pleased to see him again,' he said casually.

'Yes, of course.'

'Have you seem him often since your husband's death?'

'No.' She was puzzled by his question, but even more by the fact he was not looking at her. 'The other night was the first time since shortly after Thomas's death.'

'But you know him well.'

'Yes.' She glanced at him. 'Why are you asking? Do you think he has something to do with…with Thomas?'

'No,' he said shortly.

'Then why the questions?'

He shrugged. 'I merely wondered why you were holding his hand at Thérèse's.' He forked a piece of chicken and brought it to his mouth.

She nearly dropped her plate. He had seen that? And why ever was he bringing it up now? 'If you must know, he had just told me he lost his wife. I was offering him sympathy,' she said icily.

'I am sorry.' He was silent a moment and then he looked at her. 'Do you always hold men's hands when you offer sympathy?'

'No. Not that it is any of your concern.'

'Would you hold mine if I needed sympathy?'

Her mouth fell open. 'I beg your pardon?'

'I was merely inquiring as to how far your sympathy would extend. So, would you?'

Heat stole into her cheeks. 'This is a…a most ridiculous conversation! Have you had too much wine?' She had no idea how to read his mood. And where were Sophia and Robert?

'Not yet.' He put his fork down. 'I've made a few inquiries,' he said abruptly.

'Inquiries?' Her mind was blank for a moment. 'Oh! Have you discovered anything?' she asked.

He started to speak and then looked over her shoulder. 'Sophia and Haslett are returning.'

No further opportunities for conversation presented themselves. Robert seated himself beside her and Sophia sat next to Nicholas. They were soon joined by several other guests. Robert looked at Julia's plate. 'You have not eaten much.'

She smiled. 'It would be hard to tell with so much food.'

His mouth curved in an answering smile. 'Very true.' He sobered. 'Have you learned anything more about Thomas's death?' he asked in a low voice.

'Not very much.' She debated whether to tell him that Nicholas was helping her and decided against it. She feared it would make things more complicated.

'I will be glad to help you any way I can,' Robert said.

She flashed him a grateful smile. 'Thank you.'

'I do not like the idea of you making the sort of inquiries you did at Thérèse's.'

He was starting to sound like Nicholas. And every other male in her life. She glanced at Nicholas and found he was watching her with a cool, impenetrable stare, as if he'd caught her in some wrongdoing. Had he overheard? She hastily turned her gaze back to Robert. 'I am doing nothing dangerous. You must tell me how long you have been in England and how you find it after living away for such a time.'

He complied and they spent the rest of the meal in an easy discussion which Sophia soon joined. Julia had a difficult time keeping her mind on the conversation. She

was all too aware of Nicholas, who seemed to be engaged
in a flirtation with Lady Serena Lyndon, the dashing
daughter of the Earl of Mooreland. She was a young
woman with a sultry voice and equally sultry dark eyes.
Too sultry, in Julia's opinion, for someone who could not
be much past twenty. Despite her intention to ignore him,
she found herself glancing their way, only to be met by
the maddening sight of Nicholas actually smiling at
something Lady Serena said. She felt like throwing her
plate at him. How dare he smile at Lady Serena when he
did nothing but glare at her?

But why should he do anything else? She had done
nothing but bring him trouble and had managed to em-
broil him in her affairs. He had made it clear, perhaps
not in so many words, that he was only doing so out of
some sense of guilt over the lady he had loved.

She took a few more bites and set her plate down.
Sophia and Robert had fallen into conversation again.
Julia stood and Sophia looked up. 'I thought I might take
a short walk,' Julia said.

'Do you wish us to go with you?' Robert asked.

She shook her head and smiled. 'And disturb you when
you are so comfortable? I will not go far.'

She walked across the lawn towards the stream. She
saw George watching her and hoped he would not decide
to accompany her. She was not in the mood for his odd
remarks. However, one of his cronies said something to
him and he turned away.

A narrow dirt path ran along one side of the stream.
She started along the walk, the sun warm and pleasant
on her arms. The stream bank was shaded by trees and
a tangle of shrubs. After a while, she stopped to watch
the water as it tumbled over the rocks into a deeper pool
before continuing on its way. The gurgle of the stream

and the chirping of the birds were the only sounds she heard and she realised she had gone farther than she had intended.

She stood for a few moments and reluctantly turned around. And then gasped. Nicholas stood behind her, his arms folded across his chest. 'What the devil are you doing?' he demanded.

She lifted her chin. 'I am taking a walk, which should be quite obvious.'

'What is quite obvious is you are by yourself.'

'Not quite. You are here.' She gave him a defiant little smile.

He took a step towards her. 'Now I am.' He sounded as if he was about to lose all patience. 'Before I was not, which means you were alone. Which means, my dear, if someone decided to cause you harm, you would have no recourse.'

She had not thought of that, but she wasn't about to let him know. 'At a private picnic? How ridiculous, Lord Thayne.'

His brow snapped further down. 'You do not know that.'

'No?' she said sweetly. 'And you do not know that someone will. At any rate, my welfare is none of your concern.' She had no idea what she hoped to accomplish by goading him in such a way, but ever since she had watched him with Lady Serena she had been possessed with the strongest urge to annoy him.

'Isn't it, my dear?' He came towards her, his expression black. Despite her resolution to remain still she found herself backing towards the stream.

His face changed. 'Julia! Stop!'

But it was too late. Her foot caught in an exposed root; the next thing she knew, she was tumbling backwards down the sloping bank. She hit the water with a splash and went under for a moment before she came up, gasping. Her feet slipped on the rocks, but she managed to grab a branch before she fell again. Suddenly Nicholas was in the water beside her.

He grabbed her arms and pulled her up. She landed against his chest and he staggered as he pulled her up onto the gently sloped bank. He fell back on the bank with her and suddenly she was on top of him and staring down into his face.

'Are you all right?' he asked. 'My God! You could have drowned!'

'I can swim.' Her mouth barely formed the words. She was wet and stunned and all she could think of was the fact his brown eyes were flecked with gold and his lashes were thick and long. And his mouth was a mere breath away from her own.

His eyes darkened and suddenly she could not breathe. 'Good,' he whispered. His hand tangled in her hair and, just before he pulled her to him, she realised her bonnet was gone.

She closed her eyes. His lips were warm and firm as they moved over hers in a gentle caress. The warmth from his body seeped through the dampness of her clothes. His arm now draped across her back moulded her to his hard male curves.

Her lips parted under the insistent pressure of his mouth and his tongue slipped inside her mouth. He tasted male and intriguing. A slow heat began to form in her stomach. Through her thin damp gown she could feel the evidence of an answering desire.

Evidence that suddenly brought her to her senses. Whatever was she doing? Her eyes flew open. He abruptly removed his mouth from hers and stared at her for a moment, his expression dazed.

'Perhaps I should get up,' she whispered.

He released her. Embarrassed, she rolled off of him and sat up. Reality returned as quickly as the loss of his warmth. She was in a dirty, wet gown with her hair hanging down her back. She undoubtedly looked like a half-drowned puppy.

Nicholas had sat up beside her. She stole a quick glance and saw his breeches were wet and his coat spotted with water. 'I am sorry,' she said, averting her gaze.

'Why?'

'Because of me you are now wet. I have probably ruined your clothes.'

'The kiss more than made up for any damage you might have done to my attire.'

She started. 'The…the kiss?'

Although she still stared at the stream, she could almost see his brow rise. 'Yes, the kiss. Perhaps you recall? The exercise where our lips met and…'

This time she did look at him. His expression was quizzical. 'I know perfectly well what we did!' she snapped. 'Please, I would rather not discuss it!' It was bad enough she had allowed such a thing to happen. Worse had been her response. And her desire for much more.

He stared at her for a moment. 'Very well,' he said shortly. He stood up in one smooth movement and then held out his hand to her. 'I need to get you back to the house.'

She put her hand in his and he helped her to her feet. She started to pull her hand out of his warm grasp, but his grip only tightened. 'Wait,' he said.

She looked up at him, puzzled by his tone.

'Did you really think I meant to hurt you?' he asked.

'I beg your pardon?'

'Before you fell. You were backing away from me.' He gave a short laugh. 'As if you thought I was going to hurt you.'

For an odd moment, she glimpsed the vulnerability beneath his cool façade. 'Oh, no!' she said. 'That was not it at all. For a moment, you looked rather fierce, but I was not really afraid of you. I just stepped away and then I tripped.' Impulsively, she laid a hand on his arm. 'I do not think you would ever hurt me.'

He stood very still and looked down at her hand. 'No. I would not hurt you.'

'So you need not blame yourself. It was an accident.'

He lifted his head. 'Was the kiss an accident as well?'

'Yes. I think so.'

A slight smile touched his lips. 'You are not certain? Should we find out?'

Her pulse quickened. 'I think that is a very dangerous idea.'

'Undoubtedly. But everything about you is dangerous.' He cupped the back of her neck with a gentle hand and her eyes fluttered shut as he bent his head. His lips touched hers and then he suddenly jerked his head up. 'Damn.'

Her eyes flew open. Nicholas dropped his hands, his gaze going to something over her shoulders. With a feeling of dread, she slowly turned. George and Lady Serena stood in the clearing at the top of the slight rise from the stream. Behind them was Adam Henslowe.

George smiled. 'Well, perhaps this means there is to be an interesting announcement after all.'

Nicholas moved so he half-shielded her from the others. 'She fell into the stream,' he said coolly.

'Which, of course, explains why you were embracing her,' George said, his voice bland.

Nicholas started towards him, the look on his face murderous. Julia stood rooted, unable to move. Lady Serena gasped.

Adam caught his arm. 'Nick,' he said in a low voice. 'Lady Carrington is cold. Perhaps we should take her back to the house.'

Nicholas stopped. He stared at George in such a way, that for once, the smirk vanished from George's face.

'Was it really necessary to spoilsport, Mr Henslow?' Lady Serena inquired archly.

'Yes,' Adam said curtly. He walked down the bank to Julia's side. He asked no questions and merely removed his coat. 'Put this over your shoulders. Jessica can loan you some dry clothes.'

'Thank you.' She found she was shivering, but it was not only from the cold.

They made it back to the others without bloodshed. Adam stayed at her side as if he intended to protect her. She dared not glance at Nicholas, who walked on Adam's other side. George and Lady Serena trailed behind them in silence. When they finally reached the lawn behind the house, Sophia ran to her side, her eyes wide with worry. 'Julia? What happened?'

'I fell into the stream. Lord Thayne pulled me out.' Julia avoided looking at him.

'Nicholas?' Sophia turned to him. 'Thank goodness you were there. But how did such a thing come to happen?'

Julia touched her arm. 'It…it was such a stupid thing. I tripped.' Despite the coat she was starting to shake again.

By now the other guests had gathered around with

murmurs of sympathy and shock. Jessica appeared at her side and took her arm. 'Come, we will go in the house.'

An hour later, Julia sat in Jessica's dressing room on a chaise-longue, a quilt over her knees and a cup of hot tea on the small table next to her. Jessica had been everything that was kind, sending the maid to help Julia out of her wet clothes, and to clean the mud from her skin and hair. After that she had provided her with a change of dry clothing.

And then Jessica had left Julia in her dressing room and told her she must rest before joining the others. But now, in the quiet of the room, Julia's mind refused to co-operate. How could she have been so stupid? Not only to fall into a stream, but to allow Nicholas to kiss her? Not that it was entirely his fault. She had kissed him back, which somehow made it even worse.

And then to be discovered in such a way! She wanted to shudder every time she thought of it. Adam had said nothing but George had had a most odd gleam in his eye. And what of Lady Serena? Could she be discreet enough to keep what she saw to herself? It was only a kiss after all. And a very discreet one. Not like the first one. If the others had arrived a few minutes earlier…this time she did shudder.

Besides, neither she nor Nicholas were married, and she was a widow, not a innocent young debutante, so perhaps nothing would be made of the incident.

She could only pray so.

Adam entered the dressing room just as Nicholas finished tucking the loaned shirt into a pair of Adam's black breeches. His shoulders were broader than his cousin's and his legs longer so the items were tight, but at least they were dry.

'You look a bit more civilized,' Adam remarked, leaning against the doorway.

Nicholas grimaced. 'I feel more civilized. I will own, the swim was unexpected.'

'I doubt Lady Carrington expected it either.'

Nicholas cast a swift glance at his cousin. 'How is she?' he asked cautiously. He'd hardly blame her if she refused to speak to him again after today. His behaviour had been despicable in every regard. He'd allowed the wholly unexpected and possessive jealousy he had felt over Haslett's attentions to her override his judgment. So, when she had ended up in his arms, her soft curves pressing against him, her lovely face hovering over him, he had not been able to resist.

Of course, if that wasn't enough, he had kissed her again and then tried to mow Kingsley down.

'Jessica has loaned her dry clothing. She is in Jess's private drawing room.' Adam eyed Nicholas curiously. 'I must commend her, she seems to be quite composed considering she not only fell into a stream but was caught with you in a rather compromising position.'

To his chagrin, Nicholas felt heat creep up his neck. He gave a short laugh. 'Don't be fooled, she probably hopes she'll never lay eyes on me again.'

'I somehow doubt that,' Adam said. 'You played rather nicely into George's hands, you know. I will say nothing, but I cannot vouch for Lady Serena, although I hope she realises it would not be in her best interest to spread rumours. But Kingsley is another matter. Have you thought what you'll do if he decides to use this to further his cause?'

Nicholas turned around and stared at him. 'What will I do? As much as I am loath to give Kingsley the satisfaction, he will win his wager.' He smiled grimly. 'I will marry her.'

# Chapter Twelve

Sophia set down her coffee cup and looked at Julia, who was seated across from her at breakfast. 'I do not wish to pry, but did something happen between you and Nicholas? Beside your falling in the stream?'

Julia glanced quickly up from her nearly untouched plate of toast. 'Why do you ask?'

'You have been so subdued since yesterday. Nicholas was not much better. In fact, after you both changed your clothes and returned to the company, you appeared to be avoiding one another.' She made a little face. 'I fear I was not the only one who thought so. Did you quarrel?'

'No, we did not quarrel.' If only that had been all that had happened.

'Are you certain?' Sophia asked. 'He wore such a black look when he saw you had gone to walk along the stream and then when he followed you, I feared he meant to say something dreadful to you! And if he did, I will make him extremely sorry!'

Julia stared at her, astounded by the vehemence in her friend's voice. Sophia looked so militant, Julia feared she really would say something to Nicholas if she did not learn the truth. 'He kissed me.'

'Good heavens!' Sophia exclaimed. Her eyes widened for a moment, and then her mouth curved in a smile. 'I wondered when he would get around to doing so.'

'Sophia!'

'It is quite obvious he has wanted to for an age.' Her blue eyes sparkled with teasing laughter. 'Good heavens! I am not certain you both needed to be so glum about it, however.'

Julia sighed. 'That is not the whole of it.' She might as well confess everything. She feared it would soon reach Sophia's ears any way. 'George, Lady Serena and Mr Henslowe saw us.'

'Oh, dear.' The teasing look left Sophia's face. 'That was rather unfortunate.' She paused and then asked delicately, 'Was it a very…that is, a very complicated kiss?'

'A complicated kiss?' Julia stared for a moment and then Sophia's meaning dawned upon her. 'No, that particular kiss was not.' And then felt her face heat. She hadn't meant to disclose there had been more than one.

'Well, that isn't so bad,' Sophia said doubtfully.

'But that isn't the worst.' Julia took a deep breath. 'George made some stupid remark about whether there was to be an announcement and Nich—Lord Thayne started towards him. If Mr Henslowe had not stopped him, I think he would have knocked George down. Lady Serena accused Mr Henslowe of spoiling sport.'

'Oh, dear,' Sophia said again. 'Shall I speak to Phillip? He can handle George, although I do not know what to do about Lady Serena.'

'Please do not say anything to Phillip.' He took the promise he made to Thomas to watch over her too seriously. The rift between him and George was too great already and she did not want to widen it further. Most certainly she did not want to cause any tension between him and Nicholas.

'But…' Sophia began.

'Please, I am certain everything will be fine.' She gave Sophia a reassuring smile. 'I do not want Phillip to worry about this as well.'

'If you are certain.' Sophia pushed her coffee cup away and then eyed Julia. 'So there was another more complicated kiss?'

Julia's face heated. 'I am certain it was merely an aberration.'

'Perhaps, but did you like it?'

'Sophia!'

'Well, you must have if there was a second one. And for some reason, I expect he does it very well.' Sophia arched a delicate brow. 'Well, does he?'

'Sophia. Yes. I…I suppose so. I haven't had much experience. Just Thomas.' Which was something else that had completely bewildered her. She had never thought that after Thomas she would desire another man's kisses.

'So you did like it.'

Why lie? Sophia had always said she was too transparent to tell a believable falsehood. 'Yes, but I wish I had not.'

'It has been three years since Thomas,' Sophia said gently. 'I do not think it is wrong for you to like another man's kisses.'

'I do not wish to like his.' Julia gave Sophia a shaky smile. 'My association with him seems to be nothing but disastrous. I have made up my mind about one thing, however. I intend to avoid him until I leave London.'

'Well, I don't wish to overset you, but I fear that will be rather difficult.' She gave Julia an apologetic little smile. 'Lord Monteville has sent us an invitation to join him in his box tonight at the opera. Nicholas will be there as well.'

After breakfast, Sophia sat down at the small desk in one corner of the library to answer her correspondence. Julia paced to the window and looked out at the street. The grey sky drizzled rain. Except for the green grass in the centre of the square, she could see nothing but the buildings. A wave of homesickness for Foxwood washed over her. Barbara and Eduardo would take good care of the farm and its four-legged residents, but she missed them very much.

She turned away from the window. How much longer could she stay in London? Her search for Thomas's killer seemed to be fraught with difficulties and had become inextricably entwined with Nicholas. Perhaps Phillip was right—there was nothing more to his death than a mere robbery.

Was there a way of ever knowing?

Which was perhaps the question she had to answer before she considered leaving London. And she did not know how else to do so without involving Nicholas.

The one man she should, if she had an ounce of sense, avoid. Particularly after yesterday.

This was ridiculous. She could not afford to waste time thinking about a kiss. It had meant nothing. Not to her. Or to Nicholas. It was obvious he still cared deeply for the woman he had loved and lost, just as she still cared for Thomas. As she had told Sophia, yesterday had been an aberration for both of them.

Nicholas had just entered White's when Phillip appeared at his side. 'I need to speak to you,' he said without preamble.

'Of course. I had no idea you were back in town.'

'I arrived late last night.' From the grim look on Phillip's face, Nicholas suspected the interview was not for pleasure. Had he already got wind of yesterday's débâcle?

He followed Phillip to a table in the morning room. The older man waited until they were seated and the waiter had taken their order before speaking. 'There are rumours you have been inquiring after Thomas's death. Is this true?'

'I have made a few inquiries.'

Phillip frowned. 'Why?'

'Because the alternative is to have Lady Carrington do so.'

'She has told you her suspicions?'

'She has told me she is determined to discover who killed her husband. However, I do not think it safe for her to go about asking questions on her own.'

'And so you offered to do it for her. I see.' Phillip leaned back. 'Very wise of you, but unnecessary. I assume you have discovered nothing useful.'

'No.' Unless he counted the information Julia learned from Haslett. Information Phillip already knew.

'I thought not. Certainly not after so much time has passed.'

'But you have not been able to convince Lady Carrington of that,' Nicholas said.

'No.' Phillip's brows drew together. 'It is in a sense unfortunate she saw the ring again for it has given her hope that is most likely false. But perhaps if you continue to ask a few questions, it will satisfy her enough so she will cease asking questions on her own. I hope that in time she will let the matter rest.'

'Perhaps.' For some reason, the conversation made Nicholas uneasy but he could not quite pinpoint why.

Phillip adroitly changed the topic, but it did not concern Julia. Apparently, he had not yet heard any of the rumours. Or George had yet to spread them.

Phillip left White's an hour later. The sense of uneasiness Nicholas had felt with Phillip returned in full force. He had planned to visit Tattersall's to view the contents of a stable up for auction, but he changed his mind. Instead he headed for Grosvenor Square.

Monteville's secretary was seated at a table in the small room off the library. Colton looked up as Nicholas entered and stood. He was a serious young man with sandy hair and a pair of intelligent grey eyes.

'Good day, Lord Thayne.' He removed his spectacles. 'What may I do for you?'

Nicholas came to stand in front of the table. 'My grandfather has said you are at my disposal if needed.'

Colton nodded. 'Yes, he has said so on several occasions.'

'Then I have a task for you.' He doubted if his grandfather had quite intended that he should send his secretary out of London for a few days, but he would deal with that detail later.

# Chapter Thirteen

Phillip came to escort Sophia and Julia to the King's Theatre. Julia's apprehension that he had heard some sort of rumours about yesterday's affair appeared to be unfounded for he said nothing. She began to relax. Perhaps George and Lady Serena would not mention it after all. But as they travelled through the dark London streets, nervousness began to set in for another reason.

She dreaded meeting Nicholas.

She would pretend nothing had happened.

The street in front of the King's Theatre was filled with carriages. They were forced to wait until their carriage could stop near the entrance and then Phillip helped them down.

Julia had not been in the King's Theatre before. She was taken aback by the crowded lobby and the expensive, glittering clothing of the patrons. Sophia had told her no one was admitted unless in full dress.

She paused for a moment to let an elderly lady and two younger women pass, all dressed in magnificent silks and jewels, and then realised she had lost Sophia and Phillip in the crowd. Panic gripped her for a moment and then she calmed herself. Surely they would realize she was missing and wait for her. If not, she could ask someone to direct her to Lord Monteville's box.

And then someone touched her arm. She gasped and spun around.

Nicholas stood behind her. 'You seem to have lost your party already.'

'Oh!' Her hand went to her throat. Relief mixed with a dozen other emotions coursed through her. In pure black, relieved only by the white ruffles at his wrists and his white waistcoat and gloves, he looked incredibly handsome. Her mouth went dry, but she managed to say, 'What are you doing here?'

His brow rose quizzically. 'I am planning to watch an opera. And you?'

'The same, of course. That is, if I can determine where the rest of my party is.' She found herself smiling at him, so great was her relief.

He stared at her for a moment and then held out his arm. 'You are fortunate tonight, for I happen to be one of your party.'

'Yes.' She took his arm. 'Thank you. You do not know how worried I was. I know it is very silly of me but for a moment—' She realized she was babbling and stopped.

'For a moment you what?' He looked down at her, a slight smile on his face and for an instant, despite the crowd, she felt as if they were the only two people in the world. She was hardly aware of the voices and laughter swirling around them.

The awareness in his eyes mirrored her own. Her world suddenly seemed to shift and she caught her breath. 'I…I felt as if I was lost.'

He smiled. 'Here? But you are not. You are quite safe.'

'Yes.' She was now and she returned his smile.

'Ah. Determined to provide more fuel for the gossip mill, I see.' George appeared as if on cue beside them.

'Good evening, Kingsley,' Nicholas said coolly. He glanced down at Julia. 'Perhaps we should continue on to the box.'

Gone was the warmth that had sprang up between them. She felt bereft, as if the sun had suddenly disappeared behind a dark cloud. 'Of course.'

They proceeded across the lobby and up the staircase. George walked on Julia's other side. Apparently oblivious to the fact his presence was unwelcome, he filled Julia's ears with a steady stream of arch comments on the dress of everyone they passed. His monologue, combined with Nicholas's tense silence, threatened to set her nerves on edge.

Despite her trepidation at spending an evening in Lord Monteville's box, Julia was nearly weak with relief when they reached it. Her relief increased when she saw that Sophia and Phillip were already there with the Earl.

Nicholas released her arm. Sophia greeted them with a pleased smile and then turned to Julia. 'I do hope you are not too angry with us, but by the time I noticed you were not with us I saw that Nicholas had found you and I knew he would see you here.'

'And I found them and made certain they actually reached the box. Otherwise, I fear they intended to spend the evening in the lobby, staring at one another,' George said.

Julia's cheeks heated while Phillip gave him a cold look. 'I trust you will keep such speculations to yourself.'

George shrugged. 'I can, of course, but I fear I cannot control what others might think. I merely wished to protect Julia from gossip.'

'Since there is nothing to cause gossip, she has no need

of your protection,' Nicholas drawled. His face held supreme indifference, but his stance was that of a tiger about to spring.

'Isn't there, Thayne?' George drawled.

Nicholas took a step forward. 'What the devil do you mean by that?' he asked in a low voice.

Julia froze, the blood pounding in her ears. The scene had all the horrible familiar aspect of a recurring nightmare. They would not possibly start a brawl in front of their families and most of the *ton*?

'I fear you are both forgetting your manners,' Monteville said. His gaze rested on Julia. 'Lady Carrington would undoubtedly like to take her seat and, since you are blocking the entrance to the box, you are rendering that impossible. Lady Carrington, perhaps you would do me the honour of sitting next to me?'

His calm words broke the standstill. 'I beg your pardon,' Nicholas said stiffly. He moved aside and, without looking at him, Julia took her place next to the Earl. To her dismay, she found her hands were trembling.

George executed an elaborate bow. 'A most interesting encounter as usual. Good evening to all.'

Julia didn't dare look at anyone. Her throat was dry and her stomach was knotted and she wanted nothing more than to disappear.

'My dear, there is nothing to distress yourself about,' Monteville said gently.

She looked swiftly up at him. 'I am very sorry.'

He raised a brow. 'I cannot imagine why. Unless of course, you deliberately provoked the regrettable behaviour of both my grandson and Lord George.'

'No, I did not, my lord, but—'

'Then you've nothing to reproach yourself for. I suggest you enjoy the performance and put the rest of this from your mind.' He spoke kindly but firmly.

She managed a smile. 'I will try.'

'Good. Have you been to the King's Theatre before?' he asked.

'I have not.' She tried to follow his lead, keeping her voice polite and conversational as if nothing untoward had happened.

She found any sort of concentration impossible once the performance began. She scarcely noticed when the curtain came down and the interval arrived. Their box was suddenly filled with visitors and she found herself smiling and nodding and attempting to respond to the remarks addressed to her. The effort was tiring. Lady Middleton entered the box with her eldest daughter and soon cornered Nicholas. She only relaxed when Robert appeared and engaged her and Sophia in conversation. She glanced at Nicholas once and found him regarding her with a dark expression. She looked quickly away. What was wrong with him now?

She was taken aback, however, when they finally took their seats for the second half, to find him taking the place next to her. She cast him a startled glance. His brow shot up. 'I am merely sitting by you, not planning a ravishment.'

'I hardly thought that!'

'Good. I wouldn't want Kingsley's remarks to worry you.'

'I assure you they did not. I have scarcely given them a thought.'

'No?' He looked completely disbelieving.

'No!' She frowned at him. 'Perhaps we should watch the performance.' She turned away. They were speaking in low tones, but she feared they would be overheard.

'If you wish. Although I wasn't aware you paid much heed to the first half.'

She looked back and levelled her most cool look at him. 'And how would you know?'

'Because I was watching you.' He gave her a satisfied smile.

'You should have been watching the stage.'

'You are more interesting.'

She flushed in spite of herself. 'I assure you I am not!' She turned away again, determined not to respond to anything else he might say. To her immense relief, he said no more.

Flustered, she stared at the stage. Had he been flirting with her? No, that was completely impossible.

Nicholas stole a glance at Julia's delicate profile. From all appearances, she was so engrossed in the performance his presence was completely forgotten. The only thing that gave her away was that if he so much as shifted, her hand tensed around her fan.

Or if he stared at her as he was doing now. He slowly pulled his gaze away and back to the stage where the soprano was singing an impassioned aria. Why the devil did he persist in teasing her?

He scowled. He knew perfectly well why. Teasing her was a mask for his real desire. A desire to pull her into his arms and make love to her until she lost all resistance.

And then what? She was not the sort of woman he wanted as a mistress. His few liaisons since Mary's death had been with upper-class women who expected nothing more from him than his body and a few expensive jewels. He had quickly curtailed the one relationship that might have promised more.

But even if he were to make such a foolish proposition,

she would never accept. He'd seen the awareness in her eye, but she would fight him every step of the way. Three years ago, before Mary, before his world had shattered, he might have considered Julia a challenge and set out to seduce her with very little conscience. But that was before he learned that the emotions of others were not something that could be so carelessly dismissed in the pursuit of pleasure.

Nor were his.

With a start, he realised the audience was applauding. Had the interminable performance ended at last? Apparently so, for the music had ceased and the singers were on stage taking their final bows.

The party made their way out of the box and to one of the downstairs rooms where they waited for the carriages to be brought around. The room was crowded and conversation difficult. Although he had determined he would avoid Julia as much as possible, he was hardly gratified to find she apparently had the same thought in mind.

When they finally made their way to where the long line of carriages waited, she kept to Sophia's side.

Which was why, when she stumbled, he had no hope of catching her.

She fell directly into the street between two carriages. Sophia screamed. The startled horses shied back and heedless of the prancing animals, Nicholas shot forward, terrified she would be crushed.

She had fallen face first. He barely registered that Haslett had sprung forward to calm the horses. Nicholas reached down and lifted her into his arms and carried her out of danger. Her face was pale and her eyes fluttered open to look at him. 'Oh, dear,' she said weakly.

'Don't try to talk.' He levelled a frown at her. 'Do you hurt anywhere?'

She gave him a faint smile. 'How can I answer that if I can't talk? Please, my lord, put me down.'

'No.'

The horrified crowd had gathered around. Sophia, her face white, had just pushed past a large gentleman when someone touched Nicholas's shoulder. He turned and saw Robert Haslett at his side. His face mirrored Nicholas's own shock. 'Perhaps it would be best if you brought Julia to my carriage,' Haslett said. 'I regret to say, it is the one she nearly fell in front of.'

Hell. Haslett was one of the last persons he wanted to entrust Julia with. He was about to refuse when Sophia spoke up. 'That would be very kind. Do you not think, Nicholas?'

Julia made a movement in his arms. 'Please, I'd rather walk.'

'Not now.' He hesitated. He had no intention of putting her down. But making his way through the crowd to Stanton's or his grandfather's carriage seemed impossible.

'This is not the time to let your personal feelings overcome common sense,' Haslett said with more than a touch of irony.

Nicholas looked at him for a moment. 'You are right.'

He carried her to the carriage and set her gently on the seat. She looked as pale and fragile as she had the night she'd been hurt at Foxwood. A fierce desire to protect her surged through him. 'How do you feel?' His voice was more abrupt than he intended.

'I am fine. Just horribly mortified. To fall on my face in front of half of London.' Her voice trembled as if she was about to cry.

He resisted the urge to gently touch her cheek. 'There is no need to concern yourself over that. In the future, however, you'd best step into a carriage rather than the street.'

His feeble attempt at humour brought a faint smile to her face. Then her brow creased. 'I really had not meant to take a step at all.'

Before he could ask what she meant, he heard Phillip's voice behind him. 'How is she?'

He turned. 'Well enough under the circumstances.'

'Thank God.' Phillip's face wore a peculiar expression.

Nicholas frowned. In the commotion he realised he'd paid scant heed to the whereabouts of either Phillip or his grandfather. And the fact they had not been at Julia's side was decidedly odd. 'What is it?'

Phillip hesitated and then spoke in a low voice. 'Several witnesses claim she was pushed.'

Nicholas felt as if he'd been punched. His mind searched for any other rational explanation. 'How can they be certain? There is enough of a crowd that it would be impossible to tell. Perhaps she was merely jostled.' Even to his own ears his words sounded feeble.

'I would have said the same except for the identity of one of the witnesses. His impression I cannot question.' Phillip looked straight at him. 'You see, Monteville saw the entire incident.'

# Chapter Fourteen

Nicholas had just left his bank the following morning when he once again saw Ernest Grayson. Grayson was descending the steps of Fisk and Fisk, a business on the opposite side of the street, with the furtive air often seen in those visiting a moneylender.

Grayson was as soberly and inconspicuously dressed as he had been when he had first approached Nicholas. The older man looked down the street both ways and then started off.

Nicholas dashed across the road, heedless of the disgruntled traffic. Grayson was just about to cross the next street when Nicholas came up behind him.

He turned and his face paled. Nicholas smiled coolly. 'I have been hoping to find you again.'

Grayson eyed him with disfavour. He was a thin, neatly dressed man in his mid-thirties with the air of a harried clerk. 'Indeed, my lord. I had the most distinct impression that you had no desire to pursue the matter any further.'

'I've changed my mind. I wish to talk to you.'

Grayson gave him a hassled look. 'I do not know if the offer is still open. I would need to consult with my client first. If you will pardon me, I have another appointment.' He started across the street.

Nicholas fell into step beside him. 'Precisely who is your client? I am beginning to think I should deal with him directly.'

Grayson looked straight ahead. 'I cannot tell you.'

'You cannot or will not?'

He hesitated a fraction. 'Both.'

'I am willing to pay you handsomely for the information.'

Again hesitation. 'I think not, my lord.'

'Fisk is not known for his patience in waiting for repayment of his loans. I am certain he would not object if I offered to pay your debts. Of course, you would then be indebted to me.'

Grayson swallowed. 'I…' He cast a furtive look around as if he expected Fisk to pounce out of the shadows. 'I cannot discuss this here. Perhaps, my lord, we could meet elsewhere.'

'Your lodgings?'

'No!' He appeared almost terrified. 'I do not want you calling there. I fear that I may be followed. Tonight. At Vauxhall. I will be there with a small party. Four gentlemen and three ladies. We will arrive by boat and proceed to a private box where—'

'At the end of the Grand Walk. At eleven.' He feared the man was about to describe their supper plans next. 'And if you fail to meet me, I've no doubt I can discover your whereabouts easily enough.'

'Of course.' With a distracted expression, he dashed off.

Nicholas watched him go. He'd run Grayson to ground if the man failed to show up. After last night, he wanted more than anything to find out who was behind the attacks on Julia. He intended to make sure the man would rue his existence.

He walked to his carriage. Guilt mixed with anger had assailed him ever since last night. She had been injured under his nose. He had failed to protect her.

He could not fail again.

'Good day, Lord George!'

George urged his horse alongside the phaeton in which Lady Serena Lyndon sat with her widowed cousin, Mrs Harriet Winslet. He bowed and smiled. He knew Lady Serena's habit of driving daily in the park and had been lying in wait for her stylish phaeton.

After last night, it was time to play his hand.

Lady Serena was a notorious rumour-monger. The only thing that kept her from being ostracised was her huge fortune and the fact that most of the tales she spread had more than a hint of truth. He bestowed one of his most charming smiles upon them. 'Ah, two of England's most lovely flowers. Good day, Lady Serena, Mrs Winslet. I am delighted to see you both.'

Mrs Winslet smiled a trifle nervously. She was a timid woman who undoubtedly allowed her companion to ride roughshod over her. Lady Serena acknowledged the compliment with an insincere nod. 'And I am very delighted to see you, Lord George,' she said with a meaningful look.

'Indeed.'

'Yes.' She leaned forward a little. 'I was so concerned, as all of us were, about Lady Carrington. And since she is a guest of your aunt…I do hope she is quite well after such a terrible accident. Imagine! Being shoved in front of a carriage!'

'She is quite uninjured due to Lord Thayne's quick action in plucking her from harm's way.'

The mention of Thayne had the desired effect. Her eyes widened. 'Yes, it was fortuitous he was there. As he was near the stream. But then, he always seems to be at her side, does he not?'

'Indeed, he does seem to be underfoot a considerable amount of time. But perhaps under the circumstances it is understandable.'

'Really.' Her dark eyes opened even wider. 'But what circumstances are those?'

George smiled and shrugged apologetically. 'I fear I have said too much already. But suffice to say he has cause to be grateful to her. The highway robbery, you understand. And sometimes gratitude may lead to other…developments. As of yet, there is no announcement.' He paused and then looked uncomfortable. 'I pray you will say nothing.'

'Oh, most certainly not. I am the soul of discretion!' She settled back against the cushions with an excited air. He had no doubt she was already turning over the possibilities. He quite looked forward to the end result of her musings.

Satisfied he had fulfilled his goal of setting the cat among the pigeons, he engaged the ladies in a few more comments and insincere compliments before continuing on his way. The resulting gossip as well as a few other cats he planned to let loose should be quite effective in thrusting Julia and Thayne to the altar. And thrusting a considerable sum his way.

Nicholas took a pace around. He'd been standing in the appointed meeting place for the last ten minutes and there was no sign of Grayson. He scowled. He should have called on the man in his lodgings instead of trusting he would keep his word.

He would give him another quarter of an hour and then he'd hunt the man down. Discovering the man's lodgings had been easy enough. With a little enticement, Fisk had been more than willing to provide the information and Nicholas had already sent a servant around to verify Grayson indeed lodged there.

Nicholas had had the man followed. His servant had informed him Grayson had arrived with the party as he'd said. A half-hour before ten Grayson had slipped away and then Nicholas's man had lost him.

The path was now quiet. He could hear the sounds of the fireworks and assumed most of the crowd had gone to watch. And Grayson was not coming. He decided he would take a different path back in the chance Grayson had come another way.

He had not gone more than a few steps when he heard a rustle behind him. The hair on the back of his neck prickled. He started to turn, his hand on his pistol, But the blow came from the other direction.

He went down without a sound.

The abigail had just left the room after helping Julia dress when Sophia entered the bedchamber. Her normally calm face was filled with distress.

'Sophia?' She looked so dreadful Julia's heart slammed into her throat. 'What has happened? Are you ill?'

'No. 'Tis not me.' Sophia took a breath. 'Phillip was just here. He told me…oh, dear. It is Nicholas. He has been hurt.'

'Nicholas is hurt?' Julia stared at her, uncomprehendingly.

'He…he was attacked last night. At Vauxhall.'

The blood pounded in her head. 'Is…is he very hurt?' she whispered.

In a rush of concern, Sophia put her arm around Julia's waist. 'Oh, my dear, you must sit. Come.'

'No.' She looked into Sophia's face. 'I am fine. Please, just tell me about Nicholas. Is he conscious?'

'Oh, dear. I fear I am making a botch of this. He is conscious but with a rather nasty bump. The physician says he will be fine so you need not worry.'

'Thank God.' She sat down on the bed. 'But why was he at Vauxhall?'

'He was to meet a man there. A Mr Grayson.'

'Mr Grayson?' Julia turned to stare at Sophia. 'But that was the man who wanted to buy the ring.'

'Yes. He did not show up.' Sophia paused for a moment—still looking troubled. She sat down next to Julia and put her arm around Julia's waist. 'I fear that is not all. When Nicholas was attacked, the ring was stolen.'

'The ring?' For a moment she could hardly think what Sophia referred to and then she felt ill all over again. 'Oh, dear heaven.'

'I am so sorry. I know it meant so much to you and now it is gone again.'

'Oh, Sophia. The ring hardly matters.' She rose from the bed. 'In fact, I am beginning to think it is cursed.' She turned to look at Sophia. 'I must see Nicholas. Will you come with me?'

'Of course.' Sophia caught her hand and pressed her fingers against Julia's. 'We can leave as soon as you wish.'

# Chapter Fifteen

Nicholas scowled at his grandfather. 'I see no reason to spend my day lying about like a damnable invalid. I've a bump on my head, not an amputated limb.'

'None the less, you are to remain in bed a day.' Monteville looked down at him. 'Next time I hope you will inform us of any plans to accost suspects on your own. Particularly in secluded areas.'

'There wasn't time.' His gaze fell to his left hand and his mouth twisted bitterly. The pale line where the ring should be was a painful reminder of how much he had failed. 'I should have demanded the information from Grayson even if it meant abducting him.'

'He still may not have told you. You were fortunate you were not injured more seriously. If Grayson is to be found, I've no doubt Phillip will do so.'

Nicholas fell back against the pillows on the sofa and then winced. At least he had persuaded his grandfather to allow him downstairs in the library. He'd have felt even more like a foolish schoolboy if he had been forced to remain in his room.

The footman appeared in the doorway. 'Lady Carrington and Lady Simons, my lord.'

He sat back up and cursed. What the devil were they doing here? Julia was the last person he wanted to see. Certainly not in this condition. And not after losing the ring. 'I am obviously not receiving today.'

'I think it would be best if you were,' Monteville said. He turned to the footman. 'You may show them in.'

Nicholas forced himself to rise, and then folded his arms and stared at a point near the mantelpiece while the two ladies were shown in. His grandfather stepped forward to greet them.

'We came as soon as possible,' Sophia said. 'We were so worried about Nicholas. How…how is he?'

'You may ask me directly.' Nicholas said, taking a step. He ignored the sharp pain that shot through his head. 'I am quite well.'

'Should you not be in bed?' Sophia asked. Her wide blue eyes were filled with concern. 'You cannot be feeling at all the thing.'

'I assure you I am.'

'But you look quite pale,' she insisted. 'I think you should at least lay on the sofa.'

Julia spoke. 'I must agree with Sophia. You should not be up after such a blow.'

He turned his gaze upon her, trying not to notice how pretty her face looked beneath the wide rim of her bonnet. 'If I recall, you objected to my laying on your sofa.'

Her eyes met his. 'But this is your house and you may do as you please.'

He stared back at her. '*Touché*, my dear. And my pleasure is to remain standing. At least as long as you are.'

'Under the circumstances standing on such formality is ridiculous.'

His brow shot up. 'A pun, my dear?'

She looked as if she wanted to hit him, a circumstance

he considered most pleasing. He gave her a superior grin and leaned against the arm of the sofa.

Monteville regarded them with faint amusement. 'Perhaps you would not object to entertaining my grandson for a moment, Lady Carrington. I have recently purchased a pianoforte I intend to give to my granddaughter. I thought perhaps you would try it, Lady Simons, and give me your opinion.'

Sophia smiled. 'Of course. I would be delighted.' She ignored Julia's dismayed look.

Monteville glanced at Julia. 'I trust you will persuade my grandson to return to the sofa.'

Julia started and gave him a strained smile. 'I will try.'

Nicholas frowned after his grandfather. What the devil did he mean by leaving him alone with Julia? He stared at the panelled door as a staggering possibility hit him. Could it be his grandfather actually desired a match between himself and Julia?

The thought nearly made him reel.

'I really think you had best sit down.'

He jumped and stared at her. 'Sit down?'

'Yes.' She gave him an odd look. 'Perhaps you have heard of it, my lord? It is where one—'

'I know what it is.' He scowled at her. 'You first, my dear.'

Her face wore an odd expression and she sat on the nearest piece of furniture, an uncomfortable Queen Anne chair.

He took a seat on the sofa, remembering not to lean his head against the back. His head was beginning to hurt, but it hardly kept him from staring at her. The thought that Monteville might approve of her for his wife made his throat go dry. Not that she'd ever accept him willingly. Which would hardly stop his grandfather if he thought they were well suited. His sister's marriage was a case in point.

'Is there something wrong?' Her face now held concern. 'You look very strange.'

'Nothing is wrong.'

'Are you certain? You are pale.' The worry on her face was unnerving.

'I am fine,' he snapped. 'Did you call for a purpose?'

'Yes, if you must know,' she snapped back. 'I had wished to assure myself you were not seriously harmed, but if your rude manners are any indication you were not.'

'I beg your pardon,' he said stiffly. He rose again and went to stand near the mantelpiece. 'And I must beg your pardon for another matter as well. I fear I was robbed of your husband's ring.' He avoided her gaze.

'Sophia told me,' she said quietly.

'You are welcome to ring a peal over my head if you wish for my carelessness.'

He glanced back at her and was completely taken aback when she jumped up, fury written all over her face. 'If you must know, I do not care about the ring. What I do not understand, my lord, is why you were so idiotic to arrange such a dangerous meeting on your own in dark woods! You could have been killed!'

He stared at her as she came towards him. She stopped in front of him and glared. 'And do you know how I would have felt? Knowing you were murdered because of the stupid ring! In fact, I am glad the ring is gone! Perhaps whoever wants it is now satisfied and will stop hitting people over the head and shoving people in streets!' He blinked. She pointed a finger at his chest and he took a step back. 'And why? Why are you so horribly stubborn that you are not sitting down? Why are men so…so idiotic about these things?'

He had no idea if she was about to cry or strangle him. 'I…er…have no idea.' He caught her shoulders. 'My dear, there is no need to be so overset.'

She stared into his face. 'Yes…yes, there is.' Her voice trembled and her fine eyes filled with tears.

'Damn it,' he murmured. He pulled her into his arms and awkwardly patted her shoulder. Her body felt light and delicate against him and he leaned his head on her soft silky hair.

'Don't cry,' he murmured.

She sniffed and turned her head, but didn't pull away. His arms tightened around her and he pulled her more firmly against him. Which was a mistake. His desire to comfort her was rapidly becoming entwined with a desire to do much more. Such as complete the kiss he had started by the stream.

The sound of footsteps in the hall yanked him back to reality. He would play neatly into his grandfather's hand if he gave in to the impulse. And Kingsley's. He released her abruptly. His head did seem to be spinning. 'Perhaps you are right, I'd best sit down,' he said, his voice husky. He didn't move.

'Yes.' She looked as dazed as he felt. Her lips were slightly parted and he nearly groaned with the desire to taste them.

'Julia,' he murmured.

She swallowed. 'Should you not sit down?'

'I suppose I should.' His gaze remained fastened on her lips.

'I know Sarah will be delighted,' Sophia said from the doorway.

Nicholas jerked around and found Monteville and Sophia had both entered the room. His grandfather's look was curious, and to his embarrassment, he felt heat rise to his cheeks.

Julia backed away, her own cheeks flushed. 'I…I was just trying to persuade Lord Thayne to sit down.'

'Of course,' Monteville said blandly.

Nicholas moved to the sofa and sat. Julia took a seat as far away from him as possible. He wanted to curse. What the hell was wrong with him? He hadn't behaved in such a callow way since he was a youth in the throes of calf-love. Not even with Mary.

The thought was disturbing. And he had no idea why.

Julia forced a smile on her face as Sophia presented her to Lady Catherine Reynolds, a formidable dowager with a double chin, an intimidating bosom and a pair of sharp grey eyes. Julia and Sophia had just reached the door leading from Mrs Hawkesbury's crowded drawing room when Lady Catherine had intercepted them.

She fixed Julia with a piercing stare. 'So, you are the young woman who is causing such a stir.'

Julia was perplexed, as she had been all evening, by such mysterious remarks. She was also rather tired of them. This was the first time she and Sophia had been out in company since the opera three evenings ago. Were they referring to her being pushed in front of a carriage? She managed a polite little smile. 'Indeed. Surely such a mishap shouldn't cause that much of a stir, Lady Catherine.'

Lady Catherine cackled. 'A mishap? It was a bit more than a mere mishap, I should think. And a most fortunate one for you. As for it causing a stir, why should it not? One of the *coups* of the season.'

Julia met Sophia's eyes. She looked as confused as

Julia. Sophia turned to Lady Catherine. 'I fear we do not know what you are referring to. Lady Carrington's accident was most unfortunate and we are only thankful she was not seriously injured.'

'Which you owe to Lord Thayne, do you not?' She cackled again. 'That only served as confirmation. But I can see you intend to keep it under wraps, although it is a bit too late, I fear. Best make an announcement and get it over.'

After a few polite remarks they managed to extricate themselves from Lady Catherine and slipped into the hallway. It was only a trifle less crowded than the drawing room, but at least the staircase and front door were nearer at hand.

Sophia turned an exhausted look on Julia. 'This has been the most tiresome affair. I never thought we would escape.'

'Nor did I.' Julia pushed a strand of hair from her heated face. 'I will own I have never been so confused in my life. After Lady Catherine, I am beginning to think that they were talking about something entirely different from my fall at the Opera House.'

'I am certain they are not,' Sophia said brightly, but her face looked worried. 'We will hope that, in another day or so, it will all be forgotten. I need to find Phillip and tell him we wish to leave. Will you be all right if I leave you here?'

'Of course.' She would be glad to escape the crowded rout for a few minutes.

She waited until Sophia disappeared back into the drawing room and then moved to stand next to a table beneath a portrait of a stern man in a wig and an old-fashioned frock coat. A marble bust stood on the table under the painting.

At least, partially hidden next to the table, she could rest for a moment. The evening had been disturbing. No, not just the evening, but the entire day. She could not recall the visit to Monteville House without a blush. Whatever had possessed her to throw herself into Nicholas's arms in that fashion?

She was supposed to be avoiding him, not using every opportunity to accost him. It was just she had been so worried and he had made her so angry.

Which was no excuse at all.

'Lady Carrington.'

She glanced up and found Lady Serena standing in front of her. Her heart sank. She was not someone Julia looked forward to meeting. 'Good evening, Lady Serena.'

'I had so wanted to speak to you.'

'Indeed.' Julia said in her most discouraging tone. Not that she was hopeful it would have an effect on Lady Serena.

'Yes. To congratulate you. I dare say I should not say a thing, but there will be an announcement soon, will there not?' She managed to look guileless and shrewd at the same time.

'An announcement? I fear I have no idea what you are talking about.'

Lady Serena opened her cornflower-blue eyes very wide. 'Why, your betrothal to Lord Thayne, of course.'

# Chapter Sixteen

Colton returned to London two days after Nicholas was attacked at Vauxhall. He reported to Nicholas the morning after his return. Sitting in his grandfather's study, Nicholas listened, his uneasiness growing with every word. When Colton finished, Nicholas frowned. 'You are telling me that Halford, the elder Halford, who is reputedly senile, is not so doddering after all. And he remembers such a ring?'

Colton nodded. 'Yes, my lord.'

'You were certain he was lucid?'

'Quite. He rather puts me in mind of my own grandfather who, although he is laid up with gout, is extremely shrewd. I thought perhaps, if the information regarding Mr Halford was incorrect, that the information pertaining to the ledger was as well.'

'And was it?'

'Unfortunately not. Several of the older ledgers were burned in a fire nearly six months ago.'

That had been too much to hope for. 'Did he remember the man who sold him the ring?'

'He recalled a gentleman who spun a tale about the

ring's mysterious origins which is why he clearly remembered the ring. As well as the ring's unusual appearance.'

'Anything else? What did the man look like?' Nicholas asked.

'He could not tell me.' Colton cleared his throat. 'Unfortunately, his daughter-in-law returned just then. She appeared most displeased that he had been conversing with me and rather forcibly suggested that I leave.'

Nicholas was not able to elicit much more from Colton. After Colton departed, Nicholas stood in front of the study window. There were too many pieces he did not like. Such as why Phillip had said Halford was senile. Had Phillip actually visited the elder Mr. Halford or merely accepted the word of the younger Halford?

He could bring the information before Phillip. But for some reason he was reluctant to do so, as if he was questioning Phillip's competence in the matter—or did not trust him.

He paced away from the window and picked up a paperweight from the desk. The second attack on Julia had filled him with fury. The attack on him and the robbery of the ring had turned his fury to a cold determination. He was going to find Carrington's murderer and put a stop to this.

He set the paperweight down. Grayson's disappearance only added to his resolve. He had briefly considered Grayson as suspect and dismissed it almost as fast. His manner had been too furtive and nervous for someone who committed such well-planned attacks.

No, he was looking for someone much more devious, much more cool-headed and clever.

He was beginning to think it was time he paid a visit to Sheffield as well.

He looked up as his grandfather entered the room. In

his hand was a newspaper. 'I take it you have not seen this morning's *Post*?'

'No, sir.' The odd expression in Monteville's eyes alerted him. 'What is it?'

'I believe there is something that might interest you.' He handed Nicholas the paper. 'The third notice in the first column.'

Puzzled, Nicholas quickly perused the paragraph. 'Lady M. is to pay an extensive visit to relations in Lancashire, I see.' He glanced up at Monteville. 'Fascinating to be sure, but I fail to see how it concerns me.'

'That one may not, but the next one might.'

Nicholas turned his attention back to the paper. He froze for a moment and then slowly looked up. 'Damn him,' he said softly. 'I should call him out.'

'Which would only start a new round of rumours. I suggest you consider other alternatives,' Monteville said.

'What?' Nicholas's mouth twisted. 'According to this, her angelic ministrations during my recovery have resulted in a passion of finer feelings with an interesting announcement to be expected any day.' He slammed the paper down on the desk. 'My only alternative is to marry her.'

Monteville eyed him thoughtfully. 'Do you find the prospect that alarming?'

He glanced at his grandfather and gave a short laugh. 'You are remarkably calm. If it were not for the fact that I know you are above such machinations, I might suspect you of placing such an announcement merely to force my hand.'

'I am pleased to discover you apparently hold me above such measures,' Monteville said drily.

'I beg your pardon, sir. I did not mean to imply…' He coloured. 'I had some idea you thought Ju—Lady Carrington might be suitable for the next—' He broke off under Monteville's quizzical gaze. Now he was stammering like a schoolboy.

'The next Countess? You are correct, I have considered it, but only because I suspect neither one of you would be completely averse to the idea.'

'You are wrong on that account.' Nicholas took a wild pace around the room. 'She would rather go to the gallows than wed me. Nor do I wish to wed her.'

'You will eventually need to consider marriage.'

'I would prefer not to wed at all.'

'Because of Lady Mary?' Monteville watched him for a moment. 'I think it is time for you to let her go,' he said gently.

'I cannot.' Nicholas moved to the window and looked out at the street below.

'You will need to. If you wish your marriage to Lady Carrington to succeed.'

He looked back at his grandfather, a ghost of a smile on his lips. 'So I am to marry her?'

'I think so. She doesn't need more scandal. Nor do you.'

'I doubt she'll have me.'

'Then you will need to persuade her. Preferably as soon as possible. Once she gets wind of this, I doubt very much if she intends to remain in London much longer. I do not think Phillip will be able to keep her here.'

He stared at his grandfather, beginning to feel like a fox trapped by a pack of hounds. And when the footman entered and announced Lord Stanton was below, he knew how the fox felt when it realised its doom was imminent.

Julia found Sophia in the small drawing room off her bedchamber. She was seated at her writing desk, a pile of letters in front of her. She looked up when Julia entered and made a face. 'I fear I have been a dreadful correspondent of late.' She put her pen down and looked more closely at Julia. 'Should you be up? I doubt very much you slept much last night.'

Julia seated herself on the chair near Sophia's desk. 'As much as I was tempted, I do not think hiding away in bed past noon will solve a thing.'

Sophia considered. 'Sometimes it does. Occasionally the problem will resolve itself if one leaves it alone.'

Julia sighed. 'I do not think this one will. Which is why I have made up my mind what I must do.'

Sophia looked at her with a little frown. 'And what is that?'

'I am leaving London.'

'But, Julia, whatever for?' Sophia said, her face filled with distress.

'Oh, Sophia!' Julia said, touching her hand. 'You have been so kind and I shall miss you terribly, but I cannot stay here any longer. Not after last night.'

'Lady Serena is a dreadful gossip!'

'Sophia, surely you must see she is only saying what everyone else was thinking? That Lord Thayne and I are…are…' Julia bit her lip.

'Betrothed.'

'Yes.' Julia's face heated at the mention of the word. 'It is ridiculous! How did anyone come up with such a notion? How can I ever face him? What if he thinks I did something to encourage such fustian?'

Sophia had propped her chin on her hand and was regarding Julia with an interested look. 'I doubt if Nicholas will think such a thing.'

'But there is Lord Monteville as well. He has been more than tolerant, more than kind, and how do I repay his kindness? By attempting to trap his grandson into marriage!'

'Is that what you are doing?'

'Most certainly not! Sophia! I do not think you are taking this at all seriously!'

Sophia sighed. 'I am, but only because it is upsetting you. But I do not think everything is so dreadful that you must run from London.'

'I do. It is the only possible way to circumvent these ridiculous rumours. If I am gone then no one will see us together.'

'I am not certain that will stop the talk. They will undoubtedly invent a new tale to explain your absence. A lover's quarrel or perhaps a desire to leave so rumours of your engagement will be proved wrong until you decide it is time to make the announcement.'

'Sophia!'

'I am only teasing you. But, Julia, you cannot leave London, it may not be safe.'

'I have considered that as well. But now that the ring is stolen, I am certain nothing more will happen. I am certain the ring is the only thing this...this person wanted.' She spoke more confidently than she felt; there were still several things that puzzled her greatly. Such as why it had been necessary to push her into the street. She was beginning to think that had been a mere coincidence after all.

'Perhaps.' Sophia appeared doubtful. 'I think, dear, before you do anything we must talk with Phillip.'

'I have quite made up my mind.' No matter what Phillip had to say. She suspected he would try to talk her out of it, but this time Julia had no intention of listening.

The footman appeared in the doorway. 'Madame Blanchot is below. She wishes a word with Lady Carrington.'

'Thérèse?' Julia asked, stunned. Thérèse, always mindful of her position as the proprietor of a gaming house, rarely set foot in more respectable establishments. She feared something was very wrong. She stood. 'I shall go down directly.'

'No, you may show her in here,' Sophia said firmly. She glanced at Julia after the footman left. 'It will be more comfortable for a visit here. And besides, I have wanted to meet Madame Blanchot for an age.'

Thérèse entered the room a few moments later. There was no mistaking the fact something had shattered her natural poise. 'Lady Simons, I must apologise for calling on you in this way. But I felt I must speak to Julia without delay.'

'Of course,' Sophia said with concern. 'Are you unwell? Perhaps you should sit down.'

'You are more than kind, but, no, I am not unwell. What I have to say concerns Julia.'

'Thérèse, what is it?' Julia asked quickly. A feeling of dread was slowing creeping over her.

'Have you seen the *Morning Post* today?'

'No.' Julia realised Thérèse carried a folded newspaper. She glanced at Sophia, who appeared equally lost.

'I worried you had not.' Thérèse unfolded the paper with an agitated hand and pointed to a paragraph. 'There is something you must see.'

Sophia and Julia both peered over her shoulder. Sophia gave a little gasp. Julia stared at it and her heart took a sickening dive. 'Oh, dear heavens.' She looked at Sophia, whose face reflected her own sick dismay. 'I really think I must leave London as quickly as possible.'

The footman appeared in the doorway again. 'Lord Stanton is below. He wishes to speak to Lady Carrington.'

\* \* \*

Julia stood as Phillip was ushered into Sophia's drawing room, and wished her knees would not tremble so. She also wished Sophia and Thérèse were still present, but Phillip had insisted on speaking to her alone.

She forced a smile to her lips although her heart sank when she saw the newspaper in his hand. 'Good day, Phillip.'

He did not return her smile. 'Good day, Julia. Please sit. I have something of grave importance to impart to you.'

She sat back down on the chair. 'I suppose it is about the piece in the *Morning Post*.' She clasped her hands together. 'I have already decided what I am to do. I will leave London as quickly as possible.'

'You cannot do that, I am afraid.' He spoke in his usual firm manner, and she knew he expected her to acquiesce as she usually did.

'But I am.' She forced herself meet his eyes. 'I have made up my mind on this. I cannot stay. It is bad enough that Lord Thayne has had to endure two injuries on my account. I refuse to have him endure such outrageous nonsense as well.'

'Leaving London will not help him. Or you.'

'I am leaving tomorrow.'

'You are not.' He came to stand over her, a flinty expression in his eyes she had only seen a few times, but never before directed at her. It took all her willpower to keep from shrinking. 'Nicholas is waiting to speak to you. You will hear what he has to say. And you will accept his offer.'

'His *what*?' A nightmarish sensation washed over her.

'His offer.' He strode to the door and looked back at her. 'If you really wish to protect him from scandal, you will accept.'

She rose, her legs trembling, hardly knowing what she was about. She had never crossed swords with Phillip before, never been the recipient of his anger. The encounter left her shaking.

But even worse was the thought of facing Nicholas. Whatever was she to say to him? He couldn't possibly be planning to make her an offer.

She whirled at the footsteps behind her and clutched the back of the nearest chair for support. Her heart slammed into her ribs as she took in his expression. Nicholas looked as if he was reporting for his execution.

'I would like to speak to you,' he said grimly.

She swallowed. 'Would you? I...I cannot imagine why.'

'Can't you?' He shut the door behind him, his eyes never leaving her face, and advanced across the room.

She forced herself to stay still despite a cowardly urge to run. 'You really do not have to say a thing, my lord. In fact, I think it would be better if you did not.'

He stopped a few feet from her. 'Would you prefer my offer in writing then?'

'Actually I would prefer no offer at all.'

'That is unfortunate because I am making you one. And you are going to accept it.'

She gasped. 'I am not! I have no intention of marrying you.'

'Yes, you will.' He folded his arms and stared at her.

'And how do you know that? Are you omniscient?'

'No, but you're marrying me none the less.'

'Well, really!' She had no idea whether she wanted to hit him or burst into tears. 'I have never heard anything so...so high-handed. This whole thing is so ridiculous! You cannot possibly feel you must marry me because of that stupid thing in the paper.'

'I do.' He was beginning to look exasperated. 'Damn it, Julia, if we do not marry neither one of us will have a shred of reputation left. We've no choice.'

'If you must know, I do not give a fig for my reputation. And I would never marry a man who makes me an offer in such an arrogant, and…and callous manner. Even if he feels compelled to!' To her chagrin, her voice trembled. She gulped and looked away. She would rather die than cry in front of him.

'I beg your pardon. I seem to always be making you cry.'

She turned and glared at him. 'You did not make me cry.'

'You looked as if you were about to.'

'Well, I was not.'

He scowled at her. 'I know I'm making a botch of this. I've not had a lot of practice in making offers. In fact, last time the lady was no more pleased than you are,' he added bitterly.

She stared at him and realized he felt as confused as she did. 'I am sorry.'

'Don't be.' He frowned. 'Is there someone else? Haslett?'

'Robert?' she said in amazement.

His brow snapped down. 'You have been remarkably friendly with him.'

'He is an old friend, that is all. Besides, I think he is developing a *tendre* for Sophia.'

'Is he?' Was it possible he actually looked relieved? Before she could consider what that might mean, he spoke again. 'We do not have a choice in this matter.'

His words made her feel more trapped than his arrogance ever had. 'I don't want to marry again.'

'I know that. It won't be so bad, I promise you.'

'But Lord Monteville…he cannot possibly want this.'

To her surprise, he looked almost amused. 'Actually, on that point you are quite wrong. Consider the advantages. You will have my fortune at your disposal. If you wish to repair your farm you may.'

The generous offer only made her more wretched. 'I do not want your fortune,' she whispered.

He shrugged. 'Probably not. But my fortune and my name is what I have to offer you. But the formidable Mrs Mobley, not to mention Betty the goat, might appreciate a leak-free roof.'

She stared at him, stunned. His eyes met hers and something in his expression made her breathless. He took a step forward and reached out his hand. For an eternity they stared at each other and then he abruptly dropped his hand. He backed away. 'I will call on you tomorrow.'

'I…' But he had already turned and was out of the door before she had a chance to find her voice.

She stared at the closed door and then sank down on the sofa. She could not marry him—it was impossible. Perhaps she hadn't meant to but it had happened—she had trapped him into marriage. A loveless match. She closed her eyes. *But my fortune and my name is what I have to offer you.*

'No.' She opened her eyes. She could not do that to him. Or to herself. She would leave London even if it meant sneaking out in the dead of night.

## Chapter Seventeen

George rapped neatly on the door of Sophia's town-house. He had come directly from a musical soirée where Sophia, who fixed him with a cold stare, had informed him that Julia was home with a headache. Her brusque manner indicated he was fully to blame. His congratulations on the upcoming nuptials had no softening effect at all.

In fact, no one seemed pleased with the results of his machinations. Julia least of all, if her absence was any indication.

Which was why the news of her supposed headache aroused his suspicions. He would not put it past her to bolt.

And thus, he decided a visit to the reluctant bride-to-be was in order.

Sophia's prune-faced butler admitted him. George's request to speak with Lady Carrington was met with a frown of disapproval. 'Lady Carrington is not receiving.'

George had come prepared. He pulled a folded paper from his pocket. 'Perhaps you will give this to her and then let her decide if she is receiving or not.'

Williams took the paper between his fingers and held

it as if it were a hot coal. George watched him go and moved to idly observe one of the dull portraits the late Lord Simons seemed to favour.

After a few more minutes, Williams appeared. 'Lady Carrington will see you, Lord George. In the drawing room.'

She was standing near the mantelpiece, her whole body rigid with tension. He paused for a moment, taking in her slender figure and the soft brown of her hair. And the sensible travelling dress. He had no doubt Thayne would be most displeased if his intended bride should run off so quickly.

She looked up. 'Good evening, George.' Her voice held as much enthusiasm as William's had.

'Good evening, my dear Julia.'

A flicker of annoyance crossed her face. 'You had a message from Sophia?'

He walked towards her. 'She was concerned that you were indisposed and wished me to be certain you were not in need of a physician. Am I to assume, that since you are up and dressed, you have recovered?'

'Yes. Is that all? I do not wish to be rude, but I really cannot engage in idle conversation at this moment.'

George ran his eyes over her gown and then smiled. 'I see you are about to embark on a trip. I would like to offer my congratulations before you leave town. Most certainly the match of the season.'

'We are not going to be married,' she said flatly.

His brow arched. 'Perhaps I misunderstood. My father informed me only today of the happy event. Or perhaps the unhappy event, in this case. So you are not to be married. Have you yet informed Thayne of this?'

Her face crumpled and filled with misery. 'Please do not tease me.'

'I beg your pardon.' He watched her for a moment. 'I take it Thayne has not been informed. What are you going to do, my dear? Do you wish me to help?'

She took a deep breath. 'I must leave here. If you could take me to Thérèse's, I could then go from there to Foxwood.'

'Thérèse's? My dear, I can do better than that. I can take you to Foxwood.'

She frowned a little. 'But I wish to leave now.'

'Of course. My carriage awaits.'

'I do not wish to go to Foxwood now,' she said impatiently. 'Only to Thérèse's.'

'Very well. We will only go to Thérèse's. I suppose you have a bandbox or two.'

'Only one.' She hesitated. 'I do not want anyone to know I am leaving. At least not right away. I rather thought I would go up to bed and then leave through the servants' entrance and go through the back garden to the mews.'

'Very clandestine of you,' he remarked. 'When can you be ready? An hour?' That should give him time to track down Thayne's location. Or he could deliver her to Thérèse's and send Thayne there to retrieve his runaway fiancée.

'Yes.' She did not look very happy.

'Very well, my dear.' He smiled. 'In an hour. I will have a servant waiting for you outside the gate.'

Julia fastened the strap on the bandbox with shaky fingers. Whatever was she thinking of? Running off with George? Except she was not really running off with him, merely asking him to escort her to Thérèse's. She tried to shove aside her uneasiness. George was not the most trustworthy of men, but he had been kind to her in his own peculiar way since Thomas's death.

She would go to Thérèse's. Surely Thérèse would conceal her whereabouts until she could send for Eduardo.

She had left a note for Sophia, a very brief note for the purpose of assuring her she would be safe. Her pen had hesitated over the second note and, in the end, she had left it next to the one for Sophia. He would undoubtedly be furious with her, but relieved as well.

She picked up the bandbox and slipped out of her room. The house was quiet and she saw no one as she made her way to the back staircase. There was no one near the door that led to the garden and she made her way out unseen.

The garden was dark and shadowed. Despite her soft boots her footsteps seemed unnaturally loud on the gravel walk. She tried to stay close to the bushes and prayed no one would see her.

She reached the back wall and hesitated at the gate. Her heart was thudding loudly, but she forced herself to undo the latch and pass through.

She gasped when a man appeared out of the shadows.

'Lady Carrington?' he said softly.

'Yes.' She peered at him but could see only that he looked rather elderly and harmless.

'Come with me.'

She nodded and prayed he was George's servant. But who else would be lurking behind Sophia's house waiting for her?

The carriage stood in the side street. Her escort paused. 'Do you wish to carry your bandbox with you?' he asked courteously.

'Yes.' She clutched it to her and waited as he opened the door.

The interior was in shadow and she could not see George's face although she could see the coach was occupied. Her heart had began to thud again and her hands were clammy.

'George?' she said softly.

'Go on in, my lady,' her escort said behind her.

She climbed in and took her seat. The door closed firmly behind her and she glanced in the corner. With mounting panic she realized everything was all wrong— the man was wearing a black coat and breeches, not George's pantaloons and buff coat. And his shoulders were much too broad.

The coach began to move. 'Oh, no,' she whispered.

'Good evening, Lady Carrington,' Nicholas said.

Julia gasped. 'Wh…what are you doing here?'

Nicholas leaned back and folded his arms. 'Abducting you.'

Even in the dull light he could see the stunned look on her face. 'You cannot be.'

'Why not? It rather evens the score, does it not?'

'I don't understand. Where is George?'

He shrugged. 'Probably in his carriage somewhere near Bond Street. Not that I particularly care. Although I question your wisdom in running off with him.'

'I was not running off with him! I merely wanted him to—'

'To what? Help you escape London? Escape me?'

'No!' she snapped.

'So why were you stealing away from Sophia's house in the middle of the night, then?'

'I might ask why you were skulking around Sophia's back garden and spying on me!' she retorted.

He smiled grimly. 'Because, my dear, I suspected you might try something of this sort. When I learned you were not with Sophia, I decided I would call on you. And whom do I see but Kingsley leaving the house. Questionable under any circumstances, but when I found his carriage parked in a side street and Kingsley hovering around the garden, I decided to have a word with him.'

She stared at him aghast. 'Did you hurt him?'

He raised a brow. 'I fear he put up a bit of resistance when I informed him I intended to take his place. Along with some nonsense about how he intended to inform me of your plans.'

'But why? I still do not understand why you are doing this.'

'Because I've no intention of letting you run off. Not only because of the damnable piece in the paper, but because your life may still be in danger. And I don't trust Kingsley past my nose.'

'I see.' She looked away. 'I suppose you will take me back to Sophia's now,' she said calmly.

'No.'

'No?' Her head jerked up. 'Then where are you taking me?'

He regarded her under half-closed lids. 'I've no intention of telling you. At least for now.'

'But you cannot do this! You cannot hold me against my will!' A note of panic had crept into her voice. 'My lord! Please, take me back to Sophia's or to Thérèse's.'

'I am not planning a rape, if that is what worries you,' he said coldly. 'You will be quite safe. Trust me on this.'

'How can I? I have no idea where you are taking me.' She looked at him for a moment and then turned her head away. She sniffed.

'I don't suppose you brought a handkerchief with you. Here.' He handed her one. She looked as if she was about to refuse and then plucked it from his hand.

'Thank you,' she said in a small voice.

He stifled a groan. The anger he'd barely contained when he discovered she planned to run off with Kingsley was rapidly giving way to conscience. No doubt he had frightened her, but he had no intention of allowing her to run away, not even if she found the idea of marrying him so repulsive she would prefer to trust Kingsley over him.

Julia slowly awoke. Her arm felt cramped and her neck was cushioned by something rough. For a moment she had no idea why her bed was swaying. Then she remembered. She was in Nicholas's coach. He had kidnapped her. And she had no idea where he was taking her.

She opened her eyes and realized the rough cloth under her cheek was a masculine coat. And that she had been covered with a throw. She moved her head a little and realized with vague surprise that the early light of dawn was creeping through the windows of the coach.

She shifted. Nicholas was in the opposite corner of the coach, his eyes closed. His long legs, the muscles visible through his tight breeches, were stretched out in front of him. He wore only his waistcoat and shirt and she realised he had tucked his coat under her neck.

When had she fallen asleep? She remembered her eyes closing in spite of her resolution to remain awake. There had been a stop, she thought, but even that seemed like a dream.

Her eyes drifted over him. Sleeping, he looked oddly vulnerable. A lock of hair had fallen over his forehead, giving him a boyish air.

But there was nothing boyish about the strong masculine line of his jaw or the growth of beard around his firm mouth. Or the rest of his hard, lean body. She flushed and pulled her gaze away, feeling as if she was violating his privacy by staring at him while he slept.

The coach suddenly seemed too small and intimate. Just as hers had the night she had kidnapped him. Except this time he was not safely bound and gagged. And now she knew what it was like to have his arms around her, feel his mouth cover hers.

She must be going mad. She should not be thinking of a man who had just abducted her in such terms. Instead, she should be making plans to escape, not falling asleep as if she were at home in her own bed.

'You are awake.'

She gasped and looked over at him. He was still stretched out in the corner and looked as if he hadn't moved except to open his eyes.

'Yes.'

His gaze drifted over her. His eyes had a heavy sensuous look that reminded her of Thomas and how he had looked at her when he awoke and wanted to make love to her.

Heat rose to her cheeks. She must truly be depraved. She jerked her gaze to the window. Outside, she saw neat hedgerows and fields. 'I do not suppose you wish to tell me where we are?'

'Near Newmarket.'

'Why are we near Newmarket?' She frowned at him. Something tugged at the back of her mind.

'Monteville House is not far from here.'

'Monteville House?' A sense of panic was starting to rise in her throat. 'But why are we near Monteville House?'

'Because you are going to stay there while I go to Sheffield.'

Her hands went to her heated cheeks. 'You cannot possibly bring me to Monteville House. Are you mad? What will everyone think?'

He shrugged. 'They will think what they like. I've no doubt my grandfather will spin a plausible tale about how we decided a visit to the family would now be in order.'

'He knows about this?'

A smile tugged at his mouth. 'He does now. I left a note.'

'A note?' She undoubtedly sounded completely idiotic.

'Yes. I would be willing to wager you left a note somewhere as well.'

Her mouth nearly fell open. How dare he sit there and look so pleased with himself? He was planning to bring her to his family home? The possibilities had turned in her mind before she drifted off to sleep, but this had not been one of them. 'You cannot do this! I have brought nothing with me!'

'What is in that bandbox?'

'It is a toothbrush and a nightrail—' She broke off. 'This is ridiculous. I have no clothing.'

'Next time you decide to go off with someone you'll know to pack more,' he said kindly.

'I was not going off with someone! I had expected to go to Foxwood and I would have what I needed there. I cannot possibly arrive at your home like this!'

'No? Would you prefer to continue on to the border? Although I would prefer a change of clothing before we go on.'

'No!' She was about to fly into the boughs and then realised from the gleam in his eye that he was teasing her. In fact, he looked remarkably relaxed for a man who had just abducted a person and was planning to show up at the family home with his victim.

None of it made any sense. And she was hardly reas-

sured when they rounded a bend and she caught a
glimpse of a large manor house in the distance.

'Monteville House,' Nicholas said.

Her stomach lurched. She was beginning to wonder if
it might have been preferable if Nicholas had had improper designs on her person after all.

If the housekeeper, Mrs Burton, was shocked by the
arrival of Nicholas with a strange woman in tow shortly
after dawn, she hid it well. Her manner remained quite
calm when Nicholas said they had travelled most of the
night and Lady Carrington was in need of a bed.

She had not shown even the merest flicker of surprise
that Julia had brought only a bandbox with her as she
took the young woman upstairs then opened the door to
a bedchamber.

'I trust you will be quite comfortable here.' She held
open the door and waited for Julia to step past her.

Julia looked around at the room, taken aback by its
size and the elegance of the furnishings. She had somehow expected a chamber less grand. She realised Mrs
Burton was waiting for her to speak. 'It is lovely. Thank
you.'

'Is there anything else you require?' Mrs Burton asked.

'No, not at all.'

The housekeeper moved to the door. 'I shall send
Fanny in to help you undress, my lady.' She left the
room.

Julia stood for a moment, feeling rather lost, and finally moved towards the bed. She removed her pelisse
and laid it across a chair. A looking glass hung nearby
and she caught a glimpse of herself. With a great deal of
dismay, she saw her hair had come almost completely

out of its pins and her travelling dress was a mass of wrinkles.

Mortified, she turned away. She looked much worse than she had ever imagined. Rather like a waif someone had picked up off the streets.

She sat down on the bed. Whatever was she to do now? And, even more pressing, what did Nicholas intend to do with her?

# Chapter Eighteen

When Julia awoke again, daylight was streaming across the bed. For a moment, she thought she was in Sophia's townhouse and then her mind cleared.

She was in Monteville House. She sat up, still disoriented from her heavy slumber. From the angle of the light, she thought the hour must be well past noon.

She glanced around the room. It was a pretty, feminine room, done in colours of blue and cream. A watercolour of a garden hung on one wall. A small writing desk stood in a corner near the window and on the other side of the carved fireplace was a small wardrobe.

It was the sort of room she had dreamed of as a child, warm and inviting and with a sense of permanence, unlike the room she had occupied in her stepfather's house with its bare furnishings and drab walls. Or with Thomas, who considered rooms merely a place to rest one's head.

Which was why Foxwood had seemed so wonderful to her despite its shabbiness. A real home. A place where Thomas had finally seemed content to settle.

She threw back the bedcovers and climbed out of bed. She padded to the window and drew back the filmy muslin curtains. The day was overcast, but it failed to detract from the magnificence of the view. Below her were spread formal gardens and in the distance she saw a small lake. To the left, beyond the tree tops, she could see the rooftop of another house.

How lovely it would be to live somewhere so stately and settled. And to wake up in this cheerful, peaceful room and be able to look out of the window at gardens that were neat and civilised rather than a straggly mess. For a moment, she could almost imagine herself hiding away up here, suspended in time.

Mrs Burton's entry into the room brought her back to the present and her situation abruptly. Several muslin gowns were draped over her arm. She surveyed Julia with her placid air. 'So you are awake, my lady. I dare say you are hungry by now. A tray in your room perhaps, and then you can come downstairs for dinner. And I have brought you some gowns. They are old ones of Miss Sarah's, but since you appear to be of similar proportions they should do until your trunks have arrived.'

'Thank you,' Julia said, completely taken aback. Her trunks? Whatever had Nicholas told her?

She watched in some bewilderment as Mrs Burton bustled around opening the curtains and then the maid, Fanny, came in with a tray of food which she set on the small desk.

'After you eat and are dressed, Lord Thayne will see you,' Mrs Burton said. She hovered for a moment. 'Perhaps you should eat first, my lady.'

Julia obediently sat down and looked at the food set before her. There was cold slices of roast beef, bread and fresh strawberries. She looked up and saw Mrs Burton still watching her. She took a bite of the beef. Mrs Burton, apparently satisfied she meant to eat, finally left the room.

\* \* \*

An hour later, she had finished eating and Fanny had helped her dress. The cream-coloured gown was a little short but otherwise fitted her adequately.

The apprehension she had managed to keep at bay returned as soon as she left the sanctuary of the bedchamber. She followed Mrs Burton down the hallway and to the wide circular staircase. She descended the staircase past portraits of stern ancestors and finally across a lower hallway to a door. 'Lord Thayne is waiting for you in the library,' Mrs Burton said.

Julia thanked her and stepped past her into the room. It was large and panelled with dark wood and lined with bookshelves.

Nicholas stood near the window. She could see that it faced the lawn she had seen from her bedchamber. He had his hands clasped behind his back. He turned when she entered, then moved forward. 'I hope you rested well,' he said politely.

'Very much so.' She looked at him, uncertain of what to say next.

He had shaved and changed into buckskin breeches and boots and a dark brown coat. The informal attire only emphasised his lean masculinity. He looked at home and, despite the civilised surroundings, for the first time since last night she felt completely in his power.

'Good. Please sit.' He indicated a small settee.

She sat on the edge. He remained standing, which seemed to her an unfair advantage. 'Are you not going to sit?' she asked.

'Should I?'

'Yes, otherwise I feel as if you have called me in for a scolding.'

His mouth twitched. 'Indeed.' But instead of taking a proper seat, he perched on the edge of the desk.

She frowned at him. 'That is not a chair.'

'Would you prefer I sat next to you? That is my only alternative.'

Must he be so exasperating? 'You could pull the chair from behind the desk.'

'It is not very stable and tends to tip.'

'Really!' At least his customary stubbornness had the effect of banishing the peculiar feeling of being at his mercy. 'I would think you would have a few hundred chairs at your disposal here.'

'Yes, but I have a fondness for that particular chair.'

She sighed. 'I refuse to ask why you do not sit in it.'

'Good.' He actually smiled. 'Are you comfortable?'

'Oh, yes. My bedchamber is lovely and has such a pretty view.'

'It belonged to my sister.'

'Did it?' She was taken aback. 'I do not think I should be there. That is, I am hardly a guest and it seems rather presumptuous of me…' Her voice trailed off at his raised brow.

'My sister would be delighted to know you are in her bedchamber. And you are a guest. Is there anything else you wish to say to me?'

'I need to know why I am here,' she said quietly.

'Because I decided this would be the best place to keep you safe.'

'Safe from what? I fear I do not understand. The ring has been taken—surely that is what the thief was after. And I do not understand why I was in danger after the incident at Foxwood anyway. You were the one with the ring! It is you who should have been worried.'

He was silent for a moment. 'There are several things about the affair which do not make sense. Which is why I've no intention of allowing you out of my sight.'

'This is ridiculous! You cannot possibly consider yourself responsible for me!'

He folded his arms and stared at her. 'But I do. After all, we are going to be married.'

'We are not!' Her heart began to pound.

'I hate to contradict you, but we are. After I return from Sheffield.'

She rose. 'You are going to Sheffield? But why? Phillip said there was nothing to discover.'

'I have reason to believe, however, that the jeweller knows more than he is willing to tell.'

'Do you?' She felt a stab of fear. 'I don't want you to go.'

He looked at her, a frown on his brow. 'Why not? It may lead to the man who killed your husband.'

'Yes.' She clasped her hands tightly together and said slowly, 'I have wanted more than anything to discover the person who did this and see he was punished. I thought that I would do anything, including murder, if I had to. When I abducted you, I did not think of the consequences, that I might put someone else in danger. And I have put you in danger. You have been hurt twice because of me. And I cannot let you be hurt any more. Even if it means I never find his killer.'

He faced her. 'There is a man out there who has killed at least once. He has assaulted you twice. What if he decides assaults are not enough? That to prevent discovery he must kill again? We still do not know why you were shoved in the street or why you received a threatening note. And I've no desire to find you dead because I failed to do everything in my power to find the man.'

She stared at him, taken aback by the vehemence in his voice.

'And so you will remain here while I go to Sheffield.'

'At least let me go with you.'

'No.'

'But I wish to,' she said.

He scowled at her. 'No, and I'll place you under guard if I must.' He rose from the desk. 'I have sent for my cousin, Lady Marleigh, to chaperon you. She lives four miles from here and will arrive before dinner.'

'I see.' The thought of meeting an unknown relation of his was daunting. 'When are you leaving?'

'Tomorrow if possible.'

It was all she could do to beg him not to go. Instead, she nodded.

'You may do as you please, except I do not want you going about the grounds unattended.' When she said nothing, he frowned. 'What is it? Are you worried for your safety? You should be in no danger here. I've given instructions to the servants to admit no one unknown to them. You will be guarded when you step out the door and I trust you will do nothing foolhardy such as try to go about without a chaperon.'

'I am not worried about my safety,' she snapped.

He continued to frown. 'Then what is it?'

'It is nothing!' She could hardly admit to him that the fact he was going to leave her made her want to throw herself into his arms and beg him not to go. That she would worry about him every minute he was gone.

'Then why are you looking like that?'

'I am not looking like anything! I am merely out of sorts. Being forced into a coach and then travelling throughout the night does that to one.'

'Does it? You will have a few days to rest, then.'

She glared at him. 'I doubt that. I will most likely be wondering when I will hear of your demise!' And wanted to bite her tongue as his expression changed.

He took a step towards her. 'I see. You are worried about me.' His eye held a peculiar gleam.

She took a step backwards. 'Of course I am. I would worry about anyone.'

'Indeed.' He took another step and she found herself backed into the settee. 'I am flattered none the less. Does that mean you will miss me when I am gone? That you will be here eagerly awaiting my return?'

She flushed but forced herself to meet his gaze. 'Only because I will then be free to leave.'

His smile was rather wicked. 'Why do you think that? Perhaps I never intend to let you go. We are betrothed, you know.'

She caught her breath. 'Please don't tease me!'

Something flickered in his eye. He stepped back. 'Very well.' His voice cooled. 'The house is at your disposal. I must meet with my grandfather's agent, but you may make any requests you might have to Mrs Burton.' His voice was dismissive.

'Thank you.' She kept her voice as polite as his and walked with as much dignity as she could from the room.

And then it was all she could do to keep from bursting into ridiculous, childish tears.


His cousin, Amelia, Lady Marleigh, arrived shortly before dinner. She was shown into the study where Nicholas was seated behind the desk, staring at a pile of documents that awaited his signature.

'Good heavens, Nicholas. Whatever are you up to now?' she asked, coming into the room. She still wore her pelisse and bonnet, a confection of straw and blue that tilted fashionably on her blonde curls. She walked to his desk, stripping off her gloves. 'You have the most atrocious hand and I could scarcely make out what you wanted, except that you are in need of a chaperon. I feared I must be mistaken, for what would you be need of a chaperon for?'

He stood and came around the desk. 'You are not mistaken at all. I have a lady staying here.'

'A *lady*?'

'A person of the female persuasion such as yourself.'

She made a face and took the chair by his desk. 'Must you be difficult? Perhaps you had best tell me who this lady is and why she is here. And why ever are you at Monteville House? Should you not be in London, creating more scandal? There have been the most delicious rumours circulating about you that involve highway robbers, and a mysterious lady who nurses you back to health that you have fallen in love with—' She broke off and stared at him. 'Do not tell me you have brought her here!'

'I have. Her name is Lady Carrington.'

'Lady Carrington?' She wrinkled her brow. 'I do not know her. But you are in love with her and have brought her to Monteville House and wish me to chaperon you until you…you what?'

He fixed her with a scowl. 'I am not in love with her.'

'How disappointing.' She smiled at him. 'So, why is Lady Carrington here?'

'I abducted her.'

Her mouth fell open and then she gave a shaky laugh. 'Really, Nicholas, that is beyond the pale, even for you. I think you had best explain precisely why it was necessary to do something so deplorable.'

'I feared her life was in danger. And she was trying to leave London to escape me.' He took a pace towards the window and then turned. 'I could not think what else to do. And after I brought her here, I realised I could hardly keep her here without a chaperon. There is already enough scandal between us. You were the only person who came to mind who would not be completely shocked.'

'I am not certain whether I should be complimented or not,' Amelia said.

'There is one other thing. We are betrothed.'

She appeared momentarily stunned. 'Does Grandfather know of this?'

'It was his idea. He also knows I abducted her.'

'Heavens,' she said and then laughed. 'Of course. It all makes sense. I think you had best start at the beginning if you want me to help you.'

Julia started at the knock on the door of her bedchamber. She sat in a chair near the window and had been staring out at the garden and trying very hard to think about nothing.

She stood. 'Come in.' She was taken aback to have a tall, fashionably dressed young woman with golden hair and vivid blue eyes enter the room.

'Lady Carrington?' the young woman said. 'I am Nicholas's cousin, Lady Marleigh.'

'How do you do?' Julia felt very awkward. She had somehow thought Lady Marleigh would be much older, not someone so sophisticated and composed.

'May I come in?' Lady Marleigh asked. 'I thought I should speak to you before dinner.'

'Yes, of course. Would you care to sit down?'

'I think so. And you may take the other chair and tell me how you are. I fear Nicholas could not really say.' She took a wing chair arranged near the mantelpiece and Julia obediently sat on the other.

'I am fine,' Julia said cautiously. She had no idea what Nicholas had said to his cousin.

Lady Marleigh must have guessed her thoughts. She looked at Julia with her frank gaze. 'Nicholas told me about last night. I know you are not here willingly.' She hesitated a moment. 'I hope he did not harm you.'

'Harm me? I do not understand.' Julia stared at her and then her meaning was clear. Heat rushed to her face. 'Oh, no. He was nothing but a gentlemen.' She remembered his coat under her cheek. 'He was actually quite kind.'

Lady Marleigh smiled. 'Was he? I am glad. I did not think he would ever touch a woman without her consent, but I wanted to reassure myself. So, how did you find being abducted? I will own I always thought it might be rather romantic.'

'It wasn't really. He was angry because he thought I was running away, so we quarrelled. After that I resolved not to speak to him and then I fell asleep.'

A gurgle of laughter escaped Lady Marleigh. 'I will own that sounds quite dull. And, of course, you would quarrel with Nicholas. He has a dreadful temper. Did he scowl at you the entire time?'

Julia found herself wanting to giggle. 'Yes, but then he always does.'

'And it does not intimidate you. Splendid, he should not marry someone whom he can ride roughshod over.'

The smile left Julia's face. 'We are not going to be married,' she said quietly.

'No?' Lady Marleigh arched a brow. 'But why not?'

'Because neither of us wishes to be married. It is only because of some ridiculous gossip that is circulating in London. He feels obligated to offer me marriage, but I will not let him because it is entirely my fault we are in this stupid fix.'

'And why is that? I cannot think you could be faulted for nursing him after he was injured.'

'No, but he was injured because of me.' Julia took a deep breath. 'You see, I abducted him first because he wore my husband's ring. I wanted it back. And on the way to Foxwood, which is my farm, we were held up by highwaymen. One of the highwaymen tried to shoot me because I would not give him my pistol and Nicholas took the ball instead. So, none of this is his doing at all.'

Lady Marleigh looked stunned. 'Nicholas did not mention this.' And then she leaned forward, her eyes sparkling with laughter. 'My goodness! I am beginning to think you are quite well suited after all.'

# Chapter Nineteen

Julia paused outside the drawing room, feeling rather self-conscious. Lady Marleigh had insisted on loaning her a dress for dinner, a dark salmon silk. It was a deceptively simple gown, but the V-neckline of the bodice plunged lower than she liked. Although Lady Marleigh was several inches taller than Julia, Fanny had proved amazingly adept with the needle and had managed to put up the hem in no time. A few tucks here and there had been all that was needed to fit the bodice to Julia's more slender curves.

Lady Marleigh had supervised the dressing of Julia's hair as well and when she stood in front of the looking glass she had hardly recognised herself. She had not worn such a bold colour for an age, nor had she had her hair dressed in curls tumbling over her head.

'You look beautiful,' Lady Marleigh said. She walked around Julia. 'But your locket is not quite right. I will loan you my ruby.'

'You have done far too much already,' Julia protested.

Lady Marleigh smiled. 'Oh, not at all.'

Somehow, she had found the locket removed from her neck and a ruby and diamond necklace taking its place.

And when she had glanced back at the looking glass again, her stomach had fluttered. She looked like a woman who was set on seduction.

There was not much she could do about it now. She forced herself to enter the drawing room. To her dismay, Nicholas was the only occupant. He stood near the mantelpiece dressed in a dark coat and breeches. He looked up when she entered. The arrested expression that leapt to his eyes made her pulse leap.

She flushed as his gaze travelled over her, and lingered for a moment on the ruby above her breasts. Then he moved forward. 'Good evening, Lady Carrington.'

'Good evening, Lord Thayne.' Her own mouth was dry. Her pulse thudded as he came to stand in front of her, his eyes still on her.

His eyes searched her face and came to rest on her mouth. 'What did Amelia do to you?' he asked. His voice was husky.

'She did nothing but loan me a gown. Is that so objectionable?'

'It probably should be.' His eyes darkened. 'You look far too desirable.'

Her breath caught. 'That was not my intention.'

'No?' His mouth curved in a cynical smile. 'I've no doubt it was Amelia's.'

'I beg your pardon,' she said stiffly. Really, must he make it sound like a crime? Not only that, but she felt foolish that he seemed to think she had set out to attract him. 'I believe I will view the garden, my lord.' She started to walk past him.

He caught her arm. 'No. Wait.'

She looked up at him. 'Perhaps you would release me.'

He dropped her arm. 'I did not mean to offend you. It is just…you look lovely,' he said flatly.

The confusion in his face dissolved any hurt she had felt. She arched her brow. 'And that is what is objectionable?'

'No.' He levelled a scowl at her. 'It is not.'

'I see.' Her lips curved in a smile at his bemused expression.

His gaze sharpened and he caught his breath. 'Julia, damn it.'

'Quarrelling again?' Amelia's voice reached them from the doorway. They turned. Her gaze went from one to the other. 'Or perhaps not.' She slanted a quizzical look at Nicholas. 'I am ready to begin my duties as chaperon. That is, if you are certain you want one.'

Julia forced her mind back to Amelia's question. 'How long have I known Sophia?' She looked at Amelia blankly for a moment. 'Oh, I first met her in Vienna. It was nearly five years ago.' She gave Amelia an apologetic look. 'I am sorry, you must think I am terribly rude for not attending. I am rather tired.' They had withdrawn to the drawing room after dinner and now sat on one of the brocade sofas.

'An affliction which my cousin seems to share. I do not think he heard a thing I said all during dinner.' She patted Julia's hand. 'Do not worry. There is a cure for this, you know. A pity Nicholas is leaving tomorrow.'

'I do not want him to go. I asked him not to, but he insisted.' Julia hesitated. 'I don't suppose you could talk to him.'

'I doubt he will change his mind. He wants to protect you.'

'He doesn't need to. I have tried to tell him he is not responsible for any of this.' She had found Amelia remarkably easy to confide in, despite knowing her for a mere five hours.

'I think,' Amelia said slowly, 'that he needs to protect you. He failed with Mary and I think it is a burden he still carries. If something happens to you, it will destroy him.'

Julia sat very still. 'I did not know. In fact, I know very little about Mary at all. Except that he still loves her.'

'He told you that?'

'No, but it is quite obvious.'

Amelia fixed her clear gaze on Julia. 'Perhaps, but she is dead. And he is falling in love with you.'

Shock coursed through Julia. 'No. He cannot be.'

'But he is. Probably in spite of himself. Is that really so dreadful?' Amelia asked.

'I do not want him to be.' Julia knotted her hands together. 'I do not want anyone to be in love with me.'

'Or perhaps you are afraid to be in love with him,' Amelia said gently.

Julia looked away. 'I still love Thomas.'

'But he is dead, as Mary is. You cannot bury yourself with your husband. As Nicholas cannot bury himself with Mary. It is wrong.' Amelia turned her direct gaze on Julia. 'But he has tried. For the past two years. I had hoped…we had all hoped, when Sarah married Lord Huntington, that Nicholas would start to put the past behind him as well. But he did not, despite Huntington and Sarah's happiness and despite the fact Huntington does not hold Nicholas to blame.' She looked more closely at Julia. 'Do you know the story?'

'Only a little. I knew Mary was married and that she died.'

'Mary was betrothed to Lord Huntington when she met

Nicholas. Lord Huntington is Jessica's brother. It is another story in itself as to how Sarah came to marry him.' Amelia smiled a little and then sobered. 'Mary and Nicholas had been lovers before her wedding. I do not suppose they meant it to happen, but they had fallen in love. But Mary would not break off her betrothal to Huntington and they married. A few weeks after her wedding, Mary ran away. She had meant to stay with an old nurse of hers, but she became very ill and was forced to stop at an inn. By the time she sent for Nicholas she was dying. He has never forgiven himself for causing her death.'

Compassion and pity washed over Julia for Mary, but most of all for Nicholas who was still alive and still lived with his burden. 'I am so sorry,' she whispered. 'I had no idea.'

Amelia touched her hand. 'He needs you.'

Julia stared at her. 'But what can I do?'

'I suspect he is in his study, attempting to drink himself into oblivion. You could start by putting a stop to that. I do not think he'll be fit to travel tomorrow if he becomes thoroughly foxed. And he'll probably be stubborn enough to go anyway.'

'Perhaps it would be better if you spoke to him.'

Amelia rose. 'It would be much better if you do. Actually, I am exceedingly tired and would like to retire.' She smiled a little. 'I am in the family way.'

'How wonderful!' Julia exclaimed. 'But…oh, dear, you should not be here at all.'

'Of course I should be. I would not have missed coming for the world. And since John is away for another few days, I was quite bored.' She took Julia's hands and bent forward and kissed her on the cheek. 'I think it is time for you to go and speak to my stubborn cousin. There is no need to be afraid of him.'

Julia watched her go, her thoughts in turmoil. Nicholas was falling in love with her? He couldn't be. Not if tonight at dinner was any indication. He had said little, answering in monosyllables, clearly distracted. Once or twice, she had found him watching her, an odd expression on his face, almost one of longing. But it had nothing to do with desire. She had felt vulnerable and a little frightened, and she had no idea why.

And then she thought of Mary. And of the bleakness she had glimpsed in his face more than once. And of him alone in his study, attempting to drink his pain away. She stood. She had felt the same bleakness, the same desire to obliterate the pain in some way. Which was why she could not possibly walk away from him now.

Nicholas scowled at the decanter of brandy before him on the mahogany desk. So far it had done little to erase the empty hole that gaped inside of him. Or the damnable longing he had thought he'd buried.

Asking Amelia had been a mistake. He should have known, with her deplorable tendency towards matchmaking, that she would not leave things alone. And that damnable dress. It had caressed Julia's slender curves like a glove, the low-cut bodice revealing the creamy white mounds of her breasts. He had wanted to take her then in the drawing room and make her completely his. All of her, body, soul, and mind.

The desire to lose himself in her and with her had shot through all the barriers he had erected. And had unstopped the painful yearning for a completion he could not have.

He picked up the glass and was about to put it to his lips when the door to the study opened. He glanced up with a frown and then nearly dropped the glass when Julia stepped into the room.

She blinked and looked around as if trying to adjust to the dim light. 'Nicholas?'

His name on her lips made his hands sweat. Perhaps he was already drunk and dreaming. He rose. 'What are you doing here?'

She moved into the room. 'I came to find you. Amelia thought you might be here.' Her voice held a trace of nervousness.

'She was correct. Is there something you wanted?' She was still wearing the dress. Hell. He scowled at her. 'Otherwise I am occupied.'

'Doing what?' She took a few more steps towards him and his mouth went dry.

'Getting thoroughly foxed, if you must know.'

A frown creased her brow. 'I do not think that is a good idea at all. Will you not feel unwell in the morning?'

'Probably.'

'Then why are you drinking?'

The concern in her eyes unnerved him. 'My dear, it is none of your business,' he drawled.

The concern was replaced by a flash of anger. 'Well, it is since you are going on my business tomorrow! If you have a headache and your stomach is unwell you will hardly be able to carry out the business properly.'

He crossed his arms and leaned against the desk. 'Is there a purpose for your being here? Besides lecturing me on my drinking?' His behaviour was boorish, but the alternative was yanking her into his arms.

He was stunned when she glared at him. 'No! There is not! If you must know, the only reason I am here is because Amelia said you might need me, but I can see she is wrong!' She whirled around and marched towards the door, but not before he glimpsed her mortified expression.

Before he could say a word she had left the room, closing the door behind her with a bang.

He stared after her. She was here because Amelia said he needed her? She had come to tell him that? The look on her face had told him what it had cost her to come. His behaviour had been despicable.

He walked to the desk and picked up the glass of brandy. He stared at the amber liquid and then slammed the glass down with such force it shattered in his hand, spilling the contents across the desk. When he took his hand away, he saw, mixed with the brandy, the red of his blood.

Julia yanked the pins from her hair and threw them down on the dressing table. How could she have told him she was there because she thought he might need her? She had been so angered and so hurt by his cold behaviour that she had blurted out the first thing that came into her head. Then had wanted to die of humiliation.

And his expression. He had looked as if she had slapped him. It was obvious that she was the last person he wanted for any reason. The only thing she could hope for was that he would become so thoroughly drunk he would forget she had even appeared in his study.

The anger left her and she sank down at the dressing table in despair. Why ever had Amelia said he was in love with her? She must be mistaken, had to be mistaken. Just as she was wrong when she had said Julia was afraid to love him.

She rose and shivered. She had always been so certain there would be only one true love in her life, and that love had been Thomas. Now, she was not certain of anything.

She started at the knock on her door. Was it Amelia? Perhaps she had decided to see if Julia had succeeded in her mission. Her stomach knotted up. She could only tell Amelia the truth—that he did not want her.

She opened the door and then her heart leapt to her throat. Nicholas stood in the doorway. She took a step back, her hand to her chest. 'What are you doing here?'

His dark gaze was fixed on her face. 'I've cut my hand. May I come in?'

She looked down. He held a white handkerchief over one hand. A dark stain had seeped onto the snowy cloth.

'Oh, good heavens!' She took another step back. 'Come in, then. Whatever have you done?'

'I cut it on a glass.' He stared at her, looking slightly confused as if he couldn't comprehend that he had done so.

'Come over to the light and sit down.' When he did not move, she touched his arm. 'I need to look at it.'

He followed her obediently to the chair near the bed. A lamp stood on the table next to the bed. He sat down. She knelt down beside him and took his hand and gently unwrapped the handkerchief. The cut was on the side of his first finger and not very bad. It had stopped bleeding, but should undoubtedly be bandaged. She looked up into his tawny eyes. 'I think you will live, my lord. But I should call Mrs Burton and have her clean and wrap it.'

His head was bent towards her. 'You called me Nicholas earlier.'

'Did I?' She flushed a little. 'I do not recall.'

'When you came to find me in my study.'

Any hope he had forgotten the incident was dashed. 'I

will call for Mrs Burton.' She started to rise, only to find his hand clamped around her wrist.

He pulled her back to him. 'Don't go, Julia.' His eyes had darkened. She could smell the brandy on his breath.

'Your hand needs to be tended to.' She tried to tug her wrist out of his grasp.

'You can do it later.' His gaze drifted over her face. 'Amelia was right, you know. I need you.'

She swallowed, not quite sure what to do with his odd mood. Was he drunk? But his eyes were clear and his words unslurred. A peculiar sensation was starting in her stomach. 'I…I am certain Mrs Burton will do an admirable job of bandaging your hand.'

'I don't want Mrs Burton.' He slowly rose and pulled her to her feet. He dropped her hands and stood looking down at her, his gaze slowly travelling from her feet up over her thighs and the curve of her hip, lingering for a moment on the swell of her breasts and then over her face. Although he stood a little apart from her, not touching her at all, her entire body felt as if it was on exquisite fire.

She did not move when he stepped towards her. 'It is the dress,' he said as if explaining something very obvious. And then he pulled her into his arms.

She had expected an assault, but instead his kiss was gentle. He moved slowly across her lips, his arms so light around her she almost wondered if he held her. His mouth drifted down her neck and briefly caressed the soft skin of the top of her breast before moving upwards to claim her mouth once again.

The light pressure nearly drove her mad. She made a small sound of protest and pressed her body hard against his. Her hands crept up and entwined themselves in the thick silkiness of his hair, pulling his mouth more firmly to her own. Her tongue touched the corner of his lips.

He groaned against her mouth and lifted his head. 'I need you. Desperately.'

'I know.'

'And you do not object?'

She took a deep breath. 'No. Not tonight.'

He gave a shaky laugh. 'I suspect I should question that qualification but I won't. Not tonight.' He drew in his breath. 'Will you come to bed with me?'

'Yes.'

The flare of passion in his eyes nearly engulfed her. He held out his hand and she put hers in it. He brought it to his lips and the chaste kiss he planted on her wrist set her on fire.

'Nicholas.' His name was almost a moan.

He looked up and saw her face. And then pulled her into his arms with such fierce desire she was nearly breathless. She struggled for a moment and he instantly loosened his hold. But it was only so she could throw her arms around his neck and pull his head more firmly to hers.

# Chapter Twenty

She was not certain what brought her from the slumber she'd fallen into. But she woke and knew something was not right.

The bed was still warm from his body. She sat up, the cover falling from her bare shoulders. It took a moment for her eyes to adjust to the dark. She saw him then. He had put on his breeches and his shirt. He sat in the chair near the window, slumped forward, his head in his hands.

Without a second thought, Julia slipped from the bed. She found the quilt on the floor and picked it up and draped it around her shoulders.

She moved to his side and knelt down by the chair. 'Nicholas.'

He did not move. 'Nicholas.' She touched his hand. 'What is it?'

He lifted his head but did not look at her. 'You should be in bed.' His voice was dull.

'No.' She caught his hand. 'Let me help you.'

'You cannot. Go to bed, Julia.'

'Is it Mary?' she asked quietly. She sensed more than felt that he stiffened. 'I know about Mary. Amelia told me.'

He looked at her then and she thought she had never seen such bleakness. 'I doubt if she told you the whole of it.'

She looked at him steadily. 'She said that you blame yourself for her death.'

'I killed her.'

'How?' Her hand tightened on his. 'I do not understand.'

'When she ran from Huntington she was with child. My child. She died because she could not bear for her husband to discover she had been unfaithful before her marriage.'

His pain was tangible and more than anyone should have to bear. 'I am so sorry.' She brought his hand to her cheek. And then stood. 'Come back to bed. I want to hold you.'

He rose. 'You do not understand.'

'I understand you lost the woman you loved and you lost a child. And you bear the burden of both their deaths. It is too much for one person.'

He did not move. 'I have used you tonight. I thought if I took you to bed I could for one night erase my damnable memories. But instead, I have added one more sin to my long list. I am sorry.' He looked at her, his mouth twisting. 'You deserve better.'

'It may not help much, but I have used you, too.' She smiled a little at his expression. 'I wanted for one night to forget my pain as well. So we are even and you can, with a clear conscious, blot that sin from your ledger.'

'You are too generous.'

'It is merely the truth.' She took his hand. 'Come and sleep.'

'I have dreams.'

'I have them, too. I dream of Thomas and he is always

out of my reach. Sometimes I dream that if only I could reach him I could save him but I am always too late. And when I awaken I feel such sadness that I sometimes think I cannot bear it.'

'But you do.'

'Yes. As you do.'

He looked down at her for a moment. 'I think you are right, we should go to bed and sleep. And hope that, perhaps for the rest of the night, our demons will be held at bay.'

She led him to the bed. She waited while he removed his shirt and climbed into bed and then she slipped in beside him. He pulled her to him with one arm so her head lay on his bare chest. They lay there for a long while and gradually his breathing became heavy and even and she knew he had fallen asleep. And then she drifted away as well.

When she awoke again, she was alone. She turned to her side and clutched the pillow to her chest. His scent still faintly clung to the sheets. She felt lost.

She closed her eyes, hugging the pillow more tightly to her. Her body felt stiff, a reminder that last night had not been a dream, if the fact her body was bare beneath the sheets had not been enough of a reminder.

She had no idea whether she regretted last night or not. She supposed she should, but she had gone to him willingly…no, more than willingly. She had done everything but force him down on the bed. And she had known what she was doing—she was not an innocent virgin who knew nothing of men.

What she had told him was the truth—she had hoped that, for a night, she might banish her own emptiness. And banish some of his as well.

But she had not bargained for the sense of completeness she had found in his arms. The sense of being truly united with another soul.

Which frightened her more than any of the rest of it. For not even with Thomas had she lost herself so much in another person.

She sat up. The disorder from last night was gone. The salmon dress was neatly draped over the back of a chair and she could see her shift peeking out from underneath. Someone had already been in the room unless Nicholas had tidied up the disorder himself while she slept. The thought made her flush.

Someone knocked on the door. Amelia poked her head around. 'So, you are awake. I did not want to disturb you, but I thought you should know that Nicholas has already gone.'

'Has he? I had hoped...' She stopped and flushed. She could hardly admit that after last night she had hoped he would change his mind. And then she realised Amelia was regarding her with a peculiar look and she saw the cover had fallen away to reveal her bare shoulders. She yanked the sheet up as far as possible, embarrassed that Amelia should find her undressed.

Amelia came into the room and looked at Julia's crimson face. Her delicate brow inched up a notch. 'I can see why Nicholas appeared rather dazed this morning. Could you not have persuaded him to stay one more day?'

Pretending she did not understand Amelia's meaning would only be hypocritical. 'He left while I was asleep.' She bit her lip and forced herself to meet Amelia's face. 'I am sorry. You must think that I am ungrateful as well as immoral to engage in such behaviour while under your roof. I think it would be best if I left as soon as possible. I do not—'

Amelia's brow only inched higher. 'You cannot possibly leave. Nicholas would murder me if I let you go. And I fear my husband would be most unhappy if that happened.' She crossed the room and came to stand by the bed, her expression amused. 'Besides, it is not my roof. It is my cousin's and I doubt he found you either immoral or ungrateful.'

'But Lord Monteville…'

The laughter in Amelia's blue eyes increased. 'We are not a very proper family, I fear. My grandfather would not have been shocked although I suspect he would have insisted Nicholas remain here until you had things settled between you.'

'There is nothing to settle,' Julia said miserably. 'We both agreed it was for only a night. It will not happen again.'

'Agreements can be renegotiated.' She moved towards the door. 'I am glad you made good use of the gown.'

Her cheeks heated. 'He said it was because of it.'

Amelia laughed. 'Of course. I will send Fanny in to help you dress and then we can decide what we should do to amuse ourselves until Nicholas returns.'

Amelia kept her too busy to worry about Nicholas. She insisted on showing Julia the house. After lunch, over Julia's protest that Amelia would wear herself out, she took Julia to the lake. They sat on the bench overlooking the calm water and the swans with the summerhouse behind them, and for the first time in an age Julia felt some sense of peace.

When they returned, there was a carriage in the drive. Amelia paused and frowned. 'Nicholas did not mention a thing about visitors. And I do not recognise the coach.'

But Julia did. 'It is Sophia's carriage.'

Amelia's brow cleared. 'Sophia? Lady Simons? How delightful! Then it is all right.'

They entered the cool hallway, which already contained two trunks and several valises. With some surprise, Julia saw one of the trunks was her own. Sophia stood in one corner dressed in a stylish travelling gown, conferring with Mrs Burton. She saw them and her face lit up. She came towards Julia, hands outstretched. 'My dear, I had to come and assure myself you were all right.' She caught Julia's hands and smiled. 'Are you?'

'I am. But, Sophia, it was such a long journey for you and in the middle of the Season!'

'London already seemed dull without you.' She turned to Amelia. 'Dear Amelia, I apologise for coming so unexpectedly. But when Lord Monteville asked for Julia's trunk to be sent here I decided I would accompany it myself.'

Amelia smiled warmly. 'We are delighted to have you. Nicholas has left for a few days and so we have the house to ourselves.'

'He has left?' Sophia glanced back at Julia with a little frown. 'Perhaps that is for the best. Phillip left London yesterday morning and so George insisted on escorting me,' she said in a low voice.

'George is here?' Julia asked. She felt suddenly uneasy and then chided herself.

'I am, indeed.'

She turned and he sauntered into the hallway. Despite the journey, his coat and pantaloons were immaculate and there was not a hair out of place. She forced a smile to her face. 'Good day, George.'

'Good day, my dear Julia.' He gave her a bland look. 'There is no need to look so apprehensive. I intend to procure a room at the local inn. I do not think Lord

Thayne's hospitality quite extends to myself. In fact, I had best leave before he discovers me in his hallway.'

'You need not worry. He has gone to Sheffield,' Amelia said.

George swung around to stare at her for a moment. Then he laughed. 'How very odd of him. Not a place where one wishes to find oneself, most certainly not voluntarily.'

Amelia looked as if she was about to say something else, then glanced at Julia and stopped. 'Would you care for refreshment, Lord George?' she asked instead.

'You are most hospitable, but I believe it would be in my best interest and most likely yours, as well, to decline. Now that I have my dear aunt safely delivered, I will proceed to the inn.' He turned his enigmatic gaze on Julia. 'I trust you are not too distressed that matters did not quite play out as you intended two nights ago. I fear there was some interference.'

'I quite understand,' Julia said.

He departed a few minutes later. Sophia turned to the others with an apologetic look. 'I fear I could not persuade him to stay in London. I am grateful he did not think it would be wise for him to stay under the same roof as Nicholas. I must own I was surprised he had that much sensibility.'

'So Nicholas has a quarrel with Lord George? Whatever for?' Amelia asked.

'I have no idea,' Sophia said. 'They seem to hold one another in extreme dislike. They nearly came to blows at the Opera House because they were quarrelling over Julia.'

Julia made a face. 'Sophia! That is most untrue!'

Amelia's eyes sparkled. 'But of course. I can see this is one Season I should have insisted on going to London.

But John dislikes London and will not go unless he absolutely must. This year he used the excuse that it would be too taxing for me. Well, I suppose since Nicholas is not here we will not have a quarrel to look forward to.'

'Thank goodness,' Julia murmured. That was the last thing they needed. But as she followed Amelia and Sophia into the drawing room she could not quite shake off her sense of uneasiness. And she only hoped Nicholas was all right; if anything happened to him, she would never forgive herself.

A day after he left for Sheffield, Nicholas was shown into the Halfords' drawing room. Although the room was small, the furnishings were good. He had not thought a jeweller in a town such as this would live quite as well. And Mrs Halford, a thin woman with a narrow face and protruding teeth, was well dressed.

She smoothed down the skirt of her muslin dress in a nervous gesture, apparently flustered at having so distinguished a visitor in her drawing room. 'Please, be seated, my lord. Do you wish for refreshment?'

He remained standing. 'No, that will not be necessary. If you could tell Mr Halford, your father-in-law, that I would like a word with him.'

She avoided his eyes. 'My father-in-law is indisposed, my lord.'

'Indeed.' He looked at her, trying to decide on the best tactic. 'I would, of course, be willing to pay you well for your trouble and his. I suspect a household such as yours has considerable expenses.'

'You cannot imagine the half of it! My husband has no idea of the expense incurred to put a joint of beef on the table each Sunday, and the cost of candles to light six rooms, and he will insist on a fire except on the hottest days. And one would think such things as coats and gowns would not cost so much, but I am certain the prices are nearly as much as those in London. And...' She stopped. 'My husband does not like having him disturbed.'

'But he does not need to know.'

She eyed him with a calculating look. 'It cannot be more than a quarter of an hour. I will not have him worn out. Very well, I will get him for you.'

She started out of the drawing room and then screeched when a figure appeared at the door. Nicholas saw it was an older gentleman wearing a wig and dressed very properly in clothes of a few decades ago. He only hoped it didn't mean his mind was firmly entrenched in that period as well.

Mrs Halford had her hands over her heart. 'Why...what are you doing up? You gave me such a fright!'

'Sally said a lord had come to visit. I thought he might be here for me.'

'Why would you think that?' she asked indignantly.

'Haven't had too many lords here for you. The last one came to see Joshua.' He looked at Nicholas. 'So you wish to see me, do you? Best come to my room, then.'

'I will not have you bringing a lord to your room,' Mrs Halford said.

'I can't have a proper conversation sitting on those fancy chairs of yours.'

Mrs Halford glared at him. Nicholas followed Mr Halford down a narrow passageway to a small room. The older man stepped aside and gestured for Nicholas to go in. 'Sit down, my lord. The wing chair is the most comfortable.'

Nicholas found himself in a small crowded room that

somehow managed to hold enough furniture for two rooms. The household extravagances obviously did not extend here. The furniture was old and worn. A desk, piled high with books and papers, stood near the window squeezed between a dresser and a bookcase. All the chairs seemed to be covered with papers or books including the indicated wing chair. 'Just place the books on the bed,' Mr Halford said from behind him.

Nicholas did so and sat down. The old gentleman removed a brocade dressing gown from another chair and then seated himself. 'Well, which lord are you?' he asked eyeing Nicholas with a great deal of curiosity.

'Lord Thayne.'

'Ah. The Earl of Monteville's heir. So, what business do you have with me?'

'You had at one time in your possession an old ring.' He pulled the sketch from his pocket. 'This ring, I believe.'

Mr Halford took the sketch and looked at it. 'The old Spanish ring. I remember it. Although with the number of visitors inquiring about it recently it would have been difficult to forget it.'

'Who else has been inquiring about it?' Nicholas asked sharply.

'Nearly a week ago, a young man came who had the look of a solicitor. Said I reminded him of his grandfather. And then, a day ago, a big burly man with a Scottish accent. My daughter-in-law did not know about him,' he added with evident satisfaction.

What the devil was Mackenzie doing here? He frowned. 'Anyone else?'

'Just you, my lord.' His eyes had lost some of their blandness and had sharpened. 'So, perhaps you will tell me what your interest is in the ring.'

'The man who sold you the ring stole it from the finger of a man who was murdered. It is possible the man who sold you the ring is also the murderer.'

'That was some years ago. How did you finally come to me after this time?'

'The ring was given to me.'

'By a young lady?'

Nicholas stared at him, his gut tightening. 'Yes.'

'Very dark and pretty, but too sad for one so young. She had seen the ring in the shop window and wanted it. I was rather surprised as it was so unusual. I doubted if anyone in the village would want such a piece. I asked her where she was going but she only said north.' He looked at Nicholas. 'She bought the ring for you.'

'Yes. She is dead now.' He waited for the harsh sense of loss to grip him but it did not come.

'I am sorry.' Mr Halford looked distressed for a moment. He glanced down at Nicholas's hand. 'You do not wear it?'

'It was stolen again. Possibly by the same person or persons who took it before.'

'I see. And you wish to recover it?'

'I wish to find the man who killed Lord Carrington. His widow's life is in danger.'

Mr Halford placed the tips of his fingers together and regarded him. 'I quite understand. Perhaps not all the connections, but enough. I will tell you what I know.'

He did not add much to what Nicholas had learned from Colton, but there were a few details that Colton had not picked up. Nicholas finally rose, something else nagging at the back of his mind. It came to him just before he left Mr Halford's room. He turned. 'One more thing. You mentioned that a lord had come to see Joshua. Your son, I presume?' At Halford's nod he continued. 'Do you recall the name of the lord?'

He smiled gently. 'There are times when I find eavesdropping rather unavoidable in such a small house. His name was Lord Stanton.'

Nicholas had one last call to pay before he left Sheffield. The younger Mr Halford was not at first willing to see him, but he had taken a second look at Nicholas's grim countenance and changed his mind.

Nicholas left Halford and Sons and stood for a moment in the street outside the establishment. Halford had confirmed Nicholas's suspicions and had also let slip Mackenzie had seen him as well. Most of the unrelated pieces surrounding Carrington's death had fallen into place with cold, shocking clarity.

Two ladies glanced at him curiously as they passed by. He realised he could hardly stand in the road. He moved towards his curricle. Julia should be safe in Amelia's care and he did not want to face her until he had confronted Stanton. He only hoped he reached London before Mackenzie. Having Mackenzie hang for killing a peer would hardly do Julia good.

Besides, he wanted the pleasure of putting his fist through Phillip's face.

# Chapter Twenty-One

Amelia looked up from the note she had just received. The three ladies were seated in the drawing room looking through the most recent *Ladies Gallery*. 'Nicholas is going to London. Or is he in London? Really, I cannot make out his hurried scrawls at all.'

'I wonder why he went to London?' Sophia asked.

Julia said nothing, but was conscious of a lurch of disappointment. It had only been two days since he had left. In spite of herself, she missed him terribly. All of him, even his scowls. Worse of all, she wanted to feel his arms around her, feel his strong heartbeat under her hands and smell his particular scent.

She rose and went to the window and looked out. The sky was blue with only a few clouds floating lazily overhead. Staying in his house did not help her resolve to stay detached. Not when she saw reminders of him everywhere and there was a portrait of him done several years ago in the main hallway.

Amelia came up beside her. 'He will be home soon, I expect. I do not think he would have stayed away if it was not important.'

'No.' Julia turned and tried to smile. 'I am rather worried about him.'

'He will be safe.' Amelia looked at her for a moment with a great deal of understanding in her face. 'Sophia and I thought we would walk to the lake. Do you wish to come?'

'I think I would rather stay here if you do not mind.'

'Of course not.' Amelia touched her hand.

She stood by the window for a while longer after they left, only turning when the footman announced a visitor. She was taken aback when George was shown in.

'George? I had not thought to see you here.' He had seemed quite adamant about his refusal to set foot in Monteville House.

He smiled. 'As you can see, I changed my mind.' He glanced around the room. 'So, my dear Julia, where are your ever-present guardians?'

'They went for a walk.'

'Leaving you alone?' He raised a brow. 'My dear, I doubt if Thayne would approve of such laxness. But then he is not here, is he?'

'No, but he should be back soon. Do you wish refreshment?'

'Not now.' He moved towards her. She took a step backwards and found herself backed against the window. He stopped uncomfortably close to her and she felt a sudden flash of fear, which he must have seen. 'Afraid of me, Julia? But why? We have been neighbours for an age, even before Thomas died.'

'It is merely you are standing too close to me,' she said, trying to remain calm. 'Did you wish to sit down? Or perhaps you could catch up with Sophia and Amelia. They are going to the lake.'

'I came to see you.' He didn't move. 'Actually, I came for you.'

'I beg your pardon.'

'You are coming with me.' He pulled his hand from his pocket.

In a sort of bewildered comprehension she saw he held a pistol. 'George?'

'You are leaving the drawing room with me and then you will have a cloak brought to you. After that we will go to my carriage. Do not attempt to run or scream or indicate in any way that you are not coming with me under your own free will. Or I will be forced to shoot you and anyone else in my way. I trust you understand.'

She nodded, too frightened to speak. His eyes held a cold, steely expression and she knew he would do exactly as he said. As if in a dream, she went with him out of the drawing room and across the parquet floor of the hallway. She waited while a servant fetched her cloak. In a peculiar awareness she saw there was a fresh bouquet of flowers on the table. The footman held the door open and accepted George's explanation without a blink that he was taking Lady Carrington for a short drive and would return soon.

Then she was in his carriage and he climbed in and took the seat across from her. With a sick sensation in the pit of her stomach, she felt the carriage begin to move.

She looked at him. His eyes were on her, his expression hooded. 'Why are you doing this?' she finally asked.

'I need you for insurance, my dear. My yacht is waiting in Maldon and I want to reach it and France without impediment.'

'I do not understand.' Although a sickening thought was beginning to form.

'Don't you? I am fleeing the country and plan to disappear conveniently on the continent. As long as you are with me, no one will dare interfere. I do not think Thayne will want your blood on his hands. Or my father.' He settled back.

'Why is it necessary for you to flee England?' she asked carefully. But she already knew the answer.

'Because of the ring. A pity it surfaced. I would have been safe if it had not. But when I saw it on Thayne's hand I knew it was just a matter of time before it was recognised. I had hoped, however, you and Thayne would not cross paths. It was extremely inconvenient that you did.'

She stared at him, revolted. 'You killed Thomas.'

'Yes.' He shrugged. 'It was necessary. I could not have him exposing my, er…source of income. Selling secrets to the French proved extremely profitable and amazingly simple. I fear my sire's hope that the position of a lowly clerk would install in me a sense of honour and pride failed.' He leaned back. 'My biggest mistake was taking the ring. But I needed the money.'

His callousness shocked and horrified her. And filled her with deep rage. 'You are monstrous.'

'Perhaps. But I am a survivor.'

'I will die before I allow you to escape with me.'

His disbelieving smile made her want to slap him. 'May I remind you I hold all the cards? And I doubt, when it comes down to it, you will want to die at all.'

Nicholas resisted the urge to shove Stanton's butler against the wall. 'What do you mean he has left for Maldon?'

'He left this morning, my lord. That is all I can tell you.'

Why the hell had Stanton left for Maldon? He turned and dashed down the steps of Stanton's townhouse. Kingsley had not been at home either, although he had not been able to elicit much information of his whereabouts.

He was about to step into his carriage when someone spoke behind him. 'My lord.'

He turned. Mackenzie stood behind him. 'What the devil are you doing here?' Nicholas demanded.

'The same as yourself. Wanting a word with Stanton.' He frowned at Nicholas. 'Where's the Countess?'

'She is at my grandfather's estate. My cousin is with her. Stanton has gone to Maldon.'

Mackenzie's brow crashed down. 'The devil he has. He has a yacht there, or rather young George does.' He stared at Nicholas. 'I think, laddie, we'd best go to Maldon. And as quickly as possible.'

Julia paced around her small cramped room in George's cottage in Maldon. They had arrived last night and George had forced her into the room and taken the key. Her meals had been brought by a surly-looking woman who refused to speak to her. Julia had no doubt George had bribed the woman to pay no heed to anything she might say.

She stopped in front of the narrow window. From it, she could see the top of a mast. The sight made her stomach churn. Thank goodness the tides had not been right for leaving last night or she had no doubt they would be well on their way to France by now.

Except she had decided she would do anything to avoid getting on the ship with him. She had no idea what he planned to do with her when he reached France, but she knew it would not be pleasant.

The key turning in the door made her heart beat with a sickening thud. George entered. 'My dear, it is time to go,' he said, drawling. He held the pistol.

When she did not move, he grabbed her arm. 'Come.' He picked up the cloak from the bed and draped it around her.

She flinched and glared at him. 'I can do it myself.'

'Quiet.' He pushed the pistol into her ribs under the cloak. 'Now move.'

There was no chance to escape as she left the cottage and climbed into his carriage. The trip to the quay did not take nearly long enough. He helped her down and, as they walked out on to the quay, kept the pistol to her. He was nervous; she could tell by the way his eyes darted around. She feared he truly would shoot her if she tried to escape.

Her knees nearly gave away when she saw the boat. Although not large, it stood out among the smaller boats docked in the harbour. 'This way.' He took her arm and started towards it. A few fisherman were on the quay, but no one gave them more than a curious glance or two. 'If you scream, I will not hesitate to shoot you or anyone else,' George said in her ear.

Her stomach lurched when they reached the graceful masted boat. If she was going to do something, it would need to be soon. She looked down at the grey cold water and shivered. George pulled her on to the gangway.

'Let her go.'

George turned, his arm around her waist. Phillip stood behind them. In his hand was a deadly-looking pistol. 'Release her, George.'

'I am loath to contradict your order, but I have no intention of doing so.'

'I will shoot you without compunction.'

'Not a very paternal sentiment. However, I doubt if you will. Think of the potential scandal to the family name. You may put it about we have fallen in love and eloped.' His grip tightened on Julia's arm.

'This has gone far enough. Let her go,' Phillip said grimly. 'I will see you get to France.'

'I need her. Come, my love.' He started to move, his arm tight around her waist.

Phillip stared at him. 'I will hunt you down.'

George laughed. 'No, you won't. You will cover for me as you have done for the past three years.'

'Phillip?' Horrified, Julia stared at him. 'You knew?'

Phillip's eyes were full of regret. 'My dear…' he began.

George laughed. 'My dear Julia, of course he knew. But he was willing to do anything to protect the family honour and Arthur from scandal. The lengths he has gone to keep you from discovering the truth have been quite amazing. The highway robbery, the thief at Foxwood, the little incident at the theatre. And Mr Grayson, of course.'

Her eyes were still on Phillip. Anger mixed with horror began to seep through her numbness. 'Phillip? You hurt Nicholas?'

'No, of course he did not,' George said. 'I did. He merely sent Grayson to purchase the ring.' His voice was impatient. 'The conversation is becoming tedious. Come.' He tugged on her arm.

'No! Leave me!' She yanked her arm out of his grasp. Her anger and betrayal rendered her nearly oblivious to George and his pistol. She stared at Phillip. 'How could you? How could you do this to Thomas?'

'Get moving!' George grabbed her arm.

Furious, she stomped on his foot. Caught by surprise, he stepped backward and tripped on the edge of the gangway. He clutched at her and fell with her into the cold water below.

He released her before he hit the water. She went under, somehow remembering to take a breath, then made her way to the surface and trod water, gasping, as she tried to get her bearing. She vaguely heard shouting and voices.

She nearly screamed when an arm caught her by the shoulders. She started to flail. 'Don't fight me, Julia,' Nicholas said in her ear. 'I am going to pull you out.'

She sat in a chair by the fire Nicholas had demanded the landlady build. The inn was small and shabby, but the innkeeper had been kind. The innkeeper's daughter had found a clean muslin gown and a shawl. Despite the fire and the dry clothes she could not stop shaking.

Eduardo fetched a physician. He had examined Julia and had pronounced her to be in a state of nervous shock from the cold water. He had left a draught and said that she must sleep.

She scarcely looked up when Nicholas appeared at her side. 'You must go up to bed now,' he said.

'I do not want to sleep.'

'Julia.' He knelt beside her. 'You are safe. Eduardo is here. I am here. No one can hurt you.'

'Yes.' But her mind refused to work. She felt as cold and numb as she had when she had fallen in the water.

She made no protest when he reached down and lifted her in his arms. He carried her to the room and laid her gently on the bed. She hardly noticed when he removed the borrowed knit stockings from her feet. She took the draught without protest and slipped, at last, into a deep dreamless sleep where she knew nothing.

\* \* \*

'You have a visitor.' Barbara appeared in the doorway of the drawing room. 'Lord Monteville. He seems determined to see you. I do not think you will be able to fob him off as easily as you have the others.'

Julia looked up from her embroidery. In the fortnight that had passed since her abduction, she had found it impossible to sit without some sort of stitching in her hand. Not that she was able to sit much, for most of her waking hours were spent in restless movement. If she was not walking, she was in the garden; for the first time in several years, the garden was entirely free of weeds.

She had refused all visitors. Including Nicholas. She had not seen him since she left the inn near Maldon with Eduardo to return to Foxwood. She tried not to think of their parting, the helpless concern in his face replaced by bleakness when she said she did not think it wise for them to meet again. But how could he want her, when she felt so numb, so devoid of anything?

'Shall I show him in?' Barbara asked.

'I…' Julia rose, but Monteville had already stepped around Barbara and into the room.

'Lady Carrington,' he said. He moved forward and picked up her hand. 'I have come to see if you have recovered.'

'Thank you. I have,' she said automatically. She turned to Barbara, remembering she should at least show some courtesies. 'Perhaps you would bring Lord Monteville some refreshment.'

'Will you not be seated, Lord Monteville?' Julia said after Barbara left the room. He took the chair near the sofa and she sat back down.

He surveyed her face with a not unkind expression in his cool grey eyes. 'I do not think you have recovered at all,' he said gently.

'I am fine.'

'But you have refused to see anyone who cares about you.' He waited for a moment. 'Why?'

Her hands tightened in her lap. 'Because I can feel nothing.'

'Perhaps you are not allowing yourself, then.'

'Perhaps I have nothing left to feel.'

'I suspect that the opposite is true. You are holding such strong emotion inside that you are afraid of what might happen if you allowed yourself to feel.'

She rose and went to the window and then turned. 'I want to destroy things. I have imagined throwing every dish in the house. Or that I might scream and not stop. And then I fear I am about to go quite mad.'

'It is unlikely.' He stood and moved to stand near the mantelpiece. 'I have known Phillip for the past twenty years. I considered him one of the most intelligent and honourable men of my acquaintance. I also saw, however, he had certain weaknesses. His excessive pride in his family name. His blind devotion to Arthur, whom he saw as the embodiment of all the virtues he honoured, and his prejudice towards George, who was not.'

He looked away for a moment and back at her. 'I have, for the major part of my life, considered myself an astute judge of human character. But I failed with Phillip. I did not see, or did not want to see, how deeply his pride dictated his character. Or that his desire to protect his name would lead to such crimes against your husband and yourself. I also did not suspect the extent of George's wickedness. For that I offer my apologies to you.'

She knew how proud he was and how difficult it must be for him to admit such a thing. She realized, too, how he must feel betrayed as well. 'You do not need to, my lord.'

'I have one other confession.' He looked directly at her. 'On more than one occasion in the past fortnight, I have considered running Phillip through with a sword for the pain and betrayal he has caused his family and friends.'

'Have you?' she said, startled. 'I have thought I would like to do the very same thing. And then the fact I can feel such horrible, consuming rage frightens me. Not even after Thomas died was I so angry.'

'Yes.' He understood, she could see, and somehow his understanding began to fan the faintest flicker of hope.

'I have not wanted to feel anything,' she said. 'Not only because of the anger but because it will hurt too much when I do.'

'But you cannot stay in this state. You are hurting others as well.' He looked at her. 'And you are not allowing them to heal. Sophia has lost her nephew, and, although Phillip is not dead as George is, his betrayal has been worse than his death. She thinks you must blame her and that now she has lost your friendship as well. And there is Amelia. She is certain she is responsible for your abduction because she allowed George into the house.' He came to stand next to her. 'And my grandson. He has shut himself away again as you have. He feels he has failed you, failed to save you and so he bears the burden of that.'

Julia looked sharply at him. 'He pulled me from the water.'

'Yes, but he left you at Monteville House, and while he was gone George reached you. And he may have pulled you from the water, but he did not save you from the pain and betrayal.'

'He could not have. He has no cause to blame himself.'

'My dear, you are lost to him. And so he did fail,' he said gently.

'I am lost to him?' She looked at him, puzzled. 'How?'

'He loves you. He would help you, if he could, but you won't let him. And so, like you, he is in his own private hell.'

She stared at him, stunned. Amelia's words came rushing back. *If something happens to you, it will destroy him.* She thought of the pain he had been in that night at Monteville House. And knew she could not bear to imagine him in such pain again.

A sob rose to her throat. 'Oh, dear God.' She looked at Monteville with tears in her eyes. 'What shall I do?' she whispered.

'It is for you to decide. But you will have to go to him. I do not think he is able to come to you.' He picked up his hat and gloves. 'I will leave you, my dear. I wish you well.'

She stood for long after he left and then finally, for the first time in a fortnight, wept.

# Chapter Twenty-Two

Two days later, Julia sat in the drawing room of Sophia's townhouse. She knotted her hands together in her lap. She would hardly blame Sophia if she did not want to see her. Her treatment of Sophia had hardly been kind.

In a moment she heard familiar footsteps. And then Sophia came into the room. She paused in the doorway and Julia saw what Monteville had meant. Her face was puffed, as if she had been crying for a long while, and there were dark circles under her eyes. She stared at Julia and Julia rose. 'Sophia?'

And then Sophia dashed forward with a glad cry. 'Oh, Julia, it is you! You do not know how much I have wanted to see you!' And Julia was swept up in a joyful embrace.

The next day, she discovered from Sophia that Nicholas was rarely at home to anyone. 'Amelia does not think he has been eating or sleeping properly and he is in a foul temper most of the time.'

They were sitting in Sophia's dressing room. Julia felt sick at heart. 'I need to see him. But I do not know whether he would receive me.'

'I think you must force him to see you.' Sophia looked at her thoughtfully. 'He has been frequenting Thérèse's. You did force your acquaintance on him once before.'

'Are you suggesting I abduct him again?' Julia stared at her friend. 'He would most likely want to strangle me.'

'It would be better than what he is doing. You could take him to Foxwood again and refuse to let him go until he listens.'

'Yes, I could,' Julia said slowly. 'But how can I be sure he will be there?'

'Amelia is here in London with her husband. I think between us and Thérèse we can guarantee Nicholas will be where you want him.'

'Yes.' She had no doubt they would.

'There is one more thing.' Sophia rose. 'I will return shortly.'

Julia waited and tried not to think of all the reasons she could not abduct Nicholas again. Sophia returned. She sat down next to Julia. 'I think you should give him this.' She opened her hand and the ring lay on her palm.

'Where did you get it?' She looked slowly up at Sophia.

'From Phillip. The day after…after everything happened.' Her face was anxious. 'I know that you once said you thought it was cursed. But it was given to two people with love and perhaps it should be given once again in love.' She took Julia's hand and opened her fingers. 'Please take it.'

Julia looked it. And she slowly closed her fingers around the ring.

Nicholas glanced across the table at his opponent. 'I've relieved you of enough of your pin-money. And I'd best

take you home before your protective husband notices
you are gone.'

His cousin's smile was quite unconcerned from beneath her mask. 'Do not worry, he will not. And if he
does, he is unlikely to call you out. When you are in such
a horrid temper all the time, we are all afraid of you.'

His brow shot up. 'I had not noticed you have any
particular fear.' In fact, Amelia had hounded him un-
mercifully to take her to Thérèse's. If he did not, she
declared, she would go by herself without an escort.
However, once they arrived, she had spent much of the
evening craning her head around as if waiting for someone. If he hadn't known she was in love with her husband, he would have thought she was waiting for a lover.

'Oh, but I do. You quite terrify me.'

'You will be quite relieved to know, then, that I leave
town tomorrow.'

Something had caught her attention. She stood and
stared over his shoulder for a moment and then suddenly
fixed him with a brilliant smile. 'Actually, I think you
are leaving town tonight. I believe I will go watch the
Faro bank for a moment or two.'

'Damn it, Amelia.' But she had already left the table.

He started to rise, intending to go after her, when
someone slipped into the chair she had vacated. He
caught his breath. The woman wore a dark salmon gown
and her hair was caught up at the back of her head. For
a moment he thought he was hallucinating.

'Good evening, my lord.' Her voice was clear and unmistakable.

He sat back down. 'What the devil are you doing
here?'

'I want to play a game of cards with you.'

'And I do not want to play.' He folded his arms. 'You

made it very clear, my dear Lady Carrington, that you do not want my company in any form.'

She flinched. 'You are not very sporting.'

'I do not feel very sporting. If you will excuse me, I am going to escort my cousin home.'

'Please sit down, my lord.'

His brow shot up and then he stilled. She had a pistol pointed at him. 'What is this in aid of?'

'We are going to play a game.'

He laughed without amusement. 'Are we? So, if I refuse to co-operate you will shoot me?'

She considered. 'Yes.'

'I doubt that.' He stared at her, curious in spite of himself. Her manner was as cool as it had been that first night. Except now he knew the passion under her façade. His loins tightened. 'Very well, we'll play. The same game as before. And the terms?'

'The same as before.'

What the hell did she want? He watched her shuffle the cards. She wore gloves, but they did not diminish the memory of the feel of her hands on his body. She bent forward to deal and the movement clearly revealed the valley between her breasts. He caught his breath as desire, sharp and swift, shot through him.

She looked up and caught him watching her. She bit her lip, a gesture that told him she was not as calm as she appeared.

Her gaze on his face did not waver, however. 'Shall we begin?'

'Yes.' He watched her, paying little attention to the game. It came as no surprise when she played the winning hand.

He leaned back in the chair. 'You have won. And now perhaps you'll tell me what you want. I've no ring, although perhaps you wish money instead. Perhaps for breach of contract. We did have a betrothal of sorts or have you forgotten?'

'I have not forgotten,' she said in a low voice.

'Have you perhaps changed your mind?' He knew he was goading her, but the hurt and anger of her rejection sprang to the surface. 'You wish my fortune and title after all?'

He could see she had paled under her mask. 'I want neither your fortune nor your title.'

'Then what do you want? Revenge? Although I have no idea why. Or perhaps you wish me to admit I still desire you after all.' He ran his eyes over her face and allowed his gaze to rest on her breasts. 'Very well. I desire you. I want your lovely body with your beautiful breasts, and your graceful legs, I want to feel the curve of your hip under my hands, and I want to make love to you until you cry out with pleasure. Does that satisfy you?'

'How dare you!' She jumped up, her mouth trembling. 'I am beginning to think I should shoot you after all!'

'Go ahead.' He folded his arms. 'I find I couldn't care less one way or the other. Although I trust you can aim well enough to do the job.'

She faced him. 'How dare you talk like that! As if your life means nothing!'

He looked at her. 'Another lecture? Perhaps you would be kind enough to tell me what you want and then leave me in peace to wallow in misery as I please.'

'If you must know, I want you. And if you dare make one of your stupid, sardonic remarks I will shoot you!' She glared at him. 'So, if you will kindly get up, I am going to take you to my carriage.'

'Are you?'

'Yes!' She marched over to him. She poked him in the shoulder with the pistol. 'Stand up!'

'I suggest you do as she asks, lad.'

He nearly groaned when he heard Mackenzie's voice. The man stood in the doorway and was looking at him with a stern, unyielding expression.

Nicholas slowly rose. 'Hell.'

Julia glanced over at her captive in one corner of the carriage. He had promptly closed his eyes after settling his long frame in the seat. His temper had not been improved, as they were leaving the saloon, by the sight of Lord Marleigh standing next to Amelia near the EO bank.

Julia doubted if he was asleep. He probably wanted to avoid her. Not that she blamed him. No doubt he was extremely angry at being hauled off in a carriage at gunpoint for a second time. And even if he did desire her, it did not mean that he even liked her.

She slumped against the seat, all the energy drained from her. They would be at Foxwood soon. She would offer him a bed if he wished, and then provide him with a horse so he could return to London as soon as possible.

He opened his eyes as soon as the carriage came to a halt in the drive. 'At least there were no highwaymen,' he remarked.

'No.'

Eduardo opened the door and assisted her down. She could not quite meet Nicholas's eyes when he descended. She was aware he looked at her for a moment before he walked towards the house.

She caught up with him. 'My lord.'

He halted and looked down at her. She bit her lip. 'I wanted to tell you that you may stay here overnight and then you are free to go. I will provide you a horse in the morning and you may return to London as soon as you wish.'

'This seems to be a habit as well. You abduct me, bring me to your farm and then attempt to throw me out again as soon as possible.' He started to move towards the house again. A furry figure came out of the bushes near the front door and rubbed against his leg. 'Ah, I see my friend has come to greet me.' He bent down and rubbed the cat's head.

Barbara opened the door. 'We've been wondering when you would return. No baggage again, I see.'

'Julia needs to either warn me when she plans to kidnap me or have my valet pack a bag that she can bring with her.' He stepped into the hallway.

'So, it's like that again, is it?' Barbara looked sharply at Julia. Julia flushed and followed him in. He headed towards the staircase.

Barbara frowned and called after him. 'There is no bedchamber ready for you.'

He paused with his hand on the railing. 'I assume Julia's bedchamber is suitable.'

Julia had come to the bottom of the staircase and looked up at him. 'Then where am I to sleep?'

'With me, if you wish. Or there is the sofa in the drawing room.'

His careless tone made her want to throw something. Or cry. She turned away and looked at Barbara. 'Perhaps the drawing room, then,' she said, keeping her voice as level as possible. 'If you could bring me some bedcovers and a pillow.' She started to walk towards the drawing room.

Barbara gave her a sympathetic glance. 'He's as stubborn as ever.'

Julia pulled off her gloves and laid them on the table

near the sofa. 'I do not blame him. He is probably very angry with me.'

'I doubt that is the reason,' Barbara said as she left the room.

Julia sat down on the sofa. The curtains had not been drawn and moonlight spilled across the worn oriental carpet. Wellington jumped up beside her and began to purr.

She stroked his head. The room was quiet and peaceful. The ticking of the clock, combined with Wellington's loud purr, had a soothing effect. If she could stay in such a moment, she could perhaps bear living without him. She closed her eyes and then something soft and cool brushed her lips.

'Julia.'

She opened her eyes. Nicholas knelt in front of her. 'I need to know why you brought me here,' he said.

'It was foolish of me.'

'That is not an answer.' His eyes searched her face. 'You said you wanted me.'

'Yes.' She glanced away. 'I suppose that was foolish of me as well.'

He slowly stood. 'At Maldon, when you sent me away, I knew you were lost to me. In every way possible. I had failed you. I told myself I did not want to see you again. When I saw you tonight, I knew that was not true. I suppose I wanted to hurt you as much as you had hurt me.'

She rose as well and came to stand in front of him. 'I sent you away, not because you failed me, but because I felt so empty. I had nothing to give you and so I thought I would hurt you less if I refused to see you.'

'What changed your mind?'

'I started to feel again. And I love you.' She had nothing to lose by telling him.

He stared at her for a moment and then gave an odd strangled laugh. 'Will you marry me, then?'

She looked at him uncertainly. 'Yes. Do you still want me?'

He stepped forward and caught her hands. 'Yes. In every way possible. Shall I reiterate for you?'

Her cheeks were starting to flame. 'I believe you did once tonight.'

'Yes, although you objected strongly.' He smiled a little. 'You still have not told me what you hoped to accomplish by abducting me again.'

'I had wanted to talk to you. And…' she coloured a little '…seduce you.'

He gave her a wicked smile. 'You cannot accomplish that by sleeping in here. You had best come upstairs. But first I need to make certain this is what you want.' He slowly pulled her towards him.

In the morning Julia woke before he did. She pulled on her dressing gown and slippers and went downstairs. She returned just as he opened his eyes. Nicholas looked disoriented for a moment and then his gaze fell on her. 'When I did not find you beside me I feared last night had been a dream. Where did you go?'

'Only to the drawing room.' She sat down on the bed next to him and he sat up, the cover falling from his chest. Julia looked at his beloved face with its shadow of beard. 'I have something to give you.'

She opened her hand and held out the ring. He stared at it for a moment, then his eyes went to her face. 'Where did you get it?'

'Sophia gave it me. Phillip recovered it from George's possessions.'

'I would not be surprised if you wanted to bury it,' he said slowly.

She smiled a little. 'Perhaps once I did. But Sophia reminded me that I gave it to Thomas because I loved him and Mary gave it to you because she loved you. And if it were not for the ring, I would not have met you.'

'No.' He continued to look at her.

She hesitated. 'Perhaps it reminds you too much of Mary. That is, it is not right of me to give it to you because she first gave it to you. I...I can quite understand that.'

'But then I should not wear it because you first gave it to Thomas. Thomas is gone and so is Mary. But we are here. I once thought that I had died with Mary. But I do not feel that way now.' He cupped her face for a moment, his hand gentle. 'I love you.'

'I have not died either. And I love you as well.' She took his hand. 'Will you wear it?'

'Yes.' He watched while she slipped it on his finger. And then he slowly lowered her to the bed. She saw tenderness mixed with desire as he lay over her. When he lowered his mouth to hers, she knew their ghosts had finally been freed to rest in peace.

\* \* \* \* \*

# Miss Harcourt's Dilemma
*by*
*Anne Ashley*

**Anne Ashley** was born and educated in Leicester. She lived for a time in Scotland, but now makes her home in the West Country with two cats, her two sons and a husband, who has a wonderful and very necessary sense of humour. When not pounding away at the keys of her word processor, she likes to relax in her garden, which she has opened to the public on more than one occasion in aid of the village church funds.

# Chapter One

*1815*

It was undoubtedly the burning ambition of most well-bred young ladies of marriageable age to enjoy the heady delights of at least one London Season. Like moths to a candle's flame, they were drawn to the capital for those few short weeks each spring in the hope that at the end of the ruinously expensive social whirl, where they could mix with the Cream of Society, they would bring a gleam of satisfaction to their ambitious relatives' eyes by achieving a suitable match or, better still, an advantageous one.

So why on earth, Verity wondered, staring with scant interest through the carriage window at the passing Kentish countryside, was she journeying to the capital? She had no wish to rub shoulders with members of the top ten thousand and had absolutely no desire whatsoever to marry a member of the *ton.* She recoiled at the mere thought of ever becoming a dutiful wife and kowtowing to the whims of some well-born gentleman. So why in heaven's name had she allowed herself to be bludgeoned into agreeing to a London Season in the first place?

She could not prevent a wry little smile as she turned her head and fixed her eyes on the rather plump middle-aged widow dozing very contentedly in the opposite corner of the carriage. No one who didn't know Lady Clara Billington well would ever imagine that beneath that rather indolent but graciously charming exterior was hidden a razor-sharp manipulative mind that the most accomplished strategist would have admired.

The well-sprung carriage lurched suddenly, bringing that lady awake with a start. "Oh, great heavens!" she exclaimed, automatically raising one podgy white hand to straighten her very fashionable bonnet. "I dare swear this road gets worse each time I travel along it. Remind me to have a word with my brother Charles, Verity, my dear. Something really ought to be done about it."

After making a great play of rearranging the folds of her maroon-coloured bombazine carriage dress, Lady Billington looked up to discover her niece regarding her with a disturbingly calculating gleam in her very fine eyes. "What is the matter, my love? Why, you are looking at me as though I were a complete stranger!"

"Was I?" Like the look in her eyes, Verity's smile was not pleasant. "As a matter of fact, I am beginning to wonder just how well I do know you, Aunt Clara. I realise, of course, that since the day I left the seminary you have been scheming to get me to London for a Season. What quite amazes me, though, is that you managed to get me to agree to it eventually!"

Lady Billington's only response to this was a rather warm but decidedly vague smile before she turned her head to stare resolutely out of the window.

In point of fact her astute young niece had been only

partially right. Almost from the day of her dear brother's sad demise Lady Billington had dreamt of chaperoning his sole offspring for the duration of at least one London Season. She had not been blessed with children of her own, and had taken a keen interest in all her nieces and nephews, but Verity had quickly become her undoubted favourite. When Verity's mother had sold her Hampshire home and had returned to her native Yorkshire to keep house for her unmarried elder brother, Mr Lucius Redmond, Lady Billington had kept in contact with her sister-in-law and niece, corresponding regularly and visiting at least once a year.

When Verity's mother, too, had sadly and most unexpectedly passed away, Lady Billington had been slightly hurt to discover that Lucius had been entrusted with Verity's sole guardianship. However, being a bachelor, Mr Redmond had been more than willing to listen to her views on the rearing of a young girl, who had sadly been allowed to degenerate into something of a tomboy by her doting parent, and it had been at Lady Billington's instigation that Verity had been sent to a very select seminary in Bath.

Thankfully, by the age of sixteen, when Verity had left the school, she had outgrown her tomboyish ways and had blossomed into an exceedingly lovely young lady. Not only had she an exquisite figure and a delicately featured face, but she had been blessed with the deepest of deep blue eyes, made more striking by a riot of blue-black curls. Sadly, though, she seemed impervious to the gifts Mother Nature had so generously bestowed upon her and, apart from the occasional visit she had made to Lady Billington's home in Kent, had been more than happy to incarcerate herself in Yorkshire, helping her uncle to run his very successful newspaper business.

"That air of innocence doesn't fool me for a moment, Aunt Clara," Verity stated flatly, breaking the silence which had lengthened between them. "You are a devious, conniving woman! You know full well that had you not intimated that you were no longer going to send me those juicy snippets of information, which I find so invaluable, I wouldn't be sitting here now."

"Unjust, child!" Lady Billington countered with as much vehemence as a lady of her placid disposition could muster. "I merely wrote and told you that with that wretched Corsican upstart on the loose again, and half of Society on the Continent, there would be little enough going on in London worth mentioning and that it would be far better for you to accompany me to the capital this year so that together we might just hear enough items of gossip for you to write an interesting little piece about the Season."

Verity was far from convinced, but decided that it was not in her own best interest to comment further, for she was very well aware that without her aunt's invaluable help she would never have been able to write those articles for inclusion in her uncle's newspaper.

He had been very much against the idea at first, not wanting to sully his journal with, as he termed it, "a load of frivolous gossip", but when Verity had argued that it was not only men who read newspapers, and that an occasional article of interest to the fair sex would be much appreciated by his many female readers, her uncle had allowed her to have her way. He was old-fashioned enough, however, to believe that ladies of Verity's class had no business working at all, and had stipulated right from the start that her efforts would be an occasional feature and had limited her to just one article per month.

Verity had been more than satisfied with that. Her items on fashions, the latest way to dress one's hair and the most up-to-date beauty aids had proved of immense interest to the ladies of Yorkshire, but most popular of all had been her résumé on the events of the London Season, for which, of course, she had needed the ever-watchful Lady Billington to forward the gossip about those more colourful and well-known leaders of fashion.

"Well, if London is thin of company this Season," Verity remarked, her finely arched black brows drawing together in thought, "there is always Prinny to fall back on. He never fails to indulge in some lunacy, and I'm sure not every member of the top ten thousand has deserted our shores for the delights of Vienna… Or is it Brussels they are all flocking to now?"

"Yes, I believe it is. A pity, really." Lady Billington gave a sudden start. "I *have* heard one item of gossip whilst I've been in Kent which should interest you. It looks as though Arthur Brinley's grandson is destined to be the next Viscount Dartwood." There was no response to this and she regarded her niece in silence for a moment. "I know how fond you were of that old man, Verity, but I cannot recall your ever mentioning his grandson. Surely you are acquainted with Major Carter?"

"I knew him, yes," Verity admitted, "but I haven't set eyes on him for…oh, must be over five years now."

Once again Lady Billington studied her niece's lovely profile in silence for a moment, then said, "Am I right in thinking that you do not care for the Major very much, my dear? Do you hold him in dislike?"

Dislike…? The word seemed to echo round the con-

fines of the carriage, bringing a further thoughtful frown
to crease Verity's forehead. Did she dislike Arthur Brinley's grandson? No, she didn't think so, even though he
had hurt her rather badly once, but that seemed such a
long time ago. If she had thought about him at all in
recent years, which hadn't been often, it had been when
she had read a report in her uncle's newspaper of his
exploits during the Peninsular Campaign.

A sigh escaped her. "No, I don't dislike him, Aunt
Clara, even though he is a nincompoop." She shrugged.
"I really ought, I suppose, to think well of him, for he
has proved himself a very courageous soldier… And he
did once save my life."

"Great heavens!" Lady Billington was astounded.
"What on earth happened?"

"Oh, nothing very exciting," Verity responded with
a dismissive wave of her hand. "I came perilously close
to drowning myself once—would most certainly have
succeeded in doing so had not Brin dived into that lake
to rescue me."

Her aunt shuddered. "I suppose that occurred in the
days when you indulged in your tomboyish behaviour?"

"It most certainly did," Verity confirmed, completely
unabashed by her aunt's rather disapproving tone. She
gave a sudden start. "But you're right, you know! Brin's
coming into the title will prove of immense interest to
the ladies of Yorkshire. He's quite the local hero. It's
rumoured that he's sold his commission." Her lovely
eyes narrowed speculatively. "He hasn't returned to
Yorkshire. At least," she amended, "he hadn't when I
left last week…I wonder where he's hiding himself?"

"He may very well be in London, dear. It's rumoured
that uncle of his is deteriorating fast, and although the
dreadful creature has done everything humanly possible

to stop his nephew from coming into the title by marrying that poor child who's young enough to be his granddaughter, as I've mentioned before, it looks very likely the Major will very shortly be the new Viscount Dartwood.''

Verity gurgled with unholy amusement. ''Poor Brin! If he has been foolish enough to descend on the capital, he'll have every matchmaking mama after him.''

Lady Billington cast her niece a mildly reproachful look, and was about to inform her that she had a rather perverse sense of humour when there was a most peculiar splintering sound. The next instant she was thrown against the side of the carriage as the equipage came to a rather unexpected and abrupt halt.

''What on earth has happened?''

''I've no idea,'' Verity responded, having managed to keep her seat by retaining a firm grasp on the strap, ''but here's Ridge now, so no doubt we'll soon discover what's amiss.''

The off-side door was wrenched open and the worried face of Lady Billington's head groom appeared in the aperture. ''Are you all right, my lady?''

''Yes, Ridge. We're both fine,'' she assured him whilst trying to ease herself into a more upright position, which was no easy task as the carriage was leaning at a most peculiar angle. ''What on earth has happened?''

''The front near-side wheel's damaged and one of the traces is broke. Luckily we're within sight of Sittingbourne, ma'am. If you would care to travel in t'other carriage to The Crown, me and Clem'll walk the 'orses to the inn, and then I'll see about getting the damage repaired. Mind, there's every chance it won't be today.''

''Oh, how very tiresome! I did so want to reach London in good time to attend Lady Swayle's party this evening. Still—" she shrugged "—it cannot be helped. If you would assist Miss Verity, and then help me to alight."

Being young and slender, Verity had little trouble in scrambling out, but Lady Billington, whose girth had increased greatly in middle age, found the task no easy one, and it took the combined efforts of both niece and groom to ease her out of the carriage and onto the road.

The second coach, which had drawn to a halt a few yards behind, was not only piled high with baggage, for Lady Billington had never been known to travel light, but contained her personal maid, Dodd, the butler and what Verity considered two of the most obnoxious pets in Christendom: a green parrot and an overfed lap-dog called Horace.

Pandemonium broke out when Verity, in her usual no-nonsense manner, scooped Horace off the seat and deposited him on the hapless butler's lap. The pampered Pekinese, having taken exception to being rudely awoken from his slumber, voiced his displeasure by alternately growling and yapping which, in turn, startled the excitable parrot into vocal outbursts, and its disharmonious ear-piercing squawks continued unabated until the carriage came to a halt in the inn yard.

"That is it!" Verity snapped, alighting almost before the groom had let down the steps. "I refuse to travel another mile with those repulsive pets of yours. Why on earth you find it necessary to take the noisy blighters with you whenever you travel, I'll never know!"

"Now, now, dear, calm down," Lady Billington said soothingly, following her irate young niece into the inn. "I don't know from where you get that naughty temper of yours. Your dear papa was the most placid of creatures and I can never recall witnessing your mama ever

lose her cool. Although…'' she frowned suddenly
''…some of the Harcourts have been known to have had
a short fuse. Your great-grandfather, the fourth Duke,
was a man of almost insane temper. I recall several
members of the family remarking that he ought to have
been locked up in Bedlam.''

Verity cast her a glance of impatience. ''There's a
difference between insanity and justifiable annoyance,
Aunt Clara. Those confounded pets of yours are enough
to try the patience of a saint! And if you try to force me
to travel the rest of the way to London in the same carriage as those two monsters you'll risk losing them both,
for I shan't balk at wringing that green goose's neck or
at throwing that pampered whelp out of the window!''

Lady Billington wisely refrained from lecturing her
niece on the unforgivable wickedness of hurting dumb
creatures, and said instead, ''But, dear, you cannot possibly remain here by yourself. Why, it's unthinkable!''

''I shan't be by myself. Ridge will be with me.
Look,'' she went on hurriedly, not giving her aunt the
opportunity to point out the very obvious flaw in this
scheme, ''let us have some light refreshments whilst
we're waiting for Ridge to discover if the carriage can
be repaired today, and then decide what we're going to
do when we've spoken to him again.''

As this was the most sensible course of action Lady
Billington caught the attention of one of the inn servants
and ordered a light repast. They repaired to the coffee-
room and occupied their time while waiting for Ridge
by watching the comings and goings of the numerous
travellers moving about the very busy coaching inn.
When Ridge finally came to them his tidings were not
good. The carriage, it seemed, could not be repaired until
the morning, so he suggested he put up at the inn and

continue the journey to London the following day, once repairs had been effected.

Lady Billington had no fault to find with these arrangements, and summoned the landlord, but when Verity announced that she too would remain for the night and travel with Ridge the following day, Lady Billington's sense of propriety was deeply offended and she simply could not countenance such a scheme.

"I'm sorry, Verity, but it is out of the question. Why, it's unthinkable that you remain here without so much as a maid! I'm afraid you have no choice but to continue the journey with me."

"No!" Verity argued, stubborn to the last. "I won't travel with those wretched creatures!" She noticed Ridge's lips twitch slightly, and didn't miss the unmistakable look of sympathy in his eyes either, before she turned to the landlord, who was patiently waiting to hear whether one or two rooms would be required. "Is it possible to hire a vehicle from here?"

"Ordinarily, miss, yes, it would be. But this be a busy time o' year, with folk travelling to London for the Season, and I've nothing available. Although…" he ran a hand over his balding pate "…you might just get a seat on the mail. Mind, as your name ain't on the waybill there's no guarantee, but if there be room the coachman just might take you up."

"But you still cannot possibly travel without some female companion," her aunt put in before Verity could voice her whole-hearted approval of this solution. "And it's of no use your asking Dodd to accompany you because, as this good man has so rightly pointed out, there's no guarantee you'll get seats on the mail. Besides, I'll need Dodd to dress me for the party tonight."

"Well, ma'am, I might just be able to 'elp you out

there,'' the landlord remarked unexpectedly, much to Verity's delight and her aunt's intense irritation. ''My young niece be awaiting the mail.'' He gestured towards a corner table at which a young woman, wearing a grey cloak and bonnet, sat quite alone. ''She were in service with the Dowager Lady Longbourne, but the old lady passed on a month back and my niece be going to London to look for another position.''

Lady Billington was still far from happy over Verity's travelling to London on the mail-coach, but, after exchanging a few words with the innkeeper's niece, who seemed a very quiet and well-mannered young person, she very reluctantly acquiesced to the scheme and, as the afternoon was well advanced, wasted no further time in resuming her journey.

Once Verity had seen her aunt safely on her way, she went back inside the hostelry and sat herself down beside the innkeeper's niece. ''I suppose I ought to introduce myself as my company has been rather forced upon you,'' she remarked with her friendly smile. ''My name is Harcourt… Verity Harcourt.''

''Margaret Jones, miss. But everyone calls me Meg.''

Verity subjected her fellow traveller to a swift appraising glance. Although dressed in sensible rather than fashionable attire, she was as neat as wax. ''So, Meg, you are journeying to the capital in the hope of finding employment?''

''Yes, miss. My sister lives there, so I'll stay with her until I can find myself another situation. I have a reference from Lady Longbourne's family. I was her ladyship's personal maid, but I don't expect I'll find work as an abigail. There are plenty with far more experience than me, so I'll be happy to take anything, for there's nothing round these parts.''

Verity subjected the innkeeper's niece to a further appraising stare. Although she was quietly spoken, and evidently a little shy in the company of strangers, her clear grey eyes looked directly at one when she spoke, and Verity rather liked that.

She turned her head to stare sightlessly across the coffee-room, wondering whether to offer the young woman employment. Having always enlisted the help of one of her uncle's female servants whenever the need had arisen, Verity had never felt it necessary to employ an experienced personal maid. However, as dear Aunt Clara was so fond of reminding her, what prevailed in the wilds of Yorkshire was not necessarily acceptable in a more polished society.

She was also very well aware that her freedom would be drastically curtailed during her time in London. Jaunting about on her own would be strictly forbidden, she knew, and it was hardly fair to expect one of her aunt's servants to bear her company whenever she wished to go out for a walk, nor was it reasonable to suppose that Dodd would be willing to tend to her needs for the duration of her stay as well as those of Lady Billington.

As was her wont, Verity came to a decision swiftly. "How would you like to work for me, Meg?" she enquired, and then chuckled at the young woman's look of astonishment. "Truly, I am in earnest," she assured her. "It's high time I had a personal maid. Although I think it only fair to warn you that I live for the most part in Yorkshire, so if a quiet life in the country is not to your taste it might be best if you did seek a situation in the capital."

"Oh, no, miss. I was born and raised in the country, and Lady Longbourne never travelled far from home when I worked for her," Meg hurriedly assured her, hardly daring to believe her great good fortune. "No, it isn't that. It's just… Well, won't the lady who was with you earlier want to speak to me first? Your aunt, wasn't it?"

"Yes, Lady Billington is my aunt, but it has little to do with her, even though we shall be residing in her town house for the next few weeks. No, it's my guardian who'll be paying your wages. And Uncle Lucius will adhere to my decision, I'm sure."

"In that case, miss," Meg responded, rising from the table just as the unmistakable sound of a horn was heard heralding the arrival of the mail, "I'd better have a word with my uncle. If you aren't able to get a seat on the coach then it's my duty now to stay with you."

A few minutes later Verity watched a tall man stride purposefully into the inn by way of a side entrance. His powerful frame was swathed in a voluminous, caped grey cloak. An old-fashioned tricorn was pulled low over his brow and the lower part of his face was muffled in a dark woollen scarf so that only his eyes were visible. She assumed he must be the coachman, for he went directly across to the innkeeper and then, after exchanging a few words with Meg and her uncle, turned his head in her direction. He stared across at her for what seemed an interminable and, to her way of thinking, quite unnecessary length of time before giving an almost imperceptible nod of his head and then strode through the doorway by which he had entered.

"Yes, it's all right, Miss Harcourt," Meg came across to inform her. "The Coachman said he'd take you up, but we'd best hurry because he's a little behind schedule."

As Verity could see no sign of her aunt's groom, she asked the innkeeper to inform Ridge that she had managed to get a seat on the mail and then went outside to the inn yard to find the coach, painted in the royal livery of scarlet, maroon and black, ready and waiting to leave.

"What, no baggage, lass? I 'ope I ain't taking up no runaway!"

Momentarily startled, Verity looked up to see the Coachman peering down at her from his seat on the box. She gained the distinct impression from the wicked glint in his light brown eyes that he was laughing at her, but tactfully refrained from giving him a well-deserved set-down in case he should take umbrage and then refuse to take her. She merely contented herself with a haughty toss of her proud little head before clambering inside the rather musty-smelling equipage.

Thankfully the coach was not too crowded. A rather plump lady holding a sleeping infant on her lap, a man in rough workman's clothes, who bore all the appearance of a farmer, and a middle-aged individual of below average height, dressed in a suit of severe black cloth, occupied one seat, and Verity sat herself beside Meg on the other. Apart from a cursory glance she took little heed of her fellow travellers and began to chat away to Meg as the coach pulled out of the inn yard, telling her of her uncle's lovely home situated on the edge of the moors, and of the plans her aunt had made for the forthcoming Season.

"However," Verity went on to say, "with the unexpected turn of events in Europe my aunt doesn't envisage such a gay time in London this year, so with any luck she will not wish to remain until June."

"Ha! You speak of—how do you English say?—the Upstart's escape from Elba, no?" the man in the black suit unexpectedly remarked in a decidedly foreign accent, drawing all eyes in his direction.

"Oh, my gawd!" ejaculated the fat woman, suddenly holding the sleeping infant more tightly to her ample bosom. "Never tell me you're one of them there 'eathen Frenchies!"

"No, *madame.* I am Swiss and have papers to prove it. I am a watchmaker by trade," he went on to divulge, tapping the flat wooden box resting on his lap, "and am in your country on business."

"No doubt you had started upon your travels before news of the Emperor's escape had reached your home town, *monsieur?*" Verity remarked, unable to prevent a smile at the way the fat lady continued to regard the gentleman with blatant suspicion.

"Yes, *mademoiselle,* otherwise I would not have ventured forth, I assure you. But—" he shrugged "—I am in no danger here, I think."

"Indeed you are not, *monsieur.* We can safely put our trust in Wellington. He will not fail us," Verity assured him, a hint of pride creeping in to her voice, before turning once again to Meg, who was beginning to lose much of her shyness with her new and, what seemed to her, pleasantly friendly young mistress.

The miles sped by while Verity and Meg chatted away contentedly, and before they knew it they were drawing up in the yard of yet another busy posting house. The change of horses was effected quickly, and then they were on their way again.

It was a well-known fact that nothing was allowed to hinder mail-coaches. The guard would sound his horn to warn toll-keepers of their approach so that gates were opened without the need to stop. It came as something of a surprise to all the passengers, therefore, when for no apparent reason the coach slowed down and came to an unexpected halt.

Verity noticed the rather apprehensive glance the Swiss gentleman cast out of the window before he turned his rather hard grey eyes in her direction.

"What can be wrong, *mademoiselle?*"

Her shrug betrayed her complete lack of interest. She was in no particular hurry to reach London, so was not unduly concerned with any possible delay. She could hear the sound of voices outside and assumed that someone had flagged down the coach, possibly to warn the driver of some hazard ahead. No more than a minute or two had elapsed before they set off again, but at a much slower pace, and then, after travelling no more than a few hundred yards, they came to a halt yet again in the yard of a small wayside inn. Moments later the off-side door was thrown wide and the guard in his scarlet and gold livery appeared in the aperture.

"There's a tree fallen across the road half a mile or so ahead and vehicles building up quite some way back from it, so we'll be waiting 'ere until the road's been cleared. The Coachman says if you wants a bite to eat, make the most of the time now, 'cause he won't be stopping again 'cepting to change 'orses."

"An excellent suggestion!" Verity remarked, cutting across the fat lady's grumbles as she accepted the guard's helping hand to alight. "No one can be held responsible for what is, after all, an act of God."

"Glad t'discover tha's a sensible lass. Mayhap tha's no runaway after all," that goading, thickly-accented voice from above once again remarked, causing Verity to miss her footing. She caught the heel of her shoe in the hem of her skirts and would have fallen down the steps but for the guard's supporting hand.

"Now see what you've made me do!" she snapped, glancing down at the torn flounce before raising angrily accusing dark blue eyes up to those of the Coachman. "And I would be grateful if in the future you kept your inane reflections to yourself!"

Meg and the Coachman's wickedly taunting deep rumble of masculine laughter followed Verity into the inn. Like most volatile people, she had a temper quickly roused, but it just as swiftly abated, and she had never been known to vent her ill-humour on anyone other than the person who had instigated her wrath. So, when Meg tentatively offered to pin up the torn flounce, she thanked her but said she could manage perfectly well and then politely asked her to see about getting them some refreshments.

Apart from the mail-coach passengers there was only one other customer in the inn, a thickset man of average height, supping a tankard of ale as he stared resolutely out of the window, but even so Verity was far too modest to raise her skirts and effect temporary repairs to her torn undergarment whilst in the presence of the opposite sex, and so looked about for somewhere a little more private.

The inn was only small, and there appeared to be no private parlour, but she noticed a passageway leading off the tap and succeeded in slipping away without being noticed. As luck would have it the first door along the passageway was slightly ajar and she didn't hesitate to poke her head into the room. Thankfully it was deserted, but there were the remains of a meal on the table and, more importantly, there was a large screen placed halfway across the window which, Verity noticed as she secreted herself behind it, had been so positioned to try to prevent the considerable draught blasting through the ill-fitting windows from penetrating too far into the room.

She had just completed her task, and was placing the spare pins back into her reticule, when she heard the sound of heavy footsteps as someone entered the room. She had never suffered from shyness, not even as a child, so it would not have embarrassed her in the least to show herself and explain the very understandable reason for her presence in the room. Yet, without quite knowing why, she decided not to do so.

Peering through the crack in the screen, Verity saw a man with his back towards her, standing by the grate. She had not seen his face earlier, and she still couldn't see it now, but she had no difficulty in recognising him as the man who had been staring fixedly through the taproom window when she had first entered the inn. He was dressed in outdoor clothes, so it was safe to assume that he must be on the point of departure, she thought, but when, after several minutes had elapsed, he continued to stare down with apparent rapt interest at the logs burning brightly on the hearth she decided to make her presence known.

Reaching for her reticule, which she had placed on the rather worm-eaten windowsill, Verity was about to step out from behind the screen when she heard someone else enter the room, and an unmistakable foreign-accented voice say, "It was very clever of you, *monsieur*, to meet me here. How could you have possibly known we would be making this unscheduled stop?"

"You're not the only one with brains," the other man responded in deep, rather harsh-sounding tones, which betrayed both irritation and resentment. "I arrived early at the meeting place and learned of the tree blocking the road. It's possible for a man on horseback to get through, so I decided to ride on ahead. Mail-coaches are famed for keeping good time. I guessed the Coachman wouldn't be stopping again, except to change horses, and this place is only about half a mile away from the blockage. I was looking out for you from the window, intending to follow the rest of the way to London in the hope that I might just get the chance to pass on my master's message.''

Verity, having placed her eye to the crack in the screen again, had a perfect view of the foreigner and watched his thin lips twist into the most unpleasant and sinister smile. She had paid only scant attention to him in the coach, accepting him completely at face value. Now, however, she was far from sure that he was all that he seemed. There was something decidedly calculating in those hard grey eyes of his. He began speaking again and she listened intently.

"How obliging it was, then, of the Coachman to pull in here." His unpleasant smile faded. "We have little time and it would not be wise, I think, to be seen together. Have you anything for me?''

''Nothing yet. But my master will meet you at the usual rendezvous on Friday evening at eight o'clock.''

''Ah, yes! I remember. The inn at zee Leetle, Leetle Frampington. You English are so *drôle, n'est-ce-pas?* Very well. Inform your master I shall be there. And remind him the situation is of the most urgent. I must not delay. My beloved Emperor needs that information. He must know Wellington's plans!''

# Chapter Two

Verity had always felt justifiably proud of the noble Harcourt blood flowing through her veins. Like any other family it had certainly produced the odd black sheep, the usual smattering of rogues and rakes. The most notorious had been the third Duke, who had been suspected of murdering his first wife, although it had to be said in his defence that this had never been proved, but even those whose names were never mentioned except in whispers had always been unfailingly loyal to the crown.

Three of her young cousins were engaged in the present conflict with France, and, had Verity been born a boy, she wouldn't have hesitated to take the King's Shilling. She had never lacked for courage or daring, a circumstance which had caused Lady Billington many sleepless nights, so it would have come as something of a surprise to that lady to know that it was as much as Verity could do to stop her knees from buckling in those moments when she watched the foreigner, quickly followed by his accomplice, leave the room.

The Emperor…? Wellington…? The words seemed to reverberate off the walls like so many hammer-blows.

Dear Lord! What had she inadvertently stumbled upon? More importantly, what on earth should she do about it?

Her first impulse was to confront the foreigner, to accuse him of being a spy and have him placed in the hands of the authorities, but she curbed it. There was a very good chance she might not be believed, and truth to tell she could hardly believe it herself. It would be her word against his, after all, and no doubt he carried authentic-looking enough documents stating that he was nothing more than the innocent Swiss watchmaker he purported to be. Then, of course, there was that other man to consider. Her eyes narrowed as she recalled his words. Evidently he was merely the go-between, nothing more than a servant. But if she could get a close look at his face, and pass on an accurate description of the man to the authorities, he just might lead them to his master, the real villain of the piece.

Her course of action now clear, Verity tried to step out from her hiding place once again, only to be thwarted this time by a slatternly maidservant, whose apron was streaked with grime and whose dishevelled hair looked as though it had not seen a comb in a month of Sundays. In silent dismay she watched as the servant began, with a lassitude that was painful to witness, to pile the used dishes onto a tray. If the innkeeper had given instructions for the table to be cleared then it stood to reason that the go-between had paid his shot and was on the point of departure. There was not a moment to lose, but there was little Verity could do. It was of vital importance now that no one knew of her presence in this room, and so she had, perforce, to wait until the maid-servant had withdrawn.

It seemed to take an eternity for the girl to complete her task, but the instant the coast was clear Verity wasted not a second in returning to the entrance to the tap. She had a clear view of the counter, where the mail-coach guard stood beside the passenger who bore all the appearance of a farmer. She could also see the plump lady sitting at the corner table, feeding broth to her infant, and she could just make out the rim of her newly appointed maid's grey bonnet.

Meg was seated at the table by a substantial wooden pillar, and looked to be speaking to someone outside Verity's field of vision. In all probability it was the foreign spy, but Verity wasn't unduly concerned over this. Meg, after all, had no notion of his true profession and would, therefore, behave quite naturally. But of the go-between there was no sign. Might he have departed already?

Picking up her skirts, Verity ran back along the passageway to the door at the far end. As she had suspected it led outside to the stable yard. Since their arrival at the inn the light had deteriorated. The sky now was heavily overcast, but there was sufficient light for her to see all the outbuildings quite clearly and for her to avoid the numerous puddles, the residue of the previous day's torrential downpour, dotted across the yard as she made her way towards the stable block.

The place appeared deserted. The only sounds she detected were those made by the coach horses champing at their bits, but as she drew level with the mail-coach, brought to a halt a matter of a few yards from the stable entrance, she detected a sudden movement towards the rear of the carriage and turned her head to see the Coachman, his back towards her, staring fixedly out across the open countryside as he inhaled on a cheroot. He seemed oblivious to her presence, and as Verity was more than content to keep it that way she tiptoed across the remaining distance to the large stable only to find it, frustratingly, empty.

"And what be you about, lass, skulking out 'ere?"

Verity gave a start and swung round to see the tall figure of the Coachman standing in the doorway, effectively blocking her exit. She regarded him in exasperated silence. He really was the most irritating creature she had ever had the misfortune to encounter!

"Do you get some perverse pleasure from creeping up behind innocent damsels and scaring them half out of their wits?" she enquired, with all the haughtiness of her noble Harcourt blood.

He flicked the stub of his cheroot into a convenient puddle down by his left boot before folding his arms across his broad chest and casting his eyes over her with a slow insolence which infuriated her. "I'm beginning to wonder just 'ow innocent tha be, lass. And I can't 'elp wondering what tha be doing travelling by the mail."

Verity had grown accustomed over the years to receiving every respect and courtesy from menials, but this individual was a law unto himself. What business was it of his how she chose to travel about the country? The mannerless creature really ought to be reminded of his proper place, she decided, but the masterly set-down which rose in her throat was held in check by a sudden thought.

"How long have you been out here? Did you happen to notice a man in a grey cloak, not unlike your own, leave the inn?"

"Ha! So I were right! Tha's a runaway, after all, and thy lover's deserted you."

"Don't be nonsensical!" Verity was fast coming to the end of her tether, and only just managed to control the overwhelming desire to box his ears soundly. "I have neither the time nor the inclination to bandy words with you. Now, just answer my question, dolt!"

"Dolt, is it?" he remarked, an unmistakable edge sharpening his not unattractive deep, husky voice, and before Verity could do anything to avoid him, he had bridged the distance between them in three massive strides and had picked her up in his strong arms.

Much to her further outrage, her demands to be put down at once were sublimely ignored, and the next instant she found herself tossed unceremoniously down on a pile of hay with the Coachman's body pressed half on top of her, effectively keeping her there. More scandalised than afraid, she hit out with her small fists, only to have her wrists captured effortlessly and imprisoned above her head in one large hand. She had a glimpse of thick, slightly waving hair as the Coachman turned his head away and tossed his hat aside. Then his other hand was placed over her eyes and a firm, warm mouth was clamped over hers, silencing her angry threat of reprisals.

Only then did Verity experience a pulsating throb of fear tremble its way through her as her aunt's dire warnings of never permitting herself to be alone with a man echoed tauntingly in her ears. Now she could appreciate that sage advice, for she was brutally aware that she lacked the strength to stop this assault upon her—but equally aware that her captor was exerting only sufficient force to hold her firm. Her breasts were in no danger of being crushed beneath that broad expanse of chest, her wrists were not likely to suffer harm from that merely restraining hold, nor was her mouth in the least peril of becoming bruised beneath the featherlight touch of lips that parted hers with infinitely gentle expertise.

Never before had she found herself in such a compromising position. Never before had any man dared to take such liberties with her. She knew she ought to feel disgusted and outraged, and yet she seemed powerless to prevent her lips trembling invitingly in response when his kiss deepened. His mouth fitted so perfectly to hers that it seemed almost as if they had become as one, that she belonged to him just as surely as if they had been legally joined in wedlock, and she only knew in those moments of newly awakened desire that she didn't want those pleasurable sensations tingling through her ever to end.

"Well, now, lass, yon were right revealing." In one swift movement he had pulled away from her and had the muffler covering his face even before Verity had a chance to open her eyes. "Ne'er bin kissed afore, and enjoyed the experience, I'm thinking."

His taunting was like a slap in the face, bringing her back to reality with a cruel jolt. Scrambling to her feet, she experienced hurt and humiliation, anger and disgust in equal measures.

"How dare you use me like a—a trollop?" she snapped, doing her best to brush the clinging bits of hay from her skirts. "I shall report you to your superiors!"

It was an empty threat, spoken only in an attempt to conceal confusion and humiliation, she knew, and so, seemingly, did he, for his only response was to roar with laughter as he turned his back towards her and leaned forward on his knees to reach his tricorn.

Verity's eyes glinted dangerously. A sudden thirst for revenge was all-consuming and the target presented just a mite too tempting to ignore. So, drawing back her stoutly shod foot, she placed a well-aimed and punishing

kick to the seat of his breeches, the force of which sent
the Coachman sprawling forward into the hay.

"Why, tha little…!" Wait 'til I gets 'old o' thee!"

But Verity had no intention of waiting. One confron-
tation with this obnoxious creature was enough to last a
lifetime! She ran out of the stable and across the yard
as swiftly as her young legs would carry her, and didn't
stop running until she had re-entered the tap, where Meg
looked up at her in some concern.

"Why, Miss Verity! Wherever have you been? I was
just about to go searching for you."

With a praiseworthy attempt at appearing nonchalant
Verity seated herself at the table. "Really, Meg, I'm
deeply grateful to think that you're so concerned over
my welfare," she remarked, intentionally not lowering
her voice so that the so-called watchmaker at the next
table could not help but overhear, "but there are certain
times during the day when I demand privacy, and certain
places where modesty dictates I must go alone. And one
of those places is to be found outside in the yard."

The explanation for her long absence appeared to satisfy both listeners: Meg looked as though she had been
dipping into the rouge-pot, and the foreigner coughed
delicately before picking up his glass of wine.

This was a golden opportunity to hold the Swiss gentleman, if indeed he was Swiss, in conversation, but Verity remained frustratingly in two minds. If she suddenly
began to show a keen interest in her fellow traveller
might he not become suspicious? Added to which, honesty prompted her to admit that she felt unequal to the
task of asking seemingly innocent questions just at the
moment. Having nowhere near recovered from the rather
unnerving episode in the stable, she hadn't sufficient
wits about her to indulge in some cat-and-mouse game.

On the other hand, though, she felt it her duty to discover all she could about this man.

As it happened, the decision of how to proceed was taken out of her hands, for no sooner had she finished her now tepid cup of coffee than the guard came over to inform them that the blockage in the road had been cleared and that they would be leaving immediately.

Deliberately keeping her eyes lowered, Verity mounted the steps into the equipage, but she instinctively knew that the Coachman was staring down at her, and was no doubt deriving much amusement from her obvious discomfiture. Curse him! She knew, too, the instant they recommenced their journey, that he was deliberately tooling the vehicle at a wildly dangerous pace so as to make the ride as uncomfortable as possible… especially for her!

She clung to the strap as though her very life depended upon it, wondering how, with the exception of Meg, her fellow-travellers could doze while being jolted about in such a fashion. Even the ''watchmaker'' had his eyes closed, and, frustratingly, they remained so, which effectively prevented Verity from trying to discover anything further about him that might have been of some use to the authorities. Consequently, by the time they had arrived in London, late in the evening, she was not in the best of humours.

After requesting Meg to secure a hackney carriage, Verity was about to alight herself when she realised she had left her reticule behind. By the time she had located its whereabouts, wedged down the side of the seat, all the other passengers had alighted. Cursing under her breath, for she had wanted to keep an eye on that spy to see in which direction he went, she turned, and was about to place her foot down on the steps when she saw the Coachman, not the guard, waiting to offer a helping hand. His eyes were sparkling with devilment which, in turn, ignited an ominous glint in her own. She had borne much that day, especially from him, and the rein on her temper finally snapped.

"I shall take leave to inform you that you are the most uncouth oaf it has ever been my misfortune to encounter! And, what is more, the most cow-handed driver ever to take up the ribbons!" she informed him with brutal frankness while resisting quite beautifully the strong urge to slap his outstretched hand away. "Now, kindly remove your unprepossessing carcass out of my sight!"

His goading response, as it had been earlier, was to throw his head back and roar with laughter. Then, before Verity could formulate something else cutting to say, he placed his hands on her narrow waist and lifted her out of the coach, holding her effortlessly high in the air for several seconds, just as though she weighed no more than a child, before lowering her to her feet.

"Aye, tha's grow into a right floutersome lass, Verity 'Arcourt. And I mind tha'll suit me right well."

"You think I'd...? Well, of all the brass-faced impertinence!"

Verity swung her arm in a wide arc, but by exercising some very neat footwork the Coachman avoided the reticule making contact with his left ear, and Verity had to content herself with a further lofty toss of the head before stalking away across the yard, the Coachman's taunting laughter, for what seemed the umpteenth time that day, ringing in her ears.

"Did you happen to notice which way that foreigner went, Meg?" she asked, after having looked in vain about the yard for him.

''No, miss. I didn't. I were busy hiring this here hackney carriage.''

Knowing that it would be rather futile to try searching for him in London's busy streets, Verity gave her aunt's address to the driver and then clambered into the hired carriage.

''That dratted Coachman!'' she snapped, blaming him entirely for foiling her attempts to keep track of the spy. ''If I were a vindictive person I wouldn't think twice about reporting that oaf to his superiors. Did you see the wretch manhandling me just now?''

Meg had indeed witnessed her young mistress being assisted from the mail-coach. ''He were a bit saucy, miss,'' she responded, failing completely to suppress a chuckle. ''And very taken with you he were, too.''

''I'll give him taken with me. Such impudence! Why, if the wretch ever crosses my path again, I'll…'' Verity sat bolt-upright, gaping in astonished incredulity. ''Meg, he knows me! He knew my name.''

''Course he did, miss. I told him it, back at my uncle's inn.''

''No, Meg. We've met before today. I'd swear to it. He's a Yorkshireman. That accent of his wasn't false.'' Her eyes narrowed as she turned her head to stare blindly out of the carriage window. ''Who on earth can he be?''

## Chapter Three

Although Lady Billington would have been the first to admit that she was not one to bestir herself unduly, she had never been known to partake of breakfast in bed when she had a guest residing under her roof. None the less, when she entered the small breakfast parlour the following morning her motive for doing so was not primarily to bear her niece company for the first meal of the day but to take her roundly to task on the sheer folly of impulsively engaging servants without even so much as checking the authenticity of their references first.

Verity listened to the moderately staunchly voiced criticisms with equanimity. However, when her aunt paused to sip her coffee, she remarked in a tone bordering on the indifferent, "But didn't you read Meg's reference? I asked her last night to ensure that you got it. I felt certain you would have known Lady Longbourne, or known of her. You seem to know everyone."

"Yes, I knew her—vaguely. And, yes, Dodd did hand it to me first thing this morning and everything seems to be in order," she freely admitted, but was still far from appeased. "That doesn't alter the fact, though, that you hadn't taken the trouble to look at it yourself before offering the girl employment. You're so impulsive, child! It was against my better judgement that I left you yesterday. I cannot tell you what agonies I suffered! Why, anything might have happened to you!''

Something most definitely had, Verity mused, biting into a deliciously warm buttered roll, her mind going back to the previous day when she had entered that wayside inn. Then her aunt began speaking again and she forced herself to listen, but without any degree of real interest, to what she was saying.

''…and I learned last night from Louisa Hickox, a very old friend of mine, that your Major Carter is in town. He's staying at his friend Marcus Ravenhurst's house in Berkeley Square.''

''He isn't *my* Major Carter,'' Verity pointed out with a touch of asperity.

''Well, dear, you know what I mean. I discovered, too, that he is paying particular attention to three young ladies. So it looks as though he's thinking of settling down. And that's no bad thing if he does come into the title, which looks more likely with every passing day.''

Verity didn't bother to respond to this at all. Instead, she asked, ''Do you happen to know if Uncle Charles is in town?''

Lady Billington detected nothing amiss in this sudden and unexpected enquiry. Verity had never made any secret of the fact that Lord Charles was her favourite male member of the Harcourt family, and she had been naughty enough to suggest on more than one occasion that it was a great pity that he had not been the eldest son, for he would have made a fine duke as he was by far the most intelligent member of the family.

''I should imagine so, dear. He rarely leaves London. His only real love is his career, as you very well know.''

She shrugged one plump shoulder. "It's probably just as well he never married, I suppose."

"You appear to have marriage on the brain this morning. There are worse fates than remaining unattached, Aunt Clara," Verity remarked, rising from the table. "I think I shall pay him an impromptu visit. I haven't set eyes on him in a twelvemonth."

"Very well, dear," Lady Billington responded, her unruffled complacency having by this time returned, "but do not be too long. Remember we are to visit the dressmaker later this morning."

"I shall be back in good time," Verity assured her. "And what is more," she added, casting her eyes in the direction of the comfortable winged chair in the corner of the room in which her aunt's pampered pet lay contentedly dozing, "I shall be kind to Horace and take him with me. The only exercise that poor creature ever gets is jumping in and out of your carriage. The walk will do him good."

Lady Billington regarded her beloved pet in some concern, but a short while later, as she watched Verity leave the house with her maid, and with Horace tripping quite contentedly alongside, her dreadful fear that her precious Pekinese might betray displeasure at the forced excursion by nipping at a neatly turned ankle and end its days by being thrown into the murky grey waters of the Thames was dispelled.

Lord Charles Harcourt's residence was only a twenty-minute walk from his sister's fashionable town house in Curzon Street. Even Horace was not in the least fatigued as he clambered up the stone steps. On his best behaviour, he sat and waited patiently until the door was opened by a very morose-looking individual who, after casting an expert eye over the caller's fashionable pale blue walking dress and matching pelisse, announced that his master was not receiving that morning.

"Oh, is he not?" Verity responded lightly, with a steely look in her eyes which both her aunt and uncle would have recognised instantly but which the butler, never having seen her before, was unable to interpret until a moment later, when she all but thrust him aside as she marched resolutely into the hall. "I am not here to pay a social call. You may tell my uncle that I need to see him on a most urgent matter which will take a few minutes only of his time."

There was no mistaking the determination in the pleasant voice. There was no doubt, either, that the young person was quality born; it showed in every line of her slender form. But it was the magic word "uncle" which finally persuaded the butler to disregard his master's direct orders and disturb him.

"His lordship has someone with him at present, miss. But if you would care to step in here," he invited, opening a door on the left of the hall, "I shall inform him you are here."

Surprisingly, Verity was forced to wait in the small salon overlooking the street for no more than a minute or so before the butler returned to say that his lordship would receive her now. Leaving Horace in Meg's care, she followed the high-ranking servant across the hall and into the well-stocked library where her uncle was seated behind a huge mahogany desk.

He rose at once and came towards her to place an avuncular peck on her cheek. "My dear, you get prettier each time I see you. Can I offer you some refreshments?"

"No, thank you, Uncle Charles. I know you're extremely busy, so I shan't take up too much of your time." She frowned suddenly, casting a glance round the large, book-lined room. "I thought you had someone with you?"

"No, no, my dear. He—er—left some time ago. And I'm never too busy to see my favourite niece." Nodding dismissal to his butler, Lord Charles showed Verity to the chair placed beside the desk before resuming his own seat. "So, Clara did manage to get you to town, did she? I never thought I'd live to see you enjoying a Season."

"She certainly did manage to persuade me, but whether I enjoy the experience remains to be seen," she responded drily. "We travelled from Aunt Clara's home in Kent yesterday. And that is why I have come to talk to you, Uncle Charles."

Verity subjected him to a rather thoughtful stare. His career in politics had spanned many years, but she had never quite understood the precise nature of the work he undertook for the government—although she did know that he had travelled many times to Portugal and Spain during the Peninsular Campaign, and knew too that he was well acquainted with the Duke of Wellington.

"One of the traces broke on Aunt Clara's travelling carriage," she explained, "and as I flatly refused to travel with my aunt's pets I took a seat on the mail." She then went on to divulge in detail what had taken place in the small room at that wayside inn, and experienced a twinge of annoyance when, after learning all, he just sat there regarding her quite blandly, as though she had furnished him with nothing of more importance that the latest fashion in bonnets.

"Well?" she prompted, a touch of asperity creeping into her voice, when he still remained silent.

"Yes—er—very interesting, my dear, but I don't think we need concern ourselves unduly."

"You don't think…?" Verity regarded him in open-mouthed astonishment, unable to believe that the uncle she had always regarded so highly could say anything so crassly stupid. "Have you listened to a single word I've said, Uncle Charles?"

"Of course I have. Now, calm down, child," he said soothingly, after noting the angry flash in her violet-blue eyes. "I shall ensure that what you've told me is passed on to the—er—necessary quarter." He waved his hand in a dismissive gesture. "But we hear accounts of suspected spies all the time, and most turn out to be complete nonsense. So the best thing you can do is not to worry that pretty head of yours about it any more and forget that it ever happened."

"I see." Knowing that it would be a complete waste of breath to discuss the matter further, Verity rose to her feet. "I'm sorry I took up so much of your valuable time, Uncle Charles."

The thread of sarcasm woven into her voice did not go unnoticed, but he thought it wisest to ignore it. "Not at all, my dear. I'm always pleased to see you. Tell your aunt that I'll call on her soon, and if you can keep an evening free during your stay in town, perhaps you'll permit your old uncle Charles to take you to the theatre?"

Smiling fondly, he escorted her to the front door, but the instant he returned to his library the smile was replaced by a troubled frown. He went across to the window and followed his niece's progress along the street until she disappeared from view.

"I take it you heard all that?"

The door leading to the small ante-room was thrown wide and a tall gentleman strolled into the library. "Yes, I heard," he replied, seating himself in the chair Verity had just vacated. "Very interesting, and very valuable information. It's a pity your niece didn't get a clear view of the messenger. And it's a pity that I didn't notice anyone leave, either. But then—" he shrugged his broad shoulders "—I wasn't expecting any contact to be made with our little Frenchman at that unscheduled stop."

"It was fortuitous that Verity overheard that conversation. But I could wish she had not." Lord Charles turned away from the window and fixed his gaze on the gentleman sprawled at his ease in the chair. "You omitted to inform me that you had picked her up, m'boy."

A rather rueful smile curled the younger man's attractive mouth. "I was given strict instructions not to pick anyone up who wasn't on the waybill, but I could hardly leave her there, now, could I? I had forgotten that you two were related." He shook his head in disbelief. "I must say she has changed. I hardly recognised her."

Lord Charles, his heavy frown still very much in evidence, resumed his seat at the desk. "My memory has been equally at fault. I'd forgotten that Lucius Redmond's house in Yorkshire is quite close to your own."

"Less than three miles."

"And I suppose you knew her well at one time?"

"Very."

"Is there any possibility that she recognised you?"

"No, I'm positive she didn't. The last time we met she was little more than a child."

"Mmm." Lord Charles's worried frown grew more pronounced. "But she's a child no longer. She can be a headstrong little filly at times," he muttered, much to his visitor's evident amusement. "There's no saying what she may do now... And I didn't handle that little interview with her at all well."

* * *

Lord Charles had good reason to be concerned. Although betraying no outward signs as she made her way back to Curzon Street, nor later that morning when she accompanied her aunt to the dressmaker's, Verity was both hurt and angry over her uncle's seeming indifference to her disclosures. She was not even certain in her own mind that he would pass on the information given to him, let alone ensure that something positive was done to catch that spy and his villainous, traitorous associates. After all, hadn't her uncle pooh-poohed it as nothing important, a mere bagatelle? So what possible reliance could she place on him?

None whatsoever, she decided, glancing with scant enthusiasm at the lengths of lovely materials brought from the store-room for her inspection. Therefore it was up to her to convince him that she was not some feather-brained female who was merely overreacting… But how? What could she possibly do?

She was still pondering over this rather ticklish problem, while waiting for Lady Billington to make up her mind on whether to have one of her new gowns made up in pearl-grey or puce, when she looked up to discover she was being regarded rather thoughtfully by a young lady, modishly attired in a pale green carriage dress, seated by the window. The face beneath the dashing bonnet was quite lovely, and there was more than just a hint of amusement in the grey-green eyes which remained staring fixedly, and rather rudely, Verity considered, in her direction. She was about to bestow a look of hauteur on the ill-mannered person when the young lady unexpectedly rose from the chair and moved gracefully towards her.

"Forgive me for staring so," she said, in a voice every bit as attractive as her smile, "but am I right in thinking that you are Miss Harcourt... Miss Verity Harcourt, who used to attend Miss Tinsdale's seminary in Bath?''

''Yes, I am.'' Rising to her feet, Verity subjected the young woman's face to a rather piercing scrutiny. ''Elizabeth?'' Both expression and voice betrayed uncertainty. ''Elizabeth Beresford?''

At the nod of confirmation Verity gave an unmaidenly shriek and threw her arms round the young woman, much to the staunch disapproval of a rather forbidding-looking matron who had just entered the premises. ''I would never have recognised you,'' she said with brutal frankness. ''You're so thin!''

Far from offended, Elizabeth gurgled with laughter. ''And you haven't changed a bit. You still say precisely what you think. That was one of the many things I admired in you.''

Verity held her friend at arm's length, still somewhat bemused. Her plump, shy and rather plain schoolfriend had blossomed into such a lovely young woman. It was incredible!

''Oh, it's so good to see you again after all these years. It was such a pity we lost touch when you left the seminary, although I did write to you.'' Verity noted her friend's slight frown at this snippet of information, but as Lady Billington was approaching, she refrained from enquiring into the reason behind the slightly puzzled look.

It took Lady Billington a minute only to realise that the two girls were overjoyed to see each other again after all this time, and to come to the conclusion that her niece's friend was a sensible and well-mannered young lady. She raised no objection, therefore, when Miss Beresford suggested that, as it was such a lovely day, she and Verity would enjoy a drive round Hyde Park, and promised to restore her safely to Curzon Street later.

Verity sat herself beside Elizabeth in her friend's open carriage and for a while they reminisced about their schooldays, but then Verity changed the subject by asking her friend what she had been doing with herself since leaving the seminary.

"I well expected you to be married by now. Weren't you promised almost from birth to the son of a baronet? Quite a Gothic notion, I've always thought, but you seemed quite happy with—" Verity caught herself up abruptly when she noticed her friend's expression change suddenly, the smile vanishing and an almost closed-up look taking possession of her features. "Oh, Elizabeth, I am sorry! Have I said something I ought not?"

"No, no. Not at all!" Elizabeth responded, but the smile that accompanied the assurance was all too obviously false. "Yes, Richard and I were in a way promised to each other. Our respective fathers were great friends and had always dreamed of uniting the two families by marriage. Richard, I'm certain, would have fulfilled his father's dearest wish… Unfortunately I felt myself unable to comply. We would not have suited."

Elizabeth was looking directly at her, but Verity had the feeling that her friend was not seeing her but images from the past.

"You may recall my father died during my final year at the seminary. When I refused point-blank to become betrothed to Richard the relationship between my mother and myself, which honesty prompts me to admit had never been good, deteriorated to such an extent that I felt unable to remain under the same roof as her. I ran away to my maternal grandmother in Bristol." This time the smile was full of gentle warmth. "Best thing I ever did! I've never looked back."

Verity regarded her friend in a mixture of admiration and astonishment. The shy and highly sensitive, rather plump and plain girl she had known years ago had changed out of all recognition, and seemingly not only in looks.

"And do you still reside with your grandmother?" she found herself asking.

"Oh, yes. We are in London until the end of next week. Then we're off to join the throng in Brussels. My grandmother isn't well, Verity. I cannot allow her to make the journey alone and she is determined to go. She has a godson in the army and feels it her duty now that both his parents are dead to be near in case…" She shook her head. "I had foolishly believed that Napoleon's exile would bring an end to all this nonsense."

"Sadly it has not proved to be the case. And how many more must give their lives before it is finally over? And how many more could be saved if…?" Verity's words faded and she looked at her friend closely for a moment, hesitating, then related all she had overheard at the inn and the far from satisfactory conversation she had had with her uncle earlier that day.

Elizabeth said nothing, her expression not unlike that of Lord Charles Harcourt a couple of hours ago. Then, still without uttering a word in response, she leaned forward in her seat, gave the coachman a tap on the shoulder with her parasol and requested him to pull over as she felt the need to stretch her legs.

"So, what are you proposing to do about it now?" she asked, once they had walked several yards away from the carriage across the grass, and Verity almost sighed with relief.

"Thank heavens! I was beginning to think no one would believe me."

"I recall your being a headstrong creature, Verity," Elizabeth remarked candidly, her lips curling into a most attractively winning smile, "and I doubt you've changed that much. But you were never a liar, nor even remotely fanciful. Of course I believe you! It's a thousand pities your uncle didn't, but all is not lost. Evidently your uncle is a cautious man and requires more proof of a spy network being in operation before he is prepared to act. Therefore, you must provide him with the proof."

"Yes, but how? Short of going to this Little Frampington myself, I don't see what else I can do." Verity caught the quizzical gleam in her friend's eyes and stopped dead in her tracks. "Yes, I could go, couldn't I!" She fell silent for a moment, her mind working rapidly. "If only I could manage to leave the house without arousing my aunt's suspicions. She might appear to be feather-brained, but, believe me, she's far from it."

"And there I can be of some help to you," Elizabeth astounded her by saying. "It so happens that my grandmother intends holding a dinner-party on Friday evening. If it were not for that fact I wouldn't hesitate to accompany you, believe me." There was almost a wistful note in her soft, pleasant voice. "But the occasion will work to our advantage. What could be more natural than for me to send an invitation to you? Your aunt will suspect nothing. She saw how pleased we were to see each other. I'll send the carriage to collect you early on Friday evening. Then you can change at my grandmother's house and be on your way."

"Change?" Verity echoed, not just a little bemused. This was all going a little too fast for her.

"You cannot possibly travel all the way to Frampington and enter this inn dressed in evening garb. I rather fancy you'd stand out a trifle. Besides which, it would be highly improper for a young lady to go careering about the country on her own. Therefore you must become a youth! Don't worry," Elizabeth went on after receiving a rather startled look, "I'll get clothes for you and hire a horse."

Verity regarded her old schoolfriend with the utmost respect. "You're a marvel, Elizabeth! I should never have thought of that. Going dressed as a boy in shabby, worn clothes... Yes, the perfect solution!"

"You forget I've had experience at this sort of thing. How do you think I managed to succeed in running away from my mother's house six years ago? Although, I must confess, I did have Aggie with me."

"Aggie?" Verity echoed.

"Yes, she was our old nursemaid. She's now my personal maid. She's a dreadful scold, but a dear, and she'll do anything I ask of her. I'll get her to wait at the corner of the street for you on Friday evening. Then she can take you round to the rear of the house and up the back stairs. That way you'll not be seen by any of the other servants. Once you've changed, she will show you out to the mews where I'll arrange for the horse to be ready, saddled and awaiting you. And Aggie will watch out for you again on your return."

"Lord, Elizabeth! You've left me with absolutely nothing to do."

"Nothing except put your life in peril, Verity," she countered, looked deeply troubled now. "Oh, how I wish I could go with you!"

Verity gave her friend's arm a reassuring squeeze. "It doesn't need two of us, and I rather think it would be better if I go on my own. Now all I need to do is find out exactly where this Little Frampington is situated. I just hope it's within easy riding distance of London, otherwise we're foiled from the start.''

''We've maps back at the house. Return with me now and we can discuss everything in detail.'' Elizabeth's expression remained grave. ''Meeting up with you again after all these years has been wonderful. I just hope that I don't come to regret the encounter. It doesn't need me to warn you that these people must be dangerous, Verity. For heaven's sake, take care!''

# Chapter Four

According to Elizabeth's map, the village where Verity had to lie in wait for the spy and his accomplices appeared to be no more than an hour's ride from London. Friday evening arrived and everything went according to plan. It was an added bonus that the evening was dry and far from cold. Even the hired mount, thankfully, turned out to be a sturdy, reliable beast, sound in both wind and limb. Verity felt not in the least self-conscious in her boy's raiment, but it did take her some little time to accustom herself to riding astride again after years of being forced to sit her mount like a lady. None the less, she arrived at the turn-off to Little Frampington in good time, and, after wending her way down a series of narrow, high-hedged lanes, she finally reached her destination.

Drawing her mount to a halt in the middle of the narrow street, Verity looked about her in dismay, experiencing for the first time some slight doubts as to the wisdom of her actions. The place was nothing more than a hamlet. There wasn't even a church, and the dozen or so dwellings all looked to be in need of some urgent repairs. The inn, if one could call it so, was the most ramshackle building of the lot. There were tiles missing from its roof, there wasn't a window that didn't boast at least one broken pane of glass and the door had a hole in the bottom large enough for a cat to get through, let alone a rat! No law-abiding citizen with a modicum of intelligence would ever seek succour within its walls, for it was undoubtedly a thieves' den, a meeting place for every kind of rogue for miles around.

She hadn't formulated any plan of action. If she could manage to get close enough to overhear some snippets of the conversation which passed between the spy and his associates it would be a bonus, but even she balked at the idea of entering that place. No, she had to be sensible, as Elizabeth had urged her to be on more than one occasion during the past days. The best she could hope for now was to lie in wait and watch to see who turned up for the meeting, and then give an accurate description of all the men involved to her Uncle Charles.

Dismounting, she led her mount into the stable which, though dilapidated, was certainly in a better state of repair than the tavern, and was surprised to discover a pair of perfectly matched greys still harnessed to a very smart racing curricle. One of the fine animals whinnied at her approach, and as she ran a hand down his sleek neck she noticed a black diamond-shaped blemish in the skin beneath its silken mane.

"'Ere, what you be doing?" a rough voice demanded, and Verity, her heart almost missing a beat, swung round to see a coarse-looking man seated on a small stool down at the far end of the stable. Narrow-eyed, he looked her over with evident suspicion while he continued to whittle away at the piece of wood in his hand with an evil-looking knife.

"Nothing," she responded in a rough little voice, only

just remembering in time that she was supposed to be a youth.

"Well, gets yerself away from them there 'osses! I'm paid to look after they." Verity didn't need telling twice, and the man continued his steely-eyed piercing scrutiny as she took a step away. "What you be doing 'ere? You ain't from around these parts."

"No, I'm not. I'm—er—supposed to be meeting someone here." Verity's mind was working rapidly. He was evidently suspicious, but curious too, and she just might be able to turn this to her advantage. By keeping him talking she had an excuse to remain in the stable, where she had a clear view of the front entrance and would see anyone entering the inn.

Who yer s'posed to be meeting?"

"My uncle."

"Yer uncle, eh? Who be that, then—Old Pike the Poacher?" He guffawed at his pathetic whimsy. "What be yer uncle's name, lad?"

"Septimus Watts," she responded, hoping Lady Billington's strait-laced butler wouldn't object to her making free with his name.

"Never 'eard of 'im."

"Maybe not," Verity returned, determined to brazen it out, "but he still asked me to meet him here, outside the inn at Little Frampington."

He guffawed again, only louder this time. "Best be on yer way then, yer brainless cur. Little Frampington be a mile or so further on down the road."

"Wh-what?" It was Verity's turn to stare this time. "But this is Little Frampington, surely? I saw the signpost back along the road."

"No, it ain't! This be Frampington. And I should know…lived in this Godforsaken 'ole most all m'life.

The place you be wanting be further down the road. So best be on yer way.''

Verity had no reason to doubt him. What could he possibly gain by lying to her, after all? Without a word of farewell, which she doubted would have been appreciated anyway, she led her mount out of the stable while cursing herself silently under her breath. She ought to have studied Elizabeth's map more closely! She could have sworn, though, that there hadn't been two Frampingtons shown. Evidently this place was considered too insignificant to warrant a mention!

Not wasting a precious moment, Verity urged her mount out of the yard and into the narrow street. Although she had left London early, allowing for the possibility that she might just take a wrong turning, she knew that it must be close on eight o'clock by now, and she dug her heels hard into the gelding's flanks, but to little effect. He had proved himself to be steady and reliable, but he certainly hadn't been bred for speed, and the church clock had just finished chiming the hour as she arrived at the village of Little Frampington, which belied its name by being many times larger than its namesake back along the road.

Verity located the inn, which was situated directly opposite the church, without any difficulty. Dismounting, she led her mount into the stable and almost sighed with relief when she saw just one large bay champing away contentedly on a pile of hay. Unless that spy and his associates had made the journey on foot they had not arrived yet. She was in time!

She experienced no qualms whatsoever over entering this well-maintained building, with its whitewashed cob walls and undulating, neatly thatched roof. The interior, she discovered as she entered the tap, was further proof that mine host was both conscientious and hard-working. There was a welcoming fire in the large inglenook fireplace, the grey-stone floor had certainly seen a brush that day, and there wasn't a table—except those occupied by the customers—which had so much as a single smear to mar its highly polished surface.

Making her way over to the counter, behind which a young woman in a pristine white apron stood serving a customer, Verity cast her eyes over the other patrons, most of whom were seated at the various tables. All bore the appearance of working men, refreshing themselves after a hard day's toil. Could one of them possibly be the man who had arranged to meet that spy? She cast a further surreptitious glance over them. They appeared to be farmers or labourers, their leathery, weather-beaten faces proof enough that they were accustomed to working out of doors. It was hard to imagine that any one of them could be the spy's accomplice, unless of course he was in disguise. And one of them certainly wasn't a local, she reminded herself, recalling the large, handsome bay in the stable.

"What can I get for you, young sir?"

Verity very nearly betrayed her true sex by stupidly asking for a glass of ratafia, but managed to check herself just in time and request a tankard of ale. Quickly turning her grimace into a smile as she took her first sip, she leaned against the counter, hoping she resembled a swaggering youth.

"You keep a fine inn," she remarked.

"Why, thank you, sir! My ma and pa do like the place looking clean and tidy."

So, she was the daughter of the house, Verity mused. That might prove useful. "Yes, it's certainly better kept than a good many posting houses I've been in. Do you have rooms for hire here, or do you cater only for local trade?''

''Oh, we do have rooms, sir, but it's not often they're used. Not being on one of the main posting roads, we don't get too many travellers coming this way. Although,'' she went on, casting her rather attractive soft brown eyes about the room, ''we did have a gentleman in earlier requesting a room. Can't see him about now. Must have finished his dinner and gone back upstairs.''

Verity's eyes narrowed speculatively as she risked a further sip of the home-brewed. How very interesting. Was he merely an innocent traveller or the traitorous wretch who had arranged to meet the spy?

''My aunt travels about the country quite a bit,'' she informed the landlord's daughter in a conversational tone. ''She dislikes the noisy posting houses and much prefers to put up at quiet inns like this one. Do you happen to have a private parlour? I'm afraid she would never consider dining in the tap.''

''Yes, sir. It's upstairs. I'd willingly show it you, only it's been hired for the evening and the gentlemen will be here soon. They frequently hire the parlour for an evening.''

The ale was, surprisingly, becoming more palatable with each mouthful, Verity decided, sampling the home-brewed yet again as she watched the daughter of the house move away to serve another customer. So, these so-called gentlemen had met here before, had they? The innkeeper's daughter had been most informative, and Verity would not hesitate to pass on what she had learned to Lord Charles in the morning. A watch must be put on this place, but it might be some time before the spy met his accomplices again…and what of tonight's meeting?

Verity had well and truly got the bit between her teeth. Her Uncle Charles hadn't taken her seriously, but she was determined that he would do so after this night's escapade. Resolve added an extra sparkle to her eyes. If she remained where she was she couldn't fail to see who went upstairs to the private parlour, but now she wanted to discover more. Those men were meeting here for some purpose, possibly to make plans or maybe to exchange vital information, but no matter the reason Verity wanted to know exactly what passed between them, and the only way to achieve her objective was to hide in that upstairs parlour.

She looked across at the door, which stood slightly ajar and which in all probability led to the upper floor. After only a moment's indecision, she made her way as surreptitiously as possible towards it. One swift glance about the room was sufficient to assure her that no one was looking in her direction, and she slipped through the opening to find herself in a small lobby with the stairs rising directly ahead.

Mounting them swiftly and silently, Verity stepped onto a narrow, ill-lit landing, the only light coming from a small window at the far end. There were several doors on both left and right at intervals along the passageway. Reaching the first, she tentatively turned the knob and, poking her head into the room, discovered it to be a small and tidy bedchamber. The second led to yet another bedchamber, but the third gave access to the room she had been seeking. The curtains had been drawn across the window and candles burning brightly in their sconces bathed the small parlour in a warm, welcoming glow. There were glasses and a bottle set on the table in the centre of the room in readiness for the hirers, but nothing, not even a screen, behind which she could hide.

Disappointed, but far from disheartened, Verity closed the parlour door quietly and was pondering on what she could do when she noticed a door on the opposite side and a little further along the passageway was slightly ajar. Her eyes narrowed speculatively. Might it be possible to wait in there, keeping watch? It would offer a clear view of anyone entering the parlour. Then, when the spy and his associates had arrived, she could step across the passageway, place her ear to the door and with any luck overhear what was being said.

The only slight problem that she could envisage was if the room happened to be the bedchamber of the landlord and his wife, or their daughter, but even if this did turn out to be the case she doubted that any one of them would retire for the night until the last of the customers had departed. Yes, she would risk it!

Pushing the door open, she took a hesitant step into the room. The curtains had been drawn, effectively blocking out the rapidly fading late-evening light, but she could make out the bed at the far end and, thankfully, it wasn't occupied. She breathed a sigh of relief, and had just taken a further tentative step forward when she detected a sudden movement.

Before she knew what was happening her waist had been encircled by something strongly resembling an iron band and a large hand had been clapped over her mouth, effectively preventing the terrified squeal which rose in her throat from escaping. Dear God…! The guest! She'd completely forgotten about him.

The pulsating throb in her temples beat a vicious tattoo in her ears as her captor kicked the door shut. The heat from his powerful body penetrated her boy's raiment as she struggled wildly in a valiant attempt to break free, but her efforts were in vain. The muscular arm encircling her was immovable, and the hand over her mouth held her head firmly against a stone-hard chest. Then, without warning, he removed his arm from about her waist and tore the battered, misshapen hat from her head, allowing her silky black locks freedom to cascade about her shoulders.

"I thought as much," a vaguely familiar, accented voice growled in her ear, but Verity was in no mood to work out the possible identity of her captor.

Half out of her mind with fear at what he might do next, she felt the fingers over her mouth slacken a little and didn't hesitate to take advantage. In one slight, yet swift movement she jerked her head and sank her small white teeth hard into the fleshy part of his hand just below the thumb. A smothered oath followed as Verity made a heroic dive for the doorknob, but a moment later that well-muscled limb had her imprisoned once more and she was lifted quite off her feet.

Carrying her effortlessly under one arm, as though she weighed no more than a sack of grain, her captor strode purposefully across the bed, where he sat himself, and before Verity could do much else other than utter a gasp in protest she found herself face down over a pair of muscular thighs. Her squeals of dissent quickly turned into cries of pain as he administered half a dozen or so smarting and humiliating slaps to the seat of her breeches with the flat of his hand, before tipping her quite callously off his knee so that she landed on the floor with a further painful thud.

No one, not even her father, had ever laid a hand on her before, and a combination of anger and resentment, not to mention bruised pride, welled up inside.

Fear was suddenly a thing of the past as Verity swept the tangled mat of hair from her face and peered up at the brutish individual who had dared to treat her in such a fashion. Through the haze of tears she saw a tricorn hat pulled low over eyes, a face hidden by a muffler, and a powerful body swathed in a dark grey cloak. There could be no mistaking who it was.

"You!" she managed in a choked whisper, scarcely believing the evidence of her own eyes.

"Aye, lass. And tha can thank thy lucky stars it is. Had it been our little Frenchman or one of 'is friends, tha wouldn't be snivelling over just a walloped backside," the Coachman told her with brutal frankness. "And don't wipe thy nose on thy sleeve!"

"I haven't got a handkerchief," she muttered broodingly, and was promptly offered his own, which she accepted with as much grace as she could muster. Then, after using it thoroughly, blowing her small straight nose and wiping her eyes, she offered it back.

He regarded the crumpled ball with distaste. "Nay. Best tha keeps it. It'll be a memento, like, a reminder not to do anything so damnably foolish again." Folding his arms across his chest, he cast his eyes over her attire. "Tha don't imagine, surely, those clothes ud fool anyone? Tha's far too pretty t' be a lad."

Ignoring the compliment, she flashed him a resentful look from beneath moist lashes. "Well, and what was I supposed to do? I couldn't come here dressed in petticoats, now, could I?"

"Tha shouldn't be 'ere at all!"

"And I certainly wouldn't be if I had thought my uncle intended acting on the information I'd given him!" she countered, her spirit returning. She scrambled to her feet and moved several paces away. "And what are you doing here?" She looked at him consideringly, curiosity for the moment overriding bitter resentment. "Were you tooling that mail-coach to keep an eye on that Swiss gentleman?''

''Aye. Only 'e ain't Swiss, lass. 'E's French, one of Napoleon's top agents.''

Again she cast him a rather thoughtful look. ''Do you work for Lord Charles?''

''It'd be more accurate t'say I'm working wi' 'im at the moment. And it does 'elp our cause if t'information passed on to us is accurate. This meeting is due t' take place at nine o'clock, not eight, as you said. T'landlady kindly volunteered that snippet not long after I'd arrived.''

Verity frowned. She could have sworn the time arranged was eight o'clock. ''Well, I've learned something, too,'' she told him, determined to prove that her presence here had not been a complete waste of time. ''They've met at this place before, so it might be worthwhile keeping a watch on this inn.'' Bending, she retrieved her hat, which he had thrown on the floor. ''But, as you're here, there's no need for me to remain. I'd better be getting back to London.''

''Oh, no tha doesn't, lass!'' he growled, arresting her progress to the door. ''Tha's staying right, 'ere wi' me. I'll escort thee back t'town when us friends 'ave left. So—'' he tapped the portion of bed beside him ''—come and sit thissen down and mek thissen comfortable. We might be in for a long wait.''

''Sit?'' The malevolent look she cast him would have withered a lesser mortal. ''You've made sure I'll not be able to do that with any degree of comfort for some considerable time!''

''N' more than tha deserved,'' was his indifferent response to her hurts. ''Tha were always a 'ead strong, spoilt filly, wanting thy way in everything. And getting it most o' the time, more's the pity. Redmond ought to 'ave schooled you years ago, then it'd 'ave saved me the trouble.'' His eyes narrowed as he looked her up and down. ''And I doubt I've finished yet, tha troublesome chit!''

Verity bit back the angry rejoinder which rose in her throat as yet another thought struck her. She looked across at him keenly, but there was insufficient light to enable her to see him clearly. Besides which, the muffler hid too much of his face for her to recognise him.

''You know my Uncle Lucius, don't you? And we've met before… Who are you?''

''Aye, I knows 'im, reet enough. And I've seen thee about in Yorkshire. But as t'who I be…'Tis best tha don't know for the time being, lass, I'm merely…the Coachman.''

Verity was far from satisfied with that, but before she was able to probe further there was a noise outside on the landing, followed by the sounds of jovial voices. She cast a questioning glance at the Coachman, who placed a warning finger to his lips as he rose from the bed.

For a tall, powerfully built man he was remarkably light on his feet, hardly making a sound as he moved with lightning speed across the room. He waited a moment or two, listening intently, before opening the door a fraction and placing one eye to the crack. Verity could hear the voices clearly too, but surprisingly not one bore a trace of a foreign accent. Then the parlour door closed and the Coachman looked back at her with what could only be described as a rather suspicious glint in his eyes.

''If tha's dragged me all t' way out 'ere on some fool's errand, lass, so elp me, I'll—''

''Why? What is it? What's wrong,'' she interrupted. ''Wasn't the Frenchman with them?''

"No, 'e weren't. I'm goin' in there. And just in case tha think t' give me the slip," he added, removing the key, "I'm goin' t'take the precaution o' locking you in." Then, without giving her the opportunity to protest, he placed himself on the other side of the door, and before she could move the key turned in the lock.

Her eyes were deep blue pools of seething resentment. Confound the odious brute! He had no right to imprison her! Verity was almost beside herself with rage. She took a hasty step towards the door, intending to pound her fists against the solid wood and shout at the top of her voice, but then she checked herself as sense prevailed. By doing so she might alert the men in the room opposite, put them on their guard. Not only that, she wouldn't put it past the Coachman to return and repeat the brutish treatment he had meted out earlier if she caused a stir.

Still highly resentful, she swung round, about to take his rather insensitive advice and sit on the bed, when the floral-patterned curtains at the window caught her attention. The door might be locked...but what about the window?

Throwing back the drapes, she saw that the window was small, but certainly large enough for her to climb out. It was quite dark now, but she had no difficulty in seeing, as the window blessedly opened with ease, a single-story construction with a sloping roof directly below. Remaining only for the time it took to securely confine her long hair back in the misshapen hat, she clambered onto the sill and out into the cool night air. Then, tiptoeing lightly over the tiles, she perched herself on the edge of the roof and, with the aid of a large and conveniently placed wooden barrel, had no difficulty in reaching the ground.

She hadn't taken more than a step or two towards the stables when a door behind her opened and she swung round, her breath leaving her in a sigh of relief when she saw the landlord's daughter, wrapped in a serviceable cloak, step outside.

"Oh, it's you, young sir! I thought you'd left long since." She cast Verity one of her rather sweet, friendly smiles. "I'm just off up the road," she explained, falling into step beside the very handsome "youth", "to take this basket of food to an old lady."

"And I'm ready to leave now," Verity responded, remembering to keep her voice low. "I've—er—just been taking a stroll round this village of yours. I'm certain my aunt would be quite happy to stay overnight here."

"It's a nice quiet place, sir. I'm sorry I weren't able to show you the parlour, but old Colonel Hanbury is a funny old stick. Wouldn't like it none if he discovered someone in there when he'd paid for its hire."

"Colonel Hanbury?" Verity echoed, and the girl gurgled with laughter.

"It's supposed to be a secret, but everyone round these parts knows," she confided in a conspiratorial whisper. "Everyone except their wives, that is. The colonel, the vicar and the old doctor meet here twice a month. Their wives disapprove of gaming, you see. So for a quiet life they comes here."

Oh, God! Verity groaned inwardly. When the Coachman discovered who they were, and she didn't doubt for a moment that he would, he'd be absolutely furious with her, truly believing she had brought him out here on some wild-goose chase… And how could she prove otherwise? The sooner she departed the better!

After a hurriedly spoken farewell to the landlord's

daughter. Verity collected her mount from the stable, wincing slightly as she got into the saddle.

The ride back to London was both uncomfortable and nerve-racking. Each time she detected the sound of hoof-beats she would take a quick glance over her shoulder, expecting to see the Coachman in hot pursuit, his cloak billowing, his brow as darkly threatening as a thunder-cloud, and it was only when she had at last reached the capital, where she was able to mingle with the carriages and other riders in the surprisingly busy night streets, that she began to relax a little.

She arrived at the house Elizabeth's grandmother had hired feeling thoroughly miserable and dejected. All the carefully made plans had been for nothing. The visit to Little Frampington had been a complete and utter waste of time and effort. But what had gone wrong?

Verity just couldn't understand it at all, and shook her head in complete bewilderment. So, she might have got the time of the meeting wrong, but certainly not the place, she felt certain of that. Little Frampington, that Frenchman had said… No, he hadn't, she amended silently, her brows drawing together in deep thought. His exact words had been "zee leetle leetle Frampington."

Oh, no! Closing her eyes, Verity cursed herself for a fool. Frampington was smaller than its near neighbour, and that was what the Frenchman had meant. Of all the stupid Gallic jokes! The meeting had taken place at that rundown old tavern! She could have screamed in vexation. All that time and effort! And what had she got to show for it…? Nothing except a bruised rear!

# Chapter Five

"You must stop brooding over it, Verity, and blaming yourself. What more could you possibly have done, for heaven's sake!"

It was almost a week since she had made that futile trip to Little Frampington, and her complete lack of success had continued to weigh heavily on her mind. She had well expected a visit from an irate Lord Charles Harcourt, blaming her entirely for wasting his associate's time, but she had not set eyes on him, nor had she received any communication, written or otherwise, during the intervening days. Which was most strange, in the circumstances. Surely the Coachman wouldn't have hesitated in reporting back to him, assuring him that the meeting which had taken place at that inn had been merely a gathering of three law-abiding local inhabitants out enjoying nothing more sinister than a night's gaming?

Verity managed a wan smile, but it was an effort. "Yes, of course you're right, Elizabeth. There was nothing more I could have done. I've been pretty poor company these past days, I know. And here you are leaving tomorrow for Brussels." She gave her friend's arm an affectionate squeeze. "When shall we see each other again, I wonder?"

"Not for several months, I'm afraid. But this time, Verity, I'm determined we shan't lose touch."

"I did receive one letter from you whilst I was still at the seminary, Elizabeth, and I did write to you several times during my final year there, but never received anything further," Verity assured her, remembering the strange look on her friend's face when she had mentioned this before. This time Elizabeth was a little more forthcoming.

"After leaving the seminary, I didn't remain very long at my mother's house. She never forwarded one of your letters on to me. I foolishly assumed that you had forgotten your old schoolfriend, but I shan't make that mistake again," Elizabeth assured her. "My grandmother's courier has made all the arrangements on our behalf, and I'm not in possession of our precise direction in Brussels, but once we've arrived I shall write and let you know. And when we return you must come and stay with us in Bristol." A wickedly provocative smile hovered about her mouth. "If you're not betrothed by then, that is."

Verity pulled a face of disgust. "No fear of that, my dear friend."

There was more than a hint of derision in her voice, and Elizabeth looked at her closely. "Am I right in thinking that, when we were at school together, you mentioned you were very fond of a certain someone? In fact, I believe you said you were in love."

"Ha!" Verity scoffed, waving her hand in an impatient gesture. "Puppy love. Thank the good Lord I've more sense now!"

Elizabeth couldn't prevent a smile at the scathing tone

and, after nodding to an acquaintance who passed walking in the opposite direction, said, "What happened, Verity? How did the man whose name I'm afraid I cannot recall now give you such a dislike of him?"

"Brin Carter…now Major Carter," Verity responded after a moment's silence, staring fixedly ahead. "He once held a place in my affections but, as I've already mentioned, I was very young…and rather foolish to have thought so well of him."

"Brin…? What an unusual name!"

"He was named after his maternal grandfather. Well, it was his grandfather's surname, at any rate. It's an abbreviation. It's Brinley, really."

"What happened?" Elizabeth prompted gently.

"Oh, nothing very much. I believed myself in love with him, but my affections were not reciprocated. Brin was besotted with the daughter of the local squire. Angela Kingsley was, and still is for that matter, an ethereal creature with the face of an angel, a figure many a female would sell her soul to possess and the heart of a moneylender. Brin would never hear a word said against her. When I tried to tell him that his beloved Angela was not quite all that she seemed, he told me in no uncertain terms that I was nothing more than a spoilt and spiteful little cat who ought to be taught some manners."

Her sudden shout of laughter was a rather bitter, hollow sound. "To cut a long story short, while Brin was fighting for his country in the Peninsula, Angela, who had promised faithfully to await his return, upped and married that great tub of lard Sir Frederick Morland. Now, whether or not Brin himself believed that cock-and-bull story she put about that her family had forced her into the union, I've no idea, for I've neither spoken to him nor indeed set eyes on him in the past five years."

Elizabeth was silent for a moment, staring fixedly ahead down the park's tree-lined path, then said with that uncanny insight she had possessed even as a young girl, "I cannot help but wonder, Verity, if you are as indifferent to the Major as you claim to be. After all, you have never bestowed your affection on another."

"No, very true," she concurred. "But pray do not be under the misapprehension that I've been nursing a broken heart all this time, because I tell you plainly I have not! I simply have more sense now than to bestow affection where it is neither desired nor appreciated."

"You dismiss it lightly enough, my dear, but I suspect he hurt you very deeply."

Verity didn't attempt to respond. They had by this time arrived at Elizabeth's carriage, which had stood under the shade of some trees whilst they had taken a turn round the park. Elizabeth made to mount the steps, but Verity arrested her by placing a hand on her arm.

"I think I'll walk back to Curzon Street with Meg. So I shall bid you goodbye here." She gave Elizabeth a quick hug. "Take care, my friend."

"I shall. And let us say, rather, farewell." Concern was mirrored in Elizabeth's grey-green eyes. "Don't permit your recent disappointment at Little Frampington to shadow the rest of your stay in London. And, more importantly, don't let past hurts prevent you from forming a lasting attachment to some gentleman worthy of your affections, my dear."

Verity couldn't prevent a rather rueful little smile at this. "If I met a man whom I believed would make me happy, and I him, then I would consider marrying. But I don't expect I shall find him amongst the dashing sprigs I have met since my arrival in town. And I certainly shan't return to Yorkshire with a bruised ego if I end the Season still unattached. Be sure of that!''

As Verity watched the carriage move away and raised her hand in a final salute of farewell, she had to own that Elizabeth had given her much to ponder over. She would have been the first to admit that she didn't make friends easily, that she held only a handful of people in high esteem and that she bestowed genuine affection on very few. Was this the legacy of her once bruised and battered feelings? Surely not! She had got over Brin Carter years ago, hadn't given him more than a passing thought in a very long time. But she couldn't deny that she had tended to keep young, unattached gentlemen at a distance. Was this because she considered them for the most part nothing more than empty-headed nincompoops? Or could it possibly be that deep down she was trying to protect her young heart from being bruised and battered again?

She was still pondering over this rather disturbing possibility as she headed towards the gateway. Meg, tripping along beside her, was trying her best to draw her attention to a lady in a very fashionable bonnet, which Meg thought would suit her young mistress very well, but Verity paid little heed. Nor did she pay much attention to the very smart equipage drawing up alongside, until her name hailed in an ear-piercing, high-pitched voice broke into her rather distressing reflections and she raised her eyes to see the daughter of her Uncle Lucius's nearest neighbour.

Only it wasn't the sight of Hilary Fenner which caused Verity's heart to lurch suddenly and quite inexplicably, and caused her to blink several times, as though to dispel an image conjured up by her mind's eye, but the sight of that tall, broad-shouldered gentleman seated beside the lively auburn-haired girl in the curricle.

"I wondered if we would run across each other whilst in London, Verity," Hilary gushed in her friendly way, but in a voice which had the unfortunate tendency to grate on one after a while. "And just look who has kindly taken me for a jaunt in his smart turn-out! You remember Brin, don't you?"

Verity gazed into eyes which smiled down at her with a rather disturbing glint in their tawny depths. Silently, she was forced to admit that the years had been kind to Brin Carter. He was as devastatingly good-looking as he had been five years ago, perhaps a little more so now that time had added extra character to his face: tiny lines at the corners of his eyes and rather attractive deep clefts on either side of a mouth that was both well-shaped and rather sensual.

Her pulse continued to behave erratically, and she despised herself for being so idiotically feminine as to be beguiled, still, by his handsome face. She gave herself an inward shake, determined to overcome this foolish weakness which she believed she had conquered years ago, and, prompted by some imp of pure mischief and the strong urge to let him know that she was completely indifferent to him now, said, "Er—forgive me, sir. Your face does look vaguely familiar, but I'm afraid I cannot recall just at the moment where we have met before."

"Oh, Verity!" Miss Fenner gave a trill of laughter. "You cannot have forgotten! You were so very fond of Arthur Brinley. This is his grandson."

"Of course!" Verity was gratified to see by the slight narrowing of those attractive almond-shaped eyes that he was piqued. "You must forgive me, sir, but it has been some years since we last met."

"Indeed it has, Miss Harcourt," he concurred in a voice as richly smooth as velvet. "You were little more than a child. And may I add you have changed very little."

She looked at him sharply, suspecting his last remark of being far from complimentary, but before she could formulate a barbed response Miss Fenner interposed with, "Will you be attending Lady Morland's party tomorrow evening? Both Brin and I shall be there."

What a merry meeting that was destined to be! Verity mused, wondering if Brin had seen his beloved Angela since her marriage to the obese baronet. She lowered her eyes in an attempt to hide the wicked amusement dancing there, and her attention was drawn to the perfectly matched greys harnessed to the curricle.

Instantly her light-heartedness vanished. She had seen this turn-out before. She felt certain of it! Taking a step towards the fine gelding nearest to her, she ran her hand down his sleek neck and had no difficulty locating that tell-tale diamond-shaped blemish beneath the mane. What in the world had Brin Carter been doing at that tumbledown old tavern last Friday evening?

She looked up again, only to discover that he was staring at her rather intently. "I'm not perfectly certain what Lady Billington has planned for the evening, Hilary, but if Lady Morland has sent an invitation, no doubt we shall see one another again there."

She took a hasty step back onto the grass and forced herself to meet the Major's intent gaze. "Well, I must not detain you further. You are no doubt loath to keep these beautiful horses of yours standing too long, sir."

"To agree would show me in a very poor light, Miss Harcourt." His intent look vanished as a twitching smile pulled at the corners of his attractive mouth. "You would believe I placed the welfare of my cattle above the pleasure of conversing with you.''

''It would show sound judgement if you did, sir. One does not come across such beautiful creatures very often.''

''No, indeed one does not, Miss Harcourt,'' he agreed softly, as he continued to stare down at her fixedly, but with such a depth of warmth in his eyes now that her tongue for some inexplicable reason suddenly decided to attach itself to the roof of her mouth, and she was unable to respond to his cheerful farewell before he gave the horses their office to start.

Pulling herself together with an effort, she watched the equipage mingle with the other carriages along the busy track. Then, swinging round on her heels, she marched resolutely towards the park gate, her mind so plagued by troubled thoughts that she once again took little heed of Meg's light-hearted conversation, until she received a rather urgent tug on the arm, which was impossible to ignore, and was forced to abandon her depressing reflections.

''Yes, what is it, Meg?''

''You're going the wrong way, miss.''

''No, I'm not. I'm going to pay a call on my Uncle Charles,'' Verity informed her, her voice betraying clearly enough that she wasn't looking forward to the encounter with any degree of enthusiasm.

When she arrived at Lord Charles's house a short while later, his butler at least betrayed no signs of not being pleased to see her. He invited her quite cordially to step into the hall, where he left her while he informed his master of her arrival, and moments later she was asked to step into the library.

Leaving Meg to seat herself on one of the comfortable

chairs in the hall, Verity entered her uncle's inner sanctum to discover him seated as usual behind the huge mahogany desk, busily writing a letter. Not even by the slight raising of one greying brow did he betray any sign of surprise at her unexpected visit, but neither, which was more ominous, did his lips curl into their usual smile of greeting before he asked her to sit down.

He finished off the letter he was writing, sanded it down and then, rising to his feet, came slowly across the room towards her.

"Well, young lady, I was wondering how long it would take you to pluck up enough courage to come here and apologise for your exceedingly foolish behaviour."

"Apologise?" Verity echoed, slightly taken aback. Then she felt the first stirring of temper, and her finely arched black brows snapped together as she watched him seat himself in the chair opposite. "On the contrary, Uncle Charles, if anyone ought to apologise it is you, for allowing me to believe that you hadn't taken the information I passed on to you seriously!"

He regarded her from beneath hooded lids. "I rather think my colleague was right when he said that it's high time you were taken in hand."

"If you are referring to that obnoxious individual you sent to Little Frampington, I should be obliged, when next you see him, if you tell him from me to keep his asinine views to himself!"

"Oh, dear." There were definite signs of twitching about his lordship's mouth. "It would appear you two had a slight difference of opinion when you met the other evening."

"Difference of...? Ha! Yes, you might say that,"

Verity concurred, controlling her temper with an effort. "He's nothing but a brutish oaf!"

Lord Charles reached into his pocket and drew out a delicately painted enamel snuffbox. "His opinion of you was not—how shall I put it?—over-complimentary, either. He was not best pleased to discover you had left the premises without him. Furthermore, he was halfway to convincing himself that you had made the whole thing up, and that no meeting had ever been arranged."

"That isn't true, Uncle Charles!" Verity exclaimed, more hurt than angry now. "I would never come to you with a mouthful of lies. You know I would not!"

"Yes, my dear. I do know," he assured her without a moment's hesitation. "I can only assume, therefore, that for some reason the meeting was cancelled, or that you misheard the time and place."

"No, sir. I didn't. But what I did do was stupidly put my own interpretation on what was said," Verity explained, looking rather shamefaced, and then went on to relate, verbatim, exactly what had passed between the spy and the man in the dark cloak.

Lord Charles listened intently, nodding in agreement when she voiced her belief that the meeting had in fact taken place at eight o'clock at the tavern at the first Frampington.

"Yes, child. You may possibly be right."

"But that isn't all, sir. What is so confoundedly frustrating about the whole business is that I went to that tumbledown old tavern first. I didn't go inside," she hurriedly assured him. "One would need to take the precaution of being heavily armed before venturing into that place! But I did go into the stable, and in there I discovered a pair of fine greys harnessed to a racing curricle. It occurred to me at the time that it was a strange place for a gentleman of evident means to visit… And I saw that same turn-out in the park not an hour ago.''

He regarded her keenly, his shrewd grey eyes not wavering from her face. ''Can you be sure it was the same one?''

''Positive, sir. Perhaps both, but certainly one of those greys has a black diamond-shaped mark beneath its mane.''

''And do you happen to know the name of the person who was tooling the equipage?''

''Yes, sir.'' She lowered her eyes. She didn't want to tell him, and yet she knew she must. ''It was a certain Major Brinley Carter.''

The hand raising a pinch of snuff to one of Lord Charles's thin nostrils checked for a moment. ''How very interesting.''

Something in his tone puzzled her, and she raised her eyes to look at him again. ''Do you happen to be acquainted with the Major, sir?''

''We've met, certainly,'' he replied, returning his snuffbox to his pocket. ''Wellington speaks highly of him. A very brave man, by all accounts. Took a French Eagle in Spain. He was badly injured at Badajoz and was rewarded for his bravery with a Majority on his return to the Peninsula. Yes, a very brave man. Even the French, my dear, have a grudging respect for the men who wear rifleman-green.''

''I know of his exploits, sir,'' Verity responded softly, a distinct catch in her voice. ''He is something of a local hero to the people of Yorkshire. And it wasn't easy for me to come here and tell you this. I thought the world of the Major's grandfather, Arthur Brinley, and although I'm forced to admit I have scant regard for Brin himself,

I don't for one moment believe he would betray his country.''

"Many have done so, child. Money is a great incentive.''

"Yes, sir. And that is precisely why I cannot believe Brin is a traitor. His grandfather was a wealthy mill-owner and Brin has inherited that wealth. But…'' a sigh escaped her ''…I cannot help wondering what he was doing at Frampington last Friday evening at the appointed hour. Of course, there's always the possibility that he loaned the equipage to a friend for the evening, but…''

Giving a worried shake of her head, she rose to her feet. "I had better be on my way, sir, otherwise Aunt Clara will be wondering what has become of me.''

"Thank you for coming here today, my child.'' Lord Charles, ever the gentleman, rose also. "Your information might prove extremely valuable.''

"I hope it does, and I should like nothing better than to be of some assistance to you.'' She could not prevent a chuckle escaping at the dour look he cast her, but didn't hesitate to reassure him. "I promise I shan't go careering about the country in the dead of night on my own again. But if there is anything I can do to help, anything at all, then I hope you won't hesitate to come to me.''

Lord Charles dined alone at his house that evening, and directly afterwards walked round to his club. Seating himself at one of the tables, he whiled away the time playing cards with several acquaintances, but his shrewd grey eyes, ever alert, frequently glanced over in the direction of the door to watch the other members come and go. As the evening wore on the rooms became more crowded, but the clock in the corner had chimed midnight before the gentleman he had been hoping to see put in an appearance.

Immaculately attired in a long-tailed black coat and tight-fitting buff-coloured pantaloons, which emphasised the rippling strength in his long, muscular legs, the gentleman strolled across the room and sat himself down at the only vacant table. Lord Charles finished the hand he was playing and, excusing himself, went over to the corner table.

"I was rather hoping that I might see you here tonight." After calling to a waiter to bring a bottle and glasses, Lord Charles sat himself in the chair opposite and then looked his companion over. "Been cutting a dash in Society again, I see. Where was it tonight, m'boy?"

"Lady Gillingham's soirée." He raised his attractive eyes ceilingwards. "I managed to sit through Miss Gillingham's appalling twanging on the harp, but when some ill-favoured rascal with a squint started mouthing out some rubbishing poem he had written, I was off!"

Lord Charles's shoulders shook. "In different circumstances you might have got on very well with my niece Verity. She avoids such gatherings like the plague. And, talking of my little niece, she paid me a visit this afternoon."

"Oh, aye?" Reaching for the burgundy the waiter had just deposited on their table, Lord Charles's companion poured out two glasses. "What's the little monkey been getting up to now?"

"I get the distinct impression, m'boy, that my little Verity remains firmly fixed in your black books. And I got the distinct impression earlier that she ain't overly fond of you, either." He looked into the younger man's wickedly glinting eyes. "What happened between you two at that inn at Little Frampington last week?"

"Obviously she didn't enlighten you?"

"No, she didn't. But she did tell me something rather interesting."

His lordship wasted no further time in pleasantries, but disclosed what he had learned from his niece earlier. His companion listened intently, and when his lordship fell silent, said, "So, she saw that equipage again today in the park... Who was tooling it, did she know?"

"That, m'boy, is the most interesting fact of all." Lord Charles's smile was a trifle rueful. "The gentleman handling the ribbons was none other than a Major Brin Carter."

The younger man pursed his lips together in a silent whistle. "You're right. That is interesting! And it might turn out to be the break we've been hoping for."

"It might." Lord Charles held the younger man's gaze steadily. "And I imagine you can appreciate my rather invidious position. But what I must know is does the curricle and pair belong to the Major, and if so did he, in fact, lend the turn-out to a friend on the night in question?"

"Oh, it belongs to him, right enough," his companion responded without a moment's hesitation and, delving into his pocket, drew out a folded piece of paper which he threw down on the table.

Lord Charles picked it up and, after running his eyes over it, raised a brow. "Well, well! My little niece has turned up something well worth investigating." He shook his head. "Pity she ain't a boy. She's an observant little thing. I could have used her."

"I, on the other hand, am very glad she isn't a boy.

And I think it might be wise to give her a task to occupy her, if only to prevent her getting into more mischief.''

''What had you in mind?''

''Well, sir, it stands to reason that this—er—traitorous Major must be watched. And who better to perform that service than your delightful niece?''

Lord Charles gazed at his companion consideringly. ''What are you up to, m'boy?''

''Everything that is honourable, I assure you. You see, sir, it stands to reason that she'll need to be in the Major's company a great deal.''

''So, that's the way of it, is it?'' Lord Charles raised his glass in a silent toast. ''Well, I wish you all the luck in the world in your pursuit of my niece. But I think I should warn you that she ain't overly fond of the Major, either.''

''You know, it's funny you should say that, because I got that distinct impression too. Some childish grudge, I expect. Still—'' he shrugged ''—she'll come round. I'll see to that, never fear!''

''I don't doubt it for a moment. And I don't doubt either that you'll make my niece an ideal mate.'' Lord Charles's smile faded and his expression became thoughtful. ''But in the meantime be careful, m'boy. Verity's no fool. You might inadvertently let something slip, and if she gets wind of who owned that curricle and pair there's no saying what she may do... And I shouldn't be best pleased if harm ever came to her. I'm very fond of my little Verity.''

''Don't worry, sir. I'll take very good care of her. It'll come as no great surprise, I'm sure, when I tell you that I'm more than just a little fond of the unruly minx myself!''

# Chapter Six

Since their arrival in town Verity and her aunt had not spent above two evenings at home, and those had been through choice rather than a lack of invitations. Although Lady Billington was very gratified over this circumstance, and, indeed, over her niece's very compliant behaviour in agreeing to attend a wide variety of functions without so much as a quibble, she could not rid herself of the lowering feeling that Verity wasn't enjoying her first Season as much as she ought and that her niece's mind for the most part was quite otherwhere.

It came as something of a surprise, not to say a relief, therefore, when Verity betrayed genuine signs of enthusiasm over attending a party at Lady Morland's that evening. Lady Billington put this down to the fact that the hostess hailed from Yorkshire, and that her niece would be amongst people whom she knew well. Meg, who had been allowed more time to arrange the silky black locks in a riot of curls for the occasion, thought her young mistress's excitement stemmed from a desire to see the handsome gentleman who had drawn his curricle to a halt in the park the day before to speak to her.

In point of fact, neither was correct in her assumption.

Verity had a keen desire to attend the occasion simply because of a note she had received earlier in the day.

Verity had always been a firm favourite with Lady Billington's servants. Not only was she easy to please, but she never made any unnecessary demands on their time. Since her sojourn in Curzon Street, however, she had rocketed in their estimation simply because she had taken it upon herself to walk their mistress's pampered and rather exacting Pekinese. Horace's morning jaunts to the unfashionable Green Park, where the cows grazed contentedly and the nursemaids took their boisterous charges for an airing, so contented the little dog that he was far less troublesome for the remainder of the day.

It was while Verity had been abroad in Green Park that morning that Lord Charles had paid an unexpected call on his sister. By the time Verity had returned to the house her uncle had already departed, but he had left a note for her:

> *My dear Verity,*
> *I understand from your aunt that you are to attend a party at Sir Frederick Morland's house this evening, and I beg you will spare me a few moments of your time. I respectfully request that you meet me in the garden at ten o'clock, where I can speak to you in private.*
>
> *Yours ever, C. H.*

The only possible reason for such a request that Verity could think of was that her uncle had some news to impart regarding the further progress of his vitally important investigations. It was obvious that he didn't wish his disclosures to be overheard—consequently this request for privacy.

Verity was overjoyed to think that her uncle trusted her enough to keep her informed of any progress. And if he trusted her enough for that, it wasn't beyond the realms of possibility that he might request her further help.

Her spirits soared at the prospect, and that evening she entered Lady Billington's carriage in high good humour, much to her aunt's delight. "I'm so pleased you are looking forward to this evening, my dear. You must know Lady Morland quite well. Am I correct in thinking that she lived quite close to you before her marriage to Sir Frederick?"

"Yes." Verity pulled a face. "Too dratted close!"

Now that was most interesting! Lady Billington mused. So, Verity was not very fond of the lovely Lady Angela. Not that she was too concerned about this. Verity could be headstrong, and quite outspoken at times with people she knew well. And just what she got up to in the wilds of Yorkshire, Lady Billington dared not think! But not once had her niece given her cause to blush when in polite company. Her behaviour was always beyond reproach.

Consequently, when they arrived at their destination a short while later, Verity greeted her host and hostess graciously, not even by the blinking of an eye betraying the fact that she held Lady Morland in scant regard. Their hostess, on the other hand, looked Verity over rather keenly and for far too long, betraying, Lady Billington considered, a distinct lack of good breeding.

For the first hour Verity spent most of her time dancing. No matter where Lady Billington had chaperoned her niece, ball, rout or drum, Verity had never lacked for partners, and Lady Billington always experienced a deal of pride to see her graceful niece, never faltering over a single step, move about a dance-floor.

Sadly, though, since their arrival in town, Verity had been very impartial with her favours, and had never stood up with the same gentleman twice in any one evening. It came as no great surprise to Lady Billington, therefore, when Verity declined the invitation to dance again with the young gentleman who had claimed her hand not many minutes after their arrival, and remained quite contentedly seated beside her, staring about the crowded room.

"Where's Uncle Charles skulking, I wonder? I haven't set eyes on him at all this evening."

Lady Billington didn't attempt to hide her surprise. "Good heavens! I didn't realise he would be here. He never mentioned he would be attending when I saw him earlier today. Perhaps he's across the hall in the room set out for cards."

Verity glanced at the rather ornate clock on the mantelshelf. It was a mere five minutes to the appointed meeting time. Her uncle was a stickler for punctuality and was in all probability already awaiting her in the garden, so she decided it was high time she was making her way there, too.

Informing her aunt that she was in urgent need of some liquid refreshment after all the dancing, she made her way across the room in the direction of a large table where a footman in livery was ladling out glasses of rather weak-tasting punch.

Having acquired the knowledge of how to gain access to the garden from a very informative young gentleman who knew the lay-out of the house, and who had partnered her earlier in a dance, Verity was now aware of the precise location of the door leading to the conservatory by which one gained access to the garden.

Secreting herself behind a conveniently placed potted palm, she peered through the foliage, cast her eyes about the room just to ensure no one was looking in her direction and, fairly confident that she wasn't being observed, slipped behind the plush velvet drapes.

The air in the conservatory struck cold after the warmth of the ballroom, bringing goose pimples to that bared portion of flesh between the long evening gloves and the ornate trimmings on the tiny puff sleeves of her lovely kingfisher-blue silk gown. She shivered as she took a surreptitious glance down the long glass-built construction, for it was not an uncommon occurrence to discover amorous couples stealing a few precious minutes alone in such places. Thankfully she detected no one lurking and, opening the door leading to the garden, stepped outside into the even cooler night air.

Lifting up her skirts a little, she risked taking a few steps along the gravel path, but dared not venture very far for fear of tripping and tearing her gown. The moon, hidden behind a veil of thin cloud, offered little light to aid her, but even so she could just detect the shapes of large shrubs on her left and what appeared to be a marble cherub holding an urn aloft.

She called her uncle's name softly, tentatively, but only an eerie silence answered her. Then, just as she was about to return indoors, fearing that Lord Charles had, perhaps, been unable to attend the party for some reason, she detected a sudden movement on her right and could clearly see a small red glow.

"Who is that? Who's there?" she demanded in a voice that shook slightly, betraying alarm.

"Don't be afraid, lass."

Every nerve in her body grew taut. She couldn't mistake that husky, accented voice, and was certain of who it was even before he stepped out of the shadows and she saw that now all too familiar tricorn and cloak. Unable to suppress a tiny squeal of sheer vexation, she swung round, but before she had taken more than a step or two back towards the conservatory he was already behind her.

Pulling her back against his broad expanse of chest, the Coachman captured her wrists and pinned her arms about her slender waist, holding them there securely with his own. "Nay, lass, don't struggle so. Tha'll only end by tearing that very pretty gown o' yours," he advised gently, but with more than just a hint of amusement in his voice, and Verity, never having been able, for some obscure reason, to control her emotions when in the company of this man, felt her temper stir.

"Then let me go, you—you barbarian!"

"Shh, now. Dusta want that lot inside to hear you and come out to investigate? I'd need t'op over t'wall right sharpish, and then tha won't hear what I've come 'ere especially t'tell you."

"Well, what is it?" she snapped, her inability to break free bringing vividly to mind the humiliation she had suffered at his hands during their last encounter. More disturbing still was the effect his closeness was having on her pulse rate. He was so tall, so infinitely stronger than she was, that she would be powerless to prevent him from doing precisely what he wished to her, and yet that age-old feminine intuition assured her that he would never, ever do anything to cause her lasting harm.

"Wh-why did my uncle not come?" she prompted, trying desperately to ignore the warm breath, smelling faintly of tobacco, fanning her cheek.

"'E 'ad an unexpected visitor turn up at 'is home, lass, and so sent a message for me t'come in 'is stead."

"Then kindly pass on his message so that I can return inside!" Then, a little less sharply, "It's cold out here."

"Ain't I keeping tha warm, lass?" he husked against her left ear, before nibbling gently, and rather disturbingly, at the lobe.

"Stop that at once!" she snapped, trying desperately to ignore the delightful tingling sensation spreading down to her toes. "Right from the start you've taken the most outrageous liberties with my person. You are no gentleman, sir!"

"Oh, I can be when I choose," he returned blandly.

"Well, I've seen precious little evidence of it. In fact, you're the very worst kind of man... You're a bully!"

"Oh, I see. Tha's still smarting 'cause I walloped thy backside." He paused for a moment, as though expecting her to admit to it, but she kept her lips firmly compressed. "Nay, then, lass. That's the worst tha need ever fear from me. And tha deserved it! It were a damnably foolish thing tha did that evening, going out there by thissen. We're not dealing wi' a passel o' nursemaids."

"I know that!" she retorted, far from appeased, and even farther from forgiving him for the humiliation she had suffered at his hands. "I'm not an idiot!"

"Nay. Just a trifle spoilt," he told her infuriatingly. "But I still adore you." He placed his cheek against the soft black curls. "I can't stop thinking aboot thee, lass," he astounded her by admitting. "Tha's in m'blood. Never known a filly stir me t'way you do. And at least now I'll be able to see summat o' thee."

Verity experienced such a maelstrom of diverse emotions that for several moments she was unable to think clearly. Anger and resentment still featured strongly, but she was feminine enough to experience a deal of gratification over his evident deep attraction to her. Curiosity, too, loomed large, and she decided that at this point in their rather short and somewhat torrid acquaintanceship curiosity was perhaps the safest feeling to betray, and so asked him outright why he felt they would be seeing more of each other.

''Well, if tha wants to 'elp 'is lordship and missen in our investigations, I don't see as 'ow tha can avoid it.''

Do you mean my uncle truly wants me to help?'' Verity's most devout wish had been granted, and she experienced all the excitement of a child who had been promised a rare treat. ''But how? What does he want me to do?''

''T'information tha passed on t'Lord Charles about a certain major o' 'is acquaintance caused no little—er—interest, as tha might say. T'Major might well be completely innocent, o' course, but we needs to be certain. And that's where tha can 'elp.''

Verity didn't like the sound of this. No, she didn't like it at all. She had suffered agonising feelings of guilt after her last visit to her uncle. Surely something else hadn't been discovered about Major Carter?

''But how can I be of help?'' she asked cautiously.

''I would o' thought that were obvious, lass… Tha knows 'im, dustn't tha?''

''I knew him, certainly.''

''Well, gets to know 'im all over again. Find out 'is movements. If tha discovers t'lad's attending a certain party of an evening, make sure tha's there, too. Be in 'is company as much as possible. Find out who 'is friends be and what 'e does wi' issen during the day. Be nice to 'im, friendly-like, and 'e may let one or two things slip out.''

"What?" Verity squealed, hardly daring to believe he was being serious. "If I do that, Brin will think that I'm… He'll suppose that I'm—well—out to entrap him."

"Well? And so you are, lass," the Coachman pointed out, betraying his all-too-evident amusement once more.

"But not into marriage!" Verity countered hotly, but then began to turn the idea over in her mind. "If I do this thing it will be for one reason only—to prove Brin's innocence, not his guilt."

"Ah! So tha's a soft spot fer t'gallant Major Carter?"

"No, I have not!" The denial could not have been more forcefully spoken. "The man's a buffoon! But I was very fond of his grandfather. And for Arthur Brinley's sake, I'll prove his grandson innocent."

The Coachman was silent for what seemed an interminable length of time, and Verity sensed a change in him even before he said in a voice of such steely harshness that it brooked no argument, "Very well, then. I'll permit thee to 'elp. But we'll 'ave certain matters clearly understood at the outset. Iffen tha should uncover summat—owt at all, no matter 'ow insignificant it might seem—tha's not to act upon it thissen but inform thy uncle at once. Occasionally tha'll be contacted by missen. I'll not always be in disguise, so tha must promise t'keep thy back towards me at all times, unless I tell you otherwise. 'Tis vital my identity remains a secret if we're to stand the remotest chance of catching this unscrupulous devil who's been passing information on to the French for a number of years."

Verity nodded her head in agreement to all he had said before enquiring whether or not he had any idea who the traitor might be.

"Thanks to you, lass, we do now 'ave a possible lead.

But I can say n'more for t'present.'' And before she could even begin to ask whether he really did suspect Major Carter, he had placed his hands on her shoulders and had turned her round to face him squarely.

The muffler had been replaced by a hood. Eyes glinted wickedly down at her from behind slits cut in the leather, and it had been fashioned to leave the mouth exposed too. It gave him a rather sinister appearance, whereas before he had merely looked mysterious with his face well hidden behind the woollen scarf. Strangely, though, she experienced no fear.

It was strange, too, that it never occurred to her to struggle when he drew her closer, nor did she make the least attempt to turn her head away before his mouth fastened over hers.

Instinctively her lips parted beneath the seductive pressure of his own, and without conscious thought she raised her arms to entwine them round his neck. His response was immediate. A husky moan rose in his throat and he drew her body so firmly against his hard muscular frame that they seemed to meld together into one perfect whole, seemed inseparable, somehow. It was so strange, but still no thought of resistance entered her head. It was almost as though she belonged to him, body and soul, as though from birth she had been destined for this man alone, and nothing she said or did could detract her from this predetermined course. The very real possibility that this might be true didn't alarm her, for how could anything that felt so natural, so perfectly wonderful, be wrong?

Drawing his lips away, almost reluctantly, it seemed, he buried his face in her soft curls. '''Ere, lass, this won't do,'' he murmured, his breathing ragged. ''I must keep a clear 'ead, but that's damnably 'ard when I'm intoxicated wi' the mere thought o' you. But when this is all over, when I'm free t'be wi' you, be very sure I'll never let tha go. Tha's mine, lass… Tha always were mine. I realise that now… And I'll never let another take thee from me.''

Only then did Verity experience a frisson of fear. Although he had spoken lightly there was no mistaking the raw determination in his voice. She knew he meant it, had meant every word; knew, too, that he was as powerless to resist her as she was to resist him. Then, as if to belie this, he held her away, and her eyes betrayed both uncertainty and fear.

''Nay, lass, don't look that way.'' He ran his finger gently, reassuringly down her cheek. ''Everything will work out right fine.'' He placed a swift, featherlight kiss on her forehead. ''Go now, while I still retain t'strength t'let you go. I'll wait right 'ere until tha's safe inside.''

Half of her didn't want to go, didn't want to leave him, and yet she knew she must while she still retained that tenuous hold on both mind and body. Everything was moving too quickly, and she needed time—time for reflection and consideration, time to interpret and understand the strangely mesmeric power this sometimes infuriatingly overbearing man seemed to have over her.

She didn't look back, but instinctively knew he was watching as she entered the conservatory, and then the room beyond. Thankfully many more people had arrived during the time she had been outside, and so she had little difficulty slipping unnoticed past the group standing near the curtain, and then wending her way across the room to where she had left her aunt.

''Good heavens, child! So there you are at last! I was just about to go searching for you. Where on earth have you been all this time?''

"I slipped outside for a breath of air." She saw no reason to lie, and felt that in her present state of mind, in which strange, unfulfilled longings and a need to exercise common sense and control continued to vie for supremacy, she would make a pretty poor job of doing so if she tried. "It's so very warm in here."

It hadn't escaped Lady Billington's notice that her niece was looking rather flushed, but quite becomingly so. There was definitely an extra sparkle, too, in those blue eyes and, yes, her lips certainly did look a trifle swollen. If she didn't know better she would have suspected that Verity had been soundly kissed. Sadly, though, Verity hadn't a spark of romance in her anywhere. Rather a pity, really, she mused.

"In future, my dear, remember not to venture out on your own. One never knows who might be lurking."

How very true! Nor how one will react, Verity reflected, with more than a touch of bewilderment, not to mention shame, at her wanton behaviour in the garden. Then she became aware that she was the focal point of a pair of rather piercing blue eyes, and asked her aunt who the tall and very handsome fair-haired gentleman was staring fixedly in her direction.

Lady Billington cast a brief glance across the room. "Mr Lawrence Castleford. His uncle, Lord Castleford, knows your Uncle Charles very well, as a matter of fact. I believe Lord Castleford has something to do with the War Office, if my memory serves me correctly. He has one son, but it's common knowledge that he shows a distinct preference for that nephew of his. He really is a most unnatural father!"

Lady Billington then noticed their hostess making her way towards the exceedingly handsome Mr Castleford, and frowned slightly. "Now, perhaps you would be kind enough to satisfy my curiosity over something. Why do you dislike Lady Morland?''

"I wouldn't go as far as to say I hold her in dislike, but I have scant regard for people of that ilk.''

"I do not perfectly understand, dear. I know she's only the daughter of a country squire, but I cannot imagine it's her birth at which you cavil.''

Verity couldn't prevent a rather wicked chuckle escaping. "When you consider that one of the people I most admired was the peasant son of a whore, you might well be certain it isn't that.''

"Really, my dear!'' Lady Billington shuddered. "I wish you would learn to moderate your language.''

"I've heard Arthur Brinley described as far worse than that, I assure you.'' A tender little smile curled her lips. "One cannot help but admire a man who was born in the gutter, but who died one of the richest men in Yorkshire. One cannot help but admire anyone who strives, working all the hours God sends, to better himself. But I have scant regard for those who marry merely for social position.''

"Oh, I see!'' Lady Billington cast a further glance in their hostess's direction, and then her eyes sought the rather portly figure of their host. "So you think Lady Morland married merely for money?''

"No, I don't,'' Verity hurriedly assured her. "Had it been only for money I believe she would have married Arthur Brinley's grandson. When I went to live in Yorkshire she and Brin were already, as one might phrase it, seen as a couple.'' Verity went on to explain. "Angela wouldn't have been much above sixteen then, and Brin eighteen or nineteen. Everyone in the neighbourhood thought they would eventually make a match of it. There was a rumour at the time, and it wouldn't surprise me to learn that it had been circulated by Angela herself, that her parents would not give their consent to the match until their daughter had attained her majority. Brin went out to the Peninsula, and within three months Angela had married her obese Baronet. And that occurred a year before she had attained her majority.''

"So you think it was a title she was hankering after?''

"I certainly do, Aunt. As things have turned out, she would have been wiser to have married the weaver's spawn. She might any day now have found herself a Viscountess!''

Verity's sudden gurgle of laughter drew several pairs of eyes to turn in her direction, but she was oblivious to the stares. ''And speak of angels!''

Once again Lady Billington found herself turning her head in the direction of her niece's rather wickedly amused gaze to see a tall, powerfully built figure standing in the doorway. ''Good gracious, dear! Do you mean to tell me that that most impressive young gentleman is Arthur Brinley's grandson?''

''It is indeed!'' She was unable to suppress a further roguish chuckle. ''Just look at Brin Carter, a fine figure of a man by anyone's standards, surely, and then look at that great barrel of blubber Angela married. And if you can sit there and tell me that she didn't marry for social position, I shall think your wits are addled!''

''Well, quite!'' was all Lady Billington would permit herself to utter. Unlike her niece, who never balked at plain speaking, she often considered it wisest to keep one's reflections to oneself, but secretly she thought Verity was probably quite right.

She studied the young Major intently as he made his way across the room. His bearing was certainly that of a military gentleman. He held himself very erect, and yet he moved with an athletic, fluid grace. Nature had certainly favoured him in both face and figure. His features were good, and although she could detect little, if any, resemblance to the Carter lineage, he exuded an air of impeccable breeding.

She could not quite understand from where her niece's dislike of the Major stemmed, for she felt certain there was some slight antipathy on Verity's part at least. She made a mental note to try to get to the root of this rather puzzling circumstance, for there was nothing at all in his demeanour, from what she could see, that would give one a distaste of him. And there was nothing in his manner either, she noted, as he reached his hostess's side, to betray the fact that he had once been very attached to Lady Morland.

He took her outstretched hand in his for a few brief moments, but if the lady expected him to play the gallant and kiss the tips of her fingers she was doomed to disappointment, for he merely executed an elegant bow before releasing his slight hold on her.

"I am so very pleased you accepted my invitation, Brin. It is wonderful to see you again after all these years."

"I wouldn't have missed it for the world. It offers me the opportunity to thank you for the kindness you showed my grandfather by taking the trouble to visit him so often during my years away." He interpreted her slight frown as reluctance to discuss her philanthropy and quickly changed the subject. "You are looking well, Lady Morland. The years have been kind to you."

She pouted prettily up at him, and he could not help thinking that on a girl of sixteen the look would have been appealing enough, but on a female in her mid-twenties it seemed rather ridiculous.

"Such reserve, sir! Am I to call you Major Carter?"

"If you wish it, madam. I think our former acquaintanceship would permit a little less formality."

"We were rather more than just acquaintances, Brin," she reminded him in a husky, provocative voice, and raised limpid blue eyes in wide appeal. "Have you still not forgiven me?"

The look in his own was hard to interpret. "My dear, believe me, I bear you no ill-will. I have in recent years occasionally reflected on the rather fortunate circumstance that young ladies grow up more quickly than young gentlemen. Thankfully, you at least had the sense not to mistake close friendship for anything deeper. And for that alone I shall always be in your debt."

This was not quite the response for which she had hoped. She looked at him keenly, believing his rather unflattering observations nothing more than a smoke-screen to hide a still bruised and battered heart, and was incensed to discover that he was not even looking at her now.

She turned her head in the direction of his openly admiring scrutiny, and her eyes narrowed. "Ah! Do you remember little Verity Harcourt, Brin? What a hoyden she was, forever getting herself into some scrape or other. I recall your saying on more than one occasion what a spoilt little pest she was, forever following you about like some stray whelp."

"Did I say that?" His brows snapped together. "Well, I hope to God I had the sense not to say it to her face! Although..." His words faded and a rather twisted but not unpleasant smile curled his attractive mouth. "Yes, that just might account for it!" he finished triumphantly, if rather enigmatically.

Verity hadn't missed the glances cast in her direction

and couldn't help but wonder just what was being said about her. It crossed her mind that the Major, after their meeting in the park the previous day, might be considering asking her to dance, but if this had been his intention it was thwarted by Mr Castleford, who approached moments later requesting her to partner him in the next set of country dances.

She saw no earthly reason to refuse, even though she was impatient to begin her investigations into the Major's activities. According to her aunt, Mr Castleford was a firm favourite with the ladies, and to have refused him might have given rise to comment. And this was something that must be avoided at all costs, she knew. It was imperative, if she didn't wish to arouse suspicion, to act naturally at all times.

So, she continued to accept any gentleman's request to dance, but also ensured there were many occasions when she was seated by her aunt, thereby giving the Major numerous opportunities to approach her, but he made not the least attempt to do so. Frustration began to stir, and by the time the evening was drawing to a close she had become not just a little annoyed as well.

Guests began to depart and Lady Billington, who had enjoyed the evening enormously, suggested they too should take leave of their host and hostess. Verity dutifully rose to her feet and, determined not to be thwarted in her mission, weaved a path across the room, bidding goodnight to her numerous acquaintances as she did so, thereby trying to avoid rousing her aunt's suspicion by taking such a circuitous route.

As she drew near the Major, who was standing with his back towards her conversing with Lady Gillingham and her pretty daughter, Verity quite deliberately jogged his elbow. Unfortunately, half the contents of the glass of champagne he happened to be holding ended down the front of Miss Gillingham's very fetching primrose silk gown, drawing forth a squeal from that hapless damsel.

Verity's response was to utter an exclamation of dismay, which certainly didn't fool her aunt for a moment and which, Lady Billington suspected by the slight narrowing of his attractive tawny-coloured eyes, had gone no way to convincing the Major that it had been purely an accident, either. But Lady Gillingham, thankfully, seemed quite satisfied with Verity's rather prettily worded apology and whisked her daughter away to effect repairs.

"Wh-what an unfortunate accident!" Lady Billington remarked heroically, stepping into the breach.

"Unfortunate, certainly," was the Major's laconic response, his gaze firmly fixed on what could best be described as an unremorseful glint in a pair of violet-blue eyes. "Miss Harcourt, kindly do me the honour of introducing me to your gracious companion."

Her niece complied, and Lady Billington found her hand taken in a warm, firm clasp for a few moments. "I was slightly acquainted with your grandfather, Major," she remarked, deciding he had the most wonderful masculine smile she had ever seen. "And may I offer you my very belated condolences on his sad demise. He was well respected, I know. Verity thought highly of him."

There was a betraying twitch at the corner of the Major's finely chiselled lips. "Yes, I recall your niece was a frequent visitor to our home in her formative years, ma'am. My grandfather had the reputation of being a strict disciplinarian, but he certainly mellowed with age. Surprisingly, your niece's frequently wayward behaviour, far from arousing his wrath, rather amused him."

Out of the corner of her eye Lady Billington saw her niece stiffen, and once again stepped into the breach. Voicing the hope that they would meet again soon, she bade the Major a hurried farewell, and then whisked her niece away before Verity could compound her reprehensible actions of minutes before by saying something cutting in retaliation to the major's rather unfortunate reminiscences.

"I wonder at you sometimes, child!" she chided, once they were safely ensconced in her carriage. "You jogged Major Carter's elbow on purpose."

Verity made not the least attempt to deny it. Although she was seething with anger over Brin's rather uncalled-for remarks, the incident as a whole had not been without its amusing side. "I didn't intend that he should throw the contents of his glass over Clarissa Gillingham. What a widgeon the girl is, setting up such a screech over nothing!"

"I never for one moment suspected that that was your intention, child. What eludes me completely is why you should have gone out of your way to speak to someone you hold in contempt."

Verity was unable to meet her aunt's rather searching look, and turned her head to stare resolutely out of the window.

"We Harcourts do not appreciate being ignored," she remarked loftily. "The wretch never made the least attempt to approach me, but he most certainly found the time to speak to most every other young female in the room!"

There was more than just a hint of pique in her voice, and Lady Billington could not help but feel that her lovely young niece was not as indifferent to the handsome Major as she imagined herself to be. She could not help but wonder, too, what the Major thought now of the girl whom he had, evidently, on occasions found something of a nuisance years ago. There was no denying that he had made not the least attempt to speak to Verity, but Lady Billington had caught him glancing quite frequently in her niece's direction.

There had been something rather more than just appreciation in his gaze; something that at this early stage she decided it might be rather foolish to try to interpret. Furthermore, far from the buffoon Verity was so fond of calling him, Major Brin Carter was an intelligent man. In fact, just the man, unless she was very much mistaken, to keep her occasionally wayward niece firmly under control.

A twitching smile of contentment pulled at the corners of her mouth as she leaned against the plush velvet squabs. The future, she mused, was set fair to become not only intriguing, but highly promising too!

## Chapter Seven

If Lady Billington had hoped that the foundations of her niece's possible future happiness would be laid without delay, she was doomed to disappointment. Long before she and Verity had risen to begin a new day of frivolous enjoyment, Major Carter had already left London.

Travelling west, Brin tooled his curricle along the main post road to Oxford. It was such bliss to be in the country again after several weeks of breathing the stale air of the capital. And how he disliked town life! How the endless round of social gatherings, where each hostess vied with the other for that supreme accolade of having held the "Event of the Season," was already rapidly beginning to pall!

He was invited everywhere. A party was not considered even a moderate success if Major Brin Carter did not attend. The pile of invitation cards back in the library at Berkeley Square grew daily and the door-knocker was never still. But how many of those who now fawned about him, turning his stomach with their fulsome praises and falsely fixed-on smiles, would have given him a second look if he were not destined to be the next Viscount Dartwood?

A wry smile curled his lips. Thank God he had inherited his grandfather's sound judgement and no-nonsense common sense! Otherwise the attention he had been receiving of late might well have turned his head.

Perhaps he had not always behaved as wisely as he might have done. There had been instances in the past where, were it possible to relive, he would certainly behave differently. He had made mistakes—damned foolish ones too!—but then, who hadn't? Thankfully, though, he was a deal more discerning now than he had been in his youth.

Perhaps he had become a trifle cynical, too. That undoubtedly was the result of his years in the army, when one had had to learn to live one day at a time, never planning too far ahead. One had never known whether one would return from a mission, but one had swiftly learned whom one could trust or not. He had known both good and bad officers, both good and bad men in the lower ranks, and it was no different with those whom he had left behind in London.

Some were genuine; some most certainly were not. And there was a time, he reminded himself, when, not so discerning, he would have stigmatised all those well-bred females of Society as designing harpies and all the so-called gentlemen as mindless coffee-house fops. Five years before he would never have believed it possible that he would eventually consider a man coming from the highest echelon in Society as his most trusted friend.

He arrived at his friend's country estate early in the afternoon. The mansion, built in stone of burnished gold, was surrounded by many acres of fine rolling parkland. The main driveway swept down in a graceful arc and at its highest point offered panoramic views of the Oxfordshire countryside.

Ravenhurst was a magnificent sight by any standard. The park, laid out by "Capability" Brown during the previous century, with its sweeping lawns, clumps of stately trees and its well-stocked trout stream and lake, was a feast to the eye. At the rear of the building was the formal garden, sectioned off by neat box hedges and criss-crossed by weed-free gravel paths. Beyond that, and spreading to either side of the building, was the shrubbery, where rhododendrons when in full bloom added such vibrant splashes of rich colour to the wonderful setting that its beauty almost took one's breath away.

Brin could never come to Ravenhurst without remembering vividly the first time he had stayed at this awe-inspiring country estate. A few short weeks after he had rejoined his Regiment in the Peninsula, Wellington had taken the French-held city of Badajoz. Badly wounded in the siege, Brin had been carried back to camp on a stretcher. The army surgeon had taken one look at the festering wound in the young Captain's side and had not attempted to remove the deeply embedded lead shot.

Brin had then been placed with the dead and dying. His name would most certainly have been added quite swiftly to the long, long list of fatalities had it not been for the actions of his commanding officer, who had taken it upon himself to convey the gallant young Captain back to England where, if the worst should happen, he could at least be buried in his native Yorkshire and not be placed in some nameless grave in Spain.

Colonel Pitbury had not expected Brin to survive the rigours of the overland journey to the port. The civilian doctor who had been on board the vessel bound for Southampton, and who during the voyage had removed the ball from Brin's side and also the one lodged in his shoulder, had not expected his patient to survive. By the time they had docked in Southampton Brin's body had been racked with fever, but still he had held on to those tenuous threads of life. But for how much longer?

Colonel Pitbury had been in a quandary, not wishing to place this gallant young officer in the hands of strangers and yet fearing that Brin couldn't possibly continue to survive if he was forced to make the long journey by coach back to his native Yorkshire. Then he had recalled a letter which had come into his possession, addressed to the young Captain from a certain Mr Marcus Ravenhurst.

Of course Colonel Pitbury had not known that Captain Carter and Marcus Ravenhurst far from being friends had been barely acquainted; that they had merely found themselves earlier that year stranded at the same wayside inn for a few days. He had only experienced untold relief when, upon arrival at the vast Oxfordshire estate, the lady of the house, without the least hesitation, had ordered the Captain brought in from the post-chaise. But as the Colonel had stood there watching Brin, his young body limp, his wounds still festering, being carried by four burly footmen up the wide sweeping staircase, he had believed he was seeing him for the last time. But Colonel Pitbury had not taken into account the sheer determination and unfailing devotion of Sarah Ravenhurst.

Brin's eyes suddenly grew misty with unshed tears as memory flooded back. So deep in the throes of fever, he had been sublimely unaware of the sea voyage, let alone his arrival at this beautiful place. The first thing he had seen when the fever had broken had been the smiling face of a lovely angel peering down at him.

And Sarah Ravenhurst *was* an angel, a loving wife

and mother and the most loyal surrogate sister any man could ever wish for. She had not only healed his body three years ago, but also his mind.

He now found it difficult to believe just what an embittered young man he had been in those days. Crossed in love, and for years having been castigated as weaver's spawn, or worse, by the sons of so-called gentlemen, he had become resentful and disillusioned. But his weeks convalescing at Ravenhurst had changed all that. By the time he had left England to rejoin his regiment in Spain he had been made to appreciate his own worth.

Ashamed though he was to admit it, there had been a time when the mere thought of entering the ranks of the nobility would have terrified him, but that was no longer the case. He had proved himself to be an excellent soldier, a natural leader of men, and given time he would prove himself to be a considerate landlord and a respected member of the peerage. And he owed this confidence, this belief he now had in himself, to Marcus and Sarah Ravenhurst.

After drawing his curricle to a halt in the stable yard, and exchanging a few playful punches with Sutton, the head groom, he went round to the front entrance and was admitted by his friends' very correct butler, Stebbings, who informed him that the mistress was in the small parlour and the master was busily working in the library.

''In that case I'll inflict my company upon your mistress,'' Brin told him, handing over his hat and coat. ''But,'' he added, prompted by an imp of pure devilment, ''be good enough not to delay too long in informing your master of my arrival.''

He opened the parlour door to find Sarah Ravenhurst seated by the window, busily plying her needle. After a few moments she looked round to see who had entered. There followed a shriek of delight as the sewing was tossed aside and she came rushing forward to be enfolded in a pair of welcoming arms.

"Oh, Brin, it's lovely to see you!" The deep affection she bore him was mirrored in her lovely aquamarine-coloured eyes. "Is it just a passing visit or will you be staying?"

"Kindly unhand my wife, sir!" a deep masculine voice ordered from the doorway before Brin could open his mouth to reply. "You're never here above five minutes before you're making love to Sarah!"

"Yes, very true," that incorrigible damsel responded, not making the least attempt to break free from the Major's hold. "I'd call him out if I were you."

"Good God, madam! Do you want to be a widow? He was one of the finest marksmen in the British Army, if not the finest." Abandoning his affronted pose, Marcus Ravenhurst, one brow arching mockingly, came forward to grasp his friend's hand. "Town life not to your taste, eh?"

At the pained look on his face both husband and wife dissolved into laughter. "Yes, you can mock, both of you. Heaven spare me! It's enough to send a sane soul distracted."

"I must confess attending the endless round of parties does tend to become a trifle tedious after a time," Sarah agreed, entwining her arm round Brin's and guiding him over to the sofa. "But what can one do? One is forced to accept invitations, otherwise one is liable to give offence."

"There are quite a number I should take the greatest pleasure in offending," Brin told them roundly. "I've blessed you time without number these past weeks, Marcus, for writing that letter of introduction to Jackson's Boxing Salon. It's such a relief to get away from those matchmaking mamas, if only for a short time.''

"Bound to have happened. You're hot property at the moment, a very eligible *parti*.' Marcus handed Brin a glass of Madeira before seating himself in the chair opposite. "I must teach you how to affect a withering look. That will relieve you of any unwanted attentions. Always worked for me!''

"He doesn't need to fall into any of your bad habits,'' Sarah put in, casting her husband a disapproving glance. "I'm sure he's more than able to cope.'' She turned her attention on Brin once more, with that wicked twinkle in her eyes which he loved so much. "I cannot believe that not one of those highly finished articles hasn't taken your fancy, Brin.''

"Two or three have, as it happens. And that is why I'm here.'' Pausing to sample the excellent wine, he leaned back against the soft upholstery of the sofa. "You have been more than generous already, allowing me the use of your town house, and I know I shouldn't ask it of you, Sarah, so soon after giving birth to Julia, but I was wondering if you would be good enough to permit me to invite a party here, of not more than eight people, in the not too distant future?''

"Of course I don't mind!'' she didn't hesitate to assure him. "You mustn't pay any attention to Marcus. He fusses so. I suffered no ill effects after little Hugo's birth, and it has been no different with Julia's. I'm as fit as a fiddle and would have been happy to join you for a few weeks in Berkeley Square. But, as you very well know, I was foolish enough to marry a dictatorial creature who will have none of it, and who insists on protecting me as though I were as fragile as thistledown.''

"And I would behave just the same if you were mine." Brin smiled at her tenderly. "Not many men are as fortunate as Ravenhurst. But at least a man ought to do all he possibly can to ensure that he has made the right choice in a wife. And that is precisely why I wish to invite certain young ladies here."

Sarah's ears pricked up at this. "Oh?"

"I have singled out three who I think would be admirably suitable for a future viscountess." He fixed his gaze on an imaginary spot on the richly coloured carpet. "But I mistook a lady's feelings, a lady's true nature, once before, remember? And I have no intention of making that very foolish mistake again."

Sarah's smile faded and a hint of sadness crept into her eyes. She knew all about Brin's boyhood sweetheart and how bitterly hurt he had been when he had discovered she had married Sir Frederick Morland. "Do—do you still think about Angela, Brin? Does she still retain a place in your affections?"

"Good gracious, no!" There was no mistaking the conviction in his voice. "Of course I shall never forget her kindness to my grandfather. She continued to visit him regularly, even after she had married. I never received a letter from him without his mentioning that 't'lass has been here again." It was a wonderful thing she did, giving up so much of her time to be with a dying old man, and I shall always be beholden to her for that, but…"

His words faded and he paused to take a further sip of Madeira. "Strangely enough, last night I saw her for the first time since her marriage, when I attended a party at her house. I thought I'd feel something, and yet, Sarah, the only thing I experienced was relief that I hadn't been foolish enough to marry her."

"You are not the first man to have allowed his heart to rule his head," Marcus put in gently, "and I doubt you'll be the last."

"And that is precisely why I have no intention of making that very foolish mistake again. It is one thing to see someone for an hour or two at a party, and quite another to be in that certain someone's company for a considerable length of time, when one might observe certain—er—defects in a character which might not otherwise be apparent."

Sarah regarded him in silence for a moment, then said, "You say three young ladies have taken your eye. Have you truly no preference?"

"No, they are all equally charming." Brin suddenly raised his eyes from their further contemplation of the patterned carpet. "Oh, did I say three? Actually, there's a fourth. Unfortunately, though, she poses one or two slight problems. She frequently doesn't behave as she ought."

Sarah exchanged a meaningful glance with her spouse. "Well, of course, Brin, invite whomever you like. But, in the meantime, I assume you will be staying with us for at least one night?" At his nod of assent she rose to her feet. "In that case I shall instruct that your bedchamber is made ready for you."

Marcus gazed fixedly into the contents of his glass until the door had closed behind his wife, then raised his eyes to stare directly into those of his friend. "If you imagine for one moment that Sarah believed that bag of moonshine, then your weeks in London have addled your wits, m'boy."

"No, of course I don't think it. But I also know she would never attempt to pry."

"Very true, she would not." Marcus continued to

hold his friend's gaze steadily. "But I am quite a different proposition. Now, without further round-aboutation, may I be permitted to know the real motive behind your request?"

Verity, seated at the escritoire in the sunny front parlour overlooking the street, was trying her best to compose a letter to her uncle Lucius. In the normal course of events she would have had no difficulty in writing an account of her doings in London to her guardian, but her mind flatly refused to concentrate on the task and kept dwelling on the possible whereabouts of a certain Major of her acquaintance.

Brin had been away from London a full two weeks. Someone had spotted him tooling his curricle and pair on the main road to Oxford the day after the Morlands' party. This in itself had given little cause for concern. After all, his close friends the Ravenhursts resided in Oxfordshire. What could be more natural than for him to have paid them an impromptu visit?

Her eyes narrowed as she stared blindly out of the window. What was not so easy to understand, however, was what he had been doing two days later, travelling along the Great North Road. His eventual destination, of course, might well have been Yorkshire, but even so it was rather an odd time to decide to pay a visit to his home, just when the Season was beginning to get in full swing.

More puzzling still had been Lord Charles's attitude to the Major's sudden and unexpected absence from town. And there was no doubt in Verity's mind that Brin's decision to leave London had been made on the spur of the moment, because he had been expected to attend several functions and had arranged for notes of apology to be sent to those hostesses concerned for his unavoidable absence. But when Verity had explained this to her uncle, and had then gone on to inform him that she had learned from a very reliable source that the Major had been seen three days after his departure from London alighting from a hired post-chaise at an inn near Newark, Lord Charles had seemed sublimely unconcerned.

"I do not think there is any reason for us to be uneasy over that, my dear," he had said, with a shrug that only confirmed his complete indifference. "If it was, indeed, the Major alighting from that carriage, it is more than likely he intended paying a visit to his home."

"That occurred to me, sir. But why do so now? After all, he has been back in England for several weeks. Surely it would have made more sense to pay a visit to Yorkshire before the Season had begun?" Verity had remained suspicious. "There's something decidedly smoky about his behaviour."

"You may possibly be right, dear. But don't let us jump to conclusions. When he eventually returns, see if you cannot uncover the reason behind his unexpected departure from town. But, as I've already mentioned, there is no reason for us to be unduly concerned. I do know the precise whereabouts of our little French friend," Lord Charles had gone on to say, "and have people watching his lodgings twenty-four hours a day. He has made no attempt to leave London, so we can be fairly certain that no information has been handed over to him as yet."

So, Verity had left her uncle's house having to be satisfied with that. But the simple fact remained that she had been far from happy. And she still wasn't happy. Brin's behaviour was, to put it mildly, most odd, and her uncle's attitude, too, gave her cause for concern. If she didn't know better she would swear that Lord Charles was completely uninterested in Major Carter. But if that was the case, why then had he asked her to keep an eye on him?

The door-knocker echoing round the hall broke into her perplexing thoughts and a few moments later the butler, looking decidedly disapproving, entered the parlour to inform her that a gentleman had called to see her.

Verity raised her eyes heavenwards. Almost from her arrival in town she had been plagued by an endless stream of young men calling at her aunt's house. She ought, she supposed, to be flattered by all the attention she was receiving, and in a way she was, but she was in no danger of losing her heart to any one of them. That did not mean, however, that she would deliberately go out of her way to hurt any young gentleman's feelings, and for this reason she had never refused to receive a caller. But she was swiftly coming to the conclusion that displaying impartiality in order to avoid arousing false hopes in any one of her many young admirers was the totally wrong tactic to adopt.

"His name, Watts?"

"His name, Miss Harcourt, is Carter," a deep voice answered from the doorway, and it took every ounce of self-control Verity possessed not to gape across at the Major as he strolled, uninvited, into the room. It really was most uncanny. Whenever she spoke or thought about him he seemed to appear from nowhere!

"Why, Major! What a pleasant surprise!" The smile of welcome hid quite beautifully her astonishment as she rose from the escritoire and moved slowly towards him. "I understood you were out of town."

He slanted a mocking glance. "Keeping tabs on me, Miss Harcourt?"

"Not at all, Major." Her trill of laughter sounded affected even to her own ears. "But your absence from town has been remarked upon from time to time, and has cast certain young ladies into the mopes."

"But by your beautiful bloom I can safely assume that you are not similarly afflicted, Miss Harcourt."

Definitely I'm not! Verity thought, only just stopping herself from retorting that she would never repeat her foolishness of years before by growing fond of him. He had hurt her once, and she would never offer him the opportunity of doing so again!

"How could I possibly be one of them, sir," she responded, her smile nowhere near reaching her eyes. "You and I have known each other for years. Why, we are more like brother and sister!"

If her intention had been to dent his masculine pride it was obvious she had fallen far short of the mark, for his immediate response was, "Just what I've been endeavouring to explain to this excellent servant of your aunt's. But, as he quite correctly pointed out, it is most improper for you to entertain a gentleman caller indoors, unchaperoned. So, might I suggest that as it's such a pleasant morning we go for a turn in the park in my curricle?"

Even though spending the smallest amount of time in his company was abhorrent to her, Verity could not let this golden opportunity to begin her inquisition slip away and hurriedly accepted the invitation.

Delaying only for the time it took her to don a very becoming bonnet, she accompanied him outside into the late April sunshine to discover the curricle awaiting them, the heads of those unmistakable greys being held by a young groom.

"What superb horses these are!" Verity remarked, after the Major had ordered the groom to return to Berkeley Square and had given the pair their office to start.

"Indeed they are, Miss Harcourt."

"I cannot recall ever having seen you tool an equipage before you joined the army." There was no response. "If my memory serves me correctly you used to ride almost everywhere."

"And I still do ride frequently." She didn't miss the quizzical glance he cast her. "But when in town I believe it is expected of one to —er—cut a dash."

"So you purchased them to cut a figure in Society, sir?"

"Not entirely, no."

The horses, then, certainly did belong to him. Discovering this was a start, but there was still a great deal more she had to uncover. "Have you had them long? How does one go about acquiring such handsome beasts?"

"My, my! What a lot of questions you do ask, Miss Harcourt! Anyone would imagine that your sole purpose for accepting my invitation was to interrogate me."

Brin was far more astute than she had remembered. She must tread more warily from now on, she decided, casting him a sweet smile. "No such thing, Major! It was only that I rather have a fancy for driving myself about town. It is not only the gentlemen that cut a dash, you know."

"True. But don't expect me to encourage you in such folly." Determination hardened his voice, striking a chord of memory, but before Verity could capture the fleeting remembrance he was speaking again, in his normal, pleasant tone.

"Your Uncle Lucius would never forgive me. And, talking of your uncle, he asked me to pass on his regards." He couldn't mistake the sudden gleam of satisfaction which brightened her eyes for one unguarded moment. "Yes, Miss Harcourt, I have been in Yorkshire." His lips twitched. "Now, aren't you going to enquire what took me there?"

After counting up to ten very slowly under her breath, Verity said, "No. And I have no intention, either, of seeking your assistance in acquiring a pair of horses, because I've just remembered that Tattersall's is the place to go!"

"Not for a lady, it isn't," he countered.

"Then how the deuce does a female go about buying a decent pair?" Verity demanded, annoyed at the rather stupid codes of conduct thrust upon young, unmarried females.

"I see you haven't yet learned to control that rather naughty temper of yours, Miss Harcourt," he told her infuriatingly. "I recall my grandfather saying years ago that you needed a firmer hand than Lucius Redmond possessed."

Verity regarded his very attractive profile with narrowed, assessing eyes. For some perverse reasons best known to himself he was deliberately baiting her. Well, she wouldn't let him come out the victor from this little encounter!

"Come, come, Major Carter. You know that is a complete untruth. I recall quite clearly your saying, the very last time we met, that your grandfather looked upon me with a very indulgent eye and found my little ways quite winning."

"*Touché,* Miss Harcourt!" he acknowledged, with such an appreciative smile that Verity found her ill-humour ebbing away. "And if I were you, I would certainly find someone to advise you who knows a deal about horseflesh before you even think of attempting to purchase your own cattle."

"Is that what you did, Major?" she couldn't resist asking, out of sheer devilment and not any real desire to learn more.

"Yes, in a way. My very good friend Marcus Ravenhurst knew I was looking out for a pair and put me in the way of these fine animals."

Did he, now? Most interesting! Verity would dearly have liked to know precisely when the Major had acquired the superb greys, but, given that he was already suspicious of her many questions, she refrained from enquiring and merely remarked in a conversational way, after he had tooled his team expertly through the park gateway, whether he intended staying in London for the remainder of the Season.

"I've no fixed plans, Miss Harcourt. Much depends, of course, on circumstances."

"By that, do you mean the viscountcy?"

"Yes, but there are—er—certain other considerations," he responded, keeping his gaze firmly fixed on the carriage path ahead. "Ah! I do believe that is Lady Gillingham and her delightful daughter."

The Major drew his team to a halt beside the Gillinghams' open barouche. After greetings had been exchanged, Verity listened to the brief conversation which passed between Gillingham and Brin and had to own that his address was faultless.

There was no denying, either, that he exuded an air of quiet but unimpeachable breeding. Had he always possessed this rather charming and dignified manner? she wondered, her eyes glancing fleetingly at Clarissa who seemed in an unusually subdued frame of mind, merely responding with a "yes" or "no", or "indeed, Mama" when addressed directly.

"I hope to see you at our ball tomorrow evening, Miss Harcourt," Lady Gillingham remarked, drawing Verity's attention.

"I shouldn't miss it for the world, ma'am," she assured her. "I am reliably informed that your floral decorations are unsurpassed and that you do not conform to the present unfortunate vogue for transforming a ballroom into a silk tent."

"I can safely promise I shan't do that. And, unless you have further urgent business which is likely to call you away, Major Carter, I look forward to your company as well." And with that she gave her coachman the order to move on.

"What a very pleasant woman Lady Gillingham is," Brin remarked as he too moved off. "She has such charming, unaffected manners. It's a thousand pities there aren't more of her ilk gracing Society."

"Yes, indeed," Verity agreed. "And Clarissa is very like her, but she was certainly out of sorts today. She barely uttered a word." Eyes suddenly brimful with mischief, she cast him a sidelong glance. "I wonder if she's still a little peeved with you for throwing that glass of champagne over her at the Morlands' party?"

Brin would have been the first to admit that he had taken very little interest in Verity before he had left Yorkshire to join the army five years ago, considering her nothing more than a very pretty but decidedly spoilt child. But he had seen enough of her in her formative years to recognise that particular look and, furthermore, to know precisely what it signified.

"I shall take leave to inform you, Miss Verity Harcourt, that you are an unprincipled little baggage!"

Far from offended, Verity gurgled with laughter. "I admit, I have been known to behave a little—er—unconventionally at times. But unprincipled…? Never!"

From that moment Verity felt completely at ease in his company, just as she had done years ago, when he had behaved towards her like some indulgent elder brother. So relaxed and contented did she become that by the time they had arrived back at Curzon Street, and she was alighting from the curricle, she was not perfectly sure whether she had agreed so readily to save him a dance at Lady Gillingham's ball because it offered the ideal opportunity to quiz him further, or simply because she genuinely wanted to be with him.

# Chapter Eight

To say that Verity took little pride in her appearance would be to do the girl, Lady Billington considered, a gross injustice. Although her niece, compared to many other young ladies, spent a relatively short amount of time over her toilet, she always managed to look well-groomed. She did, however, have an unfortunate tendency to select rich, vibrant colours for her clothes: reds, dark greens and, of course, deep blues, her particular favourite. So it had come as something of a relief to Lady Billington when Verity had left the choice of materials for new gowns to her.

Of course, pastel shades were considered the only suitable colours for young, unmarried females, and Lady Billington considered it as something of an achievement to see her niece going about London dressed in pale primrose, pale blue or pink, but her greatest triumph of all, she considered, was persuading Verity to have at least one evening gown of purest white, a colour her niece had always steadfastly refused ever to consider wearing.

Lady Billington experienced no little satisfaction, therefore, when they arrived at the Gillinghams' ball on

Thursday evening. Looking particularly ethereal in a gown of white spider gauze over a white satin petticoat, with a spray of white flowers nestling in her beautifully arranged raven locks, Verity drew no little attention as they entered the crowded ballroom, but as usual she seemed oblivious to the many admiring glances cast in her direction.

"I must say, Aunt Clara, you were absolutely right," Verity announced unexpectedly as they seated themselves on two of the spindle-legged chairs placed against the wall.

"About the dress, do you mean? I know, dear. You look enchanting."

"I'm not talking about that!" Verity responded with an impatient wave of her hand. "I meant the flowers. You said Lady Gillingham's arrangements were the finest you've ever seen. And I must say they are outstanding."

"Indeed, yes. And I do believe she does them all herself."

"Then she's extremely gifted. I wish I could achieve a result half so lovely."

Lady Billington was not offered the opportunity to respond, for a young gentleman, sporting a dazzling green-and-yellow-striped silk waistcoat, approached them and whisked Verity away to join the couples taking up positions for the first set of country dances.

She followed their progress across the floor, smiling to herself. Her niece was, fundamentally, a sweet-natured girl, very generous and genuine in her praise. There was no denying, though, that Verity had on occasion allowed her temper to get the better of her, and she certainly didn't suffer fools gladly, but Lady Billington could never recall her niece deliberately hurting someone's feelings without having had very good reason. She was as happy talking with stable-boys as dukes, and had never been known to look down upon those less fortunate than herself, which certainly did the girl great credit. But Lady Billington was not blind to her niece's faults. The girl could be quite stubbornly headstrong at times and would need a man with as strong a will as her own, if not stronger, to keep her in check.

Her attention was suddenly drawn to the doorway, and she watched the entrance of two new guests. It was not her brother's unexpected appearance which brought a rather satisfied smile to her lips, however, but the arrival of the tall gentleman standing beside him. Now there was someone, unless she was very much mistaken, more than equal to the task of keeping a tight rein on a headstrong filly!

Verity was unaware of the arrival of Lord Charles and Major Carter, for at that precise moment she was moving down the floor, concentrating hard on the intricate steps. She was not allowed to return to her seat once the dance came to an end, for her hand was claimed by a second young gallant and then directly afterwards by a third. She began to think that, unless she took some drastic action, she was in the gravest danger of spending the whole evening on the dance-floor. So, as soon as that particular set came to an end, she neatly avoided a fourth young gentleman who looked perilously as if he was heading in her direction by making a bee-line for a young footman holding several glasses of champagne on a silver tray.

She quickly discovered she wasn't the only one in urgent need of refreshment. No sooner had she relieved the footman of one of the glasses than a small, slender figure appeared at her side and promptly did the same.

"Yes, it is getting rather warm in here, and rather crowded," Verity remarked. "Although, I'm certain my aunt would say that that is a definite mark of success. Your mama must be very satisfied with the evening so far," she went on when she received no response. "And the flower arrangements are the most outstanding I've ever seen."

"Mama is very gifted in so many things." A tiny sigh escaped Clarissa. "I wish I could be more like her."

Although they had never met before the Season had begun, they had always exchanged friendly words whenever they had been attending the same party of an evening, so Verity didn't consider it vulgarly forward to say, "But you are very like her, Miss Gillingham. Many people have remarked upon it."

"In looks, yes. But Mama is so very polished. She always looks so elegant, so poised, no matter in whose company she happens to be, whereas I..."

"You appear equally so, Miss Gillingham."

"Please call me Clarissa," she said with a shy smile. "I do try to behave as Mama would wish, but I sometimes make a complete mull of it. I feel much more at ease in the country. I love being with Papa, helping at the home farm."

Verity was astonished by the admission. She found it difficult to envisage such a fragile-looking creature stomping through inches of dirt and mud in serviceable boots, but evidently it was what she preferred to do.

"Mama was so looking forward to bringing me out," Clarissa continued with a plaintive little sigh. "She has worked so hard to make it all a success, and I dearly hope that I do not disappoint her by not achieving a suitable match, but..."

"I'm sure you won't disappoint her." Verity's smile

was reassuring. "No matter where I've seen you, your company is always being sought by many young gentlemen."

"I know," Clarissa responded with scant enthusiasm. "The trouble is, though, I find it difficult to converse with many of them. All they seem to think about is the latest fashion in coats or footwear—silly, unimportant things like that. Even Major Carter, whom I like above any other, doesn't seem to know very much about farming."

Verity managed to control a quivering lip, but it was an effort. "No, I don't suppose he does. Major Carter, after all, chose a career in the army, not one working on the land. Although," she added with a generosity which would have astounded her aunt, "I expect if he turned his mind to it he would make a success of land management."

She paused to sip her champagne, her eyes moving about the room. "Heavens above! Wonders will never cease! Uncle Charles is here. Will you excuse me, Clarissa? I must return to my aunt, otherwise she'll be wondering what has become of me."

Lady Billington had not been in the least concerned over Verity's long absence, for she had been keeping half an eye on her niece throughout the whole period that she had been away from her side. She had managed to keep a watch on several other persons too, while conversing with the lady seated beside her, and had been remarkably well-pleased with what she had observed.

"Dispensed with your many admirers at last?" she remarked as her niece resumed her seat, and smiled as violet-blue eyes were raised ceilingwards.

"It's really most flattering to be asked to stand up so

often, but one can have too much of a good thing. And these dratted white slippers are nipping at my toes!''

''One would never have guessed it, my dear. You always look so graceful when on the dance-floor.''

The compliment earned her aunt a warm smile, but then Verity changed the subject by saying, ''Oh, by the by, have you seen who's here?''

''Yes, dear. I saw Major Carter arrive.''

''Is he here?'' Verity glanced about the room and quickly located Brin's tall figure amongst a group of gentlemen on the opposite side of the room. ''So he is! Only I wasn't referring to him. Uncle Charles is here.''

''Yes, I know. He came in with the Major, as it happens. I didn't realise they were acquainted.''

''Er—yes. I do believe they know each other slightly,'' Verity responded guardedly. It wouldn't do to let her aunt know that she had been discussing the Major with Lord Charles. It might lead to the wildest suppositions, so she quickly changed the subject. ''Who is that middle-aged gentleman talking with my uncle? I don't believe I've ever seen him before.''

''That's Lord Castleford. You danced with his nephew at the Morlands' gathering the other week, remember?''

''Ah, yes! The handsome fair-haired one. I didn't care for him very much. He thinks a great deal too much of himself... And there was something about him...'' Verity shook her head as she glanced once again at the rather portly figure of Lord Castleford. ''Is his wife or son present this evening?''

''I should think it highly unlikely, dear. Neither of them cares for town life very much.''

''I have discovered someone else who's of a similar turn of mind,'' Verity informed her with a slight smile.

"It would seem that little Clarissa Gillingham is more at home with the sheep and cows."

"Really?" Lady Billington's brows rose. "How very interesting! I wonder if that puts her out of the running?"

Verity didn't pretend to misunderstand. Almost from the day of her arrival in London she had known the identities of the three young ladies who had found favour in the dashing Major's eyes. Before today Verity had believed that little Clarissa was the most likely candidate for the position of the future Viscountess Dartwood. There was no denying that Miss Gillingham was both pretty and sweet-natured. However, what she had learned this evening had given her pause for thought.

Clarissa would only be content if she was allowed to live a simple life in the country. But would a bucolic existence suit a man who was accustomed to excitement, accustomed to facing dangers every day? It was certainly difficult to envisage. After all, that hard life out in the Peninsula, fighting for one's country, must surely have left its mark?

Verity turned her attention on the second contender, who at that precise moment was tripping lightly down the floor in an energetic dance. Hilary Fenner, of course, had known the Major longer than Verity had herself. She was a lively and very likeable girl from a good family. It was rather a pity that her tongue tended to run on wheels, and that her voice was a constant high-pitched screech. In all other respects she might have done very well, Verity mused, casting a surreptitious glance at the third candidate.

Lady Caroline Mortimer was the only daughter of the Earl and Countess of Westbury. Verity considered her by far the prettiest of the three, but this was marred slightly by a rather haughty bearing. If Brin was, indeed, serious in his attentions towards the earl's daughter then he was aiming high. But why not? After all, the title of Viscountess was not to be sneezed at.

"May I hope, Miss Harcourt, that you have remembered to save me a dance?"

Verity came out of her musings with a guilty start, and not for the first time wished that the Major could rid himself of the unfortunate propensity he had for miraculously appearing before her just when she *occasionally* happened to be thinking about him. It really was most unnerving!

"Of course I have, sir." She rose to her feet, bestowing a smile upon him that was not completely false. "I do believe they are about to play a waltz. How very fortunate that I obtained permission to perform that particular dance from the dragon-lady herself only last week."

"For heaven's sake, child! Keep your voice down!" Lady Billington urged in a frantic undertone, before casting a surreptitious glance at that most formidable of patronesses, Mrs Drummond Burrell, who was seated a mere few feet away. "Do you want to be barred from Almack's? Ostracised from Society?"

This drew an unmistakable wicked glint to sparkle in the depths of violet eyes. "Now, there's a tempting proposition!"

"Allow me to relieve you of your niece's rather unnerving company for a short time, ma'am," the Major put in, and then whisked Verity on to the dance-floor before she could utter any further outrageous remarks to discompose her normally imperturbable chaperon.

Verity's unholy amusement vanished the instant Brin's rather shapely, long-fingered hand touched her waist. During the past week several young gentlemen had partnered her in what many seasoned members of Society considered a most improper dance, but not one had caused her pulse rate to behave so erratically. What on earth was the matter with her? Surely it wasn't possible that in some secret, dark place deep within she had retained a *tendre* for this man? The disturbing realisation that this might well prove to be the case did little to restore her equilibrium, and she found herself having to concentrate very hard as they began to swirl about the floor lest she miss a step.

"You're very quiet." The casual remark drew her head up, and he could quite easily discern unease of mind mirrored in the deep blue depths of her eyes. "What's wrong?" His usual teasing tone had been replaced by one of unmistakable concern. "What has occurred to disturb you?"

Lord, but he was astute! "Wh-why nothing!" she assured him, but so unconvincingly that it wouldn't have fooled a halfwit. "I'm still not at all proficient at this particular dance and should hate to step on your toes."

"Rest easy, child. I'm sure they would survive the encounter."

Verity was quite certain of it, too—as certain as she was that she wasn't fooling him for a moment—and she swiftly sought some change of topic. "I understand you arrived here with Lord Charles Harcourt. Are you well acquainted with my uncle?"

"I didn't arrive here with him. We merely met on the stairs," he volunteered, after only the slightest of pauses. "I do know him, however. We are both members of White's."

In that case why hadn't her uncle set himself the task of trying to discover more about the Major over a glass of port and a game of cards in the relaxing atmosphere of their club? What could have been simpler, for heaven's sake?

Verity pushed this rather puzzling thought aside and said, "I'm rather surprised to see him here tonight. He isn't one for favouring such gatherings as this with his presence."

"And neither is Lord Castleford, by all accounts," Brin returned, glancing at the two gentlemen who remained conversing in one corner. "Castleford is a close neighbour of my friend Ravenhurst, as it happens."

Is he now? Verity's eyes narrowed fractionally. And hadn't her aunt mentioned that Castleford worked at the War Office? How very interesting!

"What a pity your friend isn't in town. I wouldn't have minded having a word with him." She hadn't realised she had spoken her thoughts aloud until she glanced up and noticed that he was regarding her with a rather quizzical gleam in his eyes. "About horses, you understand. After all, if he could manage to put you in the way of those greys…"

His expression, now, was faintly mocking. "There isn't a snowball's chance in—There is no possibility whatsoever of his finding you a pair of horses, Miss Harcourt."

"Oh, and why not?"

"Firstly because he isn't in favour of ladies handling the ribbons. He would never permit his own wife to tool her own carriage. And secondly because I should veto the idea. You are far too lovely to risk your neck by indulging in what I suspect would turn out to be nothing more than a passing whim."

For a few moments it was as much as Verity could do to stop herself from giving him a well-deserved set-down for daring to suppose that he would ever be given any say in how she conducted herself, but then her sense of humour came to the fore and she found herself gurgling with laughter.

"You had the unmitigated impertinence to suggest that I was unprincipled the other day, Major Carter. I rather think that of the two of us you are the devious one. How can I possibly take you roundly to task over your lofty assumption that you could dictate how I should go on when in the next breath you pay me such a pretty compliment?"

"Spiked your guns nicely, Miss Harcourt, have I not? And to prove you bear no malice I hope you will be gracious enough to permit me to escort you in to supper later, and, of course, agree to partner me for the supper dance?"

It never crossed her mind for an instant to deny him, even though she would be breaking her golden rule of never standing up more than once with the same gentleman in any one evening. She considered their long acquaintanceship sufficient justification to disregard this excellent maxim.

Moreover, the longer she was in his company, the more likely it was that she would uncover something of importance—providing there was, in fact, something of importance to uncover.

During the following week there wasn't a day that went by when Verity was not seen in Major Carter's company, either gliding round a dance-floor on his arm in an evening, or seated beside him in his curricle during the day. Society, ever watchful for the slightest nuance, was not slow in placing its own interpretation on the sudden preference Major Carter seemed to have acquired for Miss Harcourt's company.

Naturally, conjecture was rife: was it possible that the dashing Major was considering a fourth young lady as a possible candidate for the future Viscountess Dartwood? It certainly appeared that way. And how well they looked together, that lovely, slender raven-haired girl and that broad-shouldered gentleman with those striking red-brown locks!

One would have needed to be both blind and deaf not to have known what Society was surmising, but just what Brin thought of the latest *on dits* was anyone's guess. He never failed to ask her to dance if they happened to be attending the same function of an evening, but Verity could not in all honesty say that he singled her out for particular attention, for if any one of the three young ladies to whom he had been paying court since his arrival in town happened to be present, he certainly made a point of dancing with her, too.

For her part, Verity had at first been amused by all the attention they drew whenever they were in each other's company, but as the days passed she became less and less contented, and began to experience a real sense of guilt. She tried desperately to convince herself that her pursuit of Brin was being made with the best possible intentions—for the good of the country, perhaps for the good of the man himself—but even this failed to salve her conscience. The more she was in his company, the more she grew to like him. She felt certain that he liked her too. Was it fair to continue to encourage his attentions, and thereby risk his feelings for her deepening? Of course it was not! It was heartless and unjust! Furthermore, it was not worthy of her.

Things came to a head a little over a week after the

Gillinghams' ball, when Verity entered the breakfast parlour to find her aunt, looking as excited as a child, already seated at the table.

"You will never guess what I have received this morning," she gushed, her plump face wreathed in smiles. "A letter from Sarah Ravenhurst, inviting us to stay at her country house for a few days! Here, read it for yourself."

After casting her eyes over the short missive, written in a neat, flowing hand, Verity looked across the breakfast table with a puzzled frown creasing her brow. "I didn't realise you were well acquainted with the Ravenhursts, Aunt Clara?"

"I'm not, dear. Naturally, I know Marcus Ravenhurst. He's rather a severe-looking, unapproachable gentleman. And I did meet his wife Sarah last year, when they came up to town for a few weeks. She really is the most lovely, charming young woman. But I'm not acquainted with either of them very well."

"In that case, why have we been invited to Ravenhurst?"

It was as much as Lady Billington could do to stop herself from gaping across the table at her niece. The reason was patently clear to her: Sarah Ravenhurst had issued the invitation at her good friend Brin Carter's behest. So why wasn't this apparent to Verity? she wondered, reaching for the coffee-pot and filling both their cups. After all, the girl had not made the least attempt to deny the Major her company whenever he had sought it, and Lady Billington had been secretly delighted with the way things had been progressing between the two of them.

The Major, being a gentleman of superior sense, had not been over-zealous in his attentions and was, evidently, taking things very cautiously. However, it was abundantly obvious to anyone of the meanest intelligence that they enjoyed each other's company and were well suited. It was obvious, too, that Verity had put whatever childish dislike she had had of the Major firmly behind her. What wasn't so clear, though, was the depth of her feelings.

Might her niece still consider Brin Carter as nothing more than an old friend? If that was indeed the case, then it would be advisable, Lady Billington decided with rapier-like sharpness, to tread very warily lest she throw a rub in the young Major's way. But, at the same time, it would be a grave mistake to underestimate her niece's powers of perception, she decided, handing across a cup.

"From the letter I gather that Sarah Ravenhurst is inviting several people to stay. It wouldn't surprise me if Brin hasn't asked her to invite you. After all, you two appear to have become friends again. And for my part," she went on, not offering her niece the opportunity to confirm this, "I must say it's a great honour, and I cannot deny that I should dearly love to see that house. It is reputed to be something quite out of the common way. But we shan't decide now whether or not to accept the invitation. Let us take a day or two to think it over."

Verity wasn't fooled for an instant. Her aunt had already made up her mind. And so, too, had she! To accept was out of the question. Unthinkable! It would be the cruellest thing imaginable to allow Brin to suppose that her affections were engaged. And how could he possibly think otherwise if she agreed to be what was tantamount to his guest at Ravenhurst? She realised with an acute feeling of guilt that she had been cruelly insensitive in her dealings with him, even though her intentions had been honourable enough. But how to set matters right?

More importantly, how could she flatly refuse to accept Sarah Ravenhurst's invitation without rousing her aunt's suspicions?

Lady Billington broke into her sombre reflections by speaking of the party they were to attend that evening, and Verity forced herself to listen, but as soon as breakfast was over she took herself back upstairs and changed into her outdoor clothes. Fresh air and time by herself was the order of the day.

It was a simple matter to avoid Meg's company. Her maid never came to her room unless summoned. It wasn't so easy to avoid Horace's, however. He awaited her, as he did every morning, at the foot of the stairs, his plumed tail wagging expectantly, and Verity discovered, quite surprisingly, that she just hadn't the heart to leave him behind.

She managed to slip out of the house without being observed, but as she made her way along the street and turned the corner she couldn't rid herself of the disturbing feeling that she was being followed. She looked round on several occasions, but saw nothing and no one of a suspicious nature. There were many people abroad, and she certainly received several strange looks from members of both sexes. That, of course, was only to be expected, for it was considered grossly improper for a young lady of evident quality to be out and about on her own in the streets of London, even in broad daylight.

When at last they arrived at Green Park Verity felt a little less conspicuous. Unlike Hyde Park, it was never crowded here, and to see the herd of cows, and the milkmaids dispensing glasses of warm milk, almost made one feel one was back in the peace and quiet of the countryside.

Unfortunately, Horace took exception to sharing the

park with the docile, bovine creatures. He tended to voice his displeasure rather vociferously, so Verity always kept well away from that area of park where the cows were usually to be found grazing.

After walking far enough to satisfy Horace's desire for exercise, she sat herself down on the lush grass, close to a dense area of shrubs, and began to ponder over her present, rather ticklish predicament.

A wry smile suddenly curled her lips. She had thought she had outgrown her impetuousness years ago, but apparently she most certainly had not. Since attending Miss Tinsdale's very select seminary in Bath, she had had to learn to come to terms with the many petty rules and restrictions imposed upon her sex. Women, in her opinion, were second-class citizens. They were not allowed any say in the running of their country, nor were they permitted to fight for the land of their birth.

Limitations for ladies of breeding were even more constricting. They were little more than adornments, expected only to bear children and to run a household efficiently. So was it really any wonder that she, a spirited girl of no mean intelligence, had jumped at the opportunity her uncle had offered to do something so very worthwhile? Of course it was not! But she was honest enough to admit that she had given little, if any thought to the possible consequences of her actions.

Although she had learned nothing further since the evening of the Gillinghams' ball, Verity was still certain in her own mind that Brin was no traitor to his country. But supposing she had uncovered something very much to his discredit…? Supposing she had discovered that he had been at the inn at Frampington on that particular Friday evening? Would she then have passed on the information to her uncle, knowing that Brin would in all likelihood have been taken into custody and possibly hanged as a traitor?

She shuddered convulsively. It didn't bear dwelling on. What she had succeeded in doing was bad enough, she reminded herself silently, experiencing a most unpleasant stabbing pain of guilt. Her willingness to be in his company had given him the totally wrong impression. She couldn't deny that she liked him... Yes, she liked him very well, but evidently he believed her feelings went rather deeper than mere liking. And now it was up to her to convince him otherwise without, she hoped, causing him too much pain.

"And what be tha doing out 'ere all by thissen, lass?"

Verity didn't know which of them was more startled: Horace sat bolt-upright and voiced his displeasure at the rude interruption of his pleasant doze in his usual way, and she, very nearly jumping out of her skin, inadvertently let the leash slip from her fingers. The indignant Horace wasted no time in disappearing into the shrubbery to investigate the intrusion before she could regain her hold.

"Coachman?" Verity slewed round, her eyes desperately trying to pierce the dense foliage.

"Aye, lass... And turn back round, tha troublesome chit! Remember what I told thee!"

Verity obeyed the brusque command without hesitation. "Are you not in disguise? No, of course, you're not. What an incredibly foolish thing for me to have asked!" She chuckled, feeling suddenly completely at ease knowing that he was there. "If you went about London in broad daylight dressed in mask and cloak, you would be swiftly carted off to Bow Street."

There was no response. Even her aunt's pampered

Peke had ceased his infernal yapping. "Where's Horace?" she asked, alarmed once again.

"He's right 'ere, lass." A short silence, then, "I 'ope 'e ain't thy dog. Prefer bigger ones missen."

"Of course he isn't mine! And what are you doing to him? He's very quiet." An awful suspicion occurred to her. "Oh, God! You haven't throttled him, have you? My aunt would never forgive me!"

"Course I've not. 'E's lying flat on 'is back wi' 'is legs in t'air in ecstasies over 'aving 'is middle tickled."

"Well, do be careful," she adjured him. "He does have a tendency to bite strangers."

"Animals don't bite me, lass…well, not as a rule. Only ever been attacked once in m'life… And that were by a vicious little cat. Don't think she'll ever try it again, mind. Not if she's got any sense, that is."

Verity compressed her lips together primly, flatly refusing to be drawn, but when the Coachman asked again why she was about on her own, she was forced to unlock her mouth.

"I needed to be on my own, that's why!" she snapped, resenting his adopting what could best be described as a rather authoritarian tone. "And how did you know I was here, anyway? Were you following me?"

"Aye. Often sees tha when tha's out and about… And tha never knows I'm there."

"Well, there's no need for you to keep an eye on me any longer," she told him, having by this time reached a decision. "I've decided I shan't be helping my uncle any longer."

There was a further short silence, then, in his customary rather rudely blunt fashion, "And why not?"

"Because I honestly don't believe I possess the right sort of temperament for such an undertaking."

"Come on, lass. There's more to it than that." His tone, now, was gentle, and remained so as he added, "What's occurred to upset thee?"

"Oh, nothing really. It's just…" Verity released her breath in a long sigh. "I said right from the start that I didn't think Brin was involved, and I still don't. All I've managed to uncover during this past week is that his friend Marcus Ravenhurst had something to do with acquiring those greys. Though whether the pair belonged to Ravenhurst himself, or he merely put Brin in the way of attaining them, I don't know. Brin's as cunning as an old fox!" she went on to explain, sounding decidedly nettled. "He neatly avoids responding to any questions he doesn't choose to answer, and, to be honest with you, I don't think I'm going to discover anything further from him."

"Is that the only reason why tha don't wish to continue?"

"Not entirely, no. I also feel guilty." Again she sighed. "By willingly accepting his company so often during these past days, I rather think I've given him the totally wrong impression…" You see, I've been invited to Ravenhurst for a few days."

"What of it?"

Verity raised her eyes heavenwards. Men could be so insensitive at times! "I've never met the Ravenhursts in my life, so I can only assume the invitation was instigated by Brin himself…I believe he's growing—well—fond of me."

"Bound to o' done, lass. Tha's a very lovely young woman."

Verity couldn't help feeling inordinately pleased because he considered her so. "Yes, well," she responded, her cheeks growing quite pink with pleasure. "You must see, though, that I cannot possibly accept. It would be grossly unfair. He would think his feelings were reciprocated.''

''Oh, I shouldn't worry thy pretty little head over that, if I were thee. Tha's not the only one to receive an invite. To m' certain knowledge, the earl's daughter's received one, and so too 'as that friend o' thine, the Fenner chit.''

Verity was astounded, ''How on earth can you possibly know that?''

''Makes it m' business t'know, lass. Well, 'tis common knowledge t'Major's been paying court to 'em. They received their invitations afore you.'' There was a significant pause. ''Expect you were an afterthought, as tha might say.''

''An afterthought!'' she echoed in a tiny squeal of indignation. Everything suddenly became crystal-clear. The wretch had invited her and the other ladies to Ravenhurst simply to vet them, to discover which of them would make the most suitable Viscountess. She had never been so insulted in her life!

''Course, it shows sound judgement, I s'pose,'' the Coachman remarked fair-mindedly, breaking into her vengeful deliberations, ''iffen 'e can't quite make up 'is mind which o' you 'e prefers. Personally I don't think there's the slightest doubt. Tha's much the best. But, then, each to 'is own.''

The compliment was entirely wasted, for Verity was at that moment silently bestowing a string of far from flattering epithets on the Major as she stared sightlessly across the park.

What a fool she had been to suffer pangs of conscience over that unprincipled wretch! He really was the most callous monster to play fast and loose with ladies' feelings. Not with hers, of course. She was far too sensible to be taken in by a handsome face and an outwardly pleasing manner… Vet her, indeed! Her blood was rapidly reaching boiling point. He deserved to be taught a short, sharp lesson!

"Tha's very quiet, lass."

"I'm thinking."

"What about?"

"How I can wreak my revenge on that odious toad of a Major!"

A peculiar sound, like that of a suppressed chuckle, emanated from the shrubbery. "That a girl! Go get 'im, lass! Course, it'll mean tha going to Ravenhurst."

Her eyes narrowed to slits. "I'm almost tempted."

"I would, iffen I were thee. Tha never knows, tha might discover just when Ravenhurst put 'im in t'way o' those greys. And I can always find a means of contacting you when tha's there." Leaves began to rustle. "I must be on m' way now, lass. Can't remain skulking 'ere, otherwise folks'll think I'm up t'no good. I'll be in touch."

The next instant Horace emerged from the shrubbery with something tucked beneath his collar. Verity removed it and a soft smile curled her lips. Why was it that whenever the Coachman was near she experienced the most wonderful feeling of security, the topsy-turvy world seeming to right itself at the sound of that husky, thickly accented voice?

She stared down at the delicate wild bloom resting in the palm of her hand. Dear Lord! Was it possible that she was in danger of losing her heart to that mysterious, sometimes infuriating man? Surely not! And yet…

# Chapter Nine

"Everything I've heard about this place is true!"
Lady Billington declared, totally enraptured. "Have you
ever seen anything so perfectly situated?"

Verity, staring through the post-chaise window, was
forced to admit that she had not. Since their surprise
invitation to Ravenhurst had become common knowledge, she had heard much of the quiet splendour of the
place, and had been prepared for the incomparable sight
which met her eyes as the carriage made its way down
the sweeping arc of the main driveway towards the
Georgian mansion. But what did come as a complete
surprise was the mistress of this fine house.

Verity wasn't perfectly sure just what she had been
expecting the wife of one of the richest men in the land
to be like: a little haughty, perhaps, a lady who certainly
knew her own worth, and one of impeccable manners,
formal rather than friendly. But Sarah Ravenhurst turned
out to be nothing like the lady of her imaginings, and
Verity felt instantly drawn to the very pretty young matron who, not standing on ceremony, came smilingly
across the hall to greet them with, "Oh, you poor things!
I know the journey from London is no great distance,

but it has grown so uncomfortably warm these past days and the heat this afternoon is particularly oppressive.''

"I cannot deny it is a relief to be out of that stuffy post-chaise,'' Lady Billington responded with feeling. "My niece and I decided to hire a carriage. You must have more than enough to cope with finding room for personal maids without the added burden of so many coachmen and grooms, not to mention horses.''

"That was very thoughtful of you both. Lady Gillingham was equally considerate.'' There was a decided twinkle in Sarah Ravenhurst's eyes. "We do have a more than adequate coach-house, but I'm afraid the Countess's travelling carriage is rather on the large size and takes up a good deal of space.''

"Never tell me she travelled here in that ancient landau!'' Lady Billington's pained expression betrayed quite beautifully her staunch disapproval. "The Dowager Countess had it specially made. Why, you could fit a bed inside!''

"My aunt is a fount of wisdom, Mrs Ravenhurst. There isn't much that occurs in Society as a whole which escapes her notice,'' Verity remarked wryly, drawing their hostess's eyes on her, and just for a moment she thought she could detect an arresting look in their lovely aquamarine depths, but in the next instant it was gone.

"I am not many years your senior, Miss Harcourt, so I do not think we need stand on ceremony. I hope you will call me Sarah and permit me to call you Verity. Such a pretty name, I've always thought.''

Then, without giving her young guest time to acquiesce or not, she led the way up the beautifully carved wooden staircase, explaining as she did so that they would be dining quite informally that evening, and that it was destined to be an all-female occasion as Brin was not due to arrive until much later and her husband had, unfortunately, been called away on business. This latter snippet of information drew a rather wicked smile to curl Verity's lips, but as their hostess was at that precise moment showing Lady Billington into her allotted bedchamber it went completely undetected, and by the time Sarah had turned to lead the way out of the room Verity had managed to school her features.

"I've put you in here." Sarah opened the very next door along the passageway. "I thought you would like to be near your aunt."

Verity found herself standing in a bright, airy bedchamber, decorated quite charmingly in varying shades of blue. "Oh, how lovely! Blue is my favourite colour."

"Yes, exceedingly pretty," Sarah agreed, staring fixedly at her young guest's delicately featured face. "I expect like the others you are tired after the journey, so I shall leave you to rest before dinner."

"I'm not such a poor creature. But if you're busy, please do not let me detain you."

"On the contrary, I should be more than happy to stay for a while. It will give us the opportunity to become acquainted." After making herself comfortable in the window embrasure, Sarah watched Verity untie the ribbons of her very fetching bonnet. She knew a little of her other young visitors, but where Verity was concerned Brin had not been very forthcoming, and she couldn't help wondering what lay behind his reticence. "Am I right in thinking you have known Brin for quite some time?"

"Yes. I was not much above ten years old the first time we met. My mother returned to her native Yorkshire shortly after my father died. Sadly, she outlived him by only two years, and I continued to live with

Uncle Lucius, my guardian.'' Verity's lips curled into a
tender smile as she joined Sarah on the window seat.
''He's a dear man. We get along together famously.''

''In which case you are to be envied, my dear. My
guardian was a most unpleasant individual. Quite loath-
some, in fact!'' There was a decidedly wicked little
smile playing about Sarah's lips. ''But he has made quite
a remarkably wonderful husband. I could not have found
a better man for the role.''

''Ravenhurst was your guardian?'' Verity clapped her
hands together in delight. ''Here's a lively tale! Oh, do
tell me everything!''

It had been Sarah's intention to learn as much as she
could about this vibrant young woman, but she found
herself relating a little of her own life history: of how,
three years before, she had taken it upon herself to leave
Bath; of how Ravenhurst, in hot pursuit, had run her to
earth at a wayside inn where a murder had subsequently
been committed.

Verity listened with rapt interest, her lovely eyes
bright with excitement. ''How very enlivening! And
very romantic too, of course, your falling in love and
marrying your guardian. It's a great pity he isn't here. I
would very much have liked to make his acquaintance.''

''He'll be returning in plenty of time for the party on
Friday,'' Sarah assured her. ''It was—er—most unfortunate that he was called away at such a time.''

''Wasn't it just!'' Verity agreed, but was unable to
control a quivering lip, and Sarah, her lively sense of
humour never far from the surface, dissolved into laughter.

''Oh, I can see it's a complete waste of time trying to
fool you. Yes, the wretch has left me to my own devices,'' she admitted. ''I'm afraid Marcus can be a little

intolerant at times, most especially with certain members of our sex. All in all, it was perhaps for the best that he did decide to make himself scarce.''

"In which case he has been more than generous in opening his doors to a passel of females, most of whom I'm certain are completely unknown to him," Verity responded fair-mindedly, before the glinting amusement in her own eyes began to fade. "Which is more than can be said for Major Carter. His manners leave much to be desired, it would seem. Not only does he trade on your evident close friendship by persuading you to invite certain persons to your home, but he hasn't the common courtesy to lend you his support when his guests arrive.''

Sarah could not detect so much as a trace of resentment, or even pique in the pleasant voice, only cool detachment, which she found infinitely more disturbing, and she hurriedly came to her friend's defence.

"Brin did warn me that he wouldn't be here until the evening, Verity. And please do not imagine that I was coerced into opening my home, because I tell you plainly I was not. Nothing could have pleased me more.''

She turned her head to stare out of the window at the acres of rolling parkland. "I love Ravenhurst and am more than content to spend most of the year here. I'm afraid Marcus and I are considered a very odd couple. Quite old-fashioned, in fact! We very much enjoy each other's company. Since our marriage, three years ago, I have borne him two children and have only ever spent two very short spells in London. I'm afraid I'm in the gravest danger of becoming quite anti-social. So, you see," she went on, transferring her gaze to Verity's delicate features, "when Brin offered me the opportunity to play the hostess to such a fashionable gathering of young ladies, I virtually jumped at the chance. My only fear is that you will swiftly become bored with the simple country pastimes after the sophisticated entertainments of the Season.''

Verity didn't doubt her hostess's sincerity, and was surprised to find her annoyance rapidly fading. ''I can safely promise you that I most certainly shall not. Like yourself, I much prefer the country. Believe me, your invitation to escape the capital and the endless social gatherings for a few days was a godsend!''

This assertion seemed to afford Sarah a great deal of satisfaction, and she continued to converse so openly on those subjects dearest to her heart that by the time she left the room a short while later Verity was in no doubt that the delightful Mrs Ravenhurst was touchingly devoted to Brin.

It was fair to assume that Sarah knew precisely why Brin had asked her to invite certain persons to her home, but whether she approved his motives was quite a different matter. It was evident, too, that Sarah was very much in love with her husband; had fallen in love with him soon after they had met. Therefore it was not inconceivable that she would wish the man she looked upon almost as a brother to attain the same marital bliss; that she would want Brin to be in love with the woman he eventually married.

A wry smile curled Verity's lips. Poor Sarah was doomed to disappointment, she feared. How on earth could Brin's affections be engaged when he was still considering one of four possible candidates for his future Viscountess?

Like four brood mares, Clarissa, Hilary, Lady Caroline and—curse it!—even she herself had been invited to Ravenhurst to parade for his thorough inspection. A gurgle of laughter escaped her as she moved across to the bell-pull to summon Meg. Up until her arrival her proud Harcourt blood had coursed through her veins, hotly demanding retribution on the man who had dared to suppose that she might vie for his attention and approval, but meeting Sarah Ravenhurst had had a surprisingly soothing effect upon her and, strangely, she no longer craved revenge.

The wretch still deserved to be taught a short, sharp lesson, and if the opportunity arose she doubted she would be able to resist the temptation to mete out some much needed punishment, but she had no intention, now, of going out of her way to be difficult or to cause Brin embarrassement, as she had once fully intended to do.

No, she would merely sit back and no doubt derive much amusement from the spectacle of seeing the other three young ladies being put through their paces while, at the same time, she became better acquainted with the charming Mrs Ravenhurst.

During dinner that evening Verity was given ample opportunity to study their hostess more closely. If Sarah believed she was in danger of becoming anti-social, then she betrayed no sign of it. Her manners were faultless, she was both gracious and friendly, and what Verity particularly liked was the way Sarah treated everyone equally: bestowing no undue deference towards the Countess of Westbury, who undoubtedly possessed the highest social standing.

She was also given the opportunity to study more closely the contenders for the position of Viscountess Dartwood.

Clarissa, who seemed remarkably cheerful, possibly because she was in the country again, continued to remain her firm favourite for the title. She was a kind-hearted, unassuming girl who would make any man a very comfortable wife.

There was no denying that Hilary Fenner, too, was a good-natured female. Although Hilary wasn't a particularly close friend, Verity had always got on very well with her. It was her propensity to chatter, however, which might prove to be her undoing, a fault which could never be levelled at the Countess's daughter.

Apart from the occasional "yes" or "no", when addressed directly, Lady Caroline barely uttered a word, and yet it was she who very nearly proved to be Verity's undoing when, in response to Sarah's suggestion that the ladies might like to visit a place of interest in the morning, she raised her eyes from the food on her plate and said imperiously, "We shall go to Oxford!"

Verity's eyes, glinting with unholy amusement, met those of her equally diverted hostess across the table, and it was left to the imperturbable Lady Gillingham to break the ensuing silence.

"I think that a capital notion! I have never been there and would very much like to pay a visit."

With the exception of Verity, who dared not speak lest she betray her mirth, and the Countess, who said she would forgo the pleasure as she was not a particularly good traveller in warm weather, all the other guests voiced their whole-hearted approval to the trip, and so Sarah offered to put her open carriage at their disposal.

"But we cannot all possibly fit into just the one carriage," Hilary pointed out after her mother had thanked their hostess for the kind offer.

"We can take our carriage as well, dear," Mrs Fenner suggested, but Hilary was far from satisfied with that.

"It won't be as pleasant as riding in the open air."

''I shall not be accompanying you,'' Sarah informed them. ''I shall remain here with Lady Westbury.''

''And I, too, shall forgo this trip,'' Verity announced, drawing a rather concerned look from her aunt.

''Why? You do not feel unwell, I trust?''

''No, Aunt Clara. As hale and hearty as ever. It's just that I have a fancy to explore these beautiful grounds here.''

''Well, that still leaves six of us,'' Hilary reminded them, her peevish tone making it abundantly clear to everyone that she didn't relish the prospect of being one of those forced to travel in a closed carriage, and drew an understanding smile from her hostess.

''I'm sure Brin would be only too delighted to act as your escort,'' Sarah said. ''He will probably wish to take his curricle, so one of you young ladies could travel with him.''

''I shall go in the curricle!''

Once again Lady Caroline's majestic utterance brought a glow of wicked amusement to Verity's eyes, which brightened considerably when she caught the malevolent glance that Hilary cast the imperious earl's daughter.

All in all, she mused, the next few days were set fair to affording her untold amusement. There was every chance that Hilary would come to cuffs with Lady Caroline long before the visit was over, and it would be interesting to see if the unobtrusive little Clarissa managed to gain her fair share of the gallant Major's attention. Most interesting of all would be to view her hostess's reaction to the events of the next few days, for unless she was very much mistaken, and she didn't think she was, Sarah Ravenhurst had a rather wicked sense of humour, not unlike her own.

Verity's delight at the prospect of an amusing sojourn in the country received an unexpected and rather severe knock as soon as the ladies rose from the table. They were invited to repair to the drawing-room, where a gold-painted instrument of majestic proportions had been placed near the pianoforte in one corner of the room. Sarah's suggestion that one of the ladies might like to entertain them was instantly taken up by Lady Caroline who, in her now all-too-familiar commanding way, said, "I shall play!"

She proved to be a rather gifted player, and Verity was not slow in adding her voice to the general praises when the earl's daughter had come to the end of her lively little piece. Hilary, not to be outdone, didn't hesitate to take up the position on the stool, and she, too, performed very creditably, but when Clarissa was then invited to display her skill on the harp, Verity decided that it was time she made a quick exit.

As luck would have it her chair was placed near the long French window, which had been left open to allow a little fresh air into the room. She waited only until all eyes were focused on Clarissa's dainty fingers plucking at the strings and then slipped outside, undetected, she hoped, and sped along the path, only to collide with a large, immovable object as she rounded the corner. Strong hands gripped her upper arms, steadying her, and she found herself staring up at the golden flecks in Major Carter's twinkling brown eyes.

"Here, let me pass!" she demanded, after ineffectually struggling to free herself from his hold. "Besides which, your presence is required inside."

One russet brow rose mockingly. "And yours isn't, I suppose?"

"Not at the moment, no."

He caught the faint strains of music and betrayed his immediate understanding by a twitching smile. "Evidently you are not a young lady who appreciates the finer arts."

"Not that infernal twanging, I don't!" Verity retorted, not mincing words, then found herself responding to that smile. "Now, be a gentleman, Brin, and allow me to pass before that wretched aunt of mine comes in search of me."

"Oh, so it's Brin again, is it?" he remarked, sublimely disregarding her request. "Since our first meeting in London I have been forced to contend with a very formal *Major Carter,* and during the past few days a frigidly spoken *sir.* So I can only assume that whatever I did to annoy you—though heaven knows what it was!—has been forgiven and forgotten."

He watched a decidedly guarded look replace the flicker of amusement in her eyes and prudently changed the subject. "Well, I take it you've dined already. Sarah does tend to keep country hours here at Ravenhurst. Did you have a good journey? When did you arrive?"

Her expression changed instantly now that she was on safer ground. "Several hours ago. And we were on time. Which is more than can be said for you!"

"Disappointed I wasn't here to greet you, lass?"

She looked at him sharply. Never before had she heard him use any Yorkshire term, and there was something vaguely familiar in the tone. "I've never heard you resort to any Yorkshire expression before."

"I do from time to time," he admitted, at last releasing his hold, and Verity took immediate advantage by stepping back a pace. "The men in my regiment used to find it amusing. My estimable grandparent certainly didn't, mind," he went on, his smile turning rueful.

"Many a skelping I got when I was a lad when he caught me talking broad Yorkshire. I was born the son of a gentleman, and had to speak like a gentleman."

Verity recalled Arthur Brinley referring to his grandson on numerous occasions as "quality made", and her eyes softened in memory, but only for a moment.

"Evidently he didn't beat you hard enough as you continue to fall back into your old ways."

Surprisingly he made no attempt to respond to her gentle teasing, and after a few moments she raised her eyes from the folds of his intricately tied neckcloth to look into his face, and then instantly wished she hadn't. There was such a strange look in the tawny depths of his eyes, a mixture of warm appreciation and something else—something so disturbing in its intensity that she felt the muscles of her abdomen tighten suddenly.

"You—you had better go inside and present yourself, Major Brin Carter," she forced from a suddenly dry throat. "The ladies await the pleasure of your company."

"May I not escort you back inside? I'm certain the young lady has completed her rendition."

"Thank you, no. I think I'll take a wander in the garden for a short while." She didn't add that she needed time to pull herself together. Really, she was behaving like some lovesick schoolgirl! And there was absolutely no reason for it, either! she chided silently. She had overcome her infatuation for this man years ago... Hadn't she?

She turned and walked slowly away without another word, but instinctively knew he was watching her and forced herself to control the rather childish desire to run. Only when she had turned the corner, out of sight of that disturbing gaze, did she allow herself to relax but even so she couldn't resist looking over her shoulder just to ensure that he wasn't following.

Arriving at the end of the path which ran the whole length of the moderately sized mansion, Verity found herself in the stable yard. A middle-aged, stockily-built groom was in the process of leading Brin's horses into the large stone-built stable block, talking softly to them as he encouraged the spirited pair through the doorway.

Without conscious thought she crossed what had to be the cleanest cobbled yard she had ever seen and entered the stable to discover a row of fine animals, each in its own roomy stall, some contentedly chomping away on sweet-smelling hay, whilst others stood with their heads over the doors, watching with evident rapt interest the settlement of the new arrivals.

"Evening, miss. And a very fine evening it be too."

"Yes, indeed." Verity's lips curled into a glowing smile, which many an experienced male had found irresistible, as she moved towards the friendly groom who was busily rubbing down one of Brin's greys. "Lovely animals, are they not?"

"They are that, miss. Couldn't choose between these and the master's pair, yonder." He gestured towards the end two stalls and Verity turned her head to run her eyes over the other two greys. "My master knows a thing or two about 'orseflesh, miss." His brawny shoulders shook. "Still, he ought to. Taught 'im m'self!"

Verity had made up her mind to have nothing further to do with her uncle Charles's very serious investigations. She had felt a traitor herself when she had informed him, two days before, that she simply couldn't continue working on his behalf. She would have given almost anything to do some small service for her country, and she still would, but she was sensible enough to realise that she just simply didn't possess the right sort of temperament to inform on people whom she liked. So it quite astounded her when she found herself remarking. "Ah, yes! I recall Major Carter saying that Mr Ravenhurst is an excellent judge of horseflesh. He put Brin in the way of this pair, I understand?"

"Aye, miss. That 'e did."

Let it go, Verity! Don't continue or you might regret it, the voice of conscience warned, but that strong desire to be of use to King and Country persisted like some irritating itch.

"I'm surprised he could have brought himself to part with such magnificent beasts."

"Oh, they didn't belong to the master, Miss Harcourt."

Thank heavens for that! Verity raised her eyes in silent gratitude to the Almighty for having spared her the agony of deciding whether or not to inform on Marcus Ravenhurst. Now that she knew for sure that her kindly hostess's husband was innocent of any traitorous dealings, ought she to try to discover more?

She was still debating within herself when a thought suddenly struck her. "How do you know my name?"

"Major Brin told me." There was a definite twitching at the corners of the groom's thin-lipped mouth. "'Sutton,' says 'e, 'if you sees a little lady with the deepest of deep blue eyes, and hair like a raven's wing, that'll be Miss Harcourt, and you can safely saddle up a beast of spirit for her iffen she's inclined to ride. A capital little 'orsewoman is Miss Harcourt,' says 'e."

Damned impudence! Verity thought, not flattered in the least. And just how Brin could possibly know what kind of horsewoman she was defeated her completely, since he had not seen her in the saddle for a very long time, and in those bygone days she had been forced to ride a very docile pony.

"How very considerate of him to apprise you of my ability," she forced out between gritted teeth before swallowing her ire. "I should very much like to put one of your master's beasts through its paces."

She fixed her attention upon Brin's greys once more. "One does not come across such fine animals very often. Do you happen to know how your master managed to put the Major in the way of these beauties, Sutton?"

If he considered the question more than unusually inquisitive he betrayed no signs of it. "I do that, miss. They come from the Castleford estate. Their lands border with the master's to the north."

Castleford, Verity echoed silently. Now *that* snippet of information she was prepared to pass on to Lord Charles. He would no doubt find it most interesting.

"I had better be getting back inside, otherwise your mistress will think I've got myself lost. It has been a pleasure making your acquaintance, Sutton," she told him, with such a radiant smile that he was afterwards overheard to remark that Miss Harcourt had the sweetest smile, barring the mistress's, he had ever seen, and that it was enough to melt the hardest man's heart.

Verity, little realising the effect she had had upon the Ravenhursts' head groom, made her way along the path to the front entrance and was admitted by Stebbings, who promptly handed her a letter.

"It was discovered pushed under the door, Miss Harcourt," he explained in response to her rather puzzled glance at her name written in a bold and unfamiliar hand. "It was Major Carter who noticed it when I admitted him a short while ago."

After thanking the butler, Verity didn't waste a moment in having her curiosity satisfied. Rushing up the stairs to the privacy of her room, she broke the seal to read

*Darling lass,*
  *I am nearby, as promised. If you need to contact me for any reason then go to The Three Swans at Houghton. There, ask for Thomas Stone, and he will pass on any message.*
  *Your Coachman.*

Instinctively, Verity's lips curled into yet another of those devastating smiles. Was he in truth *her* Coachman? More importantly, did she want him to be hers?

Since the evening of the Morlands' party he had, increasingly, intruded into her thoughts, and not always favourably. No one could ever have accused her of having a romantic disposition, and yet the memory of his kisses, of that hard, muscular body pressed against her own, never failed to arouse the most ardent need deep inside.

Her smile slowly began to fade and she shook her head in disbelief at her own folly. It was madness, unutterable madness to feel as she did! she told herself roundly. What did she know about him, after all? She cast her eyes once again over the few boldly written lines, conjuring up an image of that tall, mysterious figure as she did so.

He was certainly an intelligent and educated man for all that he spoke with a broad Yorkshire accent, but that, she suspected, was put on for her benefit, for there had been numerous occasions when his accent had been far from pure. That little subterfuge apart, she didn't doubt his loyalty and trustworthiness were beyond question, otherwise Lord Charles would never have chosen him for such a vitally important task. And strangely enough she trusted him too; had done so right from the first time he had kissed her in that stable. She had instinctively known that he would never really harm her.

Yet was this sufficient reason to contemplate spending the rest of her life at his side? No, of course it was not! It was foolish beyond measure even to think of marriage until she had come to know him a good deal better. It was only a feather-brained female who would ever allow her heart to rule her head!

Reaching for the book of poems that she had brought with her from London, Verity placed the letter behind the delicate wild flower which she had so carefully pressed between the book's covers, and smiled crookedly at her own folly.

"I think," she murmured, "yes, I rather think I'm in the gravest danger of becoming quite feather-brained."

# Chapter Ten

Following instructions to the letter, Perkins entered his master's bedchamber early the next morning to discover the Major, already dressed in shirt and breeches, seated at the dressing table.

He had been the Major's valet a few short weeks only, and thought that he couldn't have been blessed with a more thoughtful or less exacting master. Not once had he seen him out of temper, although the Major sometimes seemed abstracted, as though he had a great deal on his mind. This morning, however, there were no traces of worry as his master paused in his whistling of a lively ditty to bid a cheerful greeting.

"And a very pleasant morning it is too, sir," Perkins responded, handing the Major one expertly starched cravat before laying the others he carried very carefully in one of the drawers.

"Anyone up and about, Perkins?" Brin asked as he began to twist the long length of linen skilfully round his neck.

"I believe the mistress is in the breakfast parlour, sir."

Brin couldn't prevent a smile at this innocent slip of

the tongue. Perkins had been employed as footman in the Ravenhurst household for a number of years before becoming his valet, a change of situation which Sarah herself had suggested when she had learned that Brin had sold his commission in the army and would be living for a time in the capital.

"You cannot possibly continue to dress yourself, Brin," she had told him with that teasing smile of hers. "It simply isn't done! And as I cannot imagine your putting up with such a pernickety person as Marcus's valet, I suggest you ask Perkins to be your personal manservant. I know he wishes to improve himself. He's meticulous in carrying out his duties, but young enough for you to train him to your particular requirements. I think he's wasted as a footman. He would make an excellent valet."

"It might have escaped your notice, Perkins, but I don't happen to be married. You do not have a mistress…yet."

The young man coloured to the roots of his sandy-fair hair. "I do beg your pardon, sir."

"Don't fret yourself, lad. It doesn't worry me none. Although," he went on with a decided gleam in his eyes, "I doubt your former master would be any too pleased if he overheard you referring to his wife as my mistress."

"Sir, I never meant…I would never dream of suggesting…" He ceased his somewhat disjointed explanations when he realised he was being teased and his lips curled into a rather boyish half-smile. "Quite so, sir!"

"Glad to see you can take a joke, Perkins," Brin remarked approvingly. "Do you happen to know if Mrs Ravenhurst is alone?"

"One of the young ladies has already left her room, sir. I passed her on the stairs a few minutes ago."

"Which one?"

"I'm afraid I'm not familiar with their names, sir."

"Describe her."

"She was very pretty," Perkins responded, the embarrassed hue returning to his cheeks.

"That doesn't help much, lad. They're all pretty."

"Not like this one, sir," Perkins so far forgot himself to remark. "She has black hair and the loveliest deep blue eyes I've ever—"

"Say no more!" Brin, satisfied with the folds in his cravat, rose from the dressing-table. "The blue superfine, Perkins, I think."

He slipped his arms into the impeccably cut jacket, and then wasted no further time in joining Sarah and Verity in the breakfast parlour. He received a charming smile from one and a mere nod from the other in response to his cheerful greeting, before seating himself down beside his hostess.

"I don't believe our young guest is in the best of humours this morning, Sarah," he remarked provocatively while helping himself to several slices of ham. "I cannot recall her being moody as a child. Headstrong, yes, but not prone to fits of the sullens. But then—" he shrugged "—people do change as they get older, I suppose."

"Pity you haven't," came the muttered response from across the table, drawing a chuckle from both Brin and the lady of the house.

"I can see that you two do not stand upon ceremony. Which is no bad thing. But for your information, Brin, Verity isn't suffering from a fit of 'the sullens,' as you phrase it. We were having a very comfortable coze before you came in.''

One russet-coloured brow rose. ''About me, was it?''

''What on earth makes you suppose that we'd wish to start the day by discussing such a mundane topic?'' Verity interposed before Sarah could reply.

She was far from being in an offhand mood, even though she suspected that he was doing his level best to provoke her. But why must he come down to breakfast looking so damnably attractive? The mere sight of him was enough to send any young female's heart fluttering. But she was determined that he would never discover the effect he still had upon her, and if to achieve her objective meant that she must appear slightly churlish...then so be it!

''As a matter of fact, before you came in, Sarah very kindly offered to show me round this beautiful house of hers, once she's seen you all safely on your way to Oxford, that is.''

Reaching for her coffee-cup, Verity didn't see his expression change suddenly, but Sarah most certainly noticed his smile fade and a slight frown momentarily crease his brow.

''Verity decided yesterday evening that she would forgo the trip as she preferred to explore Ravenhurst. And please feel free to ride whenever you wish,'' she went on, looking back at the young woman who was beginning to intrigue her more and more with every passing minute. ''Just send a message to the stables and Sutton will ensure that a suitable mount is saddled for you. In fact, I would be grateful if you exercised my mare whilst you're here. I do not take her out nearly as often as I ought.''

"I should love to, Sarah. Unfortunately I omitted to bring my habit."

"That isn't a problem. I have several and we're much the same size. You're more than welcome to borrow one of mine."

"You shouldn't encourage her, Sarah," Brin advised, not offering Verity the chance to voice her sincere thanks. "She always did have a propensity for going off on her own. She'll only end by getting herself lost and you'll be forced to order every able-bodied man on the place out searching for her."

Verity kept her eyes lowered, suddenly finding the crusts on her plate of immense interest. She would have been the first to admit that, as a child, she had been known on occasions to go off on her own, but she had never ridden very far, nor had she ever caused either her mother or her guardian concern over her welfare by remaining away from home for any great length of time.

Since leaving the seminary, almost five years ago, she had always adhered, except on that recent occasion when she had made that unforgettable but fruitless trip to Little Frampington, to her guardian's request that she take a groom with her whenever she went riding. Consequently, she considered Brin's remarks not only completely unwarranted, but grossly unfair, and she suspected that he knew they were too.

She was now firmly convinced that he was deliberately trying to annoy her. The only possible reason for his wishing to do so that occurred to her was because he was still nettled over her behaviour towards him the previous evening.

When she had eventually returned to the salon to rejoin the other ladies, it had been to discover that Brin was already there. It had quite sickened Verity to see

how the three contenders for the title of Viscountess
Dartwood had made such an inordinate fuss of him,
clinging to his every word and giggling at his remarks
like three simpletons. Steadfastly refusing to join the little group of admirers, Verity had seated herself on the
couch with Mrs Fenner and Lady Gillingham and when,
a few minutes later, Brin had crossed the room, heading
in their direction, she had quite pointedly risen from the
couch and had gone to seat herself beside their hostess.

Raising her eyes, she risked a quick glance across the
table at him. The quizzical glint in his eyes confirmed
her suspicion, and only her resolve not to cause their
kindly hostess embarrassment prevented Verity from
yielding to his deliberate provocation and retaliating
with a few well-chosen words. She was very well aware,
though, that her tolerance level was not always high, and
quickly made an excuse to leave the table before the
temptation to toss the dregs of her coffee-cup in Brin's
direction became too strong!

Sarah was under no illusions, either, that her good
friend had gone out of his way to be deliberately aggra-
vating. Now, had it been her husband sitting beside her
at the table, she certainly wouldn't have been in the least
surprised to hear him passing some provocative remark.
He was renowned for doing just that—adorable wretch
that he was! But she had never known Brin try to put
anyone out of countenance before. So why should he
have behaved in such an uncharacteristic fashion towards Verity? It really was most intriguing!

But by the time she had risen from the breakfast table,
having had leisure to witness Brin's attitude towards the
other young ladies, all of whom entered the room shortly
after Venty's departure, she was no longer groping in

the dark for a possible reason for her friend's rather puzzling behaviour.

The instant the girls had joined them at the table Brin had returned to his usual urbane self. He had listened to Hilary's prattle with an indulgent ear, had quickly put the shy and sweet-natured Clarissa at her ease and had even managed to extract a reasonable amount of conversation from the normally taciturn Lady Caroline. In all honesty Sarah couldn't have said that he had betrayed a preference for any one of them, but instinct told her that he favoured Clarissa. But even Lady Gillingham's charming daughter had failed to ignite that certain something that Sarah had glimpsed for one unguarded moment when his eyes had rested upon Verity.

It would certainly be most interesting to see how things developed between those two in the next couple of days, Sarah mused, mounting the stairs to make her first visit of the day to the nursery. If Brin was serious in his intentions, and she was firmly convinced now that he was, and that this little interlude in the country was not the complete and utter sham she had once suspected it might be, he was certainly going about fixing his interests in a most peculiar way. Surely it made more sense to charm the girl, to pay her pretty compliments and be attentive to her every need? So why had he gone out of his way to make her hackles rise? She shook her head in puzzlement. Men did go about things in the oddest ways sometimes. Although, she supposed, they must have their reasons.

And what of the girl herself? A slight frown marred the perfection of Sarah's forehead. Verity's feelings were somewhat harder to define. There was no denying that she had made a point of keeping him at a distance the previous evening. There was no denying, either, that she seemed a completely different person when in Brin's company: coolly aloof, watchful almost. On the surface it appeared that she wasn't very fond of him at all, and yet Sarah sensed that this was far from the truth. It was almost as if Verity had built up a protective wall about herself to keep Brin firmly at bay. But if he succeeded in breaking down that barrier, by whatever method he chose, then what would be the outcome?

Sarah's smile returned. Yes, it would be most interesting to watch developments during the next few days; not interfere, of course, merely observe, and see how successful Brin was in storming the citadel!

Later that morning Verity, sublimely unaware that her every word, her every gesture was being studied with intense interest by the lady of the house, accompanied her aunt outside to the open carriage awaiting to take the ladies on their outing to Oxford.

Mrs Fenner had unfortunately succumbed to a sick headache and had decided to forgo the trip. Which meant, of course, that there was now ample room in the carriage to accommodate all the ladies. Lady Caroline was already seated in Brin's curricle, and no one attempted, or perhaps dared, to suggest that she ride in the open carriage with the others.

"Are you certain you won't change your mind and join us, dear?" Lady Billington asked as she seated herself beside Hilary. "I'm certain you'd enjoy the outing."

"I'm sure I would too," Verity agreed, "but I would prefer to stay here and explore the grounds."

"You won't be able to avoid me indefinitely," Brin's wickedly taunting voice whispered in her ear, making Verity start visibly.

She flashed him a darkling look. "Go away!" she

breathed, not mincing words, and then louder, "The ladies await your pleasure, Major."

Sarah, standing a few feet away, didn't hear the little interchange, but she couldn't mistake the look of irritation on Verity's face. Evidently Brin was persisting, with provocation as his main weapon.

"If I were you, Brin, I'd take the ladies to The Bell for luncheon," she suggested, stepping forward a pace or two. "One can always be assured of excellent fare."

"Yes, and please don't feel obliged to hurry over your meal." Verity's smile was a study in roguishness. "Remember we ladies do not enjoy gobbling down our food."

"Believe me, I shall ensure all return none the worse for their trip. And," he added, once again placing his lips close to her ear, "believe me, I shall ensure that I see you later, too."

"Not if I see you first, you won't!" she countered, completely unmoved by the challenging edge to his voice.

He looked as though he was about to say something further, but then seemed to think better of it and, after exchanging a few words of farewell with Sarah, climbed into his curricle.

As soon as Brin had given his greys the office to start and led the way up the sweep of the drive, Verity released her breath in an unmistakable sigh of relief, and then turned to discover her hostess regarding her with a not unpleasant, but quite unreadable look in her eyes.

"Are you sure you can spare the time to show me round this fine house of yours, Sarah? I'm not such a poor creature that I cannot find something to occupy me until the sightseers return. And you do now have Mrs Fenner as well as the Countess to consider."

"Of course I'm not too busy. I shall enjoy your company," Sarah assured her, entwining her arm through Verity's in a sisterly way and leading her back into the spacious hall. "The servants see to most everything. And as far as my other two guests are concerned... Lady Westbury, it seems, is more than content to pass the morning plying her needle, and Mrs Fenner assures me that a few hours in bed, with the curtains drawn across the window, is usually enough to rid her of her troublesome malady. So for the remainder of the morning, certainly, I'm more than happy to bear you company."

In view of this charming assurance Verity suffered no pangs of conscience as she spent the next couple of hours leisurely inspecting most of the rooms in the house, which managed superbly to combine both elegance and comfort. A quick visit to the nursery offered her the opportunity to meet Hugo Ravenhurst, the boisterous two-year-old who already betrayed definite signs of having inherited his father's famous scowl, and of viewing the latest addition to the family who was sound asleep in her cot. The tour ended in the library, the master's inner sanctum, a room which seemed to exude its owner's personality: solid, dependable and infinitely masculine.

The instant they entered, Verity's nostrils were assailed by an unmistakable mixture of smells: leather, brandy and tobacco. Seemingly Sarah could detect the faint odour of cheroots, too, for she went straight over to the window.

"Brin's been in here this morning," she remarked, wrinkling up her nose as she threw one of the windows wide to let in some fresh air. "I'm afraid he picked up the habit of smoking whilst out in the Peninsula, and Marcus allows him to indulge his vice in here."

Verity had been listening with only half an ear, for her attention was drawn to the painting of the master and mistress above the fireplace. She couldn't prevent a slight smile as she recalled the picture of Marcus Ravenhurst in the long gallery, painted, she guessed, several years ago, but in this likeness his features seemed far less harsh, and although he wasn't smiling precisely, he looked a man who was more than just a little contented with life.

"I think you've mellowed your husband, Sarah," she remarked.

"It's a very good likeness." The love she bore him was mirrored in her eyes. "Yes, he has changed during these past few years," she admitted. "He's far more tolerant than he used to be, but I cannot take all the credit for that. His friendship with Brin means an awful lot to him. Why, they are more like brothers!"

"Which is rather strange in itself when one considers that they haven't been acquainted for any great number of years. Although…" Verity looked thoughtfully into space "…I suppose there are those who instinctively take to each other. And there was that time Brin was convalescing here after the injuries he sustained at Badajoz."

"You know about that…? Of course, Brin must have told you. How very foolish of me!"

"No, Brin didn't tell me… You did." Verity gurgled with laughter at the look of astonished disbelief on her hostess's pretty face. "Yes, Sarah," she reiterated, "in a way it was you who told me. You wrote to Brin's grandfather on several occasions, informing him of his grandson's progress. As you probably remember, Arthur Brinley was unwell himself, too ill to make the journey to Oxfordshire. What you probably didn't know was that his eyesight was failing fast. I visited him most every day. I read your letters to him, and it was I who penned the ones he dictated in response.''

''Good heavens!'' Sarah was startled and appeared more than a little confused. ''And all this time Brin has believed…'' Her words faded as the door opened and the butler entered to inform his mistress that luncheon was now ready and that Lady Westbury and Mrs Fenner were at the present moment making their way to the dining-room.

Sarah and Verity didn't waste any time joining them. It was a relief to discover that Mrs Fenner had fully recovered from her headache, and as the Countess proved she was far more adept at the gentle art of conversation than her daughter appeared to be the meal passed very pleasantly.

Directly afterwards they all retired to the small parlour, where the conversation tended to revolve around the efficient running of a large household. Verity could summon up little enthusiasm for a topic she knew next to nothing about and found herself with increasing frequency staring out of the window at the glorious parkland sweeping away from the house in a gentle upward slope. The day was warm and dry and the countryside beckoned, so, as soon as she felt she could excuse herself without appearing rude, she slipped upstairs to collect her bonnet and parasol and to don a pair of stout calf-boots, and then wasted not another moment in venturing out of doors.

Having given little thought to viewing any particular feature of the park, Verity merely set off in a northerly direction. The landscape looked a magnificent sight, bathed as it was in bright afternoon sunshine, but Verity swiftly discovered that the temperature was not conducive to setting a strenuous pace, and so she merely strolled towards the home wood, which edged the park for quite some considerable distance.

The shade of the trees looked most inviting, but she resisted the temptation to venture beneath those leaf-laden branches and explore the undergrowth, for a brief glance back over her shoulder at the mansion, which looked quite small nestling in its hollow, was sufficient to inform her that she had already walked some considerable distance, and, having no idea of the hour, she thought perhaps she ought to be making her way back.

By the time she had reached the lake she was feeling not just a little fatigued, and decided to sit for a while to rest her weary legs on the slight bank which surrounded the breadth of glistening water. It was so peaceful, so completely unspoilt by any of those man-made eyesores most gentlemen of substance would insist on having erected on their land. She could quite understand why Sarah Ravenhurst was so blissfully contented to remain here month in, month out. But then, she suspected, Sarah Ravenhurst would find happiness anywhere providing her husband was by her side.

Verity's eyes narrowed, but not against the bright reflection of the sun's rays on the water. Would she be contented living anywhere? Would she ever come to love a man with such a depth of devotion as Sarah loved her husband? Was she, Miss Verity Harcourt, capable of caring for a man the way Sarah cared for Marcus? Up until a few weeks ago she would have responded with an emphatic "*no*." But now she wasn't so sure.

Something had certainly happened to her since she had made that eventful journey by mail-coach. She had changed. She felt, now, strangely discontented with her lot, as though something fundamental was missing from her life, as though she were no longer whole. Was this how Sarah felt when her husband was not with her? Was this gnawing ache deep within really love?

She shook her head, still unsure. The only thing she did know was that when the Coachman was with her she experienced a delicious feeling of euphoria. But how few and far between those occasions! And how long would it take before she could be with him whenever she wished? Certainly not until he had completed his present mission. And she certainly would never expect him to abandon that very important task just to be with her.

Absently, she began to twist the handle of her parasol round and round, sending its adorning tassels whirling in a lively dance. She had never known anyone quite like the Coachman before. She had certainly found him infuriating on occasions, but she had never found his company dull. Which was more than could be said for any other young gentleman of her acquaintance. No, that wasn't strictly true, she amended silently. She was never bored whenever in Brin's company. And he, like the Coachman, possessed that rather unfortunate ability to annoy her unbearably at times... How very odd that was!

"Ah, so there you are! And to think I was warning Sarah only this morning that you were likely to get yourself lost."

Verity turned her head, an expression of exasperation taking possession of her features as she watched Brin, with that elegant long-striding gait of his, coming down the slope towards her.

"Had you been born a woman, Brin Carter, and had lived a couple of centuries ago, you would have been in the gravest danger of being burned at the stake. I don't know how you manage it, but you always seem to appear from nowhere just when I happen to be—"

Verity caught herself up abruptly, but by the gleam of what looked suspiciously like satisfaction brightening his eyes she knew he had guessed what she had been about to admit.

"And I cannot imagine how you think I can possibly be lost when the mansion's looming large not five hundred yards from where I'm sitting," she finished pettishly.

Uninvited, he stretched himself out on the grass beside her. After crossing one booted leg over the other, he placed his hands beneath his head and looked so comfortably relaxed that she didn't suppose a gentle hint that she didn't require his company would meet with much success at being rid of him, so she merely enquired politely, but with little interest, how he had enjoyed the trip to Oxford.

"Most interesting," was his rather uninformative response.

This drew a decidedly sceptical arch to her left brow. "Well, no one would have guessed it. You didn't remain there very long."

"Evidently you've lost all track of time in your exploration of the grounds." He opened one eye and peered up at her from beneath the brim of his beaver-hat. "The afternoon is well-advanced."

"In that case I'd better return indoors and change for dinner."

He prevented her rising by placing a gently restraining hand on her arm. "No, don't rush away. Dinner will be a little later this evening, so you've plenty of time."

Verity didn't attempt to force the issue. She was enjoying herself just sitting and drinking in the beauty of the place. "If common report turns out to be true," she remarked, breaking the short companionable silence, "then it won't be too long before you'll be lord and master of an estate like this one. What's the latest report on your uncle's condition?"

"I know no more than you do, Verity," he surprised her by admitting. "I've never had any contact with any member of my father's family, not even by letter." There was a slight bitter twist to his lips, but his voice betrayed complete indifference as he added, "You see, I'm weaver's spawn, and never mentioned. My father married beneath him and against the wishes of his family."

"Good Lord, Brin!" Verity was deeply shocked and didn't attempt to conceal the fact. "To hear you talk anyone would think you were brought up in a hovel. Your grandfather was a wealthy man; he lived in a fine house and was well respected."

"By those who knew him, yes," he agreed. "And he did everything humanly possible to raise me correctly— sent me to Harrow; tried to rear me to be a gentleman; got my commission in the army. But in the eyes of my father's family I continue to remain a pollutant of their noble blood."

"You sound as though you don't care," she remarked softly. "But have you always been so indifferent to their contempt?"

"When I was growing up it bothered me, yes," he freely admitted. "There was a time when I did feel bitter, resentful… But not any longer."

It occurred to her then that they had never spoken this way before. When he had joined the army she had been too young, too naïve to discuss such serious topics.

She had almost attained the age of fifteen when he had left Yorkshire for the Peninsula. She had thought herself quite the young lady after spending more than two years at that seminary, but maybe in his eyes she'd still been a child. Was it really any wonder, then, that he had refused to listen to her when she had tried to put him on his guard about Angela? Was it any wonder that her advice had been interpreted as nothing more than childish spite? Or had there been more behind that vicious peal he had rung over her head? Had his resentment at the attitude of his father's family extended to all those born of a certain class?

She gazed once again at the shimmering waters of the lake. If that had been the case, he certainly had set his dislike aside when he had dived into that other lake to rescue her all those years ago.

"You're very quiet, Verity," he remarked unexpectedly, intruding into her reverie. "What are you thinking about?"

"My childhood. I was recalling that time you saved my life."

"Did I?" He looked nonplussed. "I don't recall that."

"We were all invited to the Fenners' place," she reminded him. "It was their eldest son's birthday, if my memory serves me correctly. A group of us went down to the lake." Her lips curled into a rather rueful smile. "You may recall that I was something of a daredevil in those days, so when one of the boys suggested that no female could row across to the other side of the lake and back again, I took up the challenge. I sat myself in the old rowing-boat and they pushed it into the water. No one realised the boat had a hole in the bottom. I'd reached the centre of the lake before the dratted thing began to sink. You heard my cries for help, and dived in to rescue me." She didn't add that being carried back to the house in his arms had made the whole terrifying experience extremely worthwhile.

She turned her head to look at him. He was still lying at his ease, but that intense look she had seen the evening before was back in his eyes. "Now that you mention it, I do recall the incident. You owe me a debt of gratitude, Verity Harcourt... And one day I may ask you to repay that debt."

He had spoken lightly enough, and yet she sensed he hadn't been joking. She was about to reassure him that, if it was ever within her power, she wouldn't hesitate to do so, when a plaintive little cry reached her ears and she turned her head in time to see Hilary Fenner crumple to the ground.

They were both on their feet in an instant, but could only watch in dismay as the prostrate figure rolled over and over down the slope, coming to a halt a matter of inches from where they stood.

Hilary's petticoats had ridden up to her knees, revealing an unseemly amount of stocking and lacy pantalets, and Verity could feel a hot flush of colour stain her cheeks, though she noticed that Brin didn't seem in the least disturbed by the sight of a lady's undergarments as he knelt down beside the inert figure.

"I'll go back to the house and get help," she offered, and was about to set off when she noticed the rather sardonic expression on Brin's face and transferred her attention to Hilary, studying her more closely.

One slender hand was being held in Brin's, the other was resting above her head. The posture seemed unreal somehow, too studiedly elegant to be true. She looked for all the world like a pathetic heroine in some theatrical farce. Then Verity noticed the slight movement beneath the lids. The little wretch was shamming it!

"I don't believe there's any need to alarm the others," he said, casting Verity a conspiratorial wink. "I expect it's the heat. She'll soon come round."

He was evidently offering Hilary an opportunity to redeem herself, but Verity wasn't so charitably inclined. She detested any form of artifice. And this little performance was beyond anything! Hilary deserved to be taught a lesson!"

"I expect you're right. We'll just leave her here, should we?"

"Tut! Tut! We can't do that." His resigned sigh sounded most convincing. "I suppose I'll need to carry her."

"I wouldn't if I were you," Verity advised, only just managing to keep her voice steady. "It's a warm day, and Hilary's no lightweight, you know. You might expire yourself before you've gone a hundred yards."

This was almost too much for Brin. He turned away, his shoulders shaking with suppressed laughter. "Well, what do you suggest?" he asked with a supreme effort at self-control.

"Give me your hat."

"What for?"

"I'll go over to the lake and fill it with water, then you can throw it over her. That's sure to bring her round!" Verity was far from surprised to hear the pathetic moan in response to this rather artless suggestion. "Well, well! I do believe she's coming round."

"Oh, what happened?" Eyelashes fluttered dramatically before Hilary opened her limpid blue eyes to stare up at Brin. "Oh, I feel so strange, Major Carter."

"You'll feel the toe of my boot if you don't stop this nonsense at once!" Verity threatened, having reached the end of her patience. "I've yet to witness a more nauseating spectacle!"

Hilary sat upright with remarkable speed and transferred her gaze from openly contemptuous eyes to discover sparkling amusement in brown ones.

"I—I did feel rather peculiar, Major Carter." She allowed him to help her to her feet, and then flashed a dagger look in Verity's direction. "No matter what some people may think!"

"In that case, Miss Fenner, I suggest you go back indoors and lie down for a while. I'm sure that is all that is needed to set you to rights."

His sympathetic tone won him a warm smile. Hilary then risked a rather furtive glance in Verity's direction, saw the expression on her face hadn't altered and gave a haughty toss of her head before stalking off in the direction of the house.

"I don't think she'll try that little trick again," he remarked, watching her disappear down the path leading to the shrubbery.

"There are times when I'm put to the blush by members of my own sex. What some females will stoop to to attract attention!" The look she cast him as they too set off towards the house was filled with admiration. "It's a good thing you knew at once that she was shamming it. I was all for summoning help."

"I've seen plenty of men faint during my years in the army, Verity. And I don't recall any one of them squeezing my fingers slightly."

"Is that what she did?" Her ever lively sense of the ridiculous gurgled forth. "What a ninnyhammer!"

"Be that as it may. She isn't going to forgive you in a hurry for suggesting I wouldn't be able to carry her."

"I suppose it was a little cruel, as she isn't in the least

overweight, but she deserved it after that ridiculous exhibition. I cannot abide shams.''

''No,'' he said softly, the look in his eyes bringing a perculiar wobbly feeling to her knees. ''It would never enter your head to resort to such feminine wiles.''

Verity wasn't so sure. If he continued to look at her that way she felt she would be in the gravest danger of swooning herself!

# Chapter Eleven

After changing her dress, Verity decided to pay a visit to her aunt's room. When she had returned to the house with Brin a short while earlier it was to be told that Lady Billington had retired to her room for a rest before dinner. Verity hadn't been particularly concerned over this. Lady Billington enjoyed good health, and had never suffered from any of those trifling ailments which seemed to affect so many members of their sex, but she was far from an energetic person, and if Brin had taken the ladies on an extensive tour round Oxford on foot, Lady Billington, never having been a keen walker, would most likely feel genuinely fatigued after the unaccustomed exercise.

Verity entered the bedchamber to discover her aunt, already dressed in one of her elegant evening gowns, seated before the dressing table mirror, having her hair arranged by her devoted Dodd.

"Ah! Verity my dear. I was hoping to have a chance to speak to you before joining the others downstairs."

"Oh?" Verity seated herself on the edge of the bed. "Why, have you something important that you wished to discuss with me?"

"No, not at all. I just thought it might be nice to have a little talk in private." Satisfied with the arrangement of her hair, Lady Billington nodded dismissal to her maid. "How has your day been?" she enquired after the door had closed behind Dodd. "I was informed on our return that you had gone out for a walk. I hope you haven't been too bored."

"Not in the least, Aunt. I've spent a most enjoyable time here at Ravenhurst. And how was your day?"

Lady Billington's lips curled into a strange little smile. "Very interesting... Enlightening, you might say."

"Oh?"

"Yes, dear. The more I get to know Major Carter, the more I come to like him."

"Mmm. Yes, he does have a tendency to grow on one, I must say." Verity took a moment or two to study the nails on her left hand. "And how did you enjoy the company of the other ladies? Did Lady Caroline majestically lead the way with one of her 'We shall go here' pronouncements?"

"Oh, my dear, don't! You'd think that mother of hers would check her." Her pained expression was suddenly replaced by one of approval. "But I can tell you one thing... Major Carter isn't the kind of man to put up with any of that nonsense. She tried to ride back with him in his curricle, but he told her in no uncertain terms that she couldn't because he'd already offered to take little Clarissa Gillingham up beside him. He ordered Lady Caroline to get into the barouche and she obeyed, as meek as you please." Lady Billington chuckled at the memory as she rose from the stool and led the way out of the room. "Evidently that's the way to handle the earl's daughter."

So Brin had had enough of Lady Caroline and had

opted for a change of companion on the return journey, had he? And what man in his right mind wouldn't prefer Clarissa's company? Verity mused as she accompanied her aunt down the staircase. It also went some way to explain Hilary's ludicrous performance earlier, of course. Evidently she had felt decidedly put out at being the one not to ride with Brin and, being a girl of some spirit, had put her mind to it to have her fair share of the Major's company, though whether or not feigning a swoon was the right tactic to adopt was rather debatable. And, of course, she hadn't fooled Brin for an instant. He might once have been susceptible to feminine wiles, but evidently that was no longer the case.

"Oh, it sounds as if some of the dinner-guests have arrived," Lady Billington remarked as they reached the hall.

Verity had forgotten that Sarah had mentioned that she had invited a select few of her male neighbours to dine this evening so that Brin would not feel overawed by what would otherwise have been all-female company. Not that Verity thought Sarah need have concerned herself unduly on Brin's behalf; he was more than equal to the task of coping with any company: male, female or mixed. Which was more than could be said for herself! Verity reflected, recalling with a distinct feeling of unease those moments in the garden when his look had turned her knees to jelly. It was perhaps just as well that there were going to be other gentlemen present, if not for Brin's sake…then certainly for her own!

In her confused state it was perhaps inevitable that the first person she noticed on entering the salon was Brin himself, standing by the window, conversing with a jovial individual whose ruddy complexion betrayed his fondness for port. Their eyes met across the room and

Verity found herself instinctively responding to the smile he cast her before their hostess came forward, bringing with her a slender young gentleman of only just average height whom she introduced as the Honourable Mr Claud Castleford.

The instant Verity heard the name her ears pricked up, and she gave the young gentleman, who might not otherwise have been so favoured, her full attention. Apart from a pair of intelligent and humorous bright blue eyes Lord Castleford's son, outwardly, had little to commend him. He could never be termed even moderately good-looking and his stature was far from impressive, and yet within the space of a mere few minutes Verity had already decided that she liked him. His manner was open and friendly without being too forward, and she was more than happy, therefore, to find herself a short while later seated beside him at the dining-table.

"I had the felicity of making Mr Lawrence Castleford's acquaintance whilst in London. A cousin of yours, so I understand," she remarked after helping herself from a dish of mushrooms prepared in a particularly fine sauce.

"Oh, yes. Lawrence likes to cut a dash in Society. Handsome devil, ain't he?"

"Yes, he's certainly handsome," Verity responded, betraying in her tone that she hadn't been at all impressed, and found herself being regarded in no little admiration.

"It's refreshing to meet a young lady, Miss Harcourt, who hasn't been beguiled by the Adonis in our family. I'm afraid it's a thorn in my father's flesh that I'm not more like my dashing cousin. But I much prefer the quiet life. I'm quite content to remain here looking after the estate."

She recalled then that her aunt had mentioned that Lord Castleford seemed to prefer his nephew's society to his own son's. There had been no bitterness or resentment in Claud's pleasant voice, and yet Verity felt certain that he must feel a little hurt by his father's most unnatural preference, and she found sympathy coming to the fore.

"That's no bad thing, Mr Castleford. An estate cannot run itself. And what you find to do with your time, I'm sure, is a great deal more worthwhile than cutting a dash in Society."

"I certainly think so, Miss Harcourt." He smiled suddenly. "Not that I haven't tried to play the fashionable gentleman, as you might say. Purchased a racing curricle and a fine pair of greys not so long ago. Deuced foolish thing to have done! Where do I ever go to be seen in such an expensive turn-out? And one needs to be on horseback to get about one's land."

The fork Verity had been raising to her mouth checked for a moment. It had not been her intention to enquire further into Brin's acquisition of those unmistakable greys, but now the opportunity had arisen...

"It is strange you should say that, Mr Castleford," she remarked in what she hoped sounded an innocently conversational way, "because I was thinking of acquiring an equipage for myself not so long ago. It was Major Carter, in fact, who talked me out of it. He quite correctly pointed out that I would have little use for such a smart turn-out once I was away from the capital."

"What a coincidence! It was the Major who purchased my curricle and pair."

"Really!" Verity was all wide-eyed innocence. "If only I had known you wanted to part with such fine animals! I believe I would have ignored Major Carter's sound advice had I been granted the opportunity of acquiring such handsome beasts. You are a most remarkable judge of horseflesh, Mr Castleford! But I feel quite out of charity with you,'' she went on, for the first time in her life deliberately resorting to a typically feminine trait by casting him a tiny look of resentment from beneath long, curling lashes. ''If only you had made it common knowledge that you wished to part with them!''

''Truth to tell, Miss Harcourt, I did it on the spur of the moment. Ravenhurst happened to mention that his friend was interested in purchasing a curricle and pair, so I asked my father to drive the turn-out to London when he returned to the capital at the beginning of April so that the Major could look them over.''

''How vexing! My aunt and I arrived in town at about that time. I must have missed my chance by a few days only.''

Mr Castleford, without the least prompting, was then obliging enough to tell her the exact date the equipage had been sold to Brin, which turned out to be the Monday after that Friday evening meeting at Frampington. Verity almost sighed with relief. So, as she had always thought, it hadn't been Brin at that tavern after all.

Instinctively she turned her head to stare at the head of the table, where he sat playing host in the absence of the master of the house. Coincidence or not, he happened to be looking in her direction, and one of those smiles which had so affected Ravenhurst's head groom automatically curled her lips.

Lady Gillingham, sitting on the Major's right, noticed his rather wonderful smile in response, and looked thoughtfully down at the food on her plate. Like Lady Billington, she had been offered ample opportunity to observe the Major during their trip to Oxford, and by the time they had returned to Ravenhurst she was fairly certain that not one of the young ladies who had enjoyed his company during the preceding hours held a place in his heart, not even her own Clarissa. It was a pity because Lady Gillingham liked the Major very well, and would not have been averse to calling him son-in-law, but she did not repine. Clarissa, after all, had only just turned eighteen: plenty of time, yet, for her to meet a suitable *parti*.

Soon after they had arrived back at Ravenhurst she and her daughter had joined Sarah and several of the other ladies in the small parlour. She had happened to be standing at the window, looking out at the glorious view, when she had observed the Major escorting Miss Harcourt back to the house. Evidently he had wasted no time in going in search of her, and it had crossed her mind, then, to wonder whether he had decided, long before this sojourn at Ravenhurst had been arranged, on the lady with whom he wished to spend the rest of his life. Now she was firmly convinced that this was, indeed, the case.

And Verity Harcourt would make the Major an ideal wife. She was a lovely girl who not only possessed a lively sense of humour but was intelligent enough not to bore him within weeks of the ceremony. But was Verity in love with the Major?

She was not the only one to be asking herself this question. Lady Billington too was very much on the look-out for certain signs, for she also had drawn the same conclusions as Lady Gillingham. She kept half an eye on her niece while conversing with the Reverend Mr Martin, who had been placed next to her at dinner, and later, when the gentlemen rejoined the ladies in the Salon after the meal was over, she was delighted to see Verity, without the least hesitation, agree to partner the Major in a game of whist.

They proved to be a formidable pairing and beat their opponents, the Countess and the local Squire, very convincingly before offering their places to Sarah and Mr Martin. Verity, little realising that she had been, and still was, the cynosure of several pairs of interested eyes, wandered over to the couch where Clarissa sat in earnest conversation with Mr Castleford.

"Oh, Verity, Mr Castleford has kindly invited me over to view his livestock. He has just acquired a Wessex saddleback. I should dearly love to see her, only—only I do not think Mama would permit me to ride over on my own." Clarissa cast a rather pleading glance up at the young woman whom she now looked upon as a friend. "If you were to come too I'm sure Mama would quite happily consent."

"Why don't we make up a small party?" a voice suggested over Verity's shoulder before she had chance to open her mouth. Not that she would have refused the request, because it would offer the opportunity of putting Sarah's mare through her paces, which she didn't doubt for a moment she'd enjoy, but whether she would attain the same satisfaction from stomping round a home farm was quite another matter.

"We could pay a visit to the church at Houghton on the way," Brin added. "Mr Martin assures me that the carvings on the pews are very worthwhile inspecting."

"An excellent suggestion!" Mr Castleford cast Clarissa a smile of gentle warmth. "I could ride over to the church and meet up with you there."

"They seem to be hitting it off very well," Brin remarked in an undertone as he drew Verity to one side.

She subjected his features to a quick, appraising

glance, but could detect nothing there to suggest he might be even remotely jealous. "I expect they've a deal in common. Mr Castleford, so I understand, enjoys life on his father's estate. And Clarissa too is more at home in the country. What, by the way," she added as an afterthought, "is a Wessex saddleback?"

There was a suspicion of a twitch about Brin's mouth. "I believe, my dear, it's a famous breed of pig."

"Heaven spare us!" Verity ejaculated, making not the least attempt to hide her mortification. "Pigs and pews… What an enlivening time we're destined for tomorrow!"

Although Verity was far from looking forward to the "treats" in store, she had no intention of casting a shadow over Clarissa's possible enjoyment and arose in good time the following morning so as not to keep the others waiting.

Both Lady Caroline and Hilary had been invited to join the little expedition, but both had declined: Lady Caroline because she had never been fond of riding, and Hilary because she wished to spend the morning with her mother, although Verity suspected the real reason was because she was still feeling embarrassed over her behaviour the previous afternoon. Consequently, it was just the three of them who went out to the stable yard directly after breakfast to discover Sutton had their mounts ready and awaiting them.

"I got the message to saddle the mistress's mare for you, Miss Harcourt, but don't you be setting 'er to jump no 'edges," he warned as he assisted Verity to mount. "She'll take a fence or a five-bar gate, no trouble, but the lady don't take kindly to 'edges. Unseated the mistress not long after she 'ad 'er when Mrs Ravenhurst tried to jump an 'edge."

"Don't worry, Sutton," Brin said, drawing Ravenhurst's fine bay beside the dapple-grey mare. "I'll see to it that Miss Harcourt takes heed of the warning."

"Miss Harcourt doesn't need you to see to anything," Verity countered waspishly, which drew a rather nervous chuckle from Clarissa who had overheard the little interchange. "She isn't so foolish as to ignore sound advice."

"I do believe Major Carter derives a great deal of enjoyment out of provoking you," Clarissa remarked as they set off in the direction of Houghton.

"He always has done," Verity responded, casting her tormentor a look from beneath the rim of the beaver hat, which had been dyed the exact same shade as the borrowed dark blue habit.

"And always manages to succeed so wonderfully well, you'll notice, Miss Gillingham." Brin's white, even teeth flashed in a wickedly challenging smile. "Verity, if you haven't already noticed, possesses something of a prickly temperament which makes the occasional goading remark so confoundedly irresistible."

Verity, at least, noticed the rather apprehensive look Clarissa darted at them, and didn't hesitate to reassure her. "Rest easy. I have no intention of coming to cuffs with Major Carter... Not until we're in private, that is."

"I look forward to the encounter," was his challenging response, and Verity decided it might be wisest if she changed the subject, if not for her own sake then at least for Miss Gillingham's.

They arrived at Houghton without indulging in any further slight skirmishes. It was far from a large habitation, boasting only one main street, but there were several rather neat little shops which looked to be doing some brisk trading. The church occupied a spot in the centre of the thriving little community, and directly opposite, Verity noticed as she dismounted and handed the reins to Brin, was The Three Swans, the inn she was supposed to visit if she needed to contact the Coachman.

Her attention was diverted by the arrival of Mr Castleford, mounted on a sturdy roan. After exchanging greetings they wasted no time in entering the small church to inspect the carved bench-ends, many of which depicted hunting scenes. Verity, surprisingly, found them most interesting, but it was not long before the thatched building on the opposite side of the street intruded into her thoughts. Might Thomas Stone be there now? More importantly, might this Thomas Stone turn out to be none other than her elusive Coachman?

The prospect was intriguing, and she found herself unable to quash the desire to discover if this was true or not. She had, of course, a very plausible reason for seeking him out: she would be able to inform him that she now knew for certain that it hadn't been Brin at Frampington on a certain Friday evening.

After a brief glance at the others, who had moved further along the aisle, and who were still inspecting the bench-ends with apparent rapt interest, Verity began to edge her way back towards the church door. Then, after a further glance to check that none of them were looking in her direction, she whisked herself outside, ran down the church path and across the road into the inn.

It took a moment or two before her eyes became accustomed to the dimness, then she spotted the landlord standing behind the counter and without delay enquired if there was a gentleman by the name of Thomas Stone residing under his roof.

''Mr Stone,'' he called to a person seated at a corner

table, whom Verity had not noticed before. "There be a young lady 'ere asking for you."

Mr Stone placed the journal he had been reading down on the table, and Verity knew even before he rose to his feet and came towards her that he most certainly wasn't the Coachman. Not only was he middle-aged, but he was at least half a foot smaller than the man she had been hoping to see. She hid her intense disappointment quite beautifully, however, behind one of her radiant smiles as she held out her hand.

"How do you do, sir? My name is Harcourt."

"Aye. Thought it must be," he replied, gesturing her to a chair. "We have a mutual friend, Miss Harcourt. And I assume you're here because you have something you wish me to pass on to him."

Verity nodded as she sat herself down. "Yes, I have, but I'm afraid it isn't much." She waited for him to resume his seat and then related what she had learned from Mr Castleford the evening before. "So, I think you can safely eliminate Major Brinley Carter from further enquiries."

He didn't respond, and Verity found herself being regarded very thoughtfully, and rather disconcertingly. A rather disturbing suspicion crossed her mind. "Why are you here, Mr Stone?"

"I'm not at liberty to divulge that, miss," he told her rather bluntly, but Verity, far from daunted, gave him back look for look.

"No, I don't suppose you are. But I cannot help wondering who you were sent here to keep an eye on... And I would wager a large sum that whoever it was, it most certainly wasn't Major Carter."

She rose to her feet. "I think I shall have a serious talk with my uncle when I get back to town. And you may tell our mutual friend that I shall have a thing or two to say to him when next we meet.''

"That message, Miss Harcourt, I most certainly shall pass on,'' he said with a ghost of a smile, and Verity, after casting him a further suspicious look, left without another word.

There was something decidedly smoky about this whole business, she decided, waiting for a lumbering cart, leaning precariously to one side under its heavy load, to move away so that she could retrace her steps across the road.

Right from the start she had known in her heart of hearts that Brin was no spy, and, from the time she had informed her uncle of Brin's unexpected departure from town a few weeks ago, she had sensed that Lord Charles had been very well aware of that fact too. And if he had decided Brin was innocent of any traitorous dealings then it was safe to assume that the people working with him must be of a similar mind.

So why had the Coachman encouraged her to come to Ravenhurst and continue discreet enquiries? It just didn't make sense. Furthermore, she could have sworn that Mr Stone was already in possession of the information she had just given him: he too had known that Brin was completely innocent.

So what was Mr Stone's reason for being in the area? she wondered, managing to get back across the road at last. Who was he keeping an eye on? The Castleford household perhaps? But why? Surely Claud Castleford wasn't suspected of being a traitor? No—that was ridiculous! It was much more likely to be Lord Castleford. He worked for the government, and was undoubtedly privy to a great deal of secret information. Added to which, it was Lord Castleford himself who had taken that curricle and pair to London, and it had still been in his possession on that particular Friday evening when that meeting had taken place at Frampington. Surely it made more sense for Mr Stone to be in London, keeping watch on the man who might possibly turn out to be the traitor? How very bewildering!

And that was not all she found perplexing… There was something, something lurking amongst the jumble of confused thoughts whirling round in her head, something so blatantly obvious that she ought to see it at once, and yet she remained, frustratingly, blindly groping to capture that elusive…something.

Out of the corner of her eye she detected a sudden movement in the churchyard, and just for one blissful moment her spirits soared, but then the tall figure stepped out from beneath the shading branches of the huge cedar tree and she saw that it was Brin.

"And where did you get to, miss?" he asked in that infuriatingly authoritarian tone which he sometimes adopted with her. Added to which, she suspected the question was completely unnecessary, because from where he had been standing he had had a clear view of the other side of the road and must have seen her emerge from the inn.

"Mind your own business, Brin Carter! You're not my keeper. I come and go as I please."

"Yes, more's the pity!" he responded in a half-growl, as he came to stand beside her and stared down into defiant eyes with a decidedly disapproving glint in his own. "It's high time you had your wings clipped, young woman."

At this severe judgement her feeling of irritation disappeared, and a reluctant smile curled up the corners of her mouth as she recalled that someone very dear to her heart had voiced much the same sentiment not so very long ago. How strange that was! Perhaps, though, all tall, broad-shouldered Yorkshire men were innately dictatorial?

"Now, Brin, remove that disapproving look," she coaxed. "You don't want to upset Clarissa again. Such a sensitive little creature! Where is she, by the way?"

"Wandering about the churchyard with Claud, gazing at gravestones." His good humour, too, having been restored, he smiled down at her with a rather rueful twist to his mouth. "It quite amazes me what interests some people. And here they are! Pigs next, I believe."

By the serenely happy look on Clarissa's face, as she walked beside Mr Castleford down the path towards them, Verity guessed that there was more between them than several interests in common. Unless she was very much mistaken little Miss Gillingham felt completely at ease in Mr Castleford's company. In fact, Verity would go so far as to say that she had never seen her look so radiantly happy before, and by the time they had made an extensive tour of the Castleford home farm, and were returning to collect their horses, Verity was firmly convinced that Clarissa Gillingham was in a fair way to losing her heart.

"It's a great pity you're expected back at Ravenhurst for luncheon. I would have liked to show you round the house," Mr Castleford remarked as they entered the stable yard. "Some other time, perhaps. Unfortunately it cannot be tomorrow because I'm off to the local market town to take a look at a pair of plough-horses and shan't be back until quite late in the day. Pity, really. It's a fascinating old place—secret passages, the resident ghost…the lot! I'm sure you ladies would have found it most interesting."

"I'm sure we would," Verity agreed, glancing over her shoulder at the grey stone Tudor building. "Unfortunately we're all returning to London on Saturday, so I'm afraid we'll need to forgo the pleasure. But I hope we'll at least have the felicity of your company again on Friday evening at Sarah's party."

"Wouldn't miss it for the world, Miss Harcourt! Miss Gillingham has promised to save me a dance, and I hope you also will favour me?"

"Of course, Mr Castleford," she responded as she once again mounted Sarah's lovely mare which she fervently wished belonged to her. "I'll look forward to it."

"I hope you weren't too bored," Clarissa remarked with an anxious glance at her companions as they trotted out of the stable yard.

"Not at all," Verity hurriedly assured her stoically, if not entirely truthfully. "I cannot, if I'm honest, say that I can work up much enthusiasm for pigs, nor do I consider them beautiful creatures, as you and Mr Castleford evidently do, but I must say that this estate is in remarkably good order. Which does that young man great credit. I understand his father leaves the running of his lands to his son, is that not so, Brin?"

He merely nodded in response and she regarded him rather thoughtfully. He had seemed in such a strange mood while they had been looking round the home farm. Surely he wasn't piqued over Clarissa's evident liking for Claud's society? No, she felt sure that this wasn't the case. He had certainly been unusually quiet, though, almost in a world of his own, and yet at the same time watchful. She had caught him on several occasions staring over his shoulder at the Castlefords' house, as though expecting to see someone or something. He really was in a very odd mood. She had never seen him this way before.

"How well do you know the family?" she asked in an attempt to restore his usual good humour. "Have you met Lady Castleford?"

He turned to look at her this time. "Yes, a charming lady. Pity she's away from home at the moment. Visiting a sick relative, I understand. I'm sure you and Miss Gillingham would have liked her."

"I believe Mr Castleford's father is returning before the weekend," Clarissa informed them. "He might even arrive in time for the party on Friday."

"Might he? Now, there's a gentleman I would very much like to meet," Verity remarked, staring fixedly ahead, and did not notice an alert and oddly calculating look flash into Brin's eyes.

## Chapter Twelve

They arrived back at Ravenhurst in good time to enjoy the light luncheon. During their absence Sarah had persuaded her other guests to take a trip that afternoon to one of the local beauty spots and, if there was time, to visit a small town not too far away where she assured them they would discover the most divine little milliner's shop at which she had managed to purchase several very delightful bonnets that equalled anything one could find in Bond Street. The invitation, naturally, extended to those who had visited the Castleford estate earlier.

Brin politely declined, as he had several urgent letters he needed to write, but Clarissa was eager for a further outing, and Verity decided she would go too, especially as Sarah intended making up one of the party.

The afternoon continued dry and bright, but thankfully not too hot, and the gentle stroll through the picturesque wood, which Sarah frequently visited during the spring and summer months, was very pleasant. They did find the time to visit the milliner's shop in the small town nearby, and several of the ladies were eager to part with their money. Sarah had not exaggerated the little establishment's excellence, but with so many eager customers bustling round to view the wares on offer the atmosphere very soon became oppressive, and Verity decided to await the others in the fresh air.

She had only just stepped outside into the bright afternoon sunshine when she noticed a hired carriage come to a halt on the opposite side of the road. Ordinarily she would have paid little attention, but with little to occupy her she continued to view proceedings. The carriage door opened and a man of well below average height, dressed in a suit of black cloth, stepped down on to the road. He was carrying a small wooden box and a rather battered cloak-bag. Verity blinked several times, hardly daring to believe the evidence of her own eyes. Dear God! Yes, yes, it was…! It was that French spy!

The hired carriage moved away and she had a clear view of the foreigner as he entered the inn situated a little further along that side of the street. No, she wasn't mistaken. It was he. Her fingers trembled as she raised them to a suddenly throbbing temple. What should she do…? What could she do?

"Verity, my dear, what on earth's the matter?" her aunt's concerned voice succeeded in breaking into her frantic thoughts. "You look as though you've seen a ghost."

"No, not a ghost," she murmured, "but something equally terrifying."

"What on earth are you muttering about? Don't you feel well?"

"I'm fine, Aunt." She pulled herself together with an effort. "Here comes Sarah with the others. I expect it's time we were heading back to Ravenhurst."

She didn't add "thank goodness", but she certainly thought it as she hurriedly climbed back into Sarah's open carriage, while still frantically trying to think of what she could do. There was nothing, of course, except get in touch with Mr Stone without delay. But that in itself would be no easy matter. How could she suddenly announce that she was going for a ride at this time of day without arousing suspicion? Furthermore, she doubted she would be permitted to go off on her own.

For the first time in her life Verity silently blessed Hilary Fenner for being an unremitting gabble-monger. Her incessant prattle offered little chance for the other occupants of the barouche to edge in a word, so Verity's mood of abstraction went completely unnoticed by her eagle-eyed aunt, and by the time they had arrived back at Ravenhurst Verity had been given ample opportunity to decide upon her best course of action: she would get Meg to walk to Houghton with a letter for Mr Stone.

When the ladies began to alight from the two carriages and make their way into the house, Verity dawdled in the rear, and by the time she had entered the hall all the others were heading up the staircase to their respective bedchambers to change for dinner.

She had noticed yesterday during her tour of the house that pens and an ample supply of paper were to be found in the library, but before she had taken more than a step or two towards the comfortable book-lined room its door opened and Brin came strolling out into the hall.

Struck by a sudden thought, Verity stopped dead in her tracks. Brin! She could confide in Brin! If he were suddenly to take it into his head to ride out directly after dinner no one would think it so very strange. After all, men did tend to behave quite inexplicably at times, she decided, taking a step towards him, but then checked again.

She didn't doubt for a moment that he was trustworthy, and she didn't doubt, either, that he would do as she asked, but she knew him well enough to be sure that he would demand an explanation first. And how could she possibly explain things to him without betraying that he had, if only for a short time, been suspected of being a traitor to his country. She recoiled at the mere thought of hurting such a heroic man's feelings. No, she simply couldn't do it!

"Verity, what on earth's the matter, child?" Not only his voice, but his expression too betrayed concern, and she found her fingers suddenly clasped in a pair of strong, shapely hands. "What has occurred to disturb your peace of mind?"

"Why, nothing!" She was suddenly conscious of the warmth of his touch, and was astonished to discover she liked it. "I—er—I need to write a letter, but if you're busy in the library I can come back later."

"And who might you be needing to contact so urgently?" His voice was gently teasing now, but his eyes remained probing, alert. "I'm beginning to suspect you of clandestine meetings. Have you a secret lover skulking nearby?"

"Wh-what?" Verity couldn't prevent those guilty crimson tell-tale stains from mounting her cheeks, but she at least managed to regain a little composure. "Don't be ridiculous, Brin!" She extricated her hands from his. "Who could I possibly know around these parts?"

"That's precisely what I'm endeavouring to find out." Folding his arms across his chest, he regarded her much as he might have done some wilful child. "On the evening I arrived I discovered a letter for you pushed under the door. And lo and behold, when I returned to the house a short while ago, there was another one! Stebbings!" he called across the hall. "Where did you put that letter for Miss Harcourt?"

The butler came forward bearing a silver tray. The instant Verity saw the bold writing on the letter her resentment at Brin's high-handed tone was swept away by a wave of exhilaration. Ignoring the butler's rather pointed sniff of disapproval, and the quizzical rise of a pair of rather well-shaped russet-coloured brows, she picked up the letter and, after lifting her chin slightly, which betrayed quite beautifully her complete indifference to their censorious views, swung round on her heels.

Conscious that her every movement was being scrutinised, Verity forced herself to walk slowly up the staircase, but the instant she was out of sight of those all-too-perceptive tawny-coloured eyes, she almost ran along the passageway and into her bedchamber. She acknowledged Meg's presence with a vague smile before going over to the window and breaking the letter's seal to read, disappointingly, just one rather abrupt command: *Meet me in the rose garden at midnight.*

Easier said than done, she thought, staring out of the window with a troubled frown. From where she stood she could see the entrance to the rose garden which lay just beyond the formal gardens at the back of the house. She felt fairly certain that the rose garden itself wasn't visible from any of the windows... But could she manage to leave the house without being observed?

Of course there was no question of her not making the attempt. And she *must* succeed! she thought determinedly. The Coachman's coming to Ravenhurst had spared her the necessity of trying to contact Mr Stone, but even if that were not the case she would still have moved heaven and hearth to be in the rose garden at the appointed time... How she longed to see him again!

''I'm sorry, Meg. I wasn't attending. What did you

say?'' she enquired, suddenly realising her maid had spoken.

''I wanted to know which dress you wished to wear this evening, miss?''

''Oh, I don't mind. We're dining quite informally. You choose.''

Meg's gentle reminder that it was time to dress for dinner forced Verity back to the present, but her mind refused to remain there for long. She found that throughout dinner it was an effort to concentrate on the general conversation and discovered on more than one occasion, when she had managed to come out of her dreamlike state, that she was being observed rather thoughtfully not only by her aunt, but by the far-from-obtuse Major.

Brin didn't join the ladies in the salon after dinner, but returned to the library to write further letters. At first Verity felt untold relief when she learned that they would be deprived of his company—at least she would have only her eagle-eyed aunt to contend with—but as the evening dragged on she experienced a complete change of heart, and could not help but feel that his presence would at least have provided the leaven to so much dough, as the conversation continued with monotonous regularity to return to the rather boring topics of fashions and household management.

Fortunately the ladies had swiftly accustomed themselves to country hours, and by the time the mantel-clock had chimed eleven most were ready for their beds. Verity, who had been doing her level best to smother yawns of boredom for most of the evening, aroused no suspicions in her aunt's mind when she too said she would retire for the night. They accompanied each other back up the stairs, with Verity offering a rather sleepily spoken ''goodnight'' as they reached her aunt's bedchamber door, but the instant she entered her own room she was suddenly brightly alert.

It was not unusual for her not to summon Meg to put her to bed, and she had made a point earlier of requesting her maid to lay out her night-gear, thereby making it quite clear that she wouldn't be requiring her services again. Lady Billington, on the other hand, always rang for Dodd, and Verity clearly heard someone enter her aunt's bedchamber a few minutes later.

Sarah had put all her guests, with the exception of Brin, whose room was in the west wing, in this part of the house, and for the next half-hour there was a continuous parade of footsteps along the passageway outside Verity's room, accompanied by the opening and closing of doors, but by the time the hands on her bedchamber clock showed ten minutes to midnight the house was as quiet as a tomb.

After throwing a shawl about her shoulders, Verity picked up a candle and padded across the carpet to the door. Only a faint click sounded as she turned the handle, and then she took a tentative glance up and down the passageway. Thankfully it was deserted. Even the candles in the wall sconces had already been extinguished by the servants, which suggested that they too had retired for the night.

But one could not be too careful, she told herself, as she tiptoed along the passageway in the direction of the staircase. If she should be unfortunate enough to come across anyone, guest or servant, then she would merely say that she couldn't sleep and intended selecting a book from the large choice in the library.

Thankfully she was not called upon to give any explanation for her furtive midnight wanderings. The hall itself was deserted, although there was an oil lamp, turned down low, resting on one of the highly polished tables, which clearly indicated that not everyone had retired for the night. Blowing out her candle, Verity placed the holder down by the lamp before tiptoeing across the remaining few feet of hall to the front door and drawing back the substantial black iron bolts which, blessedly kept well-oiled, made only the slightest of grating sounds.

Once outside, caution was forgotten. She sped along the path towards the stable area from where she could gain access to the formal part of the garden. She wasn't at all familiar with this particular area of the grounds, but the moon shining down from a clear starlit sky aided her progress along the criss-crossing gravel paths and she had no difficulty in locating the wicket-gate.

Here, she paused for a moment to regain her breath, and looked about for a sign of the person whom she was longing to see, but she could detect not another living soul. A little further down the path, however, she could see a large shape which looked suspiciously like the outline of a wooden seat, and made her way towards it.

She might at least make herself as comfortable as possible while awaiting the Coachman's arrival. There was no saying how long she would be forced to wait, because he no doubt had needed to travel some distance, but she didn't doubt for a moment that he would come.

Her faith in him was very soon rewarded. No sooner had she seated herself and pulled her shawl more closely about her shoulders, for the night air was surprisingly quite chilly after the warmth of the day, than she detected the crunch of a footstep on gravel, and turned her head to see that unmistakable outline of cloak and tricorn, and the inevitable red glow from the cheroot clutched between long fingers before it was flicked to the ground.

"Hello, lass," he murmured in that richly accented voice which she loved to hear. "I knew tha wouldn't fail me."

Verity rose to her feet, feeling so insignificantly small as she gazed up at the masked face looming above her but, oh, so infinitely safe now that he was here. "There was never any thought in my mind of not meeting you," she assured him softly, and the next moment she was in his arms.

There was nothing gentle in his embrace this time. Fastening her so closely against his tall, hard frame that she was intensely aware of his every powerful muscle, he kissed her hungrily, like some starving man feasting again after days of enforced abstinence. She clung to him, half-frightened, half-exhilarated by the strength of his desire and the ardent need it aroused in her to be held by him, to be touched by him, to be guided by him to wherever their mutual need of each other would ultimately lead.

His erratic breathing informed her clearly enough that he was labouring under immense strain to keep himself under control even before his far-from-steady hands took a hold of her upper arms, holding her firmly at bay when she made to take a step towards him.

"Nay, then, lass. It'll not do," he warned. "Don't be tempting me n' more, otherwise I'll not stop next time, and tha'll find thissen on t'ground wi' thy clothes ripped off and missen kissing every inch o' thee."

It was extremely improper, of course, for him even to suggest such a thing, but she couldn't suppress a thrill of excitement at the prospect all the same. Her rather unmaidenly thoughts were betrayed by glinting flashes of encouragement in her eyes which it took him no time at all to interpret.

"Tha don't know what tha's instigating, looking that way. It's as well that I knows tha's a complete innocent. And that's 'ow tha'll stay until after we're wed." He felt her stiffen slightly, and saw the provocative sparkle fade from her eyes. "What's up, lass? Tha's no doubts, 'ave thee?"

"Not when I'm with you, no," she freely admitted, but was determined he should know the doubts which assailed her when he wasn't there. "But—but I know next to nothing about you. I don't even know your name."

"Tha'll learn it soon enough, never tha fear. And don't be afraid I'll ask thee to live in a hovel, lass, after we're wed. Tha'll be mistress of a fine 'ouse. I've plenty o'brass."

Being thus assured did little to erase those qualms which persisted in tormenting her. "It doesn't surprise me to learn this. I know you're an intelligent and educated man." She sighed. "But I'm also very well aware that you've lied to me."

He pulled her back into his arms then, and pressed her head against his chest. "Tha knows I can't tell thee owt, lass. But when this is all over, then—"

"I understand that, and I wouldn't expect you to confide in me," she interrupted gently. "But there's no reason for you to tell me a deliberate lie." He couldn't mistake the almost resentful note in her voice. "You got me to come to Ravenhurst under false pretences. Both you and my uncle have never suspected Major Carter of being a traitor."

There was a significant pause before he said, "'Ow

else could I'ave persuaded yer t'come'ere. I wanted t'be near thee, lass.''

To be told this was naturally very gratifying, but Verity couldn't help but feel that there was something important he was keeping to himself, something she ought to be aware of herself, but still it continued to elude her.

She thrust frustrations and suspicions aside, however, and wasted no further time in acquainting him with the fact that the French spy had come into the area. Surprisingly he made no response to this intelligence, and she tried to pull away from him, but he kept her head firmly pressed against his chest, as though he feared her eyes had accustomed themselves too well to the darkness and that she would penetrate his disguise.

''I suppose you knew that already,'' she remarked, giving up the struggle against the secure pressure of those muscular arms.

''Nay, I didn't know, but I can't say I'm surprised. I don't doubt that 'e's been followed by another o' thy uncle's people, so there be no need for us to concern ussens.''

''It's Castleford you suspect, isn't it? That's why Mr Stone is so close by.''

''Now, then, lass! Tha mustn't be asking questions. But what I can tell thee is no information 'as bin passed on yet, otherwise t' little Frenchman wouldn't be 'ere. He'd be making for one o' t'ports.''

That was a reasonable assumption. It was also reasonable to assume that she would be seeing nothing more of the Coachman until this business was over, at least…

''I mustn't see you again while I'm here,'' she announced *sotto voce,* suddenly finding it necessary to cling more tightly to that powerful frame.

''Oh? And why not?''

The question was asked evenly enough, but she detected a slightly unnerving hard edge in his voice, certainly resentful and slightly threatening. For all that he had laughed at her, teased and provoked her during their short acquaintanceship, she sensed he would be a dangerous man if crossed. But he was also very perceptive, so it would be foolish to try to lie to him.

"Because that dratted Brin Carter is already suspicious over those letters you've sent here."

"Is 'e now? And 'ere tha's been saying 'e's nubbut a dunderhead."

"Well, he isn't a fool!" Verity announced almost resentfully. "He's extremely astute...except where women are concerned. No, that isn't strictly true, either," she amended. "I believe he's managed to rectify even that defect."

There was a short silence, then, "Oh, aye? Made a fool o'issen once, did 'e?"

"I wouldn't go as far as to say that," she responded, with complete honesty again, "but he wouldn't listen to people when they tried to warn him that a particular lady was not quite as sweetly angelic as he seemed to think. I tried to warn him... And I'll never forget the way he turned on me."

"Is that why tha don't like 'im, lass?" he asked gently, after a further short silence.

"Oh, no. I don't dislike him. In fact there are times when I like him very well." The spontaneous admission came as a surprise even to herself. "I never for one moment believed him capable of being a traitor, but there are times when he does behave in a most perplexing way."

The Coachman buried his lips in her soft black curls. "Mayhap 'e's in love, lass."

"Ha! Not he!" she scoffed. "Why, little Clarissa Gillingham has betrayed a fondness for Claud Castleford's company, but if you ask me Brin doesn't care a whit!"

"Mayhap she ain't t' one 'e's fallen in love wi'."

This gave Verity pause for thought. The Coachman was possibly quite correct, but she couldn't in all honesty say that Brin had shown any marked fondness for either Lady Caroline or Hilary Fenner. In her own mind she felt certain that he preferred Clarissa. Perhaps, though, his experience with Angela Kingsley had left him slightly cynical and he no longer looked for love and would be quite content with mutual respect in marriage.

She opened her mouth, about to echo her thoughts aloud, but the Coachman arrested her by placing a warning finger against her lips. She listened intently for a few moments, but could detect nothing.

"You heard something?" she whispered.

"Aye, lass. Best tha goes back inside now. I'll leave fust. T'sound came from over yonder, where I've left mi 'orse." He gestured to the area of ground behind the stable block. "Iffen there be someone lurking, it's best 'e comes after me. Wait 'ere a few minutes then makes your way back. I'll be seeing you soon, lass." And with that he placed a brief kiss on her lips before darting into the shrubbery.

For a few moments Verity could detect the rustle of leaves as he forged his way between the dense branches, then there was only silence. Once again she pulled her shawl more tightly about her, feeling suddenly cold after the cradling warmth of the Coachman's strong arms.

Would it always be like this? she wondered, feeling utterly bereft, totally dejected. Their brief meetings had come to mean so much to her, and yet this time she was left with such a hollow feeling inside, and with the wretched conviction that it was sheer madness to love a man who continued to remain a total enigma.

Trying desperately to dispel her sudden mood of depression, she listened intently, but could detect not a sound, not even that of distant hoof-beats. The Coachman, though, would not foolishly leave his mount close to the house, where it might be discovered. But enough time had elapsed for him to be a safe distance away, she decided, and began to retrace her steps, thankfully without detecting a single suspicious sound and, more importantly, without coming face to face with anyone else. Then disaster struck: the front door refused to open.

Cursing silently under her breath, Verity took a step away from the beautifully carved piece of oak which so effectively barred her entry. Foolishly it had never occurred to her that the bolts on the door might be noticed by a vigilant servant, who wouldn't hesitate to slide them securely back into place. Why, oh, why, hadn't she taken the precaution of leaving a downstairs window open? She chided herself silently for every kind of a fool before a sudden thought struck her. Maybe one of the downstairs windows had been left open? It was a forlorn hope, perhaps, but worth investigating.

She took several more paces back from the mansion and cast her eyes across the long front wall. There were dozens of windows on the ground floor alone, and she had little choice but to try each one in turn. She was about to begin her task when she detected a faint light coming from one of the library windows. Was it possible that Brin was still working in there? Or maybe it was Sarah, for she hadn't retired with the others.

Moving cautiously towards that certain window, Verity saw a chink in the curtains and, placing her face against the cool glass, peered into the room. The gap between the drapes wasn't large, but she could see several candles still burning in their sconces. So, raising her hand, she scratched lightly on the glass with her fingertips and waited, hopefully, but nothing happened. She tried again, tapping louder this time, and almost squealed in fright as the drapes were suddenly thrown wide and a tall figure appeared on the other side.

Unfortunately it was Brin, not Sarah, but one couldn't have everything one's own way, she supposed as she gestured imperiously for him to open the window.

"What in the world are you doing out there?" he demanded, not making the least attempt to speak softly.

"Why, nothing very much at the moment," was her rather sarcastic response, "but as soon as you move away I can at least climb back inside. And, for heaven's sake, keep your voice down! Do you want to wake the entire house?"

She thought she could detect a suspicion of a twitching smile about his mouth before he placed his hands beneath her arms and hauled her by rather rough and ready means into the room.

"Have you run mad, girl?" It sounded more statement than question, so she didn't feel obliged to answer, and merely watched as he closed the window and redrew the curtains. "What the deuce do you mean by wandering about outside at this time of night?" He looked down at her with all the suspicion of some irate but concerned elder brother. "It has something to do with that confounded letter, I know. Come on, out with it, my girl, otherwise I might feel obliged to inform Lady Billington of your escapade!"

Alarm bells began to sound. It was no empty threat. "Oh, Brin, you wouldn't serve me such a backhanded turn, surely?" she almost pleaded. "No, I cannot believe you'd stoop so low!"

The challenging lift to one russet brow did little to bring any comfort. "Oh, very well," she capitulated, if begrudgingly. "It did have something to do with that letter. I had to meet someone. But you mustn't ask me anything further for the present."

He seemed to debate within himself for several moments, then said, "Very well, but you're not to go out alone at this time of night again, understand?"

Verity kept her lips firmly compressed, forcing back the angry retort. He had no right to dictate to her! But then she was hardly in a position to argue, she reminded herself.

"Very well. I won't." The promise almost choked her, but she forced it out nevertheless.

"As you see. Stebbings very obligingly lit a fire as he knew I'd be working late. I would suggest you sit for a while and get yourself warm."

Placing his hand beneath her arm, Brin guided her to one of the comfortable winged-chairs placed near the hearth. It never entered Verity's head to protest, even though she knew it was grossly improper to be sitting alone at this time of night with a gentleman who wasn't a close relative, but she considered their long association sufficient reason to disregard this edict. Added to which, she was perfectly certain in her own mind that she had nothing to fear from Brin.

The realisation struck her forcibly, drawing a deep line of consternation to furrow her brow as she watched him move across to the decanters and pour out two glasses of wine. Yes, she did trust him; she trusted him implicitly. Perhaps that was why she had never in her heart of hearts thought that he could be a traitor to his country. Why, she felt as safe with Brin as she did…as she did the Coachman… How very odd that was!

Brin noted the rather puzzled expression. "What's causing you to frown so, child?"

"Wh-what?" Verity came out of her perplexing thoughts with a start. "Oh, nothing really." Taking the glass of wine he held out, she settled herself more comfortably in the chair, and couldn't prevent a wry little smile as she watched him take the seat opposite. "Truth to tell, I was just thinking that it would appear most odd, not to say improper, if I were caught sitting alone with you like this."

"Not as improper as being caught wandering about the grounds at this time of night," he countered, and then smiled at the guilty flush that accompanied her decidedly wary look. "Rest easy, child. I've no intention of carrying out an inquisition."

Relaxing visibly, she glanced about the room, her eyes coming to rest on the pile of papers strewn across the desk. "My, my, you have been busy! I hope you don't intend staying up all night, otherwise you'll be in no fit state to entertain the ladies in the morning."

"I'm afraid the ladies will need to amuse themselves. I shall be riding out fairly early and have no idea what time I'll get back." He could clearly read the unspoken question in her eyes. "There are one or two matters requiring my immediate attention. You may not be aware, Verity, but I had an unexpected visitor this afternoon." She watched his lips curl into a rather strange smile. "A certain Mr Jessop of Messrs. Jessop, Jessop and Wilkes, my late uncle's solicitors."

"Late uncle…? Oh, I see!" She raised her glass. "Congratulations, Lord Dartwood."

"I should prefer it if you continue to call me Brin. I

haven't informed anyone else, Verity, and I would be obliged if for the time being you kept the knowledge to yourself."

She was rather surprised by the request, but didn't hesitate to give her word. "But you do realise," she added, "it will not be long before your new status becomes common knowledge."

"I know, but just for a while…"

She watched him closely as he frowned down at the contents of his glass.

He looked so lost, so like a vulnerable child way out of its depth, that she experienced the strong urge to put her arms round him and comfort him, to assure him that no matter what the world at large chose to think of a mill owner's grandson entering the peerage, she at least didn't doubt that he would be a credit to the name he bore.

"You never wanted the title, did you, Brin?" she remarked with uncanny perception.

"I never coveted it, no," he admitted, raising his eyes to hers again. "And, in truth, up until a few months ago I never thought it would be mine. My uncle produced five children, three of whom were boys. The youngest died in infancy. The second son was reputed to be very much like my father—reckless and shiftless. Strangely they both met their fates in the same way—carriage accidents. But that still left the eldest son, Cedric. My uncle must have continued to be fairly confident that the fruits of his own loins would one day take his place. Cedric had married and had produced a child, although a daughter. No one could have foreseen Cedric's unexpected death. He had always enjoyed good health, and it seemed safe to assume, therefore, that he would produce more children. Who would have believed it possible for such a robust individual to succumb to a mere chill on the chest?''

Verity sat quietly turning over in her mind what he had said. She had never heard him ever mention his father before. It was not very surprising really, considering he had died when Brin had been little more than two years old. She had, however, heard enough about Brin's father from servants' gossip and snippets her Uncle Lucius had from time to time let fall to be very certain that she wouldn't have liked him.

Henry Carter had married Arthur Brinley's daughter after a whirlwind romance. Not many weeks after the wedding had taken place, he had left his young bride at his country house and had returned to London and his dissolute life. Brin's mother had died giving birth to him, and his father had not hesitated in placing Brin in his maternal grandfather's care. Whether or not he'd ever taken the trouble to visit his infant son, Verity wasn't certain. All she did know was that Arthur Brinley had thought the world of his grandson, and it was full credit to him that Brin had turned out so well.

''Will you be returning to the capital on Saturday with the rest of us?'' It had been an innocent enough enquiry, voiced mainly to break the silence, so she couldn't quite understand why he should frown at her so heavily. ''I'm sorry. I didn't mean to pry.''

''No, I wasn't thinking that,'' he assured her with a gentle smile. ''I was thinking about something else entirely. I don't envisage staying at Ravenhurst for that much longer, but I don't think I'll return to London just yet.''

He fell silent again. Verity knew he must have a great deal on his mind, and, thinking he might prefer to be left alone, she quickly finished her wine and rose to her feet.

"It's time I was bidding you goodnight, Brin. I should hate for us to be caught like this, especially now. You might suspect me of trying to entrap you into marriage!"

It had been intended as a joke, but there wasn't so much as a ghost of a smile around his mouth as he rose to his feet and escorted her into the hall. Without a word he re-lit her candle, and then walked with her to the foot of the stairs.

"Believe me, Miss Verity Harcourt," he said unexpectedly, his voice a gentle caress, "I can think of worse fates than being married to you." He then confounded her further her by raising her hand and brushing his lips lightly across the soft white skin.

## Chapter Thirteen

Verity awoke the next morning heavy-eyed and not in the least refreshed. She had passed the worst night she could ever remember. Plagued by dreams of Brin, dressed in cloak and tricorn, one moment taking her ruthlessly into his arms, the next, his features blurred, disappearing in a cloud of swirling grey mist with her hopelessly trying to find him, she had woken several times entangled in the bedcovers, beads of perspiration glistening on her forehead.

The idea of turning over and trying to go back to sleep was tempting, but she thought better of it. At least when awake she had some control over what happened to her, over what she said and did; in her dreams it seemed she had none at all!

Throwing the bedcovers aside, she padded across the carpet to the bell-pull, and within a relatively short space of time was making her way down to the breakfast parlour where she was surprised to discover all the other ladies present.

"Brin's already broken his fast and has gone out somewhere," Hilary informed her in disgruntled tones after polite "good mornings" had been exchanged.

"Yes, he said he would be riding out early," Verity responded without thinking, and received several surprised glances as she took her seat at the table, but it was the ever-vocal Hilary who voiced their curiosity.

"When did he inform you about that?"

Verity discovered she was the focal point of many pairs of interested eyes, but was in no danger of losing her composure as she reached for the coffee-pot. "I couldn't sleep last night, so came down to the library to select a book. I forgot Brin was in there. He told me then. And before you ask, Hilary," she went on, a slight edge to her voice now, "he didn't inform me where he was going, and I wasn't rude enough to enquire."

It was most unlike Verity to be tetchy in the mornings, and Lady Billington looked at her closely, noting the lacklustre eyes and the rather rigid set to those sweetly formed lips. Something, or someone, had put her niece very much out of humour.

She knew her niece well enough to be certain that it wouldn't take very much to rouse that occasionally ungovernable temper, and decided to intervene before Hilary was foolish enough to say anything further and find herself once again on the receiving end of a rather sharp response.

"Some of us have decided to return to that perfectly wonderful little milliner's we visited yesterday, dear," she remarked, sliding the plate of buttered rolls in her niece's direction. "I've made up my mind to have that delightful creation with the purple feathers."

Little did she realise, but she could not have suggested an outing that could have appealed to her niece less. Not only was Verity in no mood to spend the least amount of time in the claustrophobic atmosphere of that little shop with women who had only frills and furbelows on their minds, but she had no intention of returning to that market town where she might run the risk of coming face to face with that French spy. She experienced no qualms, therefore, in politely but quite forcefully declining.

"Perhaps you would care to come riding with Hilary and myself? We have decided not to go. It looks as though it will be another warm day. It will be much pleasanter exploring the countryside on horseback."

Clarissa's very kind invitation drew a smile from Verity, but even the prospect of a gallop across the park failed to tempt her. "It's kind of you, but I think I would prefer to stay indoors this morning. For some reason I didn't have a very good night's sleep. A little time by myself will be sufficient to set me to rights, I'm sure."

"It always does the trick for me," Sarah hurriedly put in when Lady Billington looked as though she was about to query further into her niece's unusual lethargy.

Lady Billington's fondness for her niece was evident, and her concern over her well-being very understandable, Sarah decided, but there were times when people just needed to be left alone. Verity didn't strike her as a young woman prone to fits of the megrims, but something had certainly put her in a very subdued frame of mind. It might, of course, be simply just the explanation offered—lack of sleep—but Sarah couldn't help wondering whether Verity's unusually quiet mood might not have something to do with Brin. She had spoken to him briefly before he had gone out earlier, and he too had seemed in a strangely preoccupied state of mind, not annoyed, precisely, but certainly in a world of his own.

She was not a prying person by nature, however, and thought that Verity would be far better if she were left to her own devices for a while, so she gave a gentle reminder to her other guests that they had best not tarry if they wished to return in time for luncheon.

Sarah, too, had planned to go out that morning to visit the sick wife of one of her husband's tenants, and so did not linger over breakfast herself. She was crossing the hall towards the front door a short while later when she chanced to see Verity again, coming out of the library with a book in her hand.

"The others have gone, have they?" she enquired, casting her a warm smile and receiving one in response. "I cannot say I blame you not wishing to return to that milliner's, Verity. It was quite stifling in there yesterday, and I fear that today is likely to be even warmer."

Verity's smile turned a trifle rueful. "I'm afraid I shall always be a slight disappointment to my aunt. I simply cannot summon up much enthusiasm for such trifling things as bonnets and find it immensely tedious shopping for such commodities."

"Oh, you do remind me of me sometimes!" Sarah exclaimed with a chuckle. "I couldn't agree more. We'll talk again when I get back, if you like. I shouldn't be too long."

…if you like, Verity echoed silently as she watched her kindly hostess leave the house. Oh dear, had she made it so obvious at the breakfast table that she wanted to be on her own? Sarah was such a lovely person, too!

Experiencing more than just a twinge of guilt, Verity wandered into the sunny back parlour, where Sarah frequently retreated for half an hour's peace and quiet. Seating herself by the window, which looked out on to the formal area of garden, Verity could only wonder at the change which had come over her during the past twelve hours. When she had hurried along those crisscross gravel paths the night before she had been so excited, so happy at the prospect of snatching a few precious moments with the Coachman again, and yet now she was experiencing such a lowliness of spirits, such a feeling of utter dissatisfaction.

The Coachman's rather abrupt departure went some way in explaining this change in her. But that wasn't the only reason she had succumbed to this rather disconsolate mood, where doubts and uncertainties now whirled round and round in her head making her question the wisdom of her own heart. No, of course it was not! It was the legacy of those rather perplexing dreams.

Why had Brin taken on the guise of the Coachman? Why had she responded so eagerly, with such utter abandon to his kisses? She was very fond of him, yes, even though he too could be quite infuriating at times, just like the Coachman. And last night when he had confided in her, looking so lost now that he had come into the title, she had experienced such a strong desire to protect him from life's knocks.

He had been very much on her mind when she had climbed into bed last night, so it was quite understandable why she had carried those thoughts of him into her dreams…

But why such intimate thoughts? That was what was so disturbing.

Brin arrived back at Ravenhurst shortly before noon. On learning that both Sarah and Verity were in the house, he wasted no time in changing his clothes and going down to the sunny back parlour where he had been assured the ladies were to be found.

He succeeded quite beautifully in concealing his disappointment when he discovered only Sarah present, and they chatted for a while about things in general. Then

Sarah unexpectedly remarked, "Are you aware that Verity spent a deal of time with your grandfather when you were in the army?"

"Did she tell you that?"

"Not exactly, no. But she did let fall that it was she who wrote those letters on his behalf when you were convalescing here."

He betrayed no surprise, and a rather tender smile curled the corners of his mouth. "Yes, I do realise that now. I knew she was very fond of him—admired him, I think. But it wasn't until I made that recent visit to Yorkshire, and spent an evening with my business partner, Jonas Penn, that I learned that it was Verity, and not Angela, who had spent so much time with the old man."

A flash of blue outside the window caught their attention, and they both watched as Verity entered the formal garden. Sarah followed her progress along the gravel path, a rather secretive smile curling her lips for a few brief moments before she gave a sudden and almost violent start.

"Oh, great heavens! Marcus has returned!" she exclaimed in anguished tones, praying that her sometimes very abrupt husband didn't say anything cutting to the stranger inspecting his grounds.

She thought she could detect that famous scowl, even from that distance, and groaned inwardly, holding her breath as Verity and Marcus approached each other. She saw him hold out his hand, taking slender white fingers into his own, and was amazed when he suddenly threw back his head and roared with laughter. She might have known she would have nothing to fear: Verity's outspokenness would appeal to his rather dry sense of humour.

"Oh, the little minx has captivated him!" Her mock

outrage hid quite beautifully her intense relief. "Look at the rogue flirting with her! Go out at once, Brin, before he becomes totally bewitched!"

He looked down at her with a mocking gleam in his eyes. "Oh, yes, and you so worried, I'm sure. But I shall go nevertheless. I want to have a talk with her as it happens."

Sarah remained by the window, not out of any desire to keep an eye on her husband, but out of sheer curiosity. She watched him take a smiling leave of Verity, and within the space of a few minutes he was entering the room and she was being held in a loving embrace.

"I shouldn't be kissing you at all, you flirt!" she admonished when she was able. "I saw you outside with Miss Harcourt."

"What an enchanting little witch she is! I mentioned I was acquainted with her uncle, the Duke of Richleigh, and she said she hoped that I wouldn't hold that against her." He found himself laughing again. "I must say I've always considered him a complete nincompoop, but of course I wouldn't have dreamt of saying so."

"No? Now you do surprise me!" Sarah responded wryly, before looking out of the window again. She caught sight of Brin entering the garden, and her secretive little smile returned. "Do you know, Marcus, I did Brin an injustice. I believed his wishing to invite certain ladies here was all a hum. But I have come to the conclusion that I was wrong… Yes, most definitely wrong."

"Oh?" His dark brows rose as he too surveyed the scene. "Well, my love, there's no denying that she's an enchanting little minx. Added to which, I have the utmost respect for your judgement."

She released her breath in an almost wistful little sigh. "I'm not as a rule a prying person, Marcus, as you know, but I wouldn't mind overhearing that little conversation taking place out there right now."

Sarah would have been quite disappointed, for the initial exchanges had been about nothing more titillating than the very attractive lay-out of the formal garden, before Brin with quite remarkable dexterity steered Verity towards the wicket-gate.

She was in the rose garden before she realised it, and was quite disappointed to discover that it was nothing like the romantic setting she had imagined the night before, for not one of the bushes was yet in bloom.

"Why have we come in here?"

"Because we were being observed from the parlour window," he enlightened her with a twitching smile, while urging her with ruthless efficiency towards that certain bench, "and I should prefer not to be observed."

This admission brought a wickedly teasing gleam to her lovely eyes. "Oh? I hope I'm in no danger of losing my virtue?"

"Not at the moment, no. But many more of those provocative looks of yours and I shan't be answerable for the consequences," he warned lightly, but she wasn't so very certain that he was joking.

She sat down beside him on the bench, and after a few moments when he didn't offer to speak she asked, not out of any particular interest, more of a means to break the silence, if he had been successful in his errands that morning.

"That remains to be seen," he answered rather guardedly, and then went on to divulge that he had decided to sell his grandfather's house in Yorkshire. "It wasn't an easy decision to make, Verity, but the right one, I'm sure, as I shall no doubt be making my home in Devonshire in the not too distant future."

Verity experienced a sudden spasm of pain in the region of her chest. She had seen nothing of Brin for several years, but now they had become acquainted again, and had—yes—become far closer than they had before he had joined the army. She dreaded the mere thought that he would not be close by when she eventually returned home.

"I suppose you're right." Her voice sounded strangely hollow even to her own ears and she wasn't in the least surprised at the questioning glance he cast her. "No, truly. I'm certain it was the right decision." She forced a smile, but it was an effort. "And, of course, you will need to concentrate on your new role in life."

"Ah, yes...the viscountcy. That in itself poses many problems."

"Oh, Brin! Surely you cannot be worried that you won't match up to people's expectations?" she said bracingly. "You'll have plenty of good people about you, only too willing to offer sound advice... Marcus Ravenhurst for one. And I shall always stand your friend."

The look he cast her was hard to interpret. "Will you, Verity?"

"You know I will."

"That's reassuring to hear. Because I'm going to need a friend to keep me safe from all those matchmaking mamas."

She couldn't prevent a rather wicked chuckle escaping at this. His past weeks in London had been far from easy, but when news of his uncle's demise became common knowledge his life would be plagued even further by ambitious mothers wishing to bring their daughters to his notice. "Well, I don't see how I can possibly help you out with that particular problem."

There was a moment's silence, then, "Oh, yes, you can…simply by becoming my affianced bride."

For several seconds Verity could only gape at him, feeling certain she couldn't possibly have heard him correctly. "You cannot possibly be serious!" she squealed, finding a semblance of her voice at last.

"I am, my dear," he responded with devastating calm. "Deadly serious. I need time to come to terms with this new role of mine. And you are the only person who can buy me that time. The engagement would not be of long duration, of course. And you could break it off whenever you wished."

He reached for her hand, and for some inexplicable reason she experienced no desire to draw it out of his clasp. "I never knew my mother, and, although I far from dislike your sex, there have been very few females I have learned to trust. Sarah, of course, I trust implicitly. And you, my dear girl, I would trust with my life."

Once again Verity found that her voice was reluctant to make itself heard, and she was forced to clear her throat rather noisily before she could force any words out.

"That, of course, is a rather wonderful compliment. But—but I still think you're resorting to rather drastic measures. A fictitious engagement is not the answer, and I think a little time for calm reflection will bring you to the same conclusion."

His sudden shout of laughter took her completely by surprise. "My darling girl, I haven't thought the solution up on the spur of the moment. I have been planning it for weeks, almost from the moment I set eyes on you again."

"What?" This was beyond anything. "Do you mean to tell me that the vast amount of attention you paid me in London was done for the sole purpose of hoodwinking Society into believing that you had a *tendre* for me?''

"Er—not exactly, no,'' he responded cautiously. "But one must try to make provisions for every eventuality. And you must admit that a few lines in the newspapers announcing our betrothal would look most odd if I hadn't paid you any attention at all. Besides which, I enjoyed being with you—still do for that matter,'' he added ingenuously. "It is no hardship being in your company, believe me.''

"Oh, isn't it? You unprincipled wretch!'' Verity snatched her hand away, as though to leave it resting in his any longer would run the risk of contamination. "And what about those poor girls you induced to come here, giving them false hopes?''

"Heaven spare me!'' he exclaimed in combined amusement and exasperation. "You don't imagine surely that either the screech owl or the zombie stands in the least danger of suffering a bruised heart? The only one I might have suffered pangs of conscience over was Clarissa Gillingham, but after watching her making sheep's eyes at Castleford yesterday, that isn't very likely.''

"She didn't make sheep's eyes at him at all,'' Verity argued unsteadily, trying desperately hard not to laugh at his rather unflattering descriptions of Hilary and Lady Caroline. "They merely have a deal in common.''

"Be that as it may. How could I have invited you here on your own? You would only have become suspicious and wouldn't have come.''

Verity regarded him searchingly for a moment. "Do you know, Brinley Carter, there's a great deal more to you than meets the eye. You're a devious, conniving rogue.''

He betrayed no visible signs of having taken offence at this unflattering description of his character. "You'll do it, then? We can announce our engagement at the party tomorrow evening."

"I haven't agreed to anything! And you can stop looking at me like that," she ordered when he appeared crestfallen, "because it doesn't fool me for a moment!"

She turned her head away to stare sightlessly at the rose bush directly in front of her. Now that she was over the initial shock his suggestion seemed less outrageously foolish. He hadn't been the only one to suffer from unwelcomed attentions, and she felt fairly certain that when she returned to London, Lady Billington's house would once again be plagued by an endless stream of foolish young men thinking themselves in love.

She found herself, surprisingly, seriously considering his scandalous suggestion. "We cannot possibly suddenly announce that we have become betrothed," she said, turning to look at him again. "If you want to fool people, you must do things properly. First of all, you'll need to contact my Uncle Lucius and ask his permission."

"I've already done that," he announced, completely taking the wind out of her sails. "Took that precaution when I visited Yorkshire a while back. He had no objections. In fact," he went on, ignoring her astounded look, "he seemed more than happy at the prospect."

"I don't believe I'm hearing this." She shook her head in disbelief. "Well, you might be able to fool Uncle Lucius, but Aunt Clara's a totally different proposition. She'll see through the sham instantly."

"I think you'll find you're mistaken." The wickedly glinting sparkle faded from his eyes and he looked at her intently. "Will you do it, Verity, for...friendship's sake? Will you become betrothed to me?"

Common sense told her it was madness even to consider doing such a thing, and every fibre of her being recoiled against such duplicity, but she found herself saying, "Very well. But only until the end of the Season."

"Believe me, my darling, that will be sufficient," he murmured, his voice as gentle as the lips he placed to the corner of her mouth.

Such a fleeting contact, no more than a brief token of affection a brother might bestow upon his sister, and yet sufficient to bring other and more passionate contacts vividly to mind, sending Verity's pulse rate soaring in alarm.

Dear Lord! What on earth would the Coachman make of all this when she told him...? As tell him she must.

## Chapter Fourteen

"Ah! There you are, Verity, my dear." Lady Billington came out of the small parlour in time to see Stebbings admitting her niece to the house. "Been out with Major Carter again in his curricle, have you?"

As she had already informed her aunt precisely where she had intended going that afternoon before she had left the house, and with whom, Verity considered the question superfluous and a response completely unnecessary, and merely smiled in a vague sort of way as she accompanied her aunt up the staircase.

"I imagine you'll want to rest before changing for the party tonight. All the other ladies have retired to their rooms. I must say, dear, I'm really looking forward to it."

You might be, Verity thought, thoroughly disgruntled with life, but I most certainly am not!

She kept her gaze firmly fixed on the hem of her skirt, wondering for perhaps the hundredth time what madness had possessed her to agree to Brin's outrageous scheme. She had been secretly "betrothed" for twenty-four hours, and hadn't enjoyed a single moment's peace of mind since foolishly acquiescing to the fiasco.

She felt as if she were being torn apart: half of her understood completely his motives and remained steadfastly determined to do all she could to help him as a friend, while the other half recoiled at the mere thought of acting out this farce which was tantamount to cozening people of whom she was genuinely fond.

She had been unable to bring herself to say anything at all to her aunt; but, as Brin had so brutally pointed out during their recent drive round the park, he had every intention of announcing their engagement at the party tonight and considered that she was being grossly unfair not to inform Lady Billington beforehand.

Unfair… The word left a rather bitter taste in her mouth. What could be more unfair or more despicable than repaying someone's kindness and loving attention over the years by coming to her with a mouthful of lies?

They had reached Lady Billington's bedchamber door and, as her niece appeared to be in a very pensive frame of mind, she made to enter, but Verity forestalled her by placing a restraining hand on her arm. "Aunt Clara, would you mind if we talked for a while? I promise I shan't stay long. You'll have plenty of time to rest before changing for the party."

Nothing could have pleased Lady Billington more. "Of course I don't mind, my dear. I've seen very little of you during the past two days. It will be pleasant to have a comfortable little coze." The rather satisfied glint in her eyes went completely unnoticed as she led the way into the room. "You seem to have spent a deal of time in Major Carter's company."

"Well, yes. And that is precisely what I want to talk to you about." The opening had been there and Verity was determined to make use of it before she'd a chance to change her mind. "Major Carter and I have—

have…'' She paused to take a deep, steadying breath while her eyes remained firmly glued to the pretty pearl brooch adorning the neckline of her aunt's gown.

''Major Carter has done me the honour of asking for my hand in marriage and I have accepted.''

There, it was out! She'd done it! The confession, strangely, brought a deep feeling of relief, but the satisfaction was short-lived. Verity raised her eyes and was appalled to see tears moistening her aunt's lashes before rolling silently down satiny pink cheeks.

''No, no, don't cry!'' She was at her aunt's side in an instant and held as much of that plump frame as she could fit into her slender arms. ''It'll be all right. I promise it will be all right!''

''Oh, my dear, I know it will. It's what I've been desperately hoping for, praying for these past weeks.''

''Wh-what?'' Verity sprang back as though she had been doused in scalding water.

''He's the very one for you, dear. I've known it from the moment I first set eyes on him at the Morlands' party.'' Delving into the pocket of her gown, Lady Billington drew out a wisp of silk and dabbed at her eyes. ''And these past days, seeing the two of you together… And last night when he hardly left your side… Oh, you've made me so very happy!''

Tears of joy, not sorrow! Verity could hardly believe it. Fearing her legs would no longer support her, she took the precaution of slumping down on the spindle-legged chair conveniently situated a little behind her. She was well and truly caught in a vicious trap. And, what made things so much worse, it was a trap of her own making. When the engagement was broken in a few weeks' time, dear Aunt Clara would be heartbroken. She simply couldn't win! If her present predicament hadn't promised to lead to rather sad repercussions she would have laughed at the absurdity of it all.

"And, my dear, he's so very much in love with you. Anyone can see that."

It was as much as Verity could do to stop herself from gaping. Things were getting progressively worse with each passing minute. "I suppose we have grown quite fond of each other." It sounded such a foolish thing to say, but she could think of nothing else. And at least it wasn't a lie!

"Fond?" Lady Billington's tinkling laughter seemed to hang tauntingly in the air. "You have kept me on tenterhooks for weeks, you wicked girl! And I must say you hid your true feelings very well. But last night I knew. When Brin joined us in the salon after dinner and went straight across to sit beside you on the sofa… Well, one would have needed to be blind not to see instantly that you were hopelessly in love with each other."

This couldn't be happening. It was like some fiendish bad dream. Feeling more than just a little dazed by it all, Verity rose very gingerly from the chair and moved slowly to the door, knowing that if she were forced to endure many more of her aunt's rather astounding utterances she would end by confessing the truth. "I'll leave you to rest now, Aunt Clara."

"There's no need, child. I'm not in the least need of a lie-down."

"But I am!" Verity responded with feeling. "We'll talk again later," she added, and whisked herself into her own bedchamber with unseemly haste, thereby denying her aunt the opportunity to utter anything further to confound her.

Untying the ribbons of her bonnet with fingers that were far from steady, Verity tossed the confection on the bed and then slumped down beside it, unable to believe the woman whom she had always believed possessed quite remarkable powers of penetration could have mouthed such absurdities. It was bad enough that Lady Billington was overjoyed at the betrothal without compounding such folly by suggesting that anyone could see that they were very much in love... Why, it was preposterous! What on earth had they ever said or done to give rise to such a ridiculous assumption?

Leaning back against the mound of pillows, Verity stretched out on the bed and frowned up at the pretty powder-blue silken canopy above her head as her mind went over the events of the previous evening.

They had dined early, as usual, and afterwards Brin and Marcus had enjoyed a game or two of billiards before rejoining the ladies in the salon. It was quite true that Brin had come straight over and sat himself down beside her on the sofa. But what had been so unusual about that? Except for that first evening at Ravenhurst, when she had deliberately avoided his company, and the night he had incarcerated himself away in the library, he had always made a point of seeking her out. Her eyes narrowed as the truth of this hit her rather forcibly. Yes, he had, hadn't he?

Absently gnawing at her bottom lip, she pondered over this rather undeniable fact, and after a minute or two had to own that perhaps there was some justification for her aunt's rather surprising assumption. Until Brin had admitted to it himself, it had never occurred to her that the cunning wretch had been singling her out for particular attention. Now, when he announced the betrothal this evening, no one would be in the least surprised. Oh, yes, he had been immensely clever; he had paved his way with such artful dexterity that even she had been blissfully unaware that she had been nothing more than a skilfully manoeuvred pawn in his rather amoral stratagem to keep himself safe from the tedious attentions of matchmaking mamas.

Well, and who could blame him for that? she mused, smiling in spite of the fact that she had been remarkably obtuse not to have realised long since. But then, in her own defence, she would have to own that she hadn't noticed any obvious changes in his attitude towards her.

Right from that very first curricle ride in Hyde Park they had, apart from the odd slight skirmish, been on very friendly terms. Why, anyone with a ha'p'orth of sense could see they behaved more like brother and sister: sometimes quarrelling, but for the most part companionably close. Added to which, he had never looked at her with that doe-eyed, rather sickening look of devotion most young gentlemen adopted when they had become captivated by a certain young damsel. And she sincerely hoped that she had never looked at him like some besotted, simpering ninnyhammer! So why was her aunt so convinced they were in love?

Oh, it was all too ridiculous for words! she decided, swiftly abandoning any further attempt to unearth the possible reason for the ludicrous supposition and, swinging her feet to the floor, went across to the bell-pull.

Meg took no time at all in arriving in answer to the summons and Verity, placing herself with complete faith in the hands of her young and remarkably skilful abigail, concentrated on getting ready for the party that evening.

After bathing and washing her hair, which took a considerable amount of time to dry as it was quite long, she donned the white dress which she had worn on the occasion of the Gillingham ball. Meg took her time in creating a more elaborate hairstyle for the evening, and had just positioned a spray of artificial white flowers amongst the riot of dusky locks when there was a knock on the door.

Believing it to be her aunt, Verity didn't hesitate to grant admittance. She clearly heard her young maid's sharp intake of breath and, turning her head, very nearly gasped herself.

She had never before seen Brin in the uniform of his regiment, the 95th Rifles. He was an impressive figure no matter what he wore, but in the full dress rifleman-green uniform, with its dolman and pelisse braided in black and with the plain crimson sash about his waist, he looked nothing short of magnificent.

A hard lump suddenly lodged itself in her throat as she nodded dismissal to her maid, and in those moments when she watched Brin close the door behind Meg and move slowly towards her she experienced the most searing pains of bitter regrets.

Having still been smarting over the peal he had rung over her head all those years ago, she had been too stupidly proud, too selfishly spoilt, to attend his farewell party before he had left Yorkshire for Portugal that very first time. He might so easily have lost his life, adding to those many thousands of British casualties—had come perilously close to doing just that at Badajoz.

Yet she had never once taken the trouble to pen him a few lines during those years he had spent fighting for his country, and had always managed to avoid coming face to face with him on those rare occasions when he had returned to Yorkshire on leave. Even after his long period of convalescence here at Ravenhurst, when he had returned home, sadly to see his grandfather for the last time, she had arranged to be away in Kent visiting her aunt, and had thereby neatly avoided having to meet him.

How incredibly petty-minded she had been! What a despicable attitude to adopt towards this brave man who had, after all, told her no more than the truth: she had been a selfish, spoilt creature whose real motive for speaking to him about his childhood sweetheart, if the truth be known, had not been motivated by any desire to spare him pain in the future, but had stemmed from her own petty jealousy.

Brin was not slow to notice tears, barely held in check, moistening her eyes, and took an urgent step towards her. "What's wrong, Verity?" Placing his hands gently beneath her elbows, he drew her up from the stool and looked down at her searchingly. "Are you having second thoughts…? Regrets?"

"Regrets, certainly," she admitted, "but not about the engagement."

"Are you sure?"

"Well, perhaps one or two," she admitted softly. "But I have no intention of rescinding on the arrangement."

His rather wonderful smile of gratitude caused the muscles in her abdomen to knot quite painfully. "That's good, because I've informed Marcus and Sarah. They're overjoyed with the news."

If this was said in the hope of making her feel any easier it fell far short of the mark. "They're not the only ones. My aunt was quite ecstatic when I informed her earlier." She had managed to control the threat of tears, but failed quite miserably in trying to prevent the grave misgivings she was experiencing from being clearly mirrored in her eyes. "I don't enjoy lying to people, Brin. You do realise, I hope, that there are going to be some searching questions asked when we break off our engagement?''

''We'll cross that bridge when we come to it,'' he responded in a tone which could best be described as indifferent. ''But in the meantime,'' he went on, delving into one of his pockets, ''I hope you will accept this as a token of my...of my very sincere regard for you, Verity Harcourt.'' And before she realised what was happening he had slid the sapphire and diamond ring down the third finger of her left hand.

Taken completely by surprise, she could only stare, awed, at the brightly sparkling stones. Never had she seen anything quite so beautiful, or so much to her taste. Just when he had acquired it and just how he had managed to purchase one that fitted so perfectly she could only wonder at. Suddenly the betrothal seemed so real, and for a few moments she was astounded to discover herself wishing with all her heart that it were true, but then common sense prevailed.

''It's beautiful.'' The words seemed to graze painfully against the sides of her throat, but she forced them out, none the less. ''I promise I shall take every care of it, Brin, and return it to you when—''

''No,'' he interrupted gently. ''As long as I breathe no other woman shall wear that ring. It's yours, and yours alone. No matter the outcome.'' And before she could enquire what he meant, he had placed his hands on her sides and his head lowered.

Verity was too stunned by her traitorous body's immediate response to put up even a token resistance. Those shapely hands, by accident or design, were gently pressing against the sides of her breasts, sending wave upon wave of such sensual pleasure to ripple throught her that when his lips merely brushed across hers in a repeat of the salute he had bestowed in the garden the day before, she found herself suffering pangs of disappointment.

"Well, that seems to have put some colour back into your cheeks," he remarked, betraying more than just a little satisfaction, and Verity discovered she was powerless to prevent the telltale guilty blush from deepening; as powerless as she was to untangle those wildly conflicting emotions which seemed to have entwined round her brain, successfully preventing any coherent thought save one—she desperately wanted him to kiss her again.

Evidently, though, he felt no similar yearning, for he moved away to collect her fringed silk shawl and placed it about her shoulders. "Sarah suggested that you might like to remain here with me after the others have left tomorrow. It's entirely up to you, of course, and I shan't press you."

Verity discovered herself incapable of making even this simple decision and turned towards him seeking guidance, just as though it were the most natural thing in the world for her to do so. He seemed to understand without being told that she was unsure of what to do, so made up her mind for her.

"I think it would be best if you remain. You'll only be plagued to death by the curiously vulgar element in Society if you go back with your aunt. I shall arrange for a few lines to appear in the Morning Post, so that by the time we return all the tattle-mongers will have been apprised of our betrothal and might just leave us in peace." He had no difficulty in detecting doubts and uncertainties, not to mention bewilderment, flit over her face. "And a few days' peace and quiet is precisely what you're urgently in need of."

There was no arguing with this, and when Brin, taking

her completely by surprise for a second time, announced their engagement as soon as they entered the drawing-room where everyone had congregated before dinner, she felt that weeks, not days, of peace and quiet would be needed to restore her to a semblance of her former self-possessed state.

Only by dint of tapping into that hitherto untouched inner reserve of iron determination did she manage to appear outwardly composed, and she could only marvel at Brin's quite remarkable sang-froid, accepting all the heartfelt congratulations with such an air of spontaneous gratification that Verity had forcibly to remind herself on more than one occasion that their betrothal was pure fabrication.

Had she not been standing right beside him, listening to his every word, watching his every gesture, she would never have believed it possible for someone to sound so utterly convincing. He really was quite superb. A born actor, in fact!

He responded to the various questions one or two of the more inquisitive ladies threw at him without so much as a pause for consideration, but when, during dinner, Lady Westbury enquired when the wedding would be taking place, and he blithely responded that he wasn't in favour of long engagements, and that it would be within weeks rather than months, Verity came perilously close to choking on a piece of game pie and was determined to check him at the first available opportunity before he carried things too far.

"What the deuce do you mean by telling people the ceremony will take place soon?" she demanded in an undertone when, directly after dinner, they all made their way across the hall to the large salon where the party was to be held. "You're digging a very big hole for yourself,'' she continued, nettled by his continued self-assured air. ''And don't expect me to aid you if you find yourself unable to get out!''

''You'll hardly be in a position to, my darling girl,'' he pointed out, his composure completely unruffled, ''as you'll be trapped in there with me. Now, stop glowering at me like an infuriated kitten and go over and talk to your aunt, there's a good girl. She's trying desperately to attract your attention. I'll come back to you in plenty of time for the first waltz.'' And with that he added insult to injury by giving the back of her arm a nip with his fingertips.

If he could feel her eyes boring into his back like dagger-points he betrayed no visible sign as he moved away to speak to the first of the Ravenhursts' neighbours to arrive, and Verity, looking far from a blissfully happy bride-to-be, went over to her aunt, who was chatting away to Mrs Fenner and her daughter.

''Why, you look as if you've had a lovers' tiff!'' Hilary screeched, with such a look of malicious satisfaction that Verity could have hit her.

''I wouldn't go as far as to say that,'' she responded with careful restraint. ''But I have never been one to turn a deaf ear when someone is deliberately going out of his, or her, way to irritate me, as you very well know, Hilary.''

Although not the most tactful of people, Hilary was far from slow-witted and sensibly refrained from saying anything further to annoy her rather quick-tempered neighbour before moving away with her mother to mingle with the other guests.

''Sarah tells me you're remaining here at Ravenhurst, dear,'' Lady Billington remarked, quickly guiding Verity towards two unoccupied seats where they could sit quietly for a while in private. ''I've no objection, of course, if that's what you want.''

''Oh, I'm sorry, Aunt Clara. I meant to tell you before we went in to dinner, but it completely slipped my mind. I haven't had the opportunity to discuss it with Sarah as yet, either. It was Brin's idea. He sort of made the decision for me.''

This was music to Lady Billington's ears. She had always had complete faith in the Major's ability to bridle a headstrong filly, and he had evidently already made a start, though she wisely chose not to voice her satisfying reflections aloud, and merely said, ''I didn't realise you intended announcing your betrothal so early in the evening. It took me quite by surprise.''

''You're not the only one,'' came the rather disgruntled response, and she looked at her niece closely.

''I didn't realise, either, that you were only contemplating a short engagement?''

''Oh, it will be short, right enough,'' Verity confirmed, her teeth set rigid in hard determination. A lot shorter than he thinks if he carries on as he has been doing! she added silently.

The quartet of musicians hired for the evening struck up and the object of Verity's far from flattering thoughts came across to claim her for the first dance. The party which had been originally planned merely as an informal social gathering had now changed to one celebrating their ''betrothal'', and for a short while they had the floor to themselves, the cynosure of all eyes, but then much to Verity's intense relief other couples began to join them.

She began to relax slightly, but still felt very conspicuous, and remained quite out of charity with the man who, she was very well aware without being told, had already taken it upon himself to organise her life.

"If you don't take that mulish look off your face, my girl, I'll kiss you right here in the middle of this dance-floor."

It was no idle threat, but Verity refused to be cowed. "You dare," she hissed like a spitting kitten, "and I'll retaliate by boxing your ears soundly. And then folk will begin to realise this engagement is not quite what it appears to be!"

His response was to throw his head back and roar with laughter which, of course, was not quite the effect she'd had in mind. Several indulgent smiles were cast in their direction, and she found to her surprise that she couldn't help smiling herself. It was a complete waste of effort trying to be angry with him for any length of time. He really was a hopeless case! He never behaved as she expected and, what was worse, seemed to possess an innate ability to make her furiously angry one minute and blissfully contented the next.

Her smile widened as she gazed up at his handsome face with its crowning mane of reddish brown hair which swept back in gentle waves from a high, intelligent forehead. She studied each attractive feature in turn and found herself loving the way his eyes crinkled at the corners whenever he smiled, just as they were doing now.

"You are a darling, you know," he said unexpectedly, and so impersonally that he might have been remarking on nothing more interesting than the weather, but the compliment lost nothing for all that. "It's a wonder you weren't snapped up years ago."

"I've more sense, that's why. It's quite an art avoiding parson's mousetrap. But you know that yourself, as you've succeeded in doing so thus far. And, of course,'' she went on after he had executed a rather neat turn in order to miss a collision with Hilary and her rather energetic young partner, ''that is in essence the reason we find ourselves indulging in this mindless folly.''

Instinctively her eyes moved towards the door, where the Ravenhursts stood greeting new arrivals. ''Surely you've at least told Marcus and Sarah the truth?''

There was a significant pause before he said, ''Naturally,'' and she looked at him sharply, unsure whether to believe him or not.

''And do they also know about your coming into the title?''

''Yes. I've informed them about that too. Like yourself, they are completely trustworthy. You can safely tell either of them anything and be certain it will go no further. I hope that during your stay here you'll become better acquainted with Marcus. He can be an abrupt devil at times, but you're too discerning to be put off by an astringent remark or two. Once you get to know him I'm certain you'll like him. He's one of the finest men—''

Verity noticed his eyes narrow fractionally and turned her head in the direction of his rather penetrating gaze to see Lord Castleford, accompanied by his son and nephew, enter the room. Why should their arrival cause Brin to lose track of what he had been saying and bring a rather thoughtful expression to his face? She looked back at him, only to discover him smiling down at her once again.

''Clarissa will no doubt be pleased now that Claud has arrived.''

''And does that concern you?''

''Good heavens, no! Why on earth should it?''

It shouldn't, Verity thought as the dance came to an

end and they began walking back towards Lady Billington. But something had certainly brought that flicker of thoughtful concern into his eyes, and if it wasn't Claud's arrival…then whose arrival had engendered that wary look?

It just so happened that her aunt was conversing with Lady Gillingham and her daughter, and Brin exchanged a brief word with each of the three ladies before moving away to ask Lady Caroline to dance. If Clarissa felt a little aggrieved at being passed over in preference to the earl's daughter she certainly betrayed no visible signs of it as she gazed fleetingly at the Castleford family, who remained in earnest conversation with their host and hostess, and then looked rather wistfully down at her hands resting in her lap.

Verity smiled to herself as she sat down beside her. "He's a very personable gentleman. It's little wonder you like him."

Clarissa made not the least attempt to dissemble, although a rather fetching blush mounted her cheeks. "Yes, I like him. He's not handsome or dashing, like his cousin, but I like him so very much better."

Verity frowned slightly at this. "You do not care for his cousin either, then?"

"No, not very much," Clarissa admitted. "I find him rather arrogant. And he has such a coldly calculating look that always managed to send shivers down my spine whenever I danced with him in London. I don't know him that well, of course, and perhaps one shouldn't make snap judgements because one can so often be wrong with first impressions."

"True. But I don't think you're so very far out in your assessment of him."

"And I wasn't so very far out in my assessment when

I told Mama that Major Carter was very fond of you. But then she knew that already. I'm so very happy for you, Verity. I think you and Major Carter are very well suited. You get along together so well.''

This was no more than Verity had decided herself earlier, but to hear someone else say much the same thing and to realise that others had come to the conclusion long since was quite disturbing. It wasn't like her to be so obtuse, and she couldn't help wondering what else others had glimpsed in her relationship with Brin which had not been patently obvious to herself, and perhaps still wasn't.

Alarm bells began to sound, but before she was given time to interpret their cautionary message, she noticed Claud and his cousin heading in their direction. Something made her cast a quick glance in Brin's direction. He was still swirling the earl's daughter round the floor. It was not really surprising to discover they were not conversing—after all, Lady Caroline seemed incapable of stringing more than four words together at any one time—but it was rather strange to discover him not concentrating on his partner at all, but staring quite pointedly in her direction with a look in his eyes that, had she not known better, appeared to be almost a warning.

''I trust you were successful in your endeavours yesterday, Mr Castleford?'' she remarked, addressing herself to Claud, as Clarissa seemed incapable of doing anything except smile rather shyly.

Lawrence Castleford took out his snuffbox and flicked open its lid with a practised finger while his lips, Verity noticed, were fixed in a faintly disdainful smirk. ''Hardly an appropriate topic of conversation, Claud,'' he remarked, cutting across his cousin's enthusiastic description of the two fine plough-horses he had acquired the day before, "especially as we have yet to felicitate Miss Harcourt on her betrothal."

Although Verity disliked becoming involved in things that did not directly concern her, she discovered she could not sit by and watch poor Claud, with quite malicious intent, being put out of countenance and came to his aid.

"On the contrary, Mr Castleford," she said, transferring her gaze to those soulless blue eyes. "Miss Gillingham, for one, would be far more interested in listening to your cousin expound on the merits of his latest acquisitions than being forced to endure further conversation about my engagement, of which too much has been spoken already. So," she added, rising to her feet, "emboldened as I am by the fact that I shall very shortly be irrevocably joined in wedlock, I do not demur at asking you to partner me in a dance."

Unfortunately her brazen attitude, far from shocking him, seemed to afford him a deal of sardonic amusement. Worse still was his slow, over-familiar appraisal of her figure as they walked on to the dance floor, which left Verity in little doubt that he knew precisely what she looked like without her shift.

Heavens above! she mused as he placed his hand with studied expertise on her narrow waist. Was that the warning Brin had been trying to convey? Had she inadvertently encouraged the advances of a hardened rake?

"I didn't realise, sir, that you were planning a visit to your uncle's home this weekend," she remarked, managing to draw his eyes away from their insolent contemplation of her evening gown's low neckline. "I wouldn't have thought that pastoral serenity was much to your taste."

"On the contrary, Miss Harcourt, I have a great fondness for Castleford Grange. Both my parents died when I was very young and I was reared in that house. I have been brought up to consider it my home and continue to make frequent visits.'' Verity watched his eyes momentarily stray in his cousin's direction and narrow fractionally. ''Claud appears to be rather taken with the Gillingham chit.'' His unpleasant smile, rather twisted and contemptuous, returned. ''Well, well! Life is full of surprises! I didn't realise my little cousin had it in him to attract a charmer.''

Poor Claud! How much back-stabbing had he been forced to endure from his elder and more sophisticated cousin during those years when they had been growing up together? A great deal, she suspected. Even now he probably had to contend with a continual barrage of barbed remarks whenever his cousin came to stay. Lawrence Castleford was undeniably a strikingly handsome man, but had little else to commend him as far as she was concerned.

She took a moment or two to study those exquisitely chiselled features more closely and could quite understand what Clarissa had meant, earlier, as she too experienced a frisson of fear scud its way down the length of her spine as she continued to watch him intently. He was staring in Claud's direction again and there was something rather more than cool contempt in that look of his: something quite calculatingly sinister.

She somehow managed not to betray her avid distaste of his company, but was far from sorry when the dance came to an end and he restored her to the protection of her aunt's side. No sooner had he moved away than a deep voice murmured in her ear, ''Be careful of that one, my little love. It's perfectly in order for you to dance with him, but never, I repeat never, be foolish enough to find yourself alone with him.''

Had Brin proffered that piece of sound advice a few days earlier she might well have told him to mind his own business, or at the very least teased him over possible feelings of jealousy, but as she turned and looked up into his face, easily detecting disquiet there, she felt the desire to do neither.

''Fortunately he isn't a frequent visitor to this house,'' he went on, following Lawrence's sauntering progress across the room. ''My friend Marcus, being a man of considerable discernment, doesn't encourage his visits. But one never knows. Castleford just might take it into his head to pay a call whilst you are here.''

''Don't worry, Brin,'' she didn't hesitate to reassure him. ''I've already come to the conclusion that he's definitely not to be trusted.'' She too peered in Lawrence's direction and watched him leading a young lady on to the floor, and was certain in her own mind that beneath that highly polished and prepossessing exterior beat the heart of a poisonously corrupt man.

''Do you know, I think he would be capable of almost anything. The look he cast poor Claud was—well—filled with enmity.''

''There's certainly no love lost between them. But don't be concerned for Claud. That young man might surprise you. Believe me, he's quite capable of looking after himself.''

No more was said on the matter, and for Verity's part she was quite content to forget that Lawrence Castleford was even present. This was not difficult to achieve, for, when not dancing with one of the Ravenhursts' neighbours, Brin rarely left her side, and she was quite surprised to discover, as the evening drew to a close, that she had thoroughly enjoyed the occasion which she had been so dreading earlier in the day.

Guests began to depart, and Lady Billington too rose to her feet. "It is time I was thinking of retiring, dear. I have no intention of making a very early start in the morning, but I do not wish to leave it too late. When will you be returning to the capital?"

"Do you know, I've absolutely no idea. I've hardly exchanged above a dozen words with Sarah all evening. Which is quite understandable, really—she has been so occupied with her other guests. And I cannot recall that Brin gave me a specific date. I'll ask him." She turned and was surprised not to find him hovering nearby. "Oh, he's disappeared somewhere."

"I thought I saw him wander outside to the terrace a few minutes ago." Lady Billington smiled to herself, more than just a little satisfied with the Major's attentiveness towards her niece throughout the evening. "Why not go and ask him? You can let me know in the morning."

Verity needed no second prompting. He stood at the far side of the terrace, one booted foot on the low stone balustrade, one elbow resting on his bent knee, a cheroot between his fingers, and was staring out at what little could be seen of the parkland. How many times had he adopted just such a negligent pose when out in the Peninsula? Yet she suspected that his relaxed stance was highly deceptive, that his senses, finely tuned after years of warfare, remained ever-alert.

And she wasn't wrong. He turned his head suddenly, as though sensing he was not alone, and that warm smile that she had glimpsed so often when he looked in her direction reached his eyes, crinkling the corners and intensifying the warmth in those brown depths.

As she came to stand beside him she watched him flick the half-finished cheroot over the balustrade. "There was no need to do that."

"I know you ladies aren't enamoured of the habit, but it's one I seem unable to break. Sarah dislikes it intensely, but she's kind enough to allow me to indulge myself."

The curl came so naturally to Verity's lips that she was hardly aware she was returning his smile. "Personally I don't object, but even if that were not the case, I still wouldn't have the right to dictate how you should go on."

"Now that's most odd," he responded with a provocative lift of one brow, "because I feel I have every right to govern your behaviour."

Verity was only too aware that he wasn't joking, and yet she couldn't find it within herself to be angry, or even moderately annoyed, but she managed to say with an attempt at conviction, "I wouldn't advise you to try. You must remember that we are not really betrothed, although…" she shook her head in wonder… "there were times this evening when I was forced to remind myself that our engagement was pure fabrication. It appeared so real, somehow."

"But it is real, Verity."

His assertion seemed to hang in the air like a softly taunting reminder of how incredibly naïve she had been not to have realised before that there had been no pretence, no playacting on his part throughout the evening. He had behaved quite naturally, simply because to him their betrothal was in deadly earnest… And to her…?

"And you want it to be real too, don't you?" He gave her no time to answer, but then he really didn't need to; had he retained any misgivings, her eager response to his lips as they fastened on hers with a possessive hunger would have dispelled them at once.

Verity wasn't certain whether the soft little moan of pleasure came from him or herself as his tongue began to explore the soft lining of her mouth and his hands burned a trail of sensual pleasure down the length of her back to the swell of her hips, holding, moulding her slender body so close to his that she didn't know where she ended and he began. The feel of him, the taste of him, the powerful masculinity of him engulfed her, a heady brew sending her senses reeling with an all-consuming desire for more…oh, much, much more.

As a young girl on the verge of womanhood she would have given almost anything to be locked in this man's arms. Now that sweetly remembered yearning, thrust aside by the passage of time, but never completely eradicated, was being fulfilled. And it felt so right, so wonderfully perfect that she knew with a clear-sighted conviction that they belonged together, bound by the unbreakable ties of an enduring love that would stand the test of time.

His body shook in gentle, silent laughter as he dragged his mouth reluctantly from hers to burn a trail of feather-light kisses to her temple. "You took me roundly to task earlier, my love, for remarking that the wedding would take place soon, but I think you'll now be forced to agree that for both our sakes it would be a grave mistake to wait. I am a man, with a man's very natural instincts and desires." His smile was rueful. "My gentlemanly inclinations only stretch so far, and you have strained them to their farthest limits during these past weeks."

Tilting up her chin, he looked down into eyes that glowed with all the love she bore him. "I've been determined to have you almost from the moment I saw you again. I could hardly believe it was you, but the hair, the eyes hadn't changed, only it was a woman I looked upon, not a girl. And you're my woman, Verity. You always were mine. And no other man shall have you. That I swear!''

His words, spoken with such fervour, ought to have filled her with untold joy, but the message was achingly familiar, striking a chord of memory that sent ice-cold darts of self-disgust to pierce every fibre of her being.

She wrenched herself away, unable to believe what had just taken place between them, unable to believe what she had so heartlessly allowed to happen. ''I can't...I never meant...'' Each word burned her throat, corrosive as acid. ''Oh, God, what have I done? There's someone else. Brin, forgive me...but there's someone else.''

He took a step towards her, searching her distraught features, but she backed away, her tear-filled eyes wild with a seemingly intensifying horror. ''No, my darling, there's no one else,'' he assured her softly. ''It is—''

He got no further. She swung away and fled back inside the house before he could reach her. He checked in his pursuit at the long French window and watched her headlong flight across the salon, knowing with heart-rending certainty that her tears couldn't be held in check for long, and that he alone was responsible for the needless suffering.

''It isn't you who should be begging forgiveness,'' he murmured, turning back to stare into the darkness. ''But will you ever forgive me...now?''

# Chapter Fifteen

Verity forced open her slightly swollen, red-rimmed eyes and was surprised to find her maid standing beside the bed, looking down at her in some concern. It was most unlike Meg to attend her mistress first thing without being summoned, but a swift glance at the clock was sufficient to explain the unusual behaviour.

"Good heavens! Is that the time!" Not even when in London had Verity risen so late, but then she had never taken so long to fall asleep before. She had heard the servants moving about, busily attending to their early-morning duties, before she had finally managed to stem what had threatened to be an inexhaustible flow of tears and had surrendered herself to the healing powers of slumber. Not that sleep had had any obvious soothing effect upon her weary body and tortured mind, but at least she had come to accept, cruelly painful though it was, the only course of action open to her.

Suddenly aware that Meg had not moved, and was still regarding her rather pensively, Verity forced herself back to the present. "Has Lady Billington left yet?"

"Yes, miss. An hour or so ago. She wanted to see

you before she went, but Major Carter said he would pass on her farewells.''

Just the mere mention of his name brought yet another wickedly piercing stab of pain to that already irreparably bruised and battered area just below her ribcage. So what agony was she likely to suffer when she came face to face with him again? She placed a hand to her throbbing temple. It didn't bear thinking about, and yet she knew she couldn't put off that inevitable interview indefinitely.

''Is the Major in the house, Meg?''

''No, miss. He went off somewhere with Mr Raven-hurst not long after your aunt's departure.''

So, she had been given a respite, had she? She wasn't so very sure whether this was such a very good thing, because she had to face him some time and the sooner that painful interview was over the better. And how much had he guessed already? He was certainly no fool, and although she felt fairly sure that she had not mentioned the Coachman directly, she had managed to tell him that there was someone else, someone who meant as much to her as Brin himself did… Oh God! What was she to do…? What could she do?

Meg's request as to whether to lay out the sprigged muslin brought Verity back to the present, once again but her mind continued to weigh so heavily with the heartbreaking course of action she was being forced to take that anyone with a ha'p'orth of sensibility could tell instantly that there was something drastically wrong.

Sarah, seeing her for the first time just before luncheon, was not slow to perceive the telltale signs of strain. She had witnessed Verity's headlong flight up the stairs the previous evening, and had glimpsed the unmistakable look of deep concern on Brin's face when he had come in from the terrace, and had assumed they had been indulging in a lovers' tiff. Now she was far from certain that that was all it had been. She seriously suspected that it was something far more serious, but she had no intention of prying. Added to which she had the utmost confidence in Brin's ability to sort everything out.

"Marcus has dragged your fiancé away to watch a mill taking place in a field just the other side of Oxford," she said, entwining her arm through Verity's as they went across the hall to the dining-room. "Though how anyone can gain pleasure in watching grown men indulging in a bout of fisticuffs, I'll never know!"

The scathing condemnation did manage to draw a smile from Verity. "It does seem strange, certainly. But I for one wouldn't attempt to deny gentlemen their amusements, very odd though some of them are, and I suspect you wouldn't either."

"Very true. But the wretches have left us to our own devices for the whole day. They are not due back until late this afternoon. I must pay a call on the Reverend Mr Martin later, Verity. Would you care to accompany me?"

"If you wouldn't mind, Sarah, I think I would prefer to exercise that darling mare of yours again. I'm not usually a slug-a-bed, but I'm now being punished for my laziness with a slight headache. A good gallop across the park will set me to rights."

Sarah wasn't so certain, but made not the least attempt to dissuade her, and half an hour later she stood watching her young guest cantering across the park in the direction of the home wood before getting into the carriage and setting off on her own visit.

Without conscious thought Verity turned Sarah's mare on to one of the many paths that criss-crossed the wood and found some relief from the heat of the afternoon sun beneath the shading canopy of the dense foliage, but she knew that the sun's bright rays had little to do with the throbbing ache which persisted at her temples. Until she had spoken with Brin, had tried to explain what had been happening to her during the past weeks, she knew there would be no relief whatsoever. She hoped, prayed he would understand, but even that might be too much to expect. After all, she hardly understood herself just how she had managed to get into such a tangled emotional mess.

She would have been the first to admit that in many ways she had been more fortunate than most. Spoilt, both Brin and the Coachman had called her, and they were right, of course. Even though she had lost both her parents at a young age she had still had people about her—Uncle Lucius and dear Aunt Clara, to name but two—who had continued to do everything humanly possible to make those years while she had been growing into womanhood as happy and carefree as they could.

Even her dear mother, bless her, had ensured that her sole offspring need never marry unless she chose to do so. Under the terms of the will Verity came into a substantial inheritance upon marriage or reaching the age of one-and-twenty. Safe in this knowledge, Verity had never seriously looked for a suitable mate. She had known many young men whom she had liked very well, but not one with whom she could have contemplated spending the rest of her life. No, not one...until the Coachman had crossed her path...until Brin had entered her life again.

Just why she had allowed herself to fall so hopelessly in love with such a dictatorial wretch as the Coachman she couldn't imagine. But she did love him...as surely as she loved Brin, though with him, of course, she had refused to acknowledge what her heart had been trying to tell her for weeks. Perhaps if she hadn't stubbornly refused to admit that she was still attracted to him, that he still retained a place in her affections, she might have been able to prevent those feelings from deepening. She wasn't sure, and it hardly mattered, anyway. It was too late now…all too hopelessly late. She loved them both; couldn't choose between them. So how could she contemplate marriage with either one of them?

Verity came out of her heartbreaking reflections with a start when she became aware that someone was shouting her name, and swung round in the saddle to see Claud Castleford waving frantically as he came cantering across the field, mounted on his sturdy roan.

"I thought you were deliberately ignoring me," he informed her, bringing his mount alongside and looking for all the world so much like a hurt schoolboy that she didn't hesitate to assure him that this wasn't so.

"Merely lost in my own thoughts and—" she looked about her "—lost in other ways, too. Where on earth am I? The last thing I knew I was in the Ravenhursts' wood."

"My, my! You have been in a world of your own. You've managed to find your way on to Castleford land." His boyish smile flashed out. "Or it might be more accurate to say that the mare found her way here. Sarah frequently rides this way."

"What a clever lady you are!" Verity gave the mare's silken neck a fond pat. "Let's hope you're clever enough to find your way back."

"Oh, I think that between us we can manage to set you on the right track. Although, if you're not in any hurry, would you like to return with me to the Grange?

Or is your fiancé frantically awaiting you at Raven-hurst?''

If Claud noticed the spasm of pain flit across her features he betrayed no visible signs of having done so. ''There's no one back at the house at present. Father is expecting a party of gentlemen later—all very hush-hush, you understand—but there's plenty of time to show you round the place if you would like?''

Verity accepted the invitation without a second thought. She had liked Claud from the first. Not only was he good-natured, but also an excellent conversationalist, although she did find the number of times he managed to allude to a certain young lady before they had arrived at the Grange's stable yard a little trying, and in the end she found herself saying in her usual no-nonsense manner, ''For heaven's sake, Mr Castleford! If you are so taken with Clarissa Gillingham, why on earth don't you do something about it? How can you possibly further your interests stuck here while she's in London? If you take my advice you'll pack your bags and make all speed for the metropolis!''

It took every ounce of self-control Verity possessed to stop herself from bursting out laughing. Anyone looking at Claud's astounded expression might have supposed that she had just suggested a visit to the other side of the world instead of a mere short sojourn in his own capital city.

''By gad, Miss Harcourt, you've hit on the very solution!'' After dismounting, Claud offered her a helping hand down from the saddle. ''Mama is due home the day after tomorrow. She'll come to London if I ask her. Not that I need her approval or support, you understand,'' he went on hurriedly as Verity looked at him rather askance, ''but squiring her about town will give me the perfect excuse to attend those places where Miss Gillingham is likely to be found.''

Verity cast him a look of the utmost respect as she stepped into the oak-panelled hall of his ancestral home. ''Brin told me that you had hidden depths, Mr Castleford, and he wasn't wrong. Excellent strategy!''

''Did he say that?'' Claud went quite pink with pleasure. ''Well, I ain't the slow-top some people take me for, Miss Harcourt, but I sometimes think it's better to keep one's own counsel about some things than to voice one's opinions and end by creating a grand fuss.''

Verity gained the distinct impression that he was referring to instances rather close to home, but steadfastly refused to pry into domestic problems which had absolutely nothing whatsoever to do with her, and focused her attention on the extremely fine interior of the early Tudor manor house.

Claud showed her into most of the downstairs rooms and ended his guided tour in the library which, like the hall, was wood-panelled, and a little gloomy, perhaps, but full of character and charmingly furnished, none the less.

''It's a wonderful old house!'' Verity remarked with total sincerity. ''No wonder you're so fond of the place!''

''Yes, I am,'' he freely admitted. ''It's been in the family for centuries and is steeped in history.'' A rather roguish smile pulled at the corners of his not unpleasant mouth. ''The Castleford tree bears two kinds of fruit, Miss Harcourt—the good and the bad. And it has produced more than just the occasional rotten apple during its long and fertile life. The ancestor who had this house built was a prime example of the not-so-palatable. He, of course, was the one who instigated the construction of the secret passageways, so that he could spy on those invited to stay and use anything he overheard to his advantage. A most unpleasant character!''

''He sounds it,'' she agreed.

''Most of the passageways were done away with when the rooms were enlarged, but the one behind here—'' he tapped a section of the panelling, and it sounded hollow ''—still exists. Lawrence and I discovered it when we were boys, but Father had the entrances nailed up, as you can overhear every word spoken in this room from the passageway. And there have been some very secret meetings taking place in this room in recent years, Miss Harcourt.''

Verity paid only scant attention to what he was saying as she was subjecting the panelling to a thorough examination. ''Why, one would never know there was a doorway here! It is quite remarkably well-hidden.''

''It's here.'' Claud pointed to a certain section. ''If you look very closely you can just make out certain of the nails which securely fasten it. The other entrance is in Lawrence's bedchamber. That is a little easier to locate. I'll show you if you like?''

It never entered Verity's head to demur at accompanying a gentleman into a bedchamber, and, intrigued, she eagerly followed Claud up the ornately carved staircase.

''Lawrence has gone off somewhere with Father, so we're unlikely to be caught in my cousin's private sanctum,'' Claud informed her as they entered the bedchamber, whose walls were also wood-panelled, but far more elaborately carved than those in either the library or the hall. ''He can be a funny devil at times—gets quite nasty if he knows someone's been in his room.''

Once again Verity only listened with half an ear as she studied the panelling with interest. It took a little time, but eventually she noticed a slight difference in one section. "It's here!" she said triumphantly. "Behind this old wooden chest."

"Very good!" Claud came across and moved the chest away from the wall. "I wager you cannot locate the device that used to open the door, though."

Verity didn't hesitate to take up the challenge. Each squared section had a carved rose in its centre. It had to be one of those, she decided, checking each one for any slight difference. Eventually she found one that turned beneath her inquisitive fingers. There was a faint click and a large section of the panelling opened a fraction.

"Good gad!" Claud could not have looked more stunned: his jaw dropped perceptively and his eyes widened in astonished disbelief. "But Father had the thing nailed up years ago. Lawrence and I were here, feeling most disgruntled, when the workmen performed the task."

He shrugged as he went over to the small table by the bedside and lit a candle. "At least it offers me the opportunity to show you where Lawrence and I used to hide ourselves when we wanted to escape from our rather boring tutor."

Verity smiled at this ingenuous admission as she followed him through the opening and down a series of stone steps. Footprints showed clearly in the fine covering of dust, betraying the fact that someone had certainly ventured down to the hideaway in recent years, and not someone wishful to escape a tutor, either.

The half-spiral stairway led to a narrow passageway, no more than twelve feet long by three feet wide. Three of its walls were stone-built, but the fourth was of wood. Cobwebs festooned down from the ceiling and the air was dank, but it was just the sort of place where two small boys could secrete themselves, no doubt plotting other ways to avoid lessons.

"Hello! What have we here?" Claud remarked, noticing the clearly discernible footprints at last, footprints that were far too large to be those of children. "Someone's been down here recently." He shrugged. "Perhaps one of the workmen came down to check all was well and effect necessary repairs. This false wall backs on to the panelling in the library and is—"

Claud caught himself up abruptly and placed a warning finger to his lips as the door leading to the library from the hall could clearly be heard opening.

Then Lawrence Castleford's voice, bored and faintly drawling, filtered through the panelling with disturbing clarity as he said, "I blame Claud entirely. What a complete waste of an afternoon!"

"You cannot blame him," Lord Castleford responded. "No doubt if we'd informed him where we were bound he'd have told us Chumley's bays were nothing more than high-steppers that would be found to be touched in the wind after no more than a mile or so. Claud might be sadly lacking in certain departments, but there ain't much the boy don't know about animals."

Verity heard something suspiciously like a grunt before Lawrence countered with, "Claud knew I had a fancy for those greys of his, and yet he deliberately went and offered them to Ravenhurst's damned friend."

"He had every right to sell them to whomsoever he pleased. And you've got no cause to complain. He never objected to you making use of the turn-out whenever you were here. And you borrowed it on more than one occasion when I brought it to London."

"He still might have offered me first refusal. I would have got the money together somehow."

"Oh, for heaven's sake, stop whining! I've more to think about than your petty grievances!" Verity detected the chink of glass before Lord Castleford said in a milder tone, "Here, get this down you. It'll help calm you. You do realise that you must entertain yourself this evening. Both you and Claud are barred from the library."

"Yes, I know. Don't concern yourself. I'll find something to occupy me."

Just what Lord Castleford would have responded to this, Verity was destined never to know, for Claud beckoned her to follow him back up the stairway.

"You are certainly in your cousin's black books," she remarked as Claud closed the panelling and slid the chest back into position.

An unmistakable gleam of wicked satisfaction brightened his eyes as he led the way out of the room and back along the passageway to the head of the stairs. "I cannot deny that I knew he was interested in relieving me of that turn-out, Miss Harcourt, but I also knew who would end by paying for it. Lawrence sometimes seems to have plenty of brass to throw about, but for the most part he's in debt and asking my father to bail him out."

The front door opened and Verity checked in her descent, suddenly finding it necessary to cling to the banister-rail for support, as a stockily built figure with grizzled hair stepped into the hall. She had seen that man once before, and she recalled vividly just where she had seen him.

"Who is that?" she asked, her voice little more than a choked whisper.

"Blackmore, my cousin's manservant," Claud responded, watching him stalk across the hall in the direction of the kitchen area. "He's devoted to Lawrence. Personally, I can't abide the fellow. Bit of a rum touch, if you ask me... Oh, confound it! Did I blow that candle out? I'd better go back and make sure. If Blackmore sees it burning he won't hesitate to inform Lawrence that someone's been in the room.''

For a few moments Verity stared sightlessly down into the hall, conjuring up clear images from the past while her mind assimilated all she had learned that day. Then, scarcely aware that Claud had left her side, she flew down the stairs and out of the house, not stopping to catch her breath until she had reached the stable yard.

Quickly mounting Sarah's mare, she galloped out of the yard and across the field in the direction of the small market town of Houghton, as though the devil himself were at her heels. So fixedly determined was she to make contact with Thomas Stone without delay, and ultimately the Coachman, that she was deaf and blind to the sights and sounds around her.

The pounding of hooves as horse and rider followed in hot pursuit went completely unnoticed, as did the hedge looming large not very far ahead, but Sarah's mare, ever alert, was only too well aware that they were getting perilously close to her particular pet hatred. Her ears went back and her eyes rolled before she took decisive and evasive action which sent her rider sailing through the air to land heavily in the ditch just in front of the offending obstacle.

Winded, and not just a little humiliated at the ease with which she had been unseated, Verity got slowly to her feet, wincing slightly as she put her weight on her right ankle.

"You faint-hearted creature!" she scolded as the mare took the precaution of moving several yards away. Then Verity at last became aware of the rider's approach and swung round, her face draining of every vestige of colour.

"Are you all right, Miss Harcourt?"

No one could have mistaken the genuine concern in Claud's voice, nor the lines of anxiety etched in his young face as he dismounted and came towards her, but Verity was suddenly alert, mistrustful, her mind whirling with hitherto unforeseen possibilities. Was it likely that Claud, too, was involved in his cousin's nefarious activities? The dreadful suspicion was swiftly quashed by common sense, coupled with age-old feminine intuition.

Placing a gentle hand beneath her arm, Claud helped her out of the shallow ditch. "Why did you rush off that way? Was it something I said, or did?" His concern increased when he noticed her limp slightly. "I'd better get you back to Ravenhurst."

"No. I must go to Houghton." Then, suddenly realising that she would be immeasurably foolish to believe herself capable of dealing with this vitally important situation on her own, she looked at him searchingly and quickly came to a decision. "Claud, I need your help. But first there are certain things you must know and if, when you've heard me out, you choose not to help, believe me, I'll quite understand."

Still watching him intently, Verity then went on to relate her encounter with the French spy, to inform him of her subsequent dealings with the Coachman and her meeting with Thomas Stone, and of her staunch belief that Blackmore was none other than the intermediary she had first seen at that small wayside inn.

When Claud had learned all, he uttered one word, "Lawrence."

"I'm so sorry," she murmured. "This must have come as a terrible shock to you."

"On the contrary, Miss Harcourt, it hasn't. I've always known what a black-hearted devil Lawrence is." His face and voice were expressionless, apathetic almost, and yet Verity knew he must be feeling something. His next words confirmed this. "It's my father I feel sorry for. I don't know what this will do to him, but in many ways he's only himself to blame."

He read the unspoken question in her eyes. "Loose talk, Miss Harcourt. My father, together with many others, has known for some time that information was being passed on to the enemy. But the family always knew when these secret meetings were taking place." He ran his fingers through his hair, suddenly looking far older than his four-and-twenty years. "I suppose he believed he could trust his family... And Lawrence has always been like a son to him.

"Well, I've stood by and done nothing for long enough. I allowed Lawrence to worm his way into my father's affections at the expense of my mother and myself. I cannot prevent the dishonour his actions will bring to the family name." Raw determination edged his voice. "But I'll be damned if I'll sit by and let him betray his country again if I can do anything to stop him! What do you want me to do, Miss Harcourt?"

The words of comfort she wished desperately to offer were set aside by the need for urgent action. "When is this meeting due to take place?"

"Directly after dinner, if it follows the usual pattern. And we dine early, at six. Do you want me to ride to Houghton and see this man Stone?" he offered, but Verity shook her head.

"No, I'll do that. He knows me. He'll know I'm not spinning some yarn."

Claud was certainly no fool, and a wry smile curled

his lips. "And, given the fact that he has no doubt been sent here for the sole purpose of keeping an eye on the members of my family, he's unlikely to listen to anything I might tell him."

She didn't waste time attempting to deny it. "I'm not even certain he'll be at the inn, so we must be prepared, if the worst come to the worst, to foil your cousin's attempt to pass information on to that spy ourselves."

Verity looked up at Claud, the anxiety she felt mirrored in her eyes. Not only was she expecting him to keep a close watch on Lawrence until the authorities could be alerted, which was tantamount to placing a noose round his cousin's neck, she was asking him to place his own life in danger. But what choice had she?

"You go back to the house and try, as best you can, to act naturally. Don't attempt to keep Lawrence with you. I should imagine he usually makes some excuse to retire early when these meetings take place, so that he has ample time to secrete himself in the passageway and overhear everything that is said. If he does so this evening, then let him."

"But how will I know if you've been successful in getting in touch with this man Stone?" he asked after a moment's intense thought.

"That's the problem, you won't…unless I can manage to get a message to you, or even come over myself."

"No, don't do that. It might arouse suspicion. I'll ensure that neither Lawrence nor Blackmore leaves the house." The muscles about his mouth grew taut. "It's the least I can do to try to restore a little honour to our name."

Claud offered her no opportunity to argue, and Verity could only watch, experiencing the gravest fears for his safety, as he made all speed back to the Grange. Then, without further delay, she turned and limped towards Sarah's mount, who, having regained her composure, had continued to graze quite contentedly.

She had almost reached the mare's side when the most ear-piercing, cacophonous tumult rent the air. An open carriage, tooled by someone who was incompetent, or inebriated, or both, came bowling along the road on the other side of the hedge. Sarah's mare pricked up her ears at the passengers' squeals and disharmonious attempts at singing, but when one of them suddenly attempted to play a tune on a yard of tin she wasted no time in making all speed back to Ravenhurst, and the quiet security of her stable, before Verity could make a grasp for the reins.

# Chapter Sixteen

Brin cast a brief glance at Marcus's profile, and then looked blindly at the road ahead. He ought never to have agreed to accompany him out. He had been poor company, and had taken precious little interest in the fine contest they had witnessed earlier, but it would have been a grave mistake to remain at Ravenhurst with Verity.

He was not in a position to explain his behaviour now, but when he was free to do so he must somehow find a way to make her understand that not for the world would he have deliberately hurt her. He had been foolishly unthinking in his dealings with her, but not deliberately cruel.

He had believed when the time came for him to explain, to confess all, she would take it all in good spirit, as a joke; now, however, he was far from certain that her lively sense of the ridiculous would be sufficient to erase the needless hurt he had caused her; would be enough to enable her to forgive him.

"Good Gad!" Marcus ejaculated suddenly, as he noticed a rather forlorn figure emerging from a gateway a little way ahead. "Isn't that Verity?"

Brin came out of his sombre reflections with a start and jumped down from the equipage before Marcus had brought his team to a halt. He cast one swift glance over the mud-stained habit and, before Verity could offer any explanation for her dishevelled appearance, picked her up in his arms and deposited her next to Marcus on the seat. All her protestations that she was perfectly all right, except for a sore ankle, and her requests to be taken to Houghton immediately fell on deaf ears. Marcus, trying desperately to school his features, as he had a pretty shrewd notion that hedges figured strongly in the young woman's recent misfortunes, kept his eyes glued to the road ahead, while Brin, adopting a dictatorial stance, informed her that she was going nowhere until a doctor had taken a look at her hurts.

Verity could have screamed in vexation, but there was little she could do, sandwiched as she was between two such immovable, authoritarian males, and she sat silently in ever-increasing seething frustration until they had arrived back at Ravenhurst's stable yard.

The instant Marcus had drawn his greys to a halt she called to Sutton, asking him to saddle up a fresh mount, only to have her request countermanded by Brin who, ignoring her vociferous demands to be put down at once, picked her up once more and carried her, wildly struggling, into the house.

"Oh, thank heavens, you've found her!" Sarah came rushing out to meet her husband. "I've just this moment learned that my mare came back without her and I was about to send men out to search. Is she badly hurt? I'll go up and see what can be done."

Marcus, his expression rather thoughtful now, placed a restraining hand on her arm. "No, my dear. Let Brin deal with it. I rather fancy there's more to that young woman's distress than a mere sprained ankle.''

"She certainly seemed distraught over something, screaming to be put down.'' A sudden smile erased her worried frown. ''But you're quite right. Brin will soon calm her. He has such a gentle way with him.''

Sarah would have been astounded had she been standing in the bedchamber a minute or so later to witness her friend taking Verity by the shoulders and shaking her so hard that the few pins remaining in her hair flew out in all directions, sending her raven locks tumbling down about her shoulders.

"Now, stop this at once!'' he ordered with steel-like harshness. ''You're behaving like an unruly child!''

"Brin, you—you don't understand.'' Breathless from the shaking, Verity cast a pleading glance up at his stern features. ''I must go to Houghton. It's vital I see someone there.'' And even in her agitated state she could see he was suddenly very alert.

"Who?'' There was no response, but Brin was not slow to note the sudden guarded look. ''You may as well get it into that pretty head of yours that you're not going anywhere, and the only person you'll be seeing, apart from Sarah, is the doctor.''

She remained stubbornly silent, and he cast her a look which not only betrayed frustration and annoyance but also managed to convey his slight feeling of hurt. ''Do you trust me so little, Verity, that you feel yourself unable to confide in me? Or is it merely that you think me incapable of acting on your behalf?''

"No, of course not! And I trust you implicitly, only—only…''

She slumped down on the bed, feeling utterly deflated. The determined glint in his eyes was enough to confirm that he had no intention of allowing her to leave, and she simply didn't possess the strength to fight him any more, not even with words. The ache in her ankle was increasing and that throbbing pain had returned to her temple. Most distressing of all was the knowledge that, unless something was done quickly, poor Claud would be left to deal with a potentially dangerous situation completely alone.

So, having little choice, Verity found herself relating her dealings with the Coachman for the second time that day, and then went on to disclose what she had discovered that afternoon.

But Brin's reaction was hardly what she would have expected.

Not once did he betray the least surprise, nor even a modicum of disbelief at anything she told him and, after learning all, merely remarked rather grimly, "So Claud Castleford is now in full possession of the facts, is he?"

She looked up at him sharply. "Claud isn't involved. I'd stake my life on it. Why, if you could have seen his face when that doorway leading to the secret passageway opened…when he realised his cousin was a traitor… No, Brin. Claud's completely innocent."

"I hope to God your instinct is right!" he responded, looking so forbidding that Verity hardly recognised him.

He wasted no further time and went straight over to the door. "I'll ensure that Stone is put in the picture." Then he paused, his hand on the doorknob, to look back at her, and flashed one of his rather wonderful smiles which managed to convey deep affection and a good deal of reassurance, too. "Don't worry, my darling. Your Coachman won't fail you."

No sooner had Brin left than the door opened again and Sarah entered, giving Verity no time at all to puzzle over Brin's parting words, or to concern herself with the possible happenings already taking place at Castleford Grange. It was only later, after the doctor had called and had confirmed nothing more seriously wrong than a sprained ankle and a smattering of painful bruises, and she had been left alone once again, that the gravest misgivings returned to torment her.

The draught the doctor had left to help her sleep remained untouched on the bedside table, as did the tray of food, until Meg re-entered shortly after nine o'clock to remove it. It seemed a very long time before the clock in her bedchamber chimed ten, and far longer before it chimed eleven, but when the hands were showing fifteen minutes to midnight, Verity had had enough of straining her ears, hoping to hear sounds heralding Brin's return. He hadn't returned simply because he had got himself involved. Perhaps he had been unable to make contact with Thomas Stone and had gone to the Grange to be of help to Claud. She ought to have taken that very real possibility into consideration before confiding in him. Dear God, she had put his life in danger, too!

Unable to stand the agony of waiting alone a moment longer, Verity tossed the bedcovers aside and went across to collect her robe. She was in no fit state, mentally or physically, to do anything positive herself, but at least she could talk to Marcus. Brin had the utmost respect for his friend's sound judgement, and Marcus might just be able to allay some of her worst anxieties.

There was no one in the hall, but Verity wasn't in the least surprised to discover the library door slightly ajar. Marcus wouldn't retire whilst his friend was still abroad. After a perfunctory knock she entered to find Sarah, surprisingly, the sole occupant.

"Why, Verity!" Setting aside her sewing, Sarah went

across and helped her to the chair on the opposite side of the hearth. "The doctor assured me that draught would keep you asleep until morning."

"I didn't take it," Verity confessed. "Where's Marcus?"

"He went with Brin earlier, and as yet neither of them has returned."

"Oh, God, no!"

Sarah watched in no little concern as Verity buried her face in suddenly trembling hands. She had known the instant her husband had said that he was accompanying Brin out again, without explaining where they were going or why, that something was very wrong. The dreadful suspicion that Verity might have been attacked had crossed her mind, but during the time she had been helping Meg to bathe her young mistress and get her comfortably settled in bed in readiness for the doctor's visit this fear had thankfully been dispelled. Verity had betrayed no signs of distress whatsoever, merely deep concern over something... But what?

Moving across to the decanters, Sarah poured out two glasses of wine. "As you refuse to take the doctor's medicine, you had better drink this, although I suspect it will go straight to your head as you didn't eat a bite of dinner. Not that I'm in any position to scold," she added wryly. "I didn't eat very much, either."

She resumed her seat and stared for several moments into deeply troubled violet-blue eyes. "Where have they gone, Verity? Do you know?"

"I suspect they are at Castleford Grange," she responded, seeing no earthly reason to lie, and then went on to divulge what she had discovered at that lovely old manor house earlier.

"Lawrence Castleford a traitor," Sarah murmured,

betraying no surprise. "Well, Marcus never trusted him, and I've never found his judgement faulty."

I'm so sorry, Sarah. I've now put your husband's life in danger, too."

"No, you haven't," Sarah countered evenly, keeping her deepest anxieties firmly under control. "It was Marcus's decision to accompany Brin. And I for one would not have attempted to dissuade him, even if I could."

A proud little smile hovered about her mouth. "Marcus has always wanted to be of service to his country during this present conflict with France. And now, of course, he has been given the opportunity to do something positive for the land of his birth. Just as you have. But how on earth did you become involved in this wretched business in the first place?"

Verity had long since come to the conclusion that Sarah Ravenhurst took a keen interest in the welfare of others, but she was neither vulgarly curious nor even moderately interfering. Whether the request stemmed from a genuine interest to learn more, or just as a means to pass the time while she waited anxiously for her husband's return, Verity wasn't sure, but because of Marcus's involvement she certainly considered that Sarah had a right to know more.

Only delaying for the time it took to make herself more comfortable in the chair, she was about to relate her dealings with the Coachman for the third time that day when she suddenly caught the sounds for which she had been longing. She sat bolt-upright again, her expression a strange mixture of joyful expectation and foreboding.

"I'll go." Sarah had almost reached the door before Verity had time to move. "Brin will not be best pleased to see you up at this time of night, without witnessing you hobbling about as well."

That was the least of her worries, but Verity didn't attempt to argue. After all, Sarah was mistress in her own home, and if it was only a messenger she didn't doubt she would be apprised of any information, good or otherwise, soon enough.

Although Sarah had closed the door, the sound of voices did manage to filter into the room, but not clearly enough for Verity to discern what was being said, or by whom, but she was certain that one of the voices belonged to a man.

The door opened again and Verity, hardly daring to breathe, waited for tidings, but when only silence ensued, she rose to her feet, the glass of wine slipping from suddenly trembling fingers when she saw who it was standing with his back towards her by the door.

"Coachman…?" She limped several steps towards him, but he didn't attempt to turn round. "You got my message, then?" It sounded such a foolish thing to say, but she was still in a state of shock over his unexpected appearance.

"Aye, lass."

"Is it over…finally over?"

"Aye, lass."

She limped closer. "And Brin…? Marcus…? Are they safe?" she forced herself to ask from a throat that was suddenly dry and painful.

"Ravenhurst be wi 'is wife, lass."

"And Brin?" There was no response, and icy talons of fear clawed at her heart. "What's happened to him? What's happened to Brin!" Panic raised her voice almost to screaming pitch. "Tell me, damn you!"

"Nay, then, lass. Don't tha fret thissen!" He swung

round and pulled the muffler from his face. "He's right here, my darling... Right here."

Verity stared up into those wickedly twinkling tawny eyes in wonder, in disbelief, almost. For endless moments she refused to credit what her senses were telling her, had been telling her for weeks. Then anger, virulent and icy-cold, at his duplicity, at the needless, senseless hurt he had inflicted on her slowly began to well, thrusting aside every coherent thought, every need save one: a thirst for revenge.

Balling her fist, she swung her arm in a wide arc and, before Brin could take evasive action, made vicious contact with his left ear, the force of which sent that infamous tricorn sailing off his head to skid across Marcus's highly polished desk, scattering papers in its wake.

"You louse!" she screamed, and would have fled from him, but Brin had other ideas.

Pinioning her arms to her sides, he carried her back across the room and, seating himself in the chair she had just vacated, continued to hold her prisoner on his lap.

He considered she had every right to feel hurt and aggrieved, and made no attempt to stem the flow of rather colourful epithets she spat at him, most of which he suspected hadn't been learned at that very select seminary in Bath, but had been picked up by spending far too much time in the stable yard, but he did take the sensible precaution of keeping her arms securely held until, frustrated and exhausted by her ineffectual attempts to break free, she resorted to a female's most effective weapon and promptly dissolved into tears.

After forcing his handkerchief into unwilling fingers, he waited until the flow began to subside. "I never meant to hurt you this way, my darling," he murmured, keeping her head firmly pressed against his shoulder, while stroking the silken black locks.

"You—you have been making a May game of—of me right from the start," she accused, regaining a little of her former spirit, and this time when she attempted to sit up he didn't try to prevent her.

"No, little one, that isn't true." A reminiscent smile pulled at the corners of his mouth. "Even though I made light of it, I knew from the very first time I kissed you that you were the girl for me. I told you so when we arrived in London, remember?"

The malevolent look remained, but he noticed a flicker of curiosity, too, and took heart. "I thought it would to be a simple matter to woo you as we were both intending to spend several weeks in London, but I realised when we met in Hyde Park that day that I had grossly miscalculated, had been arrogantly presumptuous in believing my heart's desire would be mine for the asking. Why, you looked at me as though I were a leper! Of course, I realise now why you did, but at the time I was blissfully unaware that you bore a grudge against—"

"Oh, yes, very clever!" she interrupted. "You did manage to worm a deal out of me when in the guise of the Coachman, didn't you?" She looked at him sharply and caught his rather pitiful attempt to suppress a smile, but the strong urge to box his ears soundly a second time was suppressed by rampant curiosity. "How on earth did you manage to get back inside this room so quickly the other night?"

"It wasn't easy, I can tell you. I had only just managed to hide my tricorn and cloak in the chest in the hall and bolt the front door when I heard you attempting to enter."

Verity didn't know whether she felt angrier with him

for his duplicity, or with herself for being such a simpleton as not to have realised the truth long since.

He read her thoughts with uncanny accuracy. "I played my part too well, but believe me it was never my intention to cause you pain." And this time when she searched his features she could detect nothing but bitter regret.

"As the Coachman I could see you only rarely, and it was never enough. As myself I was in a position to see you much more often and was confident that, given time, you would grow fond of me again. It seemed merely a simple case of ensuring that you were given sufficient reason for seeking my company."

Her bosom heaved. "Infamous!"

"And in that my judgement was not at fault, as last night proved," he continued, just as though she hadn't spoken. "But when in my disguise I might have coped admirably at hiding my identity, but not my feelings for you, and suffered the consequences of my foolish play-acting when I realised the torment I had needlessly caused. Truly, my darling, inflicting pain was not part of my plans."

Verity could feel herself weakening, but her rapid slide into foolishly forgiving him was halted abruptly when she looked down at the fine piece of lawn in her hand, and noted with a surge of resentment that it was an exact replica of the one he had given her at Little Frampington.

"Never meant to inflict pain?" she echoed, the light of battle returning to her eyes. "You beat me, Brin Carter!"

His shout of laughter was hardly destined to appease, but over that particular incident he remained firm. "You ought never to have gone to that place alone, and you know it! Although I suppose,'' he added grudgingly, and in a much milder tone, ''your going did lead to the successful outcome tonight.''

This ignited more than just a spark of interest and, setting aside her justifiable grievances for the present, she asked him to explain how he had become involved.

Swiftly coming to the conclusion that it was in his own best interests to be indulgent, Brin didn't think twice about satisfying her curiosity. ''I had already sold my commission, and had been back in England nearly a month when news broke of Napoleon's escape from Elba. Wellington's own intelligence network had discovered that our little Frenchman was active again. Wellington wanted him caught and, more especially, his English contacts. He sent an urgent dispatch to Lord Charles, and suggested that he make use of my services.''

Verity recalled then that her uncle had mentioned that Wellington thought highly of Brin. ''And did you and my uncle suspect Lawrence Castleford all along?''

''Good heavens, no! We were convinced it must be someone working at the War Office, but until you saw those greys at Frampington we hadn't a clue who the traitor might be.''

He cast her a look of the utmost respect. ''Do you recall the evening of the Gillinghams' ball, when your uncle was talking to Lord Castleford? Well, it was then your uncle discovered that Castleford's nephew had been making use of that curricle and pair. We suspected that both Lord Castleford and his nephew were involved. It was also possible that Claud knew about it too. It wasn't until tonight that the truth came out. Your instincts were correct. Claud was completely innocent and Castleford hadn't a clue what his nephew had been up to.'' He shook his head. "I've never seen a man look so devastated before."

She regarded him consideringly. "Did you organise this sojourn at Ravenhurst simply to give you an excuse to come here so that you could keep an eye on the Grange?"

"Not entirely, no," he admitted with a rueful smile. "I was convinced that none of you ladies would be in the least danger, otherwise I wouldn't have arranged it. I wanted to see the thing through, of course, but I knew I'd find it difficult to keep my mind on the task if I left you behind in London. Strictly speaking, Stone was the one who was sent to keep watch. I was here merely to offer assistance if it became necessary."

"So what happened tonight?" she prompted gently when he fell silent.

"Marcus was the only one I confided in with regard to the work I was undertaking on behalf of the government. When I related what you'd discovered, he offered his help. Like yourself, he was convinced Claud wasn't involved. So, as it would appear less suspicious if a neighbour was to call unexpectedly at the Grange, I sent him over with a message for Claud while I made contact with Stone. Marcus and I met up again later outside the Grange, but had to wait some time before Lawrence's servant came out the house. I shot Blackmore when he attempted to leave with the information."

He sounded so matter-of-fact about it all, but then a soft-hearted approach would hardly have served his cause. Added to which, having been a soldier, shooting someone was hardly a new experience for him.

"And Lawrence?"

"No, I didn't kill him... Claud did. The sound of my shot alerted Lawrence and he attempted to escape, but

Claud put a ball through his brain. There was no possibility of Lawrence getting away, so I assume Claud did it to save his cousin the hangman's noose. All Claud would say was that when an animal runs mad it is only humane to put it out of its misery."

"And the French spy?"

"He's in custody."

"So, it is finally over," she remarked, not without a certain amount of relief.

"It will be a while before Lord Castleford gets over the revelations of this night. But for us, my darling, yes—it's over."

He slid his arms about her narrow waist and, after the merest token resistance on her part, held her tightly to him while he contemplated the ties on her modest nightgown. "And now, before Sarah returns, which I'm certain propriety will force her to do very shortly…when shall we be married?"

Verity almost choked. She wasn't sure which shocked her more: his all-too-knowing and appreciative gaze, or his arrogant assumption that she would even consider such a thing after the way he had behaved towards her.

"You've got a crass nerve to suppose that I would even contemplate marrying a perfidious wretch such as you!"

"Well, if that's the case, my girl," he countered, making a passable attempt at appearing deeply shocked, "all I can say is you betray a sad want of conduct. I might go as far as to say a decidedly wanton side to your nature, too, to sit on a man's lap at this time of night dressed in little more than a thin cotton nightgown, which does absolutely nothing to conceal your evident charms and which, I might add, has ridden up to reveal more than just a glimpse of pretty thighs to lead an innocent lad astray.''

Her attempts to restore a semblance of modesty were expertly foiled. Pulling her roughly against him, Brin also quickly put an end to her counter-attack on the profligate behaviour of the predatory male by kissing her so thoroughly that she was left too breathless to argue further, even had she been so inclined. Which she was not.

Although her mind might continue to suggest that it would be wise to think twice before becoming tied for life to this man whose character, she very much feared, was rather closer to that of the outrageous and domineering Coachman than the gentlemanly Major, her body was in no doubt, and neither was her heart.

Brin's gentle laughter held a note of triumph as he held her away. ''I rather think after that response, my darling, you would be foolish even to attempt to resist your destiny.''

Verity couldn't prevent a rather wistful little smile at this, as she nestled herself more comfortably into the crook of her future husband's arm, because it was no more than she had been telling herself for weeks.

Perhaps she had been destined to take a seat on that mail-coach that day and, yes, perhaps destiny had decreed years ago that she would one day be tied irrevocably to this man. And who was she to argue with destiny? she mused, while at the same time thinking she was rather foolish to allow him to get away with his outrageous behaviour towards her so easily, and she found herself saying, but without any degree of conviction, ''You do realise that if you become riveted to me, Major Coachman Carter, you will live under the cat's foot. I think it only fair to warn you that I'll rule the roost with a rod of iron.''

"Don't tha fret thissen, lass," he responded, looking highly delighted at the prospect. "I'd 'ave to be a right dunderheead not to 'ave realised that long since."

Verity, raising her eyes heavenwards, thought that Lady Billington hadn't been far wrong when she had suggested there was a streak of insanity in the Harcourt family. Why else would anyone even consider becoming tied to such a reprehensible creature?

\*     \*     \*     \*     \*

# MILLS & BOON

# The Regency

## LORDS & LADIES
### COLLECTION

*Two glittering Regency
love affairs in every book*

*Available at WH Smith, Tesco, ASDA, Borders, Eason,
Sainsbury's and all good paperback bookshops*
www.millsandboon.co.uk

Be swept off your feet and into the past with award-winning authors Julia Justiss and Joanne Rock, and their stories of forbidden love...

### *Seductive Stranger* by Julia Justiss

In Regency England, dashing Lord Brandon had been entrusted to help Lord Sudley's daughters find husbands. But now spirited Ailis had fallen prey to the charms of a notorious rake and Lord Brandon had become enraptured with Caragh's quiet beauty...

### *The Wedding Knight* by Joanne Rock

The year was 1250 and Melissande Deverell, mere weeks before her final vows as a nun, found herself held fast in the arms of Lucian Barret, her childhood companion and now a warrior of great prowess...

Be whisked
away to
an age of
chivalry, where
passionate
knights and
innocent ladies
face danger
and desire...

### The Knight, the Knave and the Lady
### by Juliet Landon

Marietta Wardle *never* wanted to be someone's
wife, but Lord Alain of Thorsgeld had
no scruples about compromising her into
marriage...

### My Enemy, My Love by Julia Byrne

Kept hostage during a royal feud, Isabel de Tracy
held fast to the memory of tough, yet tender
knight, Guy fitzAlan...

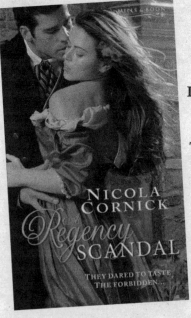

*Featuring*

**Lady Allerton's Wager**

**&**

**The Notorious Marriage**

*Two feuding families...*

*Two passionate tales...*

Against the enchanting backdrop of an island in the Bristol Channel, international bestselling author Nicola Cornick brings you two captivating stories of the feuding Mostyn and Trevithick families – and the star-crossed lovers who may bring their wilful battles to a sensual end!

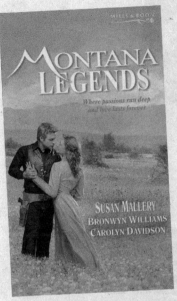

## Step back in time to the American West...

## ...where passions run deep and love lasts forever.

Introducing three captivating stories
from bestselling authors

### SUSAN MALLERY
### BRONWYN WILLIAMS
### & CAROLYN DAVIDSON

*Featuring the Kincaid brothers – three
passionate, determined men – and the women
they love in Whitehorn, Montana.*

*Celebrate
the charm of
Christmases
past in
three new
heartwarming
holiday tales!*

## COMFORT AND JOY by Margaret Moore

After a terrible accident, Griffin Branwynne gives up on the
joys of Christmas—until the indomitable Gwendolyn Davies
arrives on his doorstep and turns his world upside-down. Can
the earl resist a woman who won't take no for an answer?

## LOVE AT FIRST STEP by Terri Brisbin

While visiting friends in England for the holidays, Lord Gavin
MacLeod casts his eye upon the mysterious Elizabeth. She is
more noble beauty than serving wench, and Gavin vows to
uncover her past—at any cost!

## A CHRISTMAS SECRET by Gail Ranstrom

Miss Charity Wardlow expects a marriage proposal from her
intended while attending a Christmas wedding. But when Sir
Andrew MacGregor arrives at the manor, Charity realises that
she prefers this Scotsman with the sensual smile…

Amateur sleuth Francesca Cahill sets out to solve a new puzzling – and terrifying – case in 1900's Manhattan...

*From New York Times bestselling author*
*Brenda Joyce*

Irrepressible heiress and intrepid sleuth Francesca Cahill moves easily from her own elegant world of Fifth Avenue to the teeming underbelly of society. And despite the misgivings of her fiancé, Calder Hart, Francesca cannot turn away from the threat that is now terrorising Lower Manhattan. A madman has attacked three women – and only one has survived.

*Available at WHSmith, Tesco, ASDA, Borders, Eason, Sainsbury's and all good bookshops*

*www.millsandboon.co.uk*

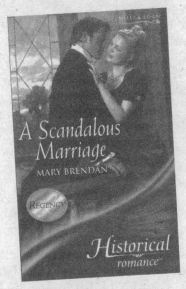